The Rules of Seduction

THE RULES OF

SEDUCTION

Daniel L. Magida

HOUGHTON MIFFLIN COMPANY

Boston • New York • London

1992

For information about permission to reproduce selections
from this book, write to Permissions, Houghton Mifflin Company,
215 Park Avenue South, New York, New York 10003.

Library of Congress Cataloging-in-Publication Data

Magida, Daniel L.
The rules of seduction / Daniel L. Magida.
p. cm.
ISBN 0-395-62049-X
PS3563.A346R85 1992
813'.54–dc20 92-5283
CIP

Printed in the United States of America

AGM 10 9 8 7 6 5 4 3 2 1

Lyrics from "Isn't It Romantic," words by Lorenz Hart,
music by Richard Rodgers, copyright © 1932 by Famous
Music Corp., used by permission.

The words from "The Bilbao Song" by Kurt Weill from
The Happy End, copyright © 1972 by Stefan S. Brecht,
reprinted by permission of Stefan S. Brecht.

For Nancy
O. L. I. H. T. S

CONTENTS

Who ever loves, if he do not propose
The right true end of love, he's one that goes
To sea for nothing but to make him sick.

—John Donne, *Elegie: Loves Progress*

The end of love is death.

—Jack Newland

PART ONE

Zig-Zaggin'
Through
Ghostland

I

HIS BIRTHDAY STARTED, more or less, at midnight, in a ball-
room. He was at a charity benefit with Boyd and Amy Cornwell
and a bunch of other people they knew from around town, and
a boy named Timothy who had somehow attached himself to their
group about two months before. There was a lot of dancing going
on, and their table kept emptying and filling as partners changed.
Timothy was a good dancer, and he danced with each of the
women in turn, as if scrupulously doing his duty. Jack doubted
whether anyone else noticed this performance, but he appreciated
it, it was the sort of thing he might have done himself not too
long ago. But Jack wasn't dancing, he was watching and drinking
Wild Turkey, and Boyd kept dragging him into the men's room
to do more cocaine from a little mirror he carried in a suede
pouch. The bourbon and the coke were helping Jack to not be
there. He'd learned at the age of thirteen that if you're not there,
nothing bad can happen, to you or to anyone else. Since he'd
spent the first part of the evening attending at a suicide, it was
a reassurance he needed.

He was a member of the board of trustees of a home where
men with AIDS could live if they had nowhere else to go — after
they'd been thrown out of their apartments or their parents'
houses, or their lovers' lives, and in between hospital stays. "Our
token straight," someone had called him, and someone else, fearing for the sensibilities of an Episcopal priest, also a trustee, had
quickly amended, "Our token rich straight." He was on the board
because he'd given them money, but he also helped out as a
volunteer, and he had stopped by that evening as he did most
Thursdays. He'd arrived to find their director arguing with two
paramedics over whether it was safe to get anywhere near a tub
filled with HIV-positive blood. The naked body in the water,
white-looking, wasted from disease even before this last indignity,
breathing faintly, might almost have been superfluous. After the

man had finally been taken down to the ambulance, Jack had put on a pair of rubber gloves and done his best to clean up the tub, and then he'd gone into another bathroom to throw up. The cocaine made him feel a lot better, and he hadn't even noticed midnight pass, and it wasn't until he got home after two that he realized he was twenty-eight.

He woke up in the morning in a kind of a panic — coke sometimes did that to him, he didn't know whether it was a physical reaction or just ordinary fear — but he pushed it down and got himself to the office. "You're looking bright-eyed and bushy-tailed," the art editor said, passing him in the hall. That's my curse, Jack thought, to look polished and clear when I feel blood-shot and messy. He got himself a cup of coffee and went to hide in his office. The magazine was in its usual pre-deadline disarray. Considering the glossy, professional appearance it always made, and the reputation for perfection it cultivated, there was something amateurish about these monthly riots, when the entire editorial staff seemed to take leave of its senses in the face of unyielding printer's deadlines. By custom, all this activity would cease at noon, when the staff would repair to a shabby bar across the street for lunch, booze, and a collective look at the next month's issue. Jack had long ago finished his contributions for this month — a review of three new movies and a report on a robber baron's very fashionable birthday party — and he sat at his desk waiting for the frenzy to be over. Through the wall he could hear the steady bass rumbling of a storyteller, punctuated intermittently by laughter. The room next door belonged to the secretarial pool, and it was customary for the writers to entertain the girls, as they were anachronistically called, until chased away by the office manager or a senior editor.

The phone rang, and he picked it up. "John Newland."

"Hello, John." It was David Lorburn, his brother-in-law. "Happy birthday."

"Hello, David. Thanks."

"I have some papers for you to sign, the ones we discussed last week."

So much for sentiment, Jack thought. He had been down at the bank the week before, talking about his trust funds in a small conference room with a large window overlooking the harbor, and while David went on in unnecessary detail, Jack found himself staring outside. The ferries and tugboats, tankers and freighters, pushed their way up and down, but no sound penetrated that hermetic, carpeted world. David would always be businesslike, he was never distracted.

Jack said, "I don't know if I can get downtown today." Not that he had anything much that needed doing. After the staff luncheon, he was planning to go to a movie that had just opened, and after that he was due at his aunt's for a sort of birthday visit, and after that he wasn't doing anything. But he didn't want to go down to Wall Street, and he didn't think he wanted to see David.

"That's all right. I can send a messenger. You'll be in the office?"

"Until lunch," he said, not committing himself.

"You'll need to have your signature notarized."

"No problem." One of the girls was a notary.

"Good. I'll send the messenger right away. And many happy returns." David hung up.

"Yeah, right," Jack said into the phone. He leaned back in his chair and put his feet up on the desk, listening to the office next door, which had suddenly gotten quiet. In another age, he thought, his meditations here would have been accompanied by the percussive clatter of typewriters rather than the soft, efficient clicking of computer keyboards — the difference between a brass band and a Japanese beetle. The decay of standards in our time, the destruction of conviviality in office life. It would make a good subject for television news, the kind of thing they liked, with no substance and a Luddite slant. He thought about David, sitting in his office at the North River Trust Company — at least he'd said "Happy birthday," even if for David it was just a mark of Jack's beneficial coming of age, the date on which the famous John White Newland Trusts terminated. The trusts his parents had set up for him.

He swiveled his chair around and turned his computer on. He didn't want to think about his parents. He looked at the screen, at the outline of an article he wanted to write on the Bogart-Bacall movies. He made some halfhearted changes and then gave it up, staring at his shoes. He felt guilty about not doing anything, but this was the last day before his vacation, and he didn't have any pressing assignments. He had turned down the opportunity to spend an all-expenses-paid week in the Hamptons nosing around the almost famous and sending back snotty reports about natural-fiber snobs and corporate raiders trying to buy respectability by the beautiful sea. His stand-in had faxed her first report the day before, and the whole scene sounded as awful as he'd imagined it would be. It was OK writing articles about the opera galas and museum benefits to which his status as a Newland got him legitimate invitations — it was another thing to tag along like a camp follower to the outposts of money that dotted Bush's America (née Reagan's) the way *plages* and spas had decorated Victorian Europe. He didn't have anything much planned for his vacation — just a few ball games with his nephew, maybe, and the usual restaurants and clubs with Boyd and Amy. His girlfriend (he wasn't allowed to call her his fiancée yet, he supposed, since they hadn't announced anything) was in Europe and wouldn't be back for another three weeks.

The messenger came from the bank. Jack signed the papers without reading them — David would sacrifice his firstborn before he would make a mistake in a business matter — and had them notarized. As he stood vaguely in a doorway, hoping not to be noticed, he saw two women, staff writers, come out of an office. One was touching the other's sleeve, as if feeling the material, and they were speaking in low tones with their heads close together. Women are so intimate with each other, he thought.

At lunch, he sat in his usual seat at the opposite end of the long, scarred table from Rob Cone, his editor. Rob, huge and hungry-looking always, was proceeding around the table, insulting the writers and needling the editors, banging a spoon on the table each time he heard something that offended one of the many rules he'd established for proper un-etiquette at a staff meeting. Jack wasn't paying much attention. He'd ordered a bourbon but wasn't drinking it. On a plate in front of him, a gray burger wallowed untouched in its natural greases. He was trying not to feel too sick from the cigarette smoke and the beery smell. They were in a back room, dark and stained, decorated with wooden signs in fake Gay Nineties script: "We do not serve Ladies to Minors" and "Tipping is not a City in China." The magazine was the plaything of a rich lady of a certain age, whose goal was to own a publication that none of her friends would read (though all of them did). She loved Rob because he offended her finely tuned sense of propriety, and she loved Jack because he didn't; she'd known his parents and grandparents and, in their world, that was the ultimate guarantee.

"And now," Rob said as menacingly as he could, "we come to the foot of the table. Do you think you can hide from me there, Newland, you little worm? What do you have planned for next month, something more than a lousy movie review, I hope. I could get three ten-year-olds to review movies, I don't need an expensive preppy for that."

"Four seven-year-olds," Jack hinted, but no one took him up on it.

"Mathematics aside, give, as they say."

"Why, Rob," Jack said sweetly, "you know I'm on vacation next month. Starting today, I'm gone for four weeks."

"Hear that, children? While we all toil away in the sweaty city, our young friend will be off in whatever places his kind go to in July. What if I cancel your vacation, you worm? What then?"

Jack smiled and lifted his arms up. "See, no strings. *Sempre libera.*"

Rob looked blank.

"Forever free," Jack supplied.

"What's that," Rob asked, pounding his spoon, "the Marine Corps motto?"

"Verdi. *La Traviata.*"

Rob snorted. "Another diseased whore. You see, I do come from a cultured background."

"Yeah," Jack said, "like penicillin."

There were general sounds of appreciation from around the table, and Rob, with a scowl, gave up on him. Jack went back to feeling mildly sick.

After lunch, he walked toward Times Square and went to the movie, which turned out to be one of those high-budget vanity productions in which the star-of-the-month revealed writing and directing talents that had hitherto, and justly, gone unnoticed.

As he walked out of the theater, his shoes sticking a little to the floor, he wondered whether he should even bother to review it. Rob had been getting on his case lately for writing only negative reviews: "You gotta like something, Newland," he'd said. Jack shook off the thought and squinted as he came out of the darkness, already hot inside his pale summer suit. There were days when Times Square was like a carnival, and there were days when it took on something of the tint of twilight and seemed soft and pliable to the dreams of those who walked in it. But this was the last day of June, and sweltering, and the place offered nothing. The sidewalks were hard and hot, stretches of desert to be crossed at peril. The surrounding buildings rose, stony and unyielding, giving nothing away except augmented heat. He took out his handkerchief and wiped his forehead, feeling dizzy.

He hailed a cab and rode uptown to his aunt Clara's apartment. She took tea every afternoon in a ritualistic fashion; he suspected that she secretly thought this was eccentric and kept it up for that reason. The last thing he wanted at that point was tea, but it was the only celebration he was likely to get that day. Anyway, it was too early for a drink.

She answered the door and gave him a kiss. "Happy birthday, dear, come in. Anne Morgan is here, and we're expecting Elizabeth anytime."

He followed her down the hallway to the living room, still feeling sick, waiting for the air conditioning to reach him. He stood in the doorway a moment to steady himself. Across the room, three windows overlooked Central Park, sealing the room off from the heat. A silver tea service sat on the low table, along with teacups in a floral pattern of green and pink. This was her summer china; her winter china had a blue border with gold rims.

Anne stood up. "Well, green eyes, happy birthday. How's life treating you?"

"Fine. And you?" Anne was famous, to him at least, for her marriages and divorces, and her love affairs, which followed one another with the regular progression of a stately dance. She seemed very beautiful to him in an autumnal way, having neither lost nor kept her looks but grown them, and he had always held her in his mind as the standard against which he compared the women of an older generation. She had been his mother's closest friend and looked as he liked to imagine his mother might have.

They sat down, his aunt in front of the tea service and Jack next to Anne. Anne said, "You look maddeningly handsome, John. Have you discovered the fountain of youth?"

"A mixture of gin and vermouth," he said flippantly, wishing for a moment that he didn't look so handsome, that he looked more the way he felt. "Or so Cole Porter said."

She laughed, as she did whenever he came up with the apt quotation. It was a game they played between themselves, she giving him feed lines, he trying to find the appropriate witticism. The laugh struck him for a moment — it was a sound he associated with rooms like this, the high-ceilinged living rooms and dining rooms in which he spent so much time. He suddenly didn't like the laugh, or the game, and he grimaced, but Anne didn't notice. She said, "Is there anything you don't know? I mean, all those articles you write." She accepted a teacup and leaned back to look at him appraisingly. "Film criticism, society parties, nightclubs, are you sure you do it all yourself?"

"We have a very small staff," he said, tired of explaining to people. He'd been hired as a film critic on the strength of his parents' friendship with the owner. For six months he had diligently turned in reviews and the occasional essay (one on the Cary Grant–Hitchcock movies, one on the Academy Award winners of 1938). One day, out of boredom more than anything else, he had tossed off a three-hundred-worder about a benefit he'd been to the night before, for the Contemporary Arts Institute. Rob had loved it. "You've caught exactly the right tone of respectful snideness," he said. "Show me more." As his parents' son, he was invited to all kinds of so-called society affairs; as Boyd and Amy's friend he went to all the hot clubs. As himself — it didn't matter much. He found a formula, crossing the basic gossip-column approach with the magazine's own snooty, New York Observed tone. He did whatever he was asked to do, whatever Rob wanted.

His aunt said, "I can't say that I much care for your magazine, John."

"Well, Aunt Clara, I don't think we write it for people like you."

She looked at him and said drily, "Don't forget that you are people like me, and that's your passport to all these parties and benefits you write about so loftily."

Anne laughed. "Touché, John. The Opera Gala, for example. What a lovely piece."

Jack had written, seven or eight months earlier:

Don Giovanni was almost incidentally the evening's excuse, and we were particularly struck by the ball scene. It is the culmination of the Don's evil that his creepy attempt to seduce the naive Zerlina takes place against the background of a minuet, the most civilized of dances. In this, Mozart and da Ponte anticipated the Met of the eighties, where a similar drama played itself out at the Gala. Hundreds of bony women stampeded the Opera House, using their finely honed elbows to clear spaces in which to be noticed, hoping to seduce the attention of someone higher up the food chain. All of this against the background of the most sublime opera by the most civilized composer (yes, we know that he was rude and fascinated with his own cah-cah).

And more in that vein. The evening had allowed Jack to play his favorite role, standing almost unnoticed and uninvolved at the side of the staircase, looking down into the milling throng in the well beneath him. He had gone alone, and as the crowd moved around him, men who knew him (or rather who knew his family, had known his parents) said distracted hellos to him. Some of the women spoke to him too, appraisingly, wondering what he was worth in the social game they were playing. He gave them no hint: in this atmosphere of seduction, his worth was as they valued him.

"But John," Anne said, "you haven't answered my question. Is there anything you don't know?"

My own heart, he thought. "The heart of a woman." She would like that better. "Here I am, twenty-eight and all alone."

"For the time being, anyway," Anne said. "The way you and Kate Welland have been going —" She left the sentence hanging in its own implications.

"Yes, John, when are you and Kate going to get engaged?" his aunt said. "I hear all about you from my friends, I saw a picture of the two of you in the newspaper last month. You've been taking her to every party in town —"

"She's been taking me," he said, trying to laugh it off.

Anne, whom he could usually count on as an ally in these discussions, said mischievously, "It's just a matter of time. He needs to pluck up his courage."

He gave her a dirty look, not wanting to be teased just then. "I promise, you will be the first to know."

The doorbell rang. It was his sister, and she made her usual elaborate entrance, full of talk, hugging Anne without touching her, finally getting to him. "Happy birthday, little brother, many happy returns." She leaned down and waved her lips past his forehead. "We got you a birthday present, but of course I forgot to bring it. We'll send it over to your apartment."

"Thank you, Elizabeth." He made an effort to rouse himself.

"Billy and Hank went shopping for it, although as usual they couldn't agree. Why do my children have such trouble getting along? I think David finally had to choose for them. I'm sure you'll love it."

He sat up. "I'm sure I will."

"Although," she went on, "any gift of ours must pale in comparison."

"To what?"

"Well, to your inheritance, of course," she said matter-of-factly. "You'll be rich as — rich as —"

"Croesus," he supplied. "No more so than you were on your twenty-eighth birthday."

"Yes, but I was already married, with two children. You're free as the air."

Their aunt intervened firmly. "I find this conversation vulgar." She poured a cup of tea for Elizabeth.

"Oh, no thank you. It's much too hot for tea. But I'll have a piece of cake. In honor of the occasion." Elizabeth never appreciated other people's fetishes, although she did, he thought, manage to ignore them without giving offense. He, on the other hand, always did what was expected of him. He imagined the two of them as travelers in some exotic land: he stopping to view decayed ruins that had no shape, visiting indigenous houses of worship, sampling native food however unappealing, making everybody happy; she sitting high up in a tourist bus, demanding a private bath, living the American plan. It was not that he was more adventurous than she, it was just the opposite.

Elizabeth picked up where she'd left off. "It's not vulgar. It's exciting. I was already married to David when Mommy and Daddy died, Billy was three and Hank was nearly two — I sometimes think I married too young —" She hesitated and then, declining to chase this hare she had so abruptly started, veered back. "But you have all the opportunity and none of the worry. Free as air," she repeated. She wasn't, he thought, much given to metaphor.

"Free?" Anne seemed determined to torture him. "We were just talking, Elizabeth, before you came, about John and Kate Welland. We think they should get married."

Elizabeth sighed, as if to imply that she thought so too but was being forbearing about it, not interfering (which almost made him laugh), and said, "Can you imagine what their children would look like? They're the perfect couple."

For you we are, he thought. Thomas Welland, Kate's father, was chairman of the North River Trust Company, the bank where David worked, the bank that managed Jack's trust fund. For Elizabeth it was a simple dynastic arrangement: marry your family into the ruling house and incidentally dispose of a somewhat problematical brother. It was a small bank, and marital affinity wouldn't hurt, especially when the Newland Trusts, Jack's and Elizabeth's and her children's, owned so much of the bank's stock.

"Even David thinks you should settle down, John," Elizabeth added. "Now that you're twenty-eight."

"What sort of birthday celebration does Kate have planned for you?" their aunt asked.

"She's in Switzerland. With her mother and her sister. They go every year, just the three of them." Girls' month off, she'd called it.

"But surely you'll have a birthday party tonight," his aunt went on, sounding pained, as if she'd slipped in her social obligations. "If we'd known, your uncle and I — that is, we were sure your friends —" She paused, on the edge of an invitation he knew she would rather not extend. She didn't want to throw together a dinner party at the last minute, his aunt and uncle never, in fact, threw anything together — her entertainments were carefully constructed events with predictable choreography, and his uncle ran on tracks as undeviating as those of the old New York Central Railroad. Jack could at least make her happy, even if he had to lie a little. "Well, I'm meeting some people later, I'm sure there'll be something. It's what I want, something spontaneous. You know Boyd and Amy."

She accepted the lie as gallantly as he had offered it and changed the subject. He told himself he didn't really want a party anyway. Being alone was bad, he thought, but it would have to be better than an evening of enforced celebration with what was left of his family.

After a few moments, Jack stood up and walked over to one of the windows. The sick feeling he'd had most of the day, which had receded here in his aunt's apartment, came back to him. At first he had put it down to a hangover, then to the weather. An emptiness in his stomach, a void hand spread out in his chest, he recognized it now. Anxiety, according to his shrink from the days after his parents' deaths. Ripley Lewis, his friend from boarding school, Churchillian for a time, called it Black Dog. Jack called it fear. Impatiently, he shrugged his shoulders and looked out the window.

Beneath him a bus pulled away from the curb with a muffled roar and a cloud of exhaust. On the sidewalk, a group of little boys in uniforms with short pants waited for the light to change, and Jack wondered what school would still be in session at the end of June. Across the street, a bum was sprawled on the ground, his back against the blackened wall of Central Park, while three girls in summer blouses and short skirts heedlessly passed. Beyond, the panorama of the park stretched out — from his vantage point he could see only the treetops interlaced. It was this, as much as the heat, that made him think: summer is here.

As a child, he had spent summers at his family's country house in northwestern Connecticut. His family and others like them from Manhattan had long ago established an enclave there, living in large houses on large properties among the valleys and hilltops of the Berkshires. It was considered more genteel than the Hamptons, less decayed than Newport, more accessible than Northeast Harbor. Something about the atmosphere implied rigor, which was then in vogue among his parents and their friends as something to be provided to children, a kind of cod liver oil for the sixties and seventies. Westfield's main street had an old-fashioned general store run by an ancient woman with a large mole on her cheek. The hardware store still in those days sold nails out of casks, the single theater showed movies that had long since ceased their runs in New York. The street terminated at the town green, a space sternly overlooked by the town hall, the post office, and two churches. There were no places where children, or more especially teenagers, could hang out unobserved, and all activity was either supervised or organized, usually both. In the face of all this implied discipline, which had felt more protective than intrusive, adolescent life centered around tennis or baseball games for boys, horseback riding for girls, and above all around the swim club.

The club was at one end of a crescent-shaped lake (overlooked by the Westfield Academy for Boys, where he'd gone to boarding school — so much of his life spent in the town of Westfield). There was a small beach, a U-shaped dock that fenced in a swimming area for little kids, a float with a slide and a diving board. Behind the beach was the clubhouse where, in the twenties and thirties, there had been weekly dances with imported New York bands, Jazz Age confections at which Jack liked to imagine Fitzgerald heroes achieving the apotheosis of cynicism. Next to the clubhouse a swimming pool and then a diving pool had been built, despite the lake, ensuring that there would always be structured activities, laps to be counted, lessons to be given. He remembered one afternoon when Chip Thomas had put on a diving exhibition. Chip was his idol — Jack was thirteen and filled with a romantic hero worship that colored everything in his life. Chip was older, around seventeen, with bronze hair and a body that he flaunted casually and gracefully around the club. That afternoon, he climbed up to the high board at the pool and, as if by chance, performed a perfect double somersault. Surfacing, he shook his head, scattering droplets over the water, and swam for the side, pulling himself out with an unbroken motion. He waited a moment at the bottom of the ladder, his hand on his cocked hip just above his bathing suit, while the person ahead of him went off. Then he climbed up and dove again, a gainer. After the third time, the other divers withdrew as dive followed dive, pikes and tucks and handstands, Jack didn't know what they were called. He was mesmerized by the sight of the golden body turning and twisting in the bright sunlight, never flawed, always beautiful. This is perfection, he thought. I love it.

His immediate reaction was emulation. He practiced diving, almost secretly, all winter long in New York, until the other boys teased him in the locker room. But it ended in disappointment when, on a gray day, the pool's surface looking oily and still, he stood on the board at the swim club where Chip had stood before him, and performed his repertoire. Some of the onlookers made nice comments afterward, but the feeling was somehow empty. He thought: I would rather watch than do, I'm cut out to love, not to be loved. Later that changed, at least the last part.

He remembered another day at the swim club, five years later, the afternoon before the annual country club dance. He was just eighteen, sitting on an overturned rowboat with three girls, idly wondering which of them he would sleep with that night. Everyone seemed to want him that summer, and he decided he would spend the night with whichever of them asked him first (in the event, it was Amy Brown who drove him back to her house, her hand resting on his thigh, and who made love to him in her pink, little-girl's bedroom). The three girls were commenting on the scene in front of them, where the boys dawdled aggressively at the water's edge. It was the kind of conversation to which men were not ordinarily privy, but Jack was an exception.

"Look at Boyd. He's cute."

"He's a dream."

"I wonder what he wears under those overalls."

Boyd Cornwell was two years younger than Jack and had taken to wearing a pair of denim overalls with no shirt, the straps and buckles rubbing against the red skin of his shoulders. Jack, as it happened, knew what Boyd wore under his overalls and said so.

"Well, what does he wear?"

Jack shook his head. "I'm not telling."

"Come on, John, that's not fair."

"I wish," Amy said, "that I could get a look inside the men's changing room."

It hadn't been in the changing room that Jack found out Boyd wore nothing under his overalls. It had been in Boyd's bedroom, at the top of an empty house, in a silence so unnatural that Jack wondered at its loudness. It had been mildly amusing, and somehow flattering, to be seduced by a younger boy. Jack glanced at Amy Brown, who said softly, "To see you, I mean. Not Boyd."

And Jack, to cool off memory and anticipation, jumped up and ran into the lake for a swim.

It hadn't occurred to him then that he would still, at the age of twenty-eight, be friendly with Boyd, or that Boyd would marry Amy. He had been happy then to luxuriate in the water as the afternoon came to an end. "Summer afternoon —" he thought, "summer afternoon; to me those have always been the two most beautiful words in the English language."

"John," Elizabeth called to him, breaking his reverie. "You're awfully quiet. What are you thinking about?"

"Henry James," he said automatically.

"Come over here and talk to me," Anne said. He obediently went and sat next to her. "It doesn't sound like you're having a very exciting birthday. I picture you in more exotic settings, I don't know, a trip on the Circle Line with champagne and strawberries, perhaps, or at least lunch at Lutèce."

"If only I could persuade you to join me," he said coyly, "I'd lunch at Lutèce any time."

She shook her head. "You're too tempting for me, green eyes. I wouldn't let myself, in your case." He wondered if this was how she seduced her men, through feigning unavailability. It was a technique with which he was familiar. She said, "I hear you visited my mother last week. It was sweet of you to go."

"I was summoned." Her mother lived in a huge apartment in a tower just up Fifth Avenue from his aunt. "She wanted me to see the redecorating job that Andrew Toller did for her."

"You are her arbiter of good taste."

"She doesn't need me for that," he said drily. Blanche Morgan's taste was legendary, although she chose to display it only to a small, shrinking group of people: the denizens of an Upper Fifth Avenue world, some of whom could remember a time before the Great War, as they still called it, all of whom were connected by filaments of blood or money. Her only memoirs, Blanche would say of those few, sad, last gray survivors, having determined that her past would die as they did, slowly and one piece at a time. "Unless," she would go on, "unless you, John, keep it alive"; for he had always been a part of her world. He said to Anne, a bit tenuously, "Do you remember, when I was a little boy, my mother would pick me up at school some days and we'd go to visit your mother. She had a huge collection of records, Broadway musicals mostly, *Anything Goes, Girl Crazy, Gypsy, Brigadoon, Guys and Dolls,* some of them were even on seventy-eights, big heavy records that whirled around on the turntable. While you all talked about whatever women talk about, I used to lie on the floor listening to those records." In short pants, his school uniform, his tie trailing across the floor, singing along with "I've Never Been in Love Before" or "The Heather on the Hill." That was how he'd learned so much about old Broadway shows, which always seemed to surprise everybody. That, and the parties his parents had given. They had been great parties, at least the sound of them, drifting up the stairs to him, had been great, and someone had always been at the piano playing Gershwin and Porter and Kern, Rogers and Hart, and, at each one, his father's favorite song, "Isn't It Romantic." The tunes had merged with his sleep, it was no wonder he could summon them up effortlessly. He said, "Do you remember the party when you sang to me at the piano?"

She looked at him speculatively. "Do you really remember that? You can't have been more than four."

"Four and a half." He did remember it, one of his earliest memories. It had been at the house in Westfield at Christmas, a legendary party, talked about for years after. Some of his memories of it came from later retellings, but some of them were real. His parents had booked all the rooms at the old Black Stag Inn, and all their friends from New York had come for the weekend. There was ice on the lake, and on Saturday afternoon his father and some of the other men played mock hockey, pretending they were thirty years younger and still in prep school. Jack sat frozen on a bench at the empty swim club and watched, and when they were done, he was allowed to walk out on the ice and take some shots at the goal. His father blocked the first few and then pretended to let him score a couple of times, to great applause from the other men, who were mostly drinking from flasks. Then his father picked him up, holding him tightly, and skated him around on the ice. There was a picture of that, but he remembered it for real. That night, when the party started, he sat at the top of the stairs, listening, watching through the bannister, being patted on the head by every man who came up to throw his wife's fur coat on his parents' bed. Much later he woke up and went into their room, the party in full swing downstairs, and hid under the coats. Anne found him there, scooped him up, half awake, and carried him off downstairs, where she sat him on top of the piano. Then she sang a very sultry, cabaret version of "Our Love Is Here to Stay," pretending to sing it to Jack, while a young man with a cigarette dangling from his mouth played along at the piano. He felt tired and warm, and he thought she was doing something special for him, even if all the grown-ups were laughing. Then his father had picked him up and taken him back to bed.

He said dreamily, "I remember what my mother was wearing. A blue dress." He realized what he had said and glanced at her before ducking his head. He didn't usually talk about himself that way, and he almost never talked about his mother.

But she only said, "We go back a long way, you and I, John."

"Twenty-eight years exactly," he said, laughing it off. But it was true, he'd been raised in a small world, and she had occupied a large place in it. His mother, Anne, Anne's mother, his aunt — it was all very certain and sure, or had been until he was thirteen. Even when he was out playing baseball or just hanging around with his friends, there was always that hum of women's talk, the lipsticked cigarettes and the smell of perfume, to return to. He thought of those women-filled days, after school when his mother took him with her on her rounds. Or sitting on the beach at the swim club in Westfield — he would run off to swim or play ball, but he'd return periodically to where she was sitting, in a group of other women. She would put a towel around his shoulders, rub him gently, not missing a beat in the female conversation that went on endlessly. How much of those discussions had he really followed, how much had stayed with him, shaping him, the ebb and flow of the words of those mothers? It wasn't, he thought, so much that he had been raised by women — he hadn't been, any more than anybody else — but that the world they had created was so definitive and whole. The rules were clear, passed down to them from their mothers and back through generations. And onward, too, he thought. Kate was one of them, she knew all the rules, the same protocol by which he had been raised. And their children, if they had any, would be raised the same way.

Elizabeth got up to leave. "Come, John, walk me down," she said.

She was quiet in the elevator, looking in her purse for something, it was a way she had of crowding people by ignoring them. He hated elevators, hated especially the way this one brought back the empty feeling to his stomach. He slumped against the back wall, and as if this were a sign, Elizabeth asked, "How is Amy? I understand she's going to be joining us on the Women's Committee for the Children's Hospital. She was such a pretty girl."

"Still pretty." He watched the floor numbers on the panel above the door, unreasonably blaming the elevator boy for not making the thing go faster, or for making it go too fast, he thought, as his stomach jumped. Randomly, he said, "Do you know a guy named Timothy Archer?"

She snapped her purse shut. "Of course. His family lived in Connecticut near us. He has a sister, too, I think." The elevator stopped with a jolt and the doors opened. In no hurry to get out, she finished her thought. "She must be a little older than you, so Timothy would be younger. Why do you ask?"

He made her wait until they'd stepped out into the lobby before answering. "He's a graduate student, at Columbia. I think. He's been hanging around, you know, with Boyd and Amy's crowd, for a couple of months now, and I didn't recognize him. He used to be an ugly little kid, I remember. Why is it always the ugly kids who turn out to be so attractive?"

She looked at him sharply. "You weren't an ugly kid. You were always —"

"Anyway, we've gotten to be pretty friendly, but he's never said anything to me about Westfield and all. I couldn't remember who he was, why he seemed to know me."

"John," she said, taking his arm as they stepped out onto the sidewalk. "I want to ask you a serious question. When are you and Kate going to get engaged?"

She'd caught him off guard, and he let his irritation show for the first time. "Hey, lay off, will you?"

She reached up and kissed him, satisfied now that she'd scored. "Happy birthday, little brother. We'll send your gift over this afternoon." And she stepped into a cab.

He watched her go, annoyed at himself for letting her get to him. The great get-Jack-married scheme. At least she was doing her own work this time. "Even David thinks you should settle down," she'd said in their aunt's apartment. That wasn't what David had said to him seven months before. David had been a lot tougher that afternoon when he'd roughed Jack up at the Knickerbocker Club; there had been none of Elizabeth's coy concern or breathless pretending. It had all gone David's way: man to man, bare-fisted and bloody.

II

HE STOOD INDECISIVELY on the sidewalk for a moment and
then crossed the street and went into the park. He didn't want
to be out in the heat, he didn't want to be walking around, and
he didn't want to be in Central Park, but somehow it seemed to
be a day to do what he didn't want. Or not to do what he did
want, if he could figure out what that was.

A crowd of Hispanic-looking boys on skateboards performed to
the music of a boom box. A fat, middle-aged man lay on a hillside,
indecently exposing his tender flesh to the sun. Four young black
women pushed four white babies in carriages. A group of little
boys played softball on a dusty diamond. The park roasted under
a slow flame. He suddenly had an idea for the review he might
or might not write of the movie he'd seen that afternoon, and he
looked for a bench and sat down. From his pocket, he took out
the little notebook he always carried and wrote: "He is not so
much an actor as an attitude." He looked at it for a minute, then
stood up, imagining that he felt his trousers sticking a little to the
bench. Probably some homeless person's home. Get a grip on
yourself, he thought; what do you want? The question David had
put to him, that evening seven months ago at the Knickerbocker
Club.

It had been a cold November afternoon, and he'd been at the
library at Lincoln Center doing some research for a film essay he
was working on. He'd come back to the office cold and disgruntled
— he liked doing research, but not when he couldn't find what
he was looking for. His ears were still burning from the cold when
the phone rang. David had many voices for him — paternal,
avuncular, fraternal, he had played all the roles in the last thirteen
years — but that day he was businesslike. It was the peremptory
summons he might make to a junior associate who was to be
reprimanded for a minor but notorious misdemeanor. "I'd like to

meet you for a drink this evening. How about the Knickerbocker Club at five-thirty?"

"I don't know, David."

"It's important, John."

Jack imagined him sitting in his office downtown, his feet up on the desk, his back resolutely turned to the plate glass beyond which the sea traffic silently toiled. Jack didn't want to hear a lecture from David, but it would be simpler to go. "All right. I'll see you there."

He left the office a little early, hurrying huddled in his coat through streets that were very cold, the hard dry cold that made ice blue. It reminded him of the air over the hockey rink at Westfield — he imagined for a moment that he could feel the vibration of the stick in his hands as he passed the puck and hear the noise of a body hitting the boards. At the club he stood in the lobby shivering a little, looking up at the Remington polo players frozen in bronze, then went up to the bar. The room, as always, seemed welcoming: the few deep chairs, the tall ceilings, and especially the paintings. Above the sideboard, Old Ironsides heeled to the wind; opposite, his back to the viewer and his head bowed with abject superiority, Cornwallis surrendered to Washington. Jack got himself a bourbon and stood a moment, getting warm.

The Knick was one of David's haunts. Jack had become a member only to please him; he had qualms about belonging to a club that wouldn't admit women. But that November he was using it more frequently, oddly enough at Kate's urging. She said she liked the idea of an all-male club, a place he could go to meet the boys, as she put it. Besides, she liked coming to the red room, the only part of the building to which women were regularly admitted, for a drink. She enjoyed the thought, she said, of sitting in that elegant room, knowing that all around her was a club full of men in deep chairs surrounded by cream-colored walls and fireplaces, all barred to her, a secret. It was an established fact in her world, her father was a member, and if Jack used the club that made him even more a part of her world. He had been going out with her for about five weeks at that point.

He carried his drink into one of the lounges and sat down. Two older members, part of an interchangeable parade who could be found playing backgammon at any hour, looked at him approvingly before going back to their doubling. They think I'm a credit to their stewardship — young, attractive, well-bred from old New York stock — little do they know. On a nearby chess table a game had been abandoned inconclusively. That's what my talk with David will be, he thought banally, a chess game. But one that Jack would automatically lose: those were, after all, the terms by which he'd agreed to play. Winning wasn't worth the cost. He sat down in an armchair and waited, sipping his bourbon while the room filled up a little and David came in. He stood in the doorway a moment, talking with an older member. He had crossed the great divide of forty and was, Jack noticed that evening, inclining toward a kind of studied portliness.

But then, Jack thought, swallowing more of his drink, David had always had an air of *gravitas*, he had never been frivolous, not a social butterfly — not even a social moth. While others of his age were chasing promiscuously after women, David had married Elizabeth. His friends had drifted through the gray years of the early seventies dispossessed of an idealism that had betrayed them and uncommitted to any faith. David had dispensed with soul-searching and had insinuated himself, quite naturally and uncynically, into the counsels of men much older than he, men like Thomas Welland, Kate's father, who soon came to rely on him. He never disappointed them, and it was the assurance (which he wordlessly conveyed) that he never would which had stood him in such good stead from the very beginning.

He came in and sat down next to Jack. "Good evening, John. It's cold out, isn't it?"

"Mmm-hmm." He would start with the weather, Jack thought and decided to play along. "It was so warm for so long, I thought it would never get cold."

"Well, they're forecasting snow for Wednesday."

Jack thought, a little sadly, We've known each other for nearly twenty years, is this the best we can do? He finished his drink and signaled to a waiter for another.

David shifted to business. "Your investment in the Watt Man-
ufacturing buyout is doing very nicely. We just got their third-
quarter numbers."

Jack could tell, from the tone of his voice, from years of experience, that this wasn't why David had summoned him, so he
stopped paying attention. He didn't know anything about in-
vesting, he trusted the money managers of the North River Trust
Company, all the bright boys Thomas Welland had assembled.
Jack could have been more assertive about his own finances; since
his twenty-fifth birthday he'd even had the right to change money
managers. But he trusted David, and besides, that would have
upset the delicate balance Elizabeth had imposed on her world
(and so by inclusion on Jack) after their parents had died. They
all had their roles to play in maintaining that balance, roles she
had assigned them from the very beginning.

His role, it seemed, was to grieve, Elizabeth's to sacrifice.
David, strong-chinned and determined, had stepped into the vac-
uum of their grief and taken charge. He had known how to suffer
nobly, how to arrange the obsequies, how, in short, to manage.
Elizabeth (for her own reasons — Jack hadn't asked for it, he was
sure of that) had determined to focus on Jack. "John is only fifteen,
it's such a vulnerable age," he heard her say more than once. She
was going to save him from the consequences of their tragedy,
and what better instrument than David: manly, effective, a role
model. Someone to step in and serve as father in all the father-
and-son chats that now would have to take place by proxy. David
had put his arm around Jack's shoulders. "We're here for you,
John, whatever you need. Whenever you want to talk." But Jack,
who knew more than he ever told anyone about things in general
and about the night his parents died in particular, sensed even
then a certain shrinking in that protective arm, as if this sort of
contact were unwelcome. For Elizabeth, though, it seemed at
least to make a pretty picture. She had disposed of Jack in a way
that submerged her own grief in selflessness, and he imagined
her saying to her friends, "David is so good with Jack." He never
questioned her about this arrangement, which continued as he
got older, because he didn't want to hurt her.

He looked out through the tall windows that fronted on the

park. The room was so warm, so comfortable, that it surprised him a moment to be reminded of the world outside, cold and gloomy and vicious. Why vicious? He wondered a moment at his thought, shivering a little. He waited for David to get to the point.

"I read your article about the Opera Gala," David said finally, settling back further into his chair. Jack smiled to himself for a moment. Discussing business, David leaned forward, lowered his voice. Personal matters somehow didn't imply the same need for intimacy that money did. Here it comes, Jack thought as David went on, "Did you think it was fair?"

Jack shrugged. He was suddenly tired — it was an accumulation of small things: the room itself, which seemed to rise up endlessly into an obscure patrician darkness, the first drink kicking in, David's reasonableness, his choice of the word "fair" to capture the high ground. He just wanted to get it over with, to make it easy for David. He said carelessly, "Oh, fairness doesn't enter into it."

"Don't you think it should?" David said, taking up the offered gambit. "I don't understand your position, John. One month you review movies, the next the opera, another the latest nightclub."

It's a small magazine, I do what I'm asked, he thought. "I observe the scene," he said loftily, reaching for his second drink.

"Yes, well. Don't you think that your entrée to the scene, as you put it, is due to your background, to your family and friends?"

"Well of course."

"And don't you think you're betraying those people by writing about them the way you do?"

"They love it." Jack gulped his drink. Didn't David realize that half the people he wrote about considered it a badge of honor? He wasn't writing scandal, after all, however scandalized David or Elizabeth might pretend to be — nothing he wrote was really that offensive. "We live in an age when to be noticed necessarily entails being insulted," he said, deliberately pedantic. "Not seriously insulted, but just a little. Those are the terms of the game. I just do what people want."

"Those women," David pursued, "at the Opera. Are they really as bad as you make them out to be?"

Jack shook his head. "David, let me ask you something. Here you are in this bastion of male superiority. How is it that you are so successful with women? Your clients, I mean."

"What are you driving at?"

"I'll tell you. You make women feel that they're at the center of things. They come to you with all their money, and you convince them that they're still in charge."

"I hope I'm not that cynical," David said with a certain amount of dignity.

"No one would ever accuse you of that. No, you really believe it. You convince them that the people who manage money for you are just glorified servants, plumbers or dressmakers, maybe, with a special expertise. But that the real power, the real enlightenment, is with the women. They love you for it." For a moment, as Jack warmed to the subject, he saw that it was true, that David lived by the same rules of seduction as he did, they were predator and prey: but David's prey were Jack's predators. Two sides of the same coin, he thought, heads he wins, tails I lose.

"I don't know what you're talking about," David said dismissively. "I'm just concerned about you, about your life. So is Elizabeth. We don't inquire, John, but we hear things."

Jack put his drink down on the small table and said carefully, "What things?"

David looked back at him levelly. "I've heard that you'll sleep with anyone who walks."

It was so unexpected, coming so coolly and in those surroundings, that Jack felt as if he were in boarding school again, lying flat on his back on a football field with the wind knocked out of him, his head banged against the ground, with the featureless autumn sky above. "That's a little exaggerated," he managed to say.

"I hope so. But from what we hear about you, your sister and I are beginning to wonder — running around all evening to clubs, spending the night with God knows who, all that liquor and for all I know drugs, going to every AIDS benefit in town —"

"You know why I go to AIDS benefits," Jack interrupted, speaking very evenly and very quietly. "It's not up for discussion. Period."

"All right." David, having won his point in such spectacular fashion, could afford to be generous. "I realize that times are different. That you and I are very different. That things which frankly would have been appalling to me and my friends are run of the mill now. That not everything means what it used to mean." He listed these points as if they were in mitigation of a sentence he'd already passed. "But you have to think about your future. Flirtation is fine in its place. But you must go ahead with your life."

— and from thence to the place of execution, Jack thought. Tried and convicted. At least he could resign gracefully. Anger was useless anyway. "You're right, David."

"John, that's easy to say. But you're drifting, and it bothers me. You have so much talent, so much ability."

I've gotten the message, Jack thought, why can't he leave me alone? He knew he was drifting, and had been for months. He thought of Kate: they had been keeping themselves more or less to themselves; it wasn't surprising that David didn't know Jack had been seeing her. David surely wouldn't have started this conversation if he'd known. Jack said, "I just need to find the right woman."

"Do you mean that?"

"Of course I do. I'll tell you what. Elizabeth is always trying to fix me up. From now on, I'll take her advice." Which was how they left it. But the discussion had depressed him, he felt as if he'd lost something or given up something against his will at the command of an imperious force that normally hid behind the confidence of its own power. Looking back at it now, after seven months, he might have dated from that conversation a kind of personal acceleration downward.

Having arrived at this conclusion, he suddenly woke up. He had wandered, in his reverie, down the Mall and behind the Zoo and now found himself on a bridge over the Lagoon, near the corner of the park at Grand Army Plaza. This was one of his favorite views of the city, and it usually seemed very romantic to him, Fifty-ninth and Fifth, an address to conjure with. But today it only made him think of the hard stone walls of New York buildings — the elegant limestone of Fifth Avenue, the regal white and green of the Plaza, the high roof of the Pierre. You could break yourself against those stones, he thought, if they didn't take you in. He was feeling sick again, and the heat was more oppressive than ever. He looked up, hoping to see storm clouds, something to clear the air. The sky was full, hazy and blank — he could almost see the electrical charges building up. There was a sort of faint greenish tinge to it, he thought, the kind of sky out of which the missiles will come. There would be a storm, but not until later. His head ached. This is getting me nowhere, I'm going home.

He lived in one of the newish apartment buildings in the Fifties between Fifth and Sixth. When he had decided to move into his own place, he had imagined himself in a loft in Tribeca — a huge space with endless shelves for his books, and stretched-out hard-wood floors and pipe racks instead of closets — or even (in his wilder moments) in a walkup in the East Village, gritty but *au courant*. Elizabeth had had another conception, had thought something contemporary to be more to the point, someplace high up with clean lines more suited to his position as man about town and observer of the scene, so he had landed in a postmodern building of questionable taste but impeccable credentials. It had a doorman and a security guard and an elevator operator (Boyd said it was easier to drop in on the secretary of defense), and a health club that he didn't use. His fellow tenants seemed largely to be foreign businessmen of all nationalities (not including the otherwise ubiquitous Japanese, this didn't seem to be one of their buildings) and their consorts of uncertain provenance. His apart-ment was on an upper floor, with windows that didn't open and a terrace that he tended to avoid. Between two opposing build-ings, he had a view of a piece of the park; between two others he could see the river. All that remained of his original vision was a book-lined study which, by way of a pull-out couch, doubled as a guest room. Though he didn't have many guests.

"Good afternoon, Mr. Newland. Your nephew is upstairs." In almost identical language, he was greeted in turn by each of his three praetorians. There was a short list — his nephews, his sister, and more recently Kate — of people who had the key and could be allowed in. He wondered, a little apprehensively, which of

Elizabeth's boys it was, until he stepped out of the elevator. From his apartment he could hear the Radiators: Billy, he thought.

Inside the apartment the music was even louder: "Zig-Zaggin' Through Ghostland." Billy, with Jack's tutoring, had lately developed a taste for southern rock. He was lying on the couch — all Jack could see of him was his sneakers tapping time with the record. There was a slight haze in the air, and the room smelled of pot. Jack shook his head, then went and looked over the edge of the couch. Billy was sprawled out, one hand holding a joint to his mouth, the other under his head. He was wearing a black T-shirt and jeans (Jack could see the hard muscles of his stomach where the shirt had pulled up), and his cuffs were stuffed into his sneakers. The laces, the color of tennis balls, were untied. He scrambled up when he saw Jack.

"Hi, Uncle John. Happy birthday."

"Thanks, Billy. Could we have the music turned down a little please."

"Sure." Billy went over and switched off the CD player.

"What are you doing here?" Jack sat down in a chair.

"Mom called from Aunt Clara's and told me to bring your birthday present over. You want to open it now?"

"Later." He knew he was being deflating. It was part of this mood he didn't seem able to shake.

"OK. You want some of this?" He held out his joint.

"No. And you shouldn't either. For one thing, it's not good for you. And your father would kill me if he found out."

Billy frowned. "You're not going to get all uncle-y on me, are you?"

"Would you rather I called David and had him get all fatherly on you?"

"Shit, no." He flopped down on the couch again and stuck his feet up on the upholstery. Jack had forgotten, if he'd ever known, how much a teenager seemed to fill a room. Especially Billy, the athlete of the family, his father's son. He never seemed to keep still, he never ceased demanding attention. It was as if some mythical beast, a young dragon perhaps, had been let into the apartment and was testing its wingspan. "Where were you this morning?" Billy asked. "I waited till almost quarter of eight."

They had an appointment to go jogging in the park three times a week. It was for Jack one of the high points of his day, the way his feet pounded purposefully on the pavement, the green of the trees or, in winter, the salmon colors of the sun's rising, and Billy next to him stride for stride. Jack sometimes dreamed about it — the two of them shoulder to shoulder, running down a leafy corridor, no sounds, no end. "I had a hangover," he said.

"And you tell me not to smoke dope? That stuff is ten times worse for you."

"I had a bad night. And don't get all nephewly on me, OK?"

Billy grinned. "Hey, is it true that you're going to marry Kate Welland?"

"Your mom sure works fast."

"What do you mean?" When Jack didn't answer, he said, "I didn't talk to her. She left a message with the housekeeper."

"Then what made you ask about Kate and me?"

Billy shrugged. "It's all Mom's been talking about practically for weeks." He got up and went into the kitchen. "You want anything?"

"No." So Elizabeth was busy talking up his engagement. He wondered whether it meant anything. "What does she say?" he called.

"About Kate?" Billy came back in with a Coke can, which he ostentatiously opened with one hand. He took a huge gulp. "She says she's perfect for you."

"That's all?"

"Jesus, John, I don't pay attention to half of what she says." He took another swallow. "I'd go bananas if I did." He burped. " 'Scuse me." He sat down again and this time put his feet, laces flapping, onto the coffee table. "So is she?"

"What?"

"Perfect for you. She's got a great body."

"Careful, Billy. Be nice."

Billy, as usual, ignored the warning. "You always get the best-looking girls. Remember that girl Judith, when you were in grad school? She was hot. What happened to her?"

"She married a priest," Jack said.

"No. Really?"

"No." He stood up. "Listen, I'm going to take a shower."

Billy looked at him as if he wanted to say something else, or as if he wanted Jack to say something else. Then he shrugged. "OK."

"Are you going to stick around?"

"Well, are you tellin' me to get out?"

Jack raised his hands. "Just asking." He went into his bedroom and undressed, then went and stood in the shower, directly under the water for a minute, letting it wash down over his face.

So Billy thought Kate had a great body. That had to be his own opinion, it wasn't something he would have heard from either of his parents. Well she did, he thought. "You always get the best-looking girls." It would be more accurate to say they got him. He hadn't realized that Judith had made such an impression on Billy, who couldn't have been more than twelve. The age for fantasies, perhaps.

Jack had been in graduate school at Yale, studying Victorian novels and writing occasional film criticism for one of the campus journals. He had gone to a party in someone's room. He remembered the room — Gothic, dark floors, a tubercular fireplace, one of those monastic steel-framed beds that Yale provided, a leaking armchair — but not his host (or hostess, perhaps). People talked about politics, it was one of those seasons when everyone seemed to be complaining about Reagan in what Jack thought was a disconnected way. No one seemed to have any frame of reference in which to put the man — they treated him as an anomaly. It irritated him, but he didn't say anything, there was no point in arguing. He leaned against the mantel drinking bad sherry, which was all that was offered (it must, he thought, have been some kind of literary party). When he left, bundled in his parka to cross the windy campus, she followed him, wrapped in a man's tweed overcoat. "Did you stand next to the fireplace on purpose?"

"Why should I?" he asked, not rudely, wanting to know.

"Firelight agrees with you. It shows you to good advantage."

He said nothing, recognizing this game and knowing its rules. Nothing was required of him. He was in her hands.

She lived on the edge of the campus in a Victorian house she shared with three other women. He walked her home and built a fire in the fireplace in her bedroom. Later, he stood naked in front of it to put another log on. "You're all fire and gold," she said softly from the tumbled bed.

Fire and gold. For a moment at the outset he had wanted to dissuade her, but she took him for all he was worth, and it was her extravagance that carried him away. He would sit in a reading room staring at her, unable for once to think of anything, imagining only the feel of her body. They once made love in the darkened stacks on the twelfth floor of the library, standing up with their clothes constricting them. On cold nights they wandered at her direction beneath the yellow-lit windows of the campus, her long hair winding smoothly between her woolen hat and the collar of her overcoat, and she told him long stories of past loves, her *summa erotica*, not boastfully (as a man would have, he reflected) but more to establish her position. One night, they stopped at the top of a snow-covered hill at the edge of the campus, where the lights of New Haven hid the stars, and she kissed him, not touching him at first except with her lips, and then more and more passionately until he felt dizzy, as if the revolving sky had descended into him. Then he slowly unzipped her pants, and he felt her shiver a little at the rush of cold air between her legs, and then his hand warmed her.

The first morning, as they lay in bed, she had said, "I hope you don't go in for a lot of bullshit."

"That depends on what you mean by bullshit."

"Complications. I'm a very straightforward person."

He paused, thinking a moment. "I'm not."

She yawned. "Oh, God. Well you're not going to turn into someone else on me, are you?"

"Who do you have in mind?"

"I've just been with too many men who start out as my lover and end up as my father or my son or my brother. Do you know what I mean?"

"I think so." He was propped up on one elbow, looking down at her face in the nest of her soft brown hair, at her brown eyes, which were focused then on a spot on the ceiling.

"Too many men," she went on, "who start out pretending that they want me, but end up wanting me to be the other half of their fantasy. Does that make any sense?" She shifted her gaze to his face. "Do you have fantasies?"

"I'm all fantasy," he said, smiling, sidestepping as neatly as he could. "Your fantasy."

She was five years older than he, which she liked, saying it made her feel decadent. Although, she said, there wasn't much corrupting to do in his case, and asked him where he'd become so good at making love.

"A lot of practice," he answered. At doing things to make people happy, he added to himself. He could have told her about his past, but didn't want to.

She wasn't interested. "If I wanted to corrupt you, how would I do it?"

"Break my heart."

"I might, you know."

It was the crime of Socrates, he told her, corrupting the youth of Athens, and commanded her to drink hemlock. He took her to New York for her birthday weekend, and their theater tickets lay unused on the dresser of their room at the Carlyle while she made long love to him. He bought her a pair of diamond earrings.

"I can't accept these."

"Why not."

"They mean — too much." She snapped the small jewel case shut.

He didn't pretend not to understand her. "They mean everything," he said extravagantly. "I love you."

"Oh, John. You can't." She looked stricken, and he suddenly felt all the fire and gold slip away from him. He knew immediately what he had done, but he couldn't call back the untimely word. He foresaw a horrible conclusion, each of them trying not to hurt the other, both of them hurt in the end. He did the only thing he could. "I was just kidding. I'm not old enough, or young enough, or something, to be in love. Just in lust." He fooled her, maybe; but the lying changed everything, for him and for her. She became impatient with him, distracted.

In the end, he thought, snapping off the shower, she left me, and that's the long and the short of it. At least she had left him, not the other way around, it hadn't been his doing. He grabbed for a towel and rubbed his hair more vigorously than he needed to. He dried himself and went out into the bedroom, the towel around his neck, and stood for a moment with his head in his hands, feeling only a kind of dumb hatred at this stupid day. He straightened stiffly when the door opened and Billy came in.

"Hey," he said. "Not a bad bod for an old guy."

"Give me a break, Billy." Jack went to his dresser, put on a pair of gym shorts, and sat down on the bed.

"I brought you this." Billy handed him an old-fashioned glass full of Wild Turkey and ice. "You looked a little green before."

"Thanks," he said and took a gulp. Billy was standing a little aimlessly in the middle of the room, his hands stuffed in his pants pockets. Whatever he has on his mind, Jack thought, it'll have to come out by itself. "How's your brother?"

"He's such a nerd." Billy seemed relieved to find a topic on which he could expound. "He's got this new friend, some fat kid with big glasses, and all the two of them do all day is come home from school and hang out in Hank's room."

"Sounds awful," Jack said and drank some more bourbon.

"Yeah, well, you wouldn't think it was so funny if you had to live with it. I had a friend over the other day and we're sitting in the kitchen? And the two of them come running in playing some stupid game about dragons or something."

If Billy was his father's son, Hank was all Elizabeth. He wasn't, at least Jack didn't think so, a nerd. He had simply, at the age of fourteen, arrived at a point in his life where all the choices seemed wrong, and he took refuge in an unpredictability of behavior. Every six months or so, he ran away from home, usually as far as Jack's apartment, sometimes not so far. He would arrive on the doorstep, usually at the most inconvenient times, when Jack was getting ready to go out, or when he and Kate had settled down with some popcorn to watch TV, with some tale of woe — a cutting remark by his parents, some infringement of his imagined rights — full of anger and remorse. Jack would cancel his plans, bundle Kate off into the bedroom, hold Hank's hand until he calmed down. He wasn't a bad kid, really, Jack kept telling Kate. He was having a rough time. Jack himself wouldn't especially want to be David's son; the standard was too high, the judgments too clear. Nor, for that matter, would he have wanted to be Billy's little brother — the ugly duckling next to the bright star.

Billy's adolescence ran true to his own form, infused with an overall certainty that Jack found himself envying at times. He hadn't escaped the usual ups and downs of growing up, and he was just as likely to bring himself to Jack in a crisis as to his father, more likely in some cases, but he did so in a more straightforward way than Hank (he had, some years before, unexpectedly asked, "How old were you when you had your first wet dream?"). Jack, however fond he was of Hank, loved Billy. But one didn't speak of love to a sixteen-year-old. "He's your brother, Billy."

"He's an asshole," Billy said sulkily.

"You're in a foul mood today."

"Yeah, well." Billy sat down on the floor and leaned against the bed. "Are you going to marry Kate Welland?"

The question of the hour. He hadn't answered his aunt, or Anne, or Elizabeth, when they'd each asked him. He hadn't even discussed it with Boyd, with whom he and Kate spent so much time. But if he were going to tell anyone, it would be Billy; he was the only one who didn't have a vested interest in the outcome, having no vested interests at all. "Can you keep a secret?"

Billy shrugged. "Sure."

"Well, then, yes, we are going to get married. We decided before she went away, but we're not telling anyone for a while. You're the only one who knows."

"That's great, John. Wow, I'm really happy for you." He twisted around on the floor a little and stuck out his hand. "Congratulations."

Jack shook his hand, which was like a puppy's, oversized with growth that he still had coming to him. "Thanks."

"When's it gonna be?"

"We haven't decided. Listen, I have a favor to ask you." He hadn't really thought about it before, but now, on the spur of the moment, he decided. "Would you be my best man?"

Billy swallowed. "You mean it?"

It would kill Hank with jealousy, but then David was the only alternative, and he was out of the question. "Of course I mean it. Who else?"

"Gosh. That's great."

He was obviously impressed, since gosh wasn't a word that was usually in his vocabulary. Jack smiled while Billy sat and took it all in. Finally Billy said, "How do you know?"

"What?"

Billy leaned his head back and looked at Jack. "How do you know if you want to marry someone? If you're in love?"

Jack shrugged. "I don't know how I know." It had somehow seemed the inevitable conclusion, it was what everybody — Elizabeth, David, Kate — wanted. He tried a shot in the dark. "How do you know anything about women?"

Billy looked away at that, and Jack thought: lucky guess. Billy said, resolutely, "I gotta ask you something." He paused. "There's this girl? We're kind of going out. She's real nice, we're having some real good times."

"And you want to know —" Jack prompted.

"Well, I think she wants to, you know, have sex. And I was wondering, sort of, how do you know what to do?"

"Oh, baby," Jack said softly, hiding a smile. "Is that it?"

"Yeah, well, it's kind of like my first time."

Jack considered the possibilities. "Do you want an anatomy lesson?"

"Shit, no," Billy said.

Jack hadn't thought it would be that. "You do what comes naturally. It's not that complicated. The important thing is to relax and have a good time. Both of you."

"That's easy for you to say," Billy said doubtfully. "What if I make a mistake?"

"What if you do?"

Billy crossed his legs and started picking at the carpet. He might, Jack thought, be his father's son, but this was the Newland vulnerability coming out in him. It was there in all of them — close to the surface in Hank, further down in Elizabeth, buried deep in Billy. "I don't know."

"Billy, you can't make a mistake. There's no such thing as a mistake. There are just things that make you both have a good time. If you really like her, you'll figure it out."

Billy looked away from him. "It's just that I'm pretty sure she's, like —" He gave it up.

Jack filled in the blank: she's experienced, and in the world of teenage boys, it was supposed to be the guy who had done it a hundred times before (Jack remembered that well enough, but he didn't think it was the right thing to bring up at this point). He decided to try a joke. "Listen," he said, "this is your uncle speaking. You and I go back a long way. If you remember, I taught you to pee standing up." Jack had been babysitting and Billy had suddenly decided to imitate him. He'd managed to hit everything in the bathroom except the water in the toilet. "I mean, if I say you have nothing to worry about, who should know better?"

Billy ducked his head. "I hate it when you tell that story."

Jack grinned. "OK. I'll save it for your kids. Or for your girl-friend if you want me to. Seriously, though," he said, becoming an uncle again, "do you have condoms?"

"Yeah. But she's taking the pill."

"How do you know?"

"She told me."

"Use a condom anyway."

Billy puzzled this out. "She doesn't have AIDS or anything," he said slowly.

Jack shook his head. "Maybe not, although you don't know that. It's your responsibility, Billy. If you're going to do this, you have to behave responsibly. You're accountable for your own actions, not anyone else."

He thought a minute. "I guess so."

Billy went home a little while later. As he was leaving, Jack reached into a drawer and tossed him a stick of cinnamon gum. "Better take this. You don't want your dad to smell anything on your breath that shouldn't be there."

"Thanks, Uncle John."

"Have a good time tonight." As he closed the door, he thought: hide your heart, Billy.

III

HE WENT BACK into the living room and stood at the window.
His body prickled as he watched the dirty heat outside the glass.
There were huge piles of clouds over New Jersey, green-edged
pyramids that disappeared upward in haze, and again he wished
for a storm. The silence in the apartment, usually so comforting,
began to disturb him. He went over to the CD player, put away
the Radiators disk, and looked indecisively at the shelf of records.
Then he remembered the package he'd gotten the day before
from Dougie, and went to open it.

Inside was a tape cassette and a note. "Dear Johnny: The Beethoven C Major Concerto with yours truly at the keyboard and the
Fairfield Chamber Symphony behind — not one of my finer efforts
but you insisted on having the complete cycle. There was some
tape left over so I recorded that Mozart sonata, the one you claimed
to know by heart." Dougie had played it over and over one spring,
and Jack had been with him most of the time. He was trying to stay
away from home as much as possible, spending all his free time
with Dougie, his best friend, his oldest friend, listening to him
practice. It was the year they turned fourteen, just before Jack
went away to boarding school, leaving Dougie behind. "See you
when I get back. Happy Birthday." Dougie was in Santa Fe, he'd
be playing the next night in the finals of a competition out there.
Jack popped the cassette in and headed for the study. He noticed,
as the familiar music began, the wrapped present that Billy had
brought — they'd never opened it.

There were four messages on the machine. The first was from
Kate in St. Moritz, crackling with satellite static: "Hello, John. I
miss you. I wish I weren't here. I wish I were with you. I guess I'll
try you later. Happy birthday. I love you." The second was from his
friend Peter Callahan, from Yale days: "Hey, Jack-o, happy birthday, kid. Sorry I'm not back in time, I'm stuck out here in the wilderness for another week." Peter had a small part in a movie that

was shooting in Oregon. "See you when I get back. Love you, 'bye." The third message was from his nephew Hank. "Uncle John? This is Hank. Billy wouldn't let me come with him. To bring your present? He's such an asshole." Jack heard some giggling in the background and assumed it was Hank's new friend. "I just wanted to say happy birthday. Anyway. Goodbye." The last message was from Boyd. "Hey, Newland. We're going to Val's later. Around nine-thirty. Got some great news. See you later." "News" was Boyd's code for coke. Great news was great coke. No news, on the other hand, was bad news. Jack rubbed his eyes and reset the machine. He was tired of cocaine. He was tired of Val's, of clubs in general. He tried not to think that he was tired of Boyd. And the whole crowd of hangers-on who trailed around after Boyd and Amy: Boyd's friends from college, and Amy's; a guy from Boyd's office who kept talking about his girlfriend's pubic hair (Jack didn't usually use the word vulgar, but it was inescapable); there was always somebody's cousin or brother from out of town. People who knew people who knew people who knew Jack, but he didn't really know any of them.

He thought about eating some dinner, but he didn't feel very hungry. He got himself another bourbon instead. He looked at the mail: two bills, four catalogues, and a birthday card from his grandmother in Palm Beach, with greetings generously inscribed by Hallmark, and only the tiniest of signatures to show that it had ever passed through her hands; her gift had been received by way of an account-to-account transfer at the bank. Ever since his parents had died, she had gone about in fear that he might some-day be foisted on her.

Occupy your mind with something else, Dr. Sanders, his shrink, had prescribed. Easy for you to say, Doc, he thought, and tried to listen to the music. Across from where he was sitting, the wall was covered with photographs: of himself, of Elizabeth, of Billy playing soccer, of Hank looking goofy, of David, of Billy in a tuxedo, of Hank as a baby, of his friends — Dougie and Peter and Ripley — of Jack's parents. No pictures of Boyd, though, or of Val's, or of vulgar friends. The other part of his life. No pictures of birthday parties, which was appropriate enough. No birthday party. Maybe he wouldn't go out at all.

But at nine o'clock he decided he would go in style. Kate had bought him a black jacket of raw silk, and a purple shirt to wear with it, and oversized pleated pants. He put them all out on the bed, fancy dress for a secret celebration, and went into the bathroom to shave. Not that he needed to, but Kate had bought him a new shaving brush, and he figured it was as good a birthday present as any. He opened the box and took it out, feeling the cleanness of the pure badger bristles (according to a little gold sticker on the tissue paper wrapping), and turned on the hot water until it steamed. He held the brush under it and was rewarded with the smell of burning badger — Texas chainsaw barbecue, he thought — and brushed soap on his face. She'd wanted to buy him a new shaving mug, but he had said no — he still used the mug from the Wedgwood Peter Rabbit set he'd had as a child. On the side, next to the painted pictures of Flopsy, Mopsy, Cottontail, and Peter, it said, "Now run along and don't get into mischief." Beatrix Potter at her best — he thought it was a salutary sentiment with which to begin each morning. When the phone rang, he thought, Let the machine get it, still lathering his lip. Then he carefully put the brush on the rim of the sink and stepped out of the bathroom stealthily, not wanting to be found out.

The bedroom was dark and very quiet, its thick carpet sucking up noise, the isolation made more insistent by the murmur of an indistinct voice from the machine in the study. He felt as if he had cotton in his ears, or as if the whole room was full of cotton. He curled his toes into the rug a moment, then edged into the living room, as if the caller might somehow know he was there. He could hear the voice more clearly now, Kate's voice, calling from Switzerland again. "— missed you again. I miss you all the time, really. This is the longest we've been apart since we met, John." He stepped forward toward the phone, thinking, I don't want to talk to her, I'm not here. He felt like a thief, standing there listening to her voice in the empty apartment, but not as empty as she thought it was. "I'll call back in the morning. It's two A.M. here. Happy birthday." She hung up.

He stood still a minute, feeling guilty, wondering if he should call her back, make up some story. Then he went back to the bathroom and picked up the razor, blaming himself. He stared at the shaving brush, feeling sorry for her, stupidly. It was such a silly present, but she had given it to him, and giving him things was so much a part of her way with him. He felt tears in his eyes and brushed them away angrily. "Kate," he said softly, leaning his hands on the edge of the vanity, looking down into the sink, thinking of how much she loved him.

He had met her at a theater party given by one of Elizabeth's friends — cocktails, the show, then dinner. Jack had been covering something else for the magazine, so he'd skipped cocktails and gone directly to the theater. It was a benefit performance, for the preservation of Broadway theaters or something, and, as he stood in the back, amid the crowd in black tie, waiting for an usher and a program, he noticed a girl standing a few rows ahead, looking back over her bare shoulder in his direction. In the closeness of the crowded theater, in the warm intimacy of the house lights, he felt that she was looking at him — but she wasn't, and he had time to study her without being noticed. She looked, almost, like a high school girl, her hair held back in a clasp, all except one artful lock that escaped across the side of her face. Her dress was red velvet with a black skirt, and he could see her in a dining room before a party, leaning over the table and lighting the candles, a last touch before guests arrived. She held her head at a certain angle and with a certain expression, as if she owned the world, or would one day.

She was, of course, one of the party to which he'd been invited, and his hostess, a woman of Elizabeth's vintage, introduced them. "So you are John Newland," Kate said, in a voice that was almost too husky. "Paul," she said to an elderly man sitting next to her, "be a pal and move over one, so John can sit down. Don't worry," she said to Jack, "Uncle Paul doesn't mind. He'll probably fall asleep anyway before the first act is over." And all through the play he was conscious of her sitting next to him, her face lit by the changing color of the light from the stage.

After the show, he helped her on with her coat, settling the sumptuous fur over her bare shoulders. At supper she ignored him, and he was corralled by a boring woman who took issue with something he'd written about a movie. He kept watching Kate, as she walked by him two or three times, her head held straight, not looking at him. It was as if she possessed this world, the closed little circle of old New York (as old as it got these days, anyway), so completely that she must also possess everything in it, including him. If she didn't always stop to count her possessions, that was only to be expected from a princess. He was already making up stories about her.

It was only at the very end of the evening, when coffee had been cleared away and brandy served, that she came and sat down next to him. "I know your brother-in-law," she said.

"And I know your father."

"And of course I've met Elizabeth."

It was the old conversation. They'd known each other, re- motely, as children — their fathers were associated in various business ventures, but the families didn't spend much time to- gether and so they'd lost touch with each other. She went to school in Virginia, and to college in Boston. Her family spent the summers at Newport, and she lived, for two years after college, in Washington. She knew boys he'd known at summer camp or at Westfield, he knew girls she'd gone to college with, and they laughed, wondering, at how small the world was, yet they hadn't met in all those years. Now she was back in New York, working for a publisher of art books that ran a small gallery on the side. It all went exactly as it always went on such occasions, the way of their world, except that she was more beautiful than anyone had been before, and at the very end she said, "Would you like to have dinner with me one night. Soon?"

"I'd love to."

"How about Wednesday, then?" They were standing in the hallway, waiting to say goodbye to their hostess. Kate had come with her uncle Paul and was going home with him. There was no opening for Jack, even if he'd wanted to, to see her home. "Shall I make the reservation?" she prompted.

"No, no," he said, coming to his senses. "I'll pick you up around eight. Where would you like to go?"

She gave him a last smile. "Someplace very expensive. Or very cheap. You decide."

They embarked on what he called, to himself, an evening ro- mance. He would meet her at her apartment on East Seventy-ninth Street and they would go to dinner or the theater, the opera or a movie — not to dinner parties because people didn't know, then, to invite them as a couple. He would see her home, but she never asked him in, she vanished inside and left him on the doorstep with the illusion of propriety. He was sure it was an illusion because he'd never met a woman before who so thoroughly radiated a romantic consciousness, as if her every gesture was calculated for its erotic effect. Or not calculated, because it all seemed so natural, part of her nature. He would wander away from her door and walk for blocks down Fifth Avenue, all the way home sometimes, thinking of wild animals, things of great beauty and violence, capable of acts of incredible grace while killing casually for food, whose nature it is not to know themselves. He felt as if he were drunk on her.

One night, about two months after he'd met her, he was sitting uncomfortably in her parents' living room, having a drink with her father. They were all going to the bank's annual Founders' Dinner. It would mark, in a way, a milestone in his relations with Kate, a kind of public affirmation of whatever it was they were to each other. Elizabeth and David would be there, of course, and maybe that was why Jack felt a little nervous. Also, Thomas Welland had always been a distant figure of authority to Jack, the keeper of the Newland Trusts, and the final arbiter of disputes with David. "You'll have to clear that with Mr. Welland," had been an occasional refrain, especially in the case of some of Jack's contributions to exotic and often AIDS-related charities, which David considered undeserving recipients of the family gold. Thomas Welland had always loomed in his imagination like Oz the great and powerful, a loud voice surrounded by smoke. Now, he was addressing Jack on the subject of the trade deficit, when Kate appeared to rescue him.

"Daddy," she said, taking Jack's glass and refilling it for him, "I'm going to show John around the house. Mommy'll be down in ten minutes."

She led him out of the room and up the stairs. "I want to show you something." Her dress rustled as she went up ahead of him, and he wondered what secret he was to be let in on, since she'd been so careful up to now to keep her secrets.

They went into a large room on the second floor, overlooking the street. It was furnished as a sitting room or den, except for a series of old glass-fronted cabinets against the walls. On the shelves, behind the glass, was arranged an assortment of carved jade objects, some as much as eighteen inches tall, others exquisitely small. He looked at them, walking from case to case, while Kate hovered in the background. "May I take one out?" he asked, opening a door. He picked up, from the black stand on which it rested, a figurine of an elderly man in flowing robes with a wispy beard. The sculptor had used minor variations in the color of the stone to give the piece a sort of comical effect.

"That's from the late sixteenth century," she said.

"It's very beautiful."

"The color of your eyes," she said. She took it from his hand and put it back in the case. He looked at another piece, a rugged mountain carved out of gray stone, with the abrupt contours of the landscapes he'd seen in advertisements for tours to China. Kate said, "That is the gray jade mountain of longevity."

"This is your collection?" he asked, somehow having assumed that it had been passed down through the family from some last-century robber baron.

"It was started by my great-grandmother, but nobody seems to have been very interested in it before me. I'm mad about jade, I don't know why. I see a piece, a good piece, and I have to have it."

"The acquisitive instinct."

She led him over to a table by the window. On it was a carved chess set, all in jade, red and white, two imperial armies facing each other over a board inlaid with jade. "It's very highly developed in me, you know."

"What is?" He picked up a rook, a white elephant, its trunk trumpeting.

"The acquisitive instinct. When I see something I want, I have to have it." She laughed at herself. "That sounds so spoiled, but it's in my genes, I guess. My family has bought and sold everything — railroads, oil wells, yachts, houses. I'm reduced to buying jade."

"I can't see," he said, putting down the elephant and picking up a pawn, "that it's much of a comedown."

"No? We even have a branch of our family tree that once owned slaves."

He looked at her and thought again how self-willed she was. It was extraordinary to him how much this trait, which might have been mere egotism in someone else, appeared in her as the product of a clear-sighted focus on what she wanted. She was one of those people who set a value on all things — who know what everything is worth, because they have always and simply known what they want. If it was ownership she valued, she was above all self-possessed.

"Come see this," she said, indicating a rectangular stand with gold pegs at each corner. Held in place by the pegs were six or eight slabs of white jade. On the top one he could see incised Chinese characters filled in with gold leaf. "That's a jade book, it's very rare. It's supposed to be the handwriting of the Emperor Kangxi." She touched it with the tip of her finger. "He had hundreds of slaves — concubines, men, children, eunuchs. I sometimes wonder what it would be like to own another person."

"You can't possess people," he said, making a joke out of it, "unless of course you're the devil." He saw, now, where she was going. He had only to stand still, no matter how close she got, and eventually she would pounce.

"Does anything possess you?" she asked, not putting it off.

"Only —"

"And if I," she added after a moment, "wanted to add you to my collection —?"

"And do you?"

She put her hand behind his neck, and he felt her breath as she pulled his face to hers.

He had been drifting — it hadn't taken a lecture from David in the mannish precincts of the Knick to tell him that. Since graduate school there had been nothing in his life, apart from his job at the magazine, that had lasted, nothing to which he felt committed. He had gone out with a lot of women, but never for more than a few weeks with any one of them; he'd even tried celibacy for a while, in a quasi-religious way. He had a few friends. There was a loosely knit group of old Westfield boys, inhabitants by day of the financial district, with whom he went to baseball games or bars. A group from Yale gave elaborate dinner parties on the floors of shared apartments on the far West Side or frequented Tribeca lofts, and with three of them he played a drunken game of bridge every Tuesday night. Peter Callahan, his closest friend from college, had gotten married. In fact, most of his friends were gradually settling into domesticity, and as they approached thirty, marriage was becoming more and more common; even the occasional infant appeared on the scene. Dougie had been living most of those years in Philadelphia, where he'd had a fellowship at Curtis. Jack was left, more and more, to Boyd and Amy and their crowd, to events that he attended in his capacity as observer of the scene, and to more exclusive private dinner parties, where he was valued as an extra man. He would leave some woman's apartment at two or three or four in the morning, his suit pants wrinkled from having been dropped on the floor or a chair, his tie draped around his neck. He'd stand on the empty corners of empty avenues waiting for a cab, shivering in the cold of night or breathing heavily in the heat of summer. In the cab he would put his head back and look at the passing buildings, half asleep and numb, smelling to himself like sex and a woman, wondering if the cabby could smell it. Then he would stumble up to his apartment and into bed, and wake up the next morning looking unscathed but feeling it terribly. Looking back, he thought, it was in this time that he gave up his childhood and gained a hardness that would, he hoped, prevent him from ever again being the occasion for pain. He developed his persona as an observer, a toy balloon that floated high above the city, drifting, until Kate arrested him by grabbing the string that night in the midst of her jade.

He woke the next morning in her bed in her apartment. He could hear her starting coffee in the kitchen. He propped the pillow against the wall and put his arms behind his head, waiting to see what would happen. She came back in a blaze of yellow — a silk bathrobe, orange juice, coffee mugs with a wide windowpane pattern. "Good morning," she said, putting the tray on the night table and sitting down next to him. He pushed a strand of hair off her face. "Good morning," he answered.

She leaned down and kissed his lips and then his chest just below the breastbone. Her hand strayed over his thighs beneath the sheet. "What about breakfast?" he said half-heartedly, but she ignored him.

That first afternoon, as they strolled along a Madison Avenue that was busily preparing for Christmas, she took him into a small store that sold Italian clothes. I hate Italian clothes, he protested softly, but she bought him a sweater. She loved buying him things, it didn't seem to matter what, and price was no object: sweaters, shirts, a shaving brush; flowers, obscene candy, cuff links; even a pair of ice skates when she wanted to go skating at Wolman Rink and he told her his skates were at the house in Connecticut. He bought her flowers, corsages, in a very old-fashioned way before they went out, and minor jewelry; once he wanted to buy her a piece of jade. But she laughed this off, telling him she was more likely to find something really good herself. She had, after all, her standards.

And he came up to her standards, or so it seemed. He fit perfectly into her life, more perfectly than he had ever fit in before. She managed to place everybody that way, inserting them into her private taxonomy, reminding him, sometimes, of a biology teacher he'd had at Westfield: "Any living thing can be identified by class and family and genus and species." There had even been a chart, the Tree of Life, illustrating, say, the exotic clouded leopard (*Neofelis nebulosa*) in the Animal Kingdom, or the more prosaic red oak (*Quercus rubra*) in the Plantae. For Kate, the hierarchy was less important than having a fixed and certain slot in which to put a specimen. David and Elizabeth were easy, their place pre-existing, *in loco parentis*. Billy functioned as a sort of sidekick, someone she could tease instead of Jack, but on whom they would rely if they ever needed to. Hank was just a baby to her: the fact that Jack "looked out for Hank," as she put it, only served to make him more lovable in her eyes.

They went out one night to the Rainbow Room. Jack was giving a birthday party for Dougie — Douglas Green, as he was known now that he was winning piano competitions. It was a small group; Dougie had been living out of town for so long that he didn't know very many people, so Jack had just invited his college friend Peter Callahan and Peter's wife, Linda. He thought Dougie would

like Peter, who was an actor, and he thought Linda might have
some single friends to introduce Dougie to. Kate was in her element. She fit Peter in right away; he'd gone to Yale with Jack,
and she understood Yale men, or thought she did, and she
charmed him. Of course, Jack thought, it's Peter's great weakness
that he's easily charmed — the way I charmed him years ago.

Kate turned her attention to Dougie. "We'll give a party," she
said after some preliminaries, "if you'll play for us. I heard the
tape you made for John — those Mozart sonatas — you're fantastic. A musical evening," she added, as if envisioning something
out of a nineteenth-century novel.

Dougie, uncharacteristically modest, Jack thought, said, "Oh,
I don't know —"

But Kate had seized the idea. Jack could tell that she liked
Dougie, she wasn't just out to charm him. He was the kind of
man she would like, he thought, attractive, accomplished. (So
what does she see in me, he wondered momentarily, by contrast
with Dougie. He had always, a little, worshiped Dougie, loved
him a little more than he loved any of his other friends.) She said,
laughing, "It'll be a conspiracy, we'll invite the board of the Philharmonic. My mother's done a lot of work with them."

But Dougie, annoyingly, wasn't playing. "I don't think so,
Kate."

"Why not? I've always wanted to do something like that. Don't
you think it would be fun, John?"

Dougie didn't let him answer. "I can't. Not right now, anyway.
I'm going to be entering a competition in Santa Fe this summer,
and I've got to play a concerto. So I'm only going to be practicing
orchestral works for a while."

It was almost too obviously an excuse. Dougie had dozens of
solo pieces he could rattle off at will: recently, after work, Jack
had been stopping at Dougie's mother's house, lying on the couch
with a drink while Dougie played sonatas and fantasies, polonaises
and impromptus, while the room got dark around them. The way
he'd gone to Dougie's house and listened to him practice when
they were young boys together. Jack was angry. He'd been basking in Kate's unfailing ability to make a place for anyone, so that

everyone felt comfortable and safe, the arranging of a perfect life. Dougie seemed suddenly boorish in comparison.

Later in the evening, he was standing at the railing, looking down on the tables and the dancers, having gone to the men's room. Dougie came and stood next to him. They watched in silence for a moment, and then Dougie said, "I don't get it, Johnny."

His little-boy name. Dougie was the only one left who was allowed to call him that. "What?" Jack said dully, knowing what was coming.

"You're not the person she thinks you are."

Jack put his hand in his jacket pocket and made a fist. "You're always saying that kind of thing to me." Remembering the last time Dougie had said that to him ("I don't know who you are anymore"), remembering that Dougie had been right then.

"I don't always say it." Dougie sounded irritated. "I only say it when it's true. And don't dodge the issue. I know you too well."

Better than anyone, Jack thought. The only person left who knew me before I started having to be someone else, before I started having to be no one at all. It was a useless thought. "So what, anyway? Suppose I like the person she thinks I am, even if it's not me. It hasn't been so great all the time, being me, you know."

"I know."

Of course he did, Jack thought. If anyone knew, it would be Dougie. He said softly, "Give me a break, OK?"

All this time they'd been watching the dance floor, and Dougie didn't look at him now. All he said was, "Sure, John. She really is terrific. I mean it."

And Jack thought, It's not Kate he's worried about in all this, it's me. And he should know.

Dougie aside, everything went along the way it was supposed to. At first he thought this was the result of her skill, or of the new maturity he attributed to himself. But gradually he came to believe that it was because they were in love. This thought, which occurred to him first on a very warm day at the end of March, he kept to himself. He knew better than to let it out, he wasn't sure he trusted it. Love was like a genie in a bottle to him. Leave it locked up, and one couldn't very well see what it was, still less understand or even recognize it when it appeared. But let it out, and it was liable to say, as the Ifrit did to the Fisherman in Scheherazade's tale: Whoso shall release me, him will I slay. Gradually, as the spring wore on, he saw that Elizabeth and David, Boyd and Amy, his friends from Westfield and from Yale, Kate and her parents and her friends, everyone began to assume that marriage would ensue, only the timing being in question. Without saying a word, they talked him into proposing. It was what everybody wanted.

There was the usual Friday-night crowd on the sidewalk behind the velvet ropes outside Val's when he got there. Every few months he swore he would never go to another club with velvet ropes again, it was like his vow to quit doing cocaine. But he never had to stand in line, or not for long, and the coke helped him to not be there, so he didn't have to keep either promise. He was waved in at the door and went inside, squeezing through the narrow entrance past the coat room. He hated coat rooms because he always lost the claim check. If I added up all the hours I spend trying to get my coat back, he thought —

The room was awash with cigarette smoke and people dressed in black. Black jeans, black makeup, black leather pants — the light seemed swallowed up in all the blackness. People shouldn't be allowed to wear black more than once a week, he thought, looking at his own black silk jacket. At least he hadn't dyed his hair. Long on top, yellow or orangey, and shaved short on the sides was mostly the current fashion. A very tall man with a sunken chest and a fifties-style shirt jostled past Jack, shrieking, "Ooh, there she is, there she is." Somebody blew cigarette smoke in his face and he coughed. "Sorry, dearie," a woman said, but he couldn't tell if she was talking to him. The bar was already crowded with people, all of whom seemed to have drink tickets, which they were waving around. He wanted a drink, but he didn't feel like fighting for one. He went out into the main room and stood, watching.

Val claimed to have come out of the mists of the distant past from New Orleans, and she had made her club a simulation of what the unsuspecting might think was Bourbon Street. The wallpaper was whorehouse red and there were little sconces with black-fringed shades. A couple of tiers of galleries with wrought iron railings overlooked the dance floor. Some were divided into cubicles with curtains, which presumably could be drawn to hide naughty goings-on. There wasn't much of that now that promiscuity had gone into eclipse ("sicklied o'er with the pale cast of thought"). Perhaps that was the appeal the upper floors held for the out-of-towners, nostalgia for the days of casual sex. The cognoscenti preferred the ground floor, nearer the dancing and the bar, and the bathrooms, where most of today's naughtiness was confined. The groundlings, transported, looked down on their betters.

The cigarette smoke was starting to make him feel nauseous. If he got a drink he'd feel better — he looked indecisively back into the bar. A girl (in black, with art deco jewelry) was giving him the eye, and he knew she wanted him to ask her to dance, so he looked away. Sometimes, before he'd met Kate, when things weren't so crowded, he would sit at the bar of some club or other waiting for a woman to sit down next to him. This had amused Boyd for some reason. The girl was edging closer, but Jack didn't feel like moving. A crowd of people walked by, huddled together like a school of fish in the shark's shadow — he recognized a model who had been famous a few months before — before dispersing around a table at the edge of the dance floor. "Aren't you John Newland?" the girl in black asked.

Yes; no; maybe — he didn't want to commit himself. He saw Val waving to him across the way. "Excuse me." He hadn't had to look at her at all.

Val was a large fake blonde on the near side of fifty. She was standing under an overhang beneath one of the mammoth speakers that blared music to the dancers. It was a dead spot, probably the only one in the place, and she didn't have to shout to be heard. "When are you going to write an article about me?" she flirted, thrusting her arm through his.

"Do you want me to?"

"Well, darling," she said in a lower voice, "I love having you around because you're so decorative, don't get me wrong. But a little bit of the right kind of publicity never hurt, did it."

He laughed. "You don't need any help from me."

She raised her arm, taking in the crowd. "Look around, John. All this can disappear as fast as it happened. I knew one day we were going to make it, and I'll know one day that we've passed the peak. I'd just like to postpone the day of reckoning."

When they'd first started coming to Val's, a few months before, there had been a blood-in-the-water feeling, trendsetters wondering if they'd backed a loser. Val's was Uptown, and nobody knew whether being Uptown was going to be cool — New York geography. Then Uptown had become the place to be (there had always been an element, the rich kids, who hadn't really liked trekking Downtown every night, it sometimes got to be a pain in the ass trying to remember where you were at two in the morning after too many hits off a coke blaster), and Val's was a winner. He asked her, "When did you know you were going to make it?"

She smiled at him. "Well, when the famous John Newland came in, what more could I want?"

"Be serious." In front of them, at the side of the dance floor, was a raised round stand. At first Val had thought she would hire professional dancers, a sort of throwback to the go-go dancers of the sixties, but it hadn't worked out. Now, a man and a woman had climbed up onto the pedestal and were showing off to a circle of admirers. The man had straight white-blond hair that seemed to move independently of his body, and the woman had the vacant stare that comes from being on two or three different highs at once and not being able to choose among them.

Val went on, "Honey, I am serious. Amy Cornwell, a couple of people from Soho, some rich young things. A museum curator. A network anchor. Two or three tall models. Two or three gay designers — they have to be the right ones, not too old, not too diseased —"

"You're heartless."

"— and you. That's what makes it. I know you'll all go on to some other place pretty soon and make them a hit. I'd just like to get a bit of publicity in before you go."

"I'll see what I can do." After all, it was no different, really, from another type of encounter. He'd allowed himself to be enticed by Val, now he had to deliver. It hadn't really occurred to him before that he had the kind of influence she ascribed to him.

"That's all I ask, sugar." She let go of his arm. "Any requests tonight?"

He thought of Billy, and the Radiators. "Something from 'Zig-Zaggin' Through Ghostland'?"

"A New Orleans band? I'll see what I can do."

Boyd and Amy were at a table against the wall, under the overhang of the balcony, with their motley crew. He surveyed them for a moment, trying not to feel too depressed. Boyd's vulgar co-worker, a couple of women who worked with Amy, the hangers-on. Sitting next to Boyd was a young man, younger than Jack, a lawyer at one of the big Wall Street firms, with the usual breathless good looks, who tried hard to smolder. He had amused Jack at first, being so obviously available, a condition that Jack understood too well (it was, in a way, the territory he inhabited himself). This availability had registered in their crowd, and the lawyer was now the object of a fierce rivalry between a girl from Pittsburgh named Laura and an older man who taught at a local college. The lawyer maintained a studied ambivalence about his sexual orientation, and more particularly about which of his two suitors he preferred. In best soap opera fashion, this little drama refused to resolve itself, and like all soap operas it had gone on too long. It was all very dull. They were all very dull. Except maybe, he thought, Timothy Archer, who seemed out of place in the tarnished crowd. At least he wasn't wearing black.

"Well, guys," he said, sitting down, trying to sound cheerful. "Here we are again."

Boyd pushed a glass of Wild Turkey over to him. "I saw you coming so I got you this."

"Thanks." He took a big swallow.

Amy said, "What was Val so busy whispering in your ear about?"

"She wants me to write an article about her."

"I wouldn't if I were you. It's too late. Passé." She disposed of Val's. He remembered her as the prettiest girl at the swim club for all of that one long summer. She had been totally unaware then, not so much of sex, as Billy was, but of the way the commerce worked, the tradeoffs in love, the buying and selling. She wasn't unaware anymore, she had become self-conscious and sophisticated, worked at one of the big fashion magazines, which was how she was able to pick winners on the club scene, or maybe even to make them. And then there was Boyd. He had been even more innocent than Amy, just fooling around, as he'd put it. He'd since lost whatever it was that had made him desirable at the age of sixteen, had gotten heavier perhaps, or his hair a little thinner, or his face a little puffier (I slept with each of them that summer, Jack thought, and now they're married to each other). Jack frowned, annoyed at himself for thinking of Boyd that way, and said to Amy, "Maybe we should start our own club."

"We have enough experience," she said, leaning over the table toward him. "What do you think?"

He had, as a matter of fact, thought about what the ideal club would be like, mostly during the half-stoned time while he watched dance floors from behind glasses of bourbon. It would be called Broken Images, and it would have no fixed existence, appearing as if by chance in decaying industrial spaces around town: in the cavernous piers of the Manhattan Bridge, in an unused subway station, under the abandoned West Side Highway. People would just know when and where to show up, and when they left in the pale morning, looking behind to find it gone, they would wonder whether it had happened at all. There would be no velvet ropes, no doorkeeper, no door. The music would be live and nonstop. "For you know only a heap of broken images," he said.

"What?"

"T. S. Eliot," he said quickly. And then, just to be contrary, he went on, "Val's isn't so bad."

"It's getting old," Boyd said. "Maybe everything's getting old. Do you feel old, Newland?"

"Why?" He wondered if, after all, he was going to have a birthday party. "Do I look old?"

"Ancient," Amy said. "Do you want to dance?"

He danced with Amy. He danced with Amy's college roommate's sister, who was in town for a week. He danced with the girl from Pittsburgh, who only wanted to talk to him about the lawyer, putting her mouth close to his ear so she wouldn't have to shout over the music. He couldn't hear her anyway. In between, he sat at the table and listened to the conversation —

someone was buying a co-op and someone else was talking about leveraging the purchase price, and someone else was talking about appreciation. He only caught bits of the discussion, but whenever he returned to the table, it was going on, like a mini-series where he'd skipped a few episodes but hadn't missed anything.

"Newland," Boyd said, "come on in the bathroom with me."

"Later." Postponing the inevitable. He drank more bourbon and stared off into the middle distance, trying to smile at appropriate times. The dance floor was crowded, and he tried to make out a pattern to the couples, the way they placed themselves. Concentric circles, maybe, with the best dancers at the center. Or a spiral, with the people who went to the most clubs in the middle. Timothy Archer was sitting next to Amy, saying to her, "I bet the lawyer finally gives in to the professor tonight." Timothy and Jack always talked about them that way — the lawyer, the professor, the girl from Pittsburgh, as if the whole thing were an allegory, which, Jack had once proclaimed, it was. They were rooting for the girl, neither of them liked the professor. Jack sighed and said romantically, "Ah, the old story. Girl meets boy. Older man meets boy. Love at first sight. And second sight." He looked out at the dance floor, where the lawyer was dancing, perversely, with Amy's old roommate. "What's going to happen? Are we going to have a major scene here — tears and accusations, maybe even a fistfight?"

"No, I shouldn't think so." Timothy paused, and Jack thought there was something a little odd about him, something foreign and between-the-wars, as if he were a character from Masterpiece Theater, Evelyn Waugh-ish. His blond hair was piled up a little messily on top of his head, and his eyes, Jack noticed, even in the unhelpful light, were a bright deep blue. Timothy said, "I've got it figured like this. The lawyer won't have the girl because she's dense. He's just using her for cover until something better comes along. Our professor — what does he profess anyway? — isn't something better exactly, but he has staying power. Odds on, the lawyer decides tonight."

"But Timothy," Amy said reprovingly, "you don't really think he's gay or anything."

Timothy laughed. "No, Amy. Not gay. Just ambivalent. Right?"

Jack tipped his head noncommittally. He had had his own encounter with the lawyer, who had asked him up to his apartment for a drink one night. Jack had been very drunk, which was the only reason he'd gone in the first place. The lawyer had dithered, clearly knowing what he thought he wanted but not how to get it, and Jack had had no interest in helping him out. He'd left after a while.

Boyd came over and said into Jack's ear, "Come on to the boys' room with me," and Jack went this time.

The bathroom seemed bright after the mottled light outside. The stalls had half-doors that pushed open in the middle, louvered slats that didn't conceal much. Val had known what she was doing, even here. He and Boyd went into the end stall, the large one for handicapped people. Boyd sat down on the seat and got out his little mirror and a vial and blade and began cutting four lines. Jack took out a ten-dollar bill and rolled it up into a straw, Andrew Jackson staring at him disapprovingly. The summer after he'd graduated from Westfield he had gone to the bank and gotten a Grover to do coke with Ripley, but they'd done a lot of stupid things he didn't like to think about. "This is stupid," he said.

Boyd looked up. "What is?"

"Well, hanging around a bathroom to do drugs. I mean, how do we know some guy wasn't in here ten minutes ago puking or something."

"Why? Do you smell anything?" Boyd went back to his work.

"No, Boyd, I don't smell anything. Don't you ever think this is wrong? I mean, they're killing people in Colombia because of this."

"Hey, we're not addicts or anything. Just a little recreational toot isn't going to hurt anyone."

The bathroom door opened. From where he stood, leaning against the stainless steel railing for wheelchair access, Jack could see over the top of the stall doors. The newcomer was a thin young man wearing a torn T-shirt and black jeans. He looked incuriously at Jack in the mirror and then went into the stall next to theirs. Jack heard the sound of the toilet seat being lifted, and then, after a moment, the noise of metal on porcelain. He looked at Boyd, who grinned, but at that moment Jack didn't find it funny. "Jesus. He's snorting it off the toilet." There was the sound of inhaling from the next stall. "That's revolting. I mean, piss drips all over the place."

"Gimme a break, man," the guy in the next stall said, his voice distorted from trying not to breathe out of his nose.

Jack was imagining the sticky yellow spots on men's room toilets. "This is disgusting."

"Calm down, Newland."

They heard their neighbor do up another line. Then he stood and opened the stall door. Jack looked away. "Asshole," the guy said, and left.

"I can't believe that, Boyd."

Boyd held the mirror out to him. "Take it easy. Do a line. You'll feel better."

"I don't —"

"Come on."

"No, Boyd. I don't want to." He shook his head for emphasis, like a little child.

"Boyd knows best. Dr. Cornwell's patent remedy."

Jack looked at the mirror and thought, If you would avoid sin, avoid the occasion of sin. Next time he wouldn't come into the bathroom. He took the rolled bill and did a line. Then he tipped his head back and looked at the ceiling, feeling the coke in his nose. Good news, he thought.

Boyd took the mirror and the bill. When he'd finished, he said, "You know, Newland, your problem is you're too intellectual for this kind of life."

This struck Jack as unreasonable. "Great, Boyd. You've known me for fifteen years and you're just finding out that I'm intellectual. Terrific."

"Take it easy. Here, do your other one." He gave the mirror back to Jack before continuing. "You know, I'm just a bond trader. I sit in a huge room with maybe fifty other guys, everybody on the phone, watching the Quotron all day. Little green numbers on the screen, the high point of the day is some announcement from Washington that usually comes at eight-thirty in the morning. If I can get an extra thirty-second of a point on a hundred-million-dollar deal, the firm is thirty thousand bucks ahead. If fifty of us do that, we're a million five ahead. If we do it once a week, we're seventy-five million ahead at the end of the year. Above our regular profit." He sounded to Jack as if his life were a fairy tale, a chronicle of things as they might be. "At night I come home, meet Amy, go to clubs. We have great sex." He took the mirror back and bent over it, and Jack, with a strange mixture of emotions — fondness, discomfort — watched the top of his head. Boyd looked up. "Why does it have to be so complicated, John?"

Jack slumped against the tile wall. "I don't know, Boyd. It just is."

"You need Kate back. When's she coming home?"

"Three weeks," he answered, knowing that having Kate back wouldn't solve anything.

"Give yourself a rest, John," Boyd said, uncharacteristically serious. "You want something to worry about, imagine what it's like to be a bond trader in this market. Fucked up the ass. Getting that extra thirty thousand bucks isn't so easy anymore. I don't even know if I'm going to have a job in a month." He held out the mirror. "Want some more?"

"No thanks."

"Last licks?"

Jack shook his head, so Boyd rubbed the mirror, then sucked his finger. He looked like a little boy for a moment, and Jack laughed. "Come on. Let's get out of here."

He felt elated all of a sudden. His mood, the beast that had been stalking him all day, finally retreated — not defeated, only stymied — but he could at least think about it now without a surge of fear. He was wrapped up in a web of affection, for Boyd, for Amy, for all these good people who were his friends, who cared about him. He danced with Amy, and then with a girl he didn't know, feeling wonderful. He knew it was the coke, cascading through his head in a shower of silver stars, and he knew it was only temporary, but he kept it going as long as he could, banking it carefully to avoid letting the beastie close in again. A little later, he was back in the bathroom, Boyd in the stall and Jack and Timothy (who'd come at Jack's invitation) standing by the sinks. Jack had his Wild Turkey with him, and he clinked the ice against the side of the glass. He said to Timothy, "I've decided you're right. About the lawyer."

"Oh. Why?"

"I'll tell you." He took another swallow, then steadied himself by leaning against a sink. "It's the law of the jungle. That poor girl —" he had another thought and pursued it, "— you know her name is Laura. Why does she insist on telling everybody, all the time, that she's from Pittsburgh? To establish her identity, I guess. Anyway. She can't make up her mind whether she's the hunter or the hunted."

Timothy went over to a urinal and unzipped his fly. "That's enigmatic. What do you mean?"

"This. She wants to be swept off her feet. That's her idea of romance. But she wants the lawyer to do it, and when he wouldn't she started to pursue him. But that was impossible, obviously."

Timothy flushed the toilet. "It put them both in a false position."

"Exactly," Jack said. "You catch on quickly." He wondered at this, as Timothy washed his hands. "That's why the lawyer is going home with the professor," Jack went on in a dreamy voice, "the lawyer doesn't want to come out into the open. The professor knows that, he'll let the lawyer stay in the underbrush, the professor's a predator. Poor Laura isn't, and that's the end of her. She doesn't realize that the lawyer wants to be seduced." Timothy came over and pulled a paper towel out of the dispenser behind Jack's shoulder. Jack said, his voice becoming suddenly hard, "The need to be seduced, to avoid taking a stand."

He heard Timothy suck in his breath and then say, very gently, "Hey. Are you OK?"

Jack turned to him. They were standing very close together, and again Jack noticed how very blue his eyes were. He shook his head. "No," he said, his voice catching in his throat. "No, I'm not OK."

Boyd called out. "Who's on deck? Come on, Newland."

Jack looked at Timothy for a moment longer and shook his head. He went into the stall and did up his lines, and called for Timothy.

"Oh. No thanks," he said politely.

"What?" Boyd said. "Come on, it's great stuff."

"No thanks. You do it. It's not my kind of thing."

Jack could imagine the incredulous look on Boyd's face. But it's great, he would say, as if Timothy spoke a foreign language. Jack went ahead and did one of the remaining lines. "Here you go, Boyd. Finish it up."

As they left the men's room, he heard the music, "Zig-Zaggin' Through Ghostland," his request. A New Orleans band, Val had said, in her best Val's-of-Bourbon-Street manner. She hadn't been in New Orleans in twenty years, Jack thought, suddenly annoyed at everything. Timothy said to him, "Come have a drink with me." They went over to the bar and Jack got them a couple of drinks. He was wary now; he'd surprised himself by what he'd said in the bathroom, even if it was the truth, it wasn't like him to spill confidences so recklessly. He should have known better, and he felt a little scared again, the culmination of this awful day. He wondered what it was about Timothy Archer that had made him loosen up so much, and he told himself not to get involved. What he really wanted was not to be pressed any further — he didn't want this to turn into one of those dreary confessional evenings.

But Timothy had, it seemed, endless reserves of tact. He thanked Jack for his drink and then kept silent as they stood in a corner of the bar. The place was full of unleashed yuppies, pretending that Friday night made a difference, that they wouldn't all be diligently toiling away the next day, bragging to each other about how hard they worked. Finally, Jack said, "Why didn't you tell me who you were?"

"Well, you obviously didn't remember, and" — Timothy blushed — "actually, I didn't want you to think I was trying to capitalize on a tenuous acquaintance."

Again Jack had a sense of foreignness. There was something definitely not New York about him. "Silly."

"You probably would have thought of me as just that snotty-nosed kid who used to hang around the swim club. Wanting to be included in everything. Ugly and importunate."

"You're not ugly anymore, anyway." Jack looked at his face, at his blond hair, which was tousled, a little, from all the dancing he'd done. Then he looked away. "I said to my sister this afternoon that it's always the ugly kids who turn out to be so attractive."

"Do you think I'm attractive?"

Oh God, Jack thought, here we go. For the second time this evening he'd let his guard down, had said what he felt, and this was what happened. Now he'd have to go through all the trouble of extricating himself, because whatever he might have done in the past with anyone else, he wasn't going to do anything with Timothy. But when he looked up, he saw that the question had been asked innocently, the way Billy might ask it of him, not meaning anything by it. A question, not a gambit. Jack drained his glass. "Sure you are," he said, and the idea depressed him for some reason.

When they got back to the table, they found that they had missed the evening's excitement. Laura was sitting and crying, being comforted by Amy's old roommate and her sister. The lawyer and the professor had disappeared. Amy looked at Timothy as if it were his fault. "It was the way you said. I'm going to take her home, Boyd."

"Oh, come on. The night's still young. I don't want to go home."

"Tell you what," Amy said efficiently. "She lives in Chelsea somewhere. Why don't you all go someplace downtown and we'll meet you."

"I don't want to go downtown," Boyd said grouchily.

"Don't be difficult, sweetheart."

Jack was watching Laura. She looked awful, huddled on a chair, her face streaked, eye makeup running down her cheeks. He thought of the conversation he'd just had with Timothy. They were all so attractive, it was almost like a credential of admission. Laura didn't look attractive anymore, and he wondered if she ever would again, to any of them. What would happen to her in that case? She'd become like a ghost at a banquet, fading, fading, until she was unseen and went away. All that these people value, he thought, is looking good, you didn't even have to have money if you looked cool. And then he thought, You may know a person by the company he keeps. Thinking of himself.

Boyd and Amy had decided where to meet, and they all moved toward the door, the women forming a phalanx around Laura. When they stepped outside, the first thing that hit them was the heat, which was unabated, and the second was a huge clap of thunder, reverberating among the buildings. "Christ," Boyd said.

"It's going to rain. Just what we need on top of this." Jack looked at the line of people on the sidewalk, longer now than it had been before. They all looked back at him hopefully, all he was to them was another empty place inside that they might be allowed to fill. The women got into a cab, and Boyd waved angrily for another. "Dumb twit. Anyone could have seen she wasn't getting anywhere. What a way to ruin a good evening."

It was suddenly too much for Jack. "Shut up, Boyd."

"Oh cut it out, Newland." There was another thunderclap. "You didn't care any more about her than I did. I heard you guys talking about her, but you didn't do anything about it. You were enjoying it."

"Shut up." Jack had a vague idea that he was shouting. It wasn't because Boyd was wrong, it was because he was right. "Just shut up." Then he stepped away from the door and walked down the sidewalk, past the velvet ropes and the crowd waiting to get in. He heard Boyd calling to him. Halfway down the next block, a cab pulled up by him. Boyd rolled down the window. "Come on, Newland. Get in the cab."

"Fuck off, Boyd." A huge raindrop hit him on the head and he flinched.

"Come on, John." The cab had slowed to a walking pace. Boyd said, "Cool off and get in."

Jack turned down a one-way street, where the cab couldn't follow.

He was alone in the city. The block on which he found himself was devoid of movement, and the activity on the avenues before and behind him seemed impossibly distant. The townhouses and apartment buildings that lined the sidewalks walled off the usual city noises, and the sky above was close and angry-colored, street-light off storm clouds. He was frightened for a moment by another great crack of thunder, and then he listened, grinning crazily as it rolled on and on, bouncing among the buildings, endlessly dying away. "Blow, winds, and crack your cheeks," he thought, then wished he hadn't. It seemed all too real that he might summon cataracts and hurricanes to their destructive work. He was alone in the city and free to do what he wanted, had no appointment, no nephew waiting, no lover weeping. He was free. He knew this block, he realized, stopping in front of a red brick building the width of two townhouses and protected behind a black iron railing. As a little boy he'd come here to school in a dark gray flannel uniform of short pants and knee socks, old New York. His mother had picked him up at the end of the day, loaded down with Bergdorf bags. He remembered, in the winter, walking with his face pressed against the prickly perfumed warmth of her fur coat. Another crack of thunder came, and more early raindrops. Withhold the flood a moment more, he thought, I am free. No deadline to meet, no curfew, no parents waiting up. At the corner he dashed across the avenue, half fearful that Boyd in his phantom taxi would appear: nothing less than a celestial omnibus would do for him tonight. He was conscious of the hunter behind him, the soft steps by the stream, but he saw no one. Boyd had abandoned him, he thought, he was alone in the city. One of his counselors from sailing camp, Donny Schaefer lived on this block, he could go up and have a drink, pretend that the past hadn't happened. The summer he was twelve, he woke up in his bunk in the cold sea air of a Cape Cod night, with Donny above him softly saying, "Come with me." He got up in his thin pajamas and went with Donny down to the dock and they took out a boat for a midnight sail. Donny said, "Are you cold? Come over here, let me see," and Jack obediently sat next to him on the deck, while Donny put his arm around him. He'd felt warm and safe, dreamily looking up at Donny's face. Jack paused in front of the building and then went on. No schoolboy crushes weighing him down, he thought, no hearts broken on his doorstep, no candles to blow out. Two blocks away was the building where Missy Reardon's parents lived. He'd met her in Switzerland. Under the pine trees overlooking St. Moritz, on the sticky summer grass, they shared a few joints and a lot of kisses, a year after his parents had died, and one Christmas vacation, the year he was seventeen, she invited him for dinner. Alone in her parents' apartment, while New York snow fell outside, they made love, his first time. He hadn't heard from her in years. I'm free, he thought again, no pulled heartstrings, no ex-lovers lurking behind the remote-camera-swept façades of the wealthy townhouses, no woman closer than the Alps. He'd grown up in an apartment a couple of blocks away, he'd walked this stretch of sidewalk practically every day, stood on this corner with Dougie while they waited for the bus to take them to school at Collegiate across the park. Dougie had practically lived at Jack's the year they'd been ten or eleven—Dougie's parents were getting a divorce, and he didn't want to hear them fighting, over property, over money, over Dougie. When Jack got to be thirteen, they reversed the arrangement: he practically lived at Dougie's, listened to Dougie practice the piano on hot afternoons, tried not to think about his own home, and then Jack went off to boarding school. The following summer Dougie said, I don't know who you are anymore, and Jack thought, I'm not anyone anymore, I'm not here, because if you're not here nothing bad can happen—and maybe that was why he was here tonight, wandering these streets where every step held a memory but nothing held him. He was free and alone, no home to go to, no friends caring, no parents living. He came out onto Fifth Avenue opposite the Metropolitan, floodlit with fountains, as the thunder pealed again and the heavens opened finally. Heedlessly, he crossed the avenue and walked past the pool, churned to violence in the rain, and stood at the foot of the great flight of steps, looking up at the palatial front. The rain ran down through his hair and over his jacket. His pants stuck to his knees. He held his arms a little apart from his sides, looking up at the great gray façade, alone in the city, free. This was his kingdom, on the day of his inheritance.

PART TWO

Westfield

～～～～～

IV

THERE WAS an odd gray light and the air smelled of roses. He sat up and checked to be sure he was alone in the bed.

The room looked vaguely familiar. The walls were papered in a tight floral pattern, there was a dresser in light varnish and a braided rug on the floor. His clothes were piled on a rocking chair in the corner. The bed was a four-poster and high off the floor, the kind of bed he was always afraid he would fall out of. Thin white curtains were drawn over the window, letting in the gray light. It was warm in the room. He felt a little drugged.

He stretched, and lay back on the pillow, his hands behind his head. The house was very quiet, but he could feel it all around him, a big house. He hadn't seen much of it the night before and hadn't been in any condition to take in much of what he had seen, but there was a big feel to it, the deep silences of size and comfort, like the country houses of his boyhood — old, rambling New England houses with a weight of history and money in them. His parents had owned a house like this (actually, it now belonged jointly to him and Elizabeth, although Jack didn't use it much), all his childhood friends had weekend homes like this, he'd spent enough nights in guest rooms to recognize this one. He yawned, and wondered where he was.

It didn't seem a very pressing question. Only two things tugged at his mind: the smell of roses and the thin gray light. He lay quietly, not caring for the moment to investigate, wondering what would happen next. It seemed indecently luxurious to lie naked beneath the sheets. Perhaps, in a little while, someone would come in with coffee and some buttered toast on a tray with the morning's newspaper. The coffee cup would be thin bone china with a crimson border, and there would be small silver pots with honey and jam, the butter would run off the sides of the toast, and the crumbs would stick to his upper lip or fall on his bare chest.

Ten minutes later, he awoke again, this time with a start. He'd had a bad dream, a messy morning dream: he'd been in some complicated building, all the doors seemed to lead to secret passages or winding complex staircases, and just as he approached the room where his family was being held prisoner, a huge black shape reared up in front of him, blocking the way. He knew what it meant, but its familiarity, like that of some revisited room of childhood, had lost all magnitude and was now only ordinary. (All right, Dr. Sanders, he said to himself, to his former shrink, I'm still having The Dream. You didn't like The Dream, it wasn't good "material," it wasn't Freudian enough for you. So I stopped telling you about it and you stopped asking. I was always eager to please.) He threw off the sheet and swung his legs down onto the floor. It made him feel dizzy a moment, but he was determined to get out of bed. He stood up carefully, putting one arm out in a practiced motion that he'd found useful to balance himself against the air. He didn't see a robe, so he walked to the window and parted the curtains cautiously. At first he couldn't understand what he was looking at — it all appeared so ghostly that for a moment he wondered (it passed over him like a kind of mental shiver) if he were still asleep. Then he laughed, realizing, and pulled the curtain open all the way. Outside, a thick fog filled the air, accounting for the gray light and the spectral shapes, which now were revealed as dimly seen trees. Below him, a flagstone terrace was bordered by a finished stone wall. To his left, a striped awning on a frame of steel pipes covered more of the terrace, while to his right a garden faded into the mist. He opened the window and stuck his head out. The air was warm and wet, but not unpleasantly so, and smelled of summer. From beyond the fog no sound came, and he was no closer to discovering his whereabouts. It all might have been arranged, deliberately, to keep him in the dark.

He turned back to the room and noticed his wristwatch lying on the dresser. It read twenty past three and he thought, I've slept all day. He smelled roses again and looked down. While he'd slept, someone had come into the room and placed a single red rose in a bud vase on the night table, next to where he'd been lying. The petals were still damp from the fog outside. He picked it up and sniffed it speculatively.

Like all good guest rooms, this one had a bathroom. The tub was huge, with brass taps and faucets, and a glass half-panel instead of a shower curtain. The checkerboard tiling, black and white, extended halfway up the walls. Huge fluffy towels were hung neatly over a heated towel rack. A collection of bottles rested on a shelf above the tub — shampoo, bath oil, foaming bath gel. He grinned, turned the hot water on, and shut the drain plug, waiting until the steam began to rise before turning on the cold water just a little. Then he poured some bath gel in and sat on the edge of the tub while bubbles formed, breathing the faint hypnotic scent. He stood at the toilet urinating, splashing a little (he thought of the men's room at Val's and made himself think of something else) and then got into the tub. It was big enough for him to really stretch out, and he lay with just his head above the water, his limbs spread out a little, bubbles all around him.

He stayed there for fifteen or twenty minutes, trying not to think of anything and mostly succeeding. Every so often he lifted his hand and turned on the hot water tap for a few minutes. Occasionally he raised his legs — he always found the feel of bubbles bursting against his skin mildly exciting. His friend Ripley had told him when they were in school that a bubble bath was the best place to jerk off, but Jack had never tried it. Then he abruptly sat up, shedding water, and opened the drain, and when the water was nearly gone, stood up and turned on the shower.

He found soap and a shaving brush and a razor in the medicine chest and a silver-backed military hairbrush on a glass shelf over the sink. When he came out of the bathroom, freshly shaved and brushed and wrapped in a towel, he found Timothy lying on the bed, propped up on one arm and munching a cookie. The smell of fresh coffee had replaced the fragrance of the rose. Timothy said, "Good afternoon."

"Hi," Jack said shyly.

"Do you feel OK?"

"I feel great."

"Terrific. Want some coffee?" On the bed next to him was a

tray with a plate of cookies and a pot of coffee and a cup and saucer (the border was dark blue and gold, not crimson). With his free hand, Timothy poured, and held the cup and saucer out to Jack.

Jack sat down in the rocking chair, still wrapped in the towel, and looked at Timothy. He was wearing a pair of loose-fitting white cotton pants and a faded, ancient, blue tennis shirt. Out of New York, out of the affected lighting of the clubs where Jack had mostly seen him, Timothy looked younger. His bare feet on the bed might have been a boy's. "How old are you?" Jack asked.

"Twenty-five. Actually, I'll be twenty-six in December." He took another cookie. "Did you find everything you needed in the bathroom?"

"Yeah. Timothy — where are we?"

He grinned. "In a house. My parents' house, although they're not here, thank God. Just us and the caretakers — Mr. and Mrs. Prescott."

"Yes, but where? I mean, what town are we in? What state are we in?" He shivered.

"Are you cold?" Timothy asked. "Put something on."

Jack looked away from him. It was always the same, he thought sadly. Sooner or later he was always asked to pay up, and he knew exactly how the bill would be presented and in what currency he would be expected to make settlement. He had just wanted to postpone the reckoning. Somehow, despite all the history of his life, he'd had the hope that Timothy would be different. He stood up, ready to do his part if he had to.

But Timothy reached down and picked up a robe off the floor. "Here, I brought you this. I forgot to leave it before." As if he'd been guessing Jack's thoughts, he said, sounding amused, "I'm not after a cheap thrill. And Jack, this is the same house my parents had when we were kids. We're in Westfield."

"Oh, Jesus." Jack put on the robe and pulled off the towel. He didn't want to be here, he never liked to be here — the town where he'd spent the summers of his childhood, where Elizabeth brought her family, where he'd gone to boarding school, where his parents had died. It was a measure of how far he'd come in the past few hours (since, really, he'd left Boyd standing at the doorway of Val's) that he didn't want to be where someone might know him. He remembered, the night before, clinging obstinately to his sense of being alone: as haunted as that was, it was somehow better than being with people. On the other hand, if he had to be with anyone, he'd just as soon be with Timothy, who seemed in some way a part of Jack's new mood. "I —"

Timothy sat up on the bed, and again Jack had the feeling his mind was being read. "I thought you wouldn't come if you knew where it was. So I just kidnaped you. We're all alone and nobody has to know."

"Thanks," he said, accepting for the moment Timothy's understanding. He added, "I really do feel great."

"I'm glad. It was — kind of hard getting you out of the rain at the museum."

"Yeah. Sorry about that."

He remembered sitting on the steps in front of the Metropolitan, his head in his hands, the rain running down his face mixing with his tears. And a voice, quite near, almost drowned in the thunder, which seemed nearly constant, said, "Hello, Jack." It was said with such gentleness that Jack almost assumed it was a phantasmic echo of his own thoughts. Then he looked up and saw Timothy. "What are you doing here?" Jack said.

"I followed you."

"What for?"

Timothy, ignoring the rain that was sweeping across the plaza in marked gusts, said, "I have a present for you." He took a flat box out of his pocket.

Jack couldn't understand. "A present?"

"I know it's your birthday, I asked around." His fair hair was dark in the rain, but his eyes still blazed in his face. He licked some water away from his lips. "I've got a cab," he said, gesturing toward the street. "Why don't you come with me?"

Jack shook himself. "Leave me alone."

"OK." Timothy seemed prepared to wait all night. "Why don't you open it?"

Jack looked down at the box. The wrapping paper was beginning to dissolve in his hands. "Later." It was what he'd told Billy, and they'd never gotten around to it.

"No way. Half the fun of giving a present to someone is watching them open it. Come on." There was something brutal about his matter-of-factness, his complete disdain for the macabre surroundings, the thunder, the rain. Jack opened the box. Inside was a digital wristwatch, a child's watch with a black face, on which was painted the Star Wars logo and pictures of R2D2 and C3PO. Timothy had been with them one night when Jack had tried to convince everyone that *The Empire Strikes Back* was the best movie of the decade. He had been drunk, but he'd half meant it, although he hadn't thought anyone had noticed. He started to cry again.

"I'm glad you like it," Timothy said seriously.

"Oh, God."

"Let's go home, Jack."

That had begun a strange nocturnal journey; he'd been reminded of nights when, as a kid, he would fall asleep in the back seat and then be moved to the rear of the station wagon to lie down, then finally be carried into his own bed. This night had that same groggy stop-and-go feel to it. They went first to a garage where Timothy picked up his car and then to Jack's apartment where, at Timothy's direction, he changed and put some clothes in a bag. And then back into the car, where he passed out pretty quickly. He slept fitfully, wakening now and then to find himself looking at Timothy's profile against the rain-dotted glass. Once he'd asked Timothy, Why are you doing this, but that must have been a dream because the answer had been, Because I love you. The scenery, what little he'd seen of it, had seemed familiar, but that had only added to the dreamlike quality of the whole experience.

He said, "Thanks. For rescuing me."

"Any time."

There was a deep stillness in the room, which suddenly felt full of feeling. He wasn't used to that, schooled as he was in keeping his feelings to himself — he couldn't quite accustom himself to the abandon with which Timothy carelessly spent his. Jack waited for something to happen, for Timothy to make a move, to interrupt the silence. But Timothy seemed comfortable with the quiet and evidently saw no need to break it. He was still stretched out on the bed, wholly absorbed in finishing another cookie. When he had, he said, "Are you hungry?"

"Hungry?"

"Yes. Hungry."

Jack nodded. "I guess I am. I don't think I ate dinner last night — or lunch, come to think of it. Jesus, all that bourbon on an empty stomach."

"Don't brag." Timothy sat up. "Why don't you get dressed, and I'll go see what I can find in the kitchen. It's Mrs. Prescott's day off, although she said she'd be back to cook us some dinner. I can probably manage some scrambled eggs in the interim if that's OK." He stood up. "I'll be in the kitchen. You'll find your way." He went out of the room.

Jack finished dressing, then stood outside his bedroom door for a moment, taking in the feeling of spaciousness he'd sensed already. He was at one end of a long wide hallway. Three or four other doors led off the hall at intervals, all closed, magnifying the dignified silence. Between the doors, pushed against the walls, were pieces of dark, polished furniture, antique pieces on which rested china bowls filled with flowers. The walls held a miscellany of nautical and sporting prints (one of them, a horse standing at attention, was called "Sir James Hogwood's Dancer"). He walked quietly down the hall over a thick green carpet, stopping once to admire a pair of Japanese vases that stood, empty, on a side table.

At the end of the hallway was a landing from which a stairway curved like a nautilus shell down to a large entryway. Across the landing, another hallway led into the other wing of the house. He walked down the staircase, feeling a little grand on its sweep, and stood a moment in the front hall, looking around. One wide doorway led into a living room, another into a library. A table held the familiar vase of flowers. He walked toward the back of the house and found the kitchen.

Timothy was sitting on a counter, a bowl in his lap, beating some eggs. "I hope you don't mind them plain. I mean, nothing fancy because I haven't a clue where the herbs and all that stuff are kept."

"That'll be great," Jack said. He smelled roses again, from a vase on a table, and he thought of the flower upstairs in his bedroom. "The flowers are beautiful," he prompted, "especially the roses."

But Timothy took him at face value. "Thanks. Mr. Prescott grows them."

"Oh." Jack wasn't sure whether he'd been rebuffed, or even what he'd meant by the compliment. In New York, in clubs with Boyd and Amy, in his life with Elizabeth and David, in his love affair with Kate, nothing was straightforward, they all protected themselves behind layers of implication like complicated codes. Everything anyone said might have a deeper, or at least a different, meaning: it was how they fashioned their world. But Timothy, almost deliberately it seemed, refused to be complicated. He took things at face value, and he meant only what he said, or seemed to. Jack felt as if he had been living in a dim place, where he had recognized people (and himself most of all) only by their shadows. Now, a light had been turned on to the darkness, and he was blinking his eyes. Having accustomed himself to a realm of innuendo, he didn't know what things signified anymore — here with Timothy it seemed that things were only themselves, that they didn't signify anything. The myth of the cave, he thought, Behold! humanity in an underground cavern. He said, "Timothy. Who are you?"

Timothy stopped beating the eggs and hopped down off the counter. He took a skillet from a hook and set it on the burner. "How do you want me to answer that question?"

Jack was silent. He didn't know what he wanted. He looked at the fog moving over the grass outside.

"Jack, I —"

"Tell me this," he interrupted. "How come you call me Jack? No one else does." Almost no one, he thought.

"It's what you call yourself," Timothy answered, as if that should have been obvious. "One night when we were all out, you said to yourself, 'Take it easy, Jack.' " He added simply, "I heard you."

"Oh, God. Was I that obvious?"

Timothy poured the eggs into the skillet. "No one else heard you. I think you must have been pretty high."

"Really." It sounded reasonable. It's what he would have said to himself if he'd had too much to drink and too much cocaine and felt it all getting out of control.

"Boyd and Amy and everyone called you John all the time, so I did too. But now Jack just seems more natural."

He didn't, Jack noticed, ask permission or approval. "I've known Boyd and Amy a long time," he said, then realized that might be considered a snub. "But —"

"But somehow they're not the type of people you'd be intimate with."

"Well," Jack said wryly, "it depends what you mean by intimate."

Timothy didn't take up the hint. He slid the eggs out onto a stoneware plate. "I mean that, as nice as Boyd is, you'd rather do coke with him than tell him to call you Jack. He's limited, in his thinking, in his feelings, and you're not."

"Neither are you, it seems," Jack murmured.

"Oh, I always say what I think," he answered imperiously. "It's my one vice."

Jack ate his eggs, thinking this over.

"Where are your parents?" he asked after they'd finished clearing away the dishes.

"I'm not sure. I think they're in Alaska or Canada. Someplace."

"You don't know?"

"Nope." He wiped his hands on a striped dishtowel and tossed it onto the counter. "We don't exactly see eye to eye. My father and me, anyway. Come on." He picked up the pot of coffee and they went into the living room. It was a wide room with French doors along one wall leading out to the garden. There seemed to be a lot of furniture in the room, mostly couches and chairs, and an old writing desk and a grand piano. Timothy put the pot on a table and flopped down on a couch, one leg curled under him. "My dad and I just don't get along. He's a great guy, and I admire him for a lot of things, but somehow —"

Jack sat down on a chair and poured a cup of coffee. "What does he do?"

"He's an architect. You've heard of him."

"Archer/MacNeill?" Jack had heard of them, staunch defenders of an orthodox modernity against the heretical onslaught of post-modernism. "I love their work."

"Everybody does," Timothy said glumly. "I somehow wouldn't have thought you would, though. Modernism isn't in anymore, and you're supposed to be the chronicler of what's in."

"You're teasing me." Jack slipped off his loafers and propped his feet up on the couch. "Actually, I prefer the classical: clean lines, strength of form, Beethoven over Berlioz, Pollack over Picasso —"

"That's an odd juxtaposition."

"About your father," Jack reminded him.

"Oh, my father," He tipped his head back and looked at the ceiling. "We're a textbook case, him and me — psychology textbook, that is. Like when I was six, and he tried to teach me how to ride my bicycle without training wheels. I remember him holding on to the bike and running next to me, and then he let go and I fell over and cut my chin. There I was, sitting in the gutter, wiping blood off my face, howling. He was trying to be helpful, but after a while he sort of got impatient, and wanted me to climb back on and try again, which was the last thing I wanted. He finally picked me up and tried to sit me on the bike, but I was kicking too hard. So we went home. He kept trying — for two weeks we'd go out along the driveway or down to the school parking lot and try again, but I was terrified. Finally he gave up. He's never really forgiven me."

"Isn't that a little extreme?" Jack was thinking about his own father.

"I mean," Timothy had found a hole in his shirt and was poking a finger through it, "I mean that it formed his opinion of me, and he's never really changed it since. He thinks I'm soft or something. Do you think I'm soft?"

Jack thought, in fact, that anyone who was so candid would have to be hard, the way an athlete's body is hard, used to punishment. "What happened?"

"To what?"

"With the bike riding."

"Oh. I finally went out and taught myself one day."

"Maybe that's what he can't forgive you for," Jack observed drily.

Timothy extracted his finger from the hole in his shirt and looked up at Jack. "It's not like that," he said, and his voice had a stubbornness to it, as if this was a debate he'd had before. "I used to tell my sister that I'm the son my father never had. We're so totally different. He has all this technical training, of course, and he loves to tinker with things, to work around the house, fix the dryer, that kind of thing. And me, I'm totally hopeless at that sort of thing, I can't even remember which way to turn a bolt to loosen it. In the end, he would always get impatient with me, and I would try not to cry — just imagine a thirteen-year-old boy crying because he couldn't unscrew the toaster. You can imagine how well that went over."

"Unfinished business from adolescence." Jack thought of Dr. Sanders, whose favorite diagnosis had been "adjustment reaction." Jack had seen that written every month on the insurance form which he got from David and gave to the doctor and which he then, humiliatingly, had to return to David.

"I hate it when they use technical terms like that," Timothy said, echoing Jack's thoughts. "It seems so clinical. Although it is kind of true, sometimes. There was a period when every time I thought of my father, I had this mental picture of a giant penis."

Jack giggled. "You made that up for a shrink."

"No, really. Actually, what I used to make up for the shrink was dreams. My real dreams were totally boring — this was in college and I used to dream that I was in class or studying or something — so I made things up."

"I never made anything up," Jack said. "I had enough stuff going on in my life that I didn't have to. But a lot of the time I just didn't tell him things. It seemed easier that way."

"What was he like?" Timothy uncurled his leg and sat on the other one. "I collect psychiatrists. I'm going to mount their heads on the wall one day and then donate them to the Museum of Natural History."

"You'd like mine then. Dr. Sanders. Like the Colonel. My brother-in-law found him. It was when I was in school, at Westfield, he was who teenagers saw around here. He tried to be so hip. His idea of hip was a big Billy Joel poster in his waiting room." He leaned back a little and slid down so the bottom of his spine rested near the edge of the chair. It was the pose he'd adopted most of the time in Dr. Sanders's office. "And the tissue box. There was always a box of tissues, and sometimes things would get pretty emotional and I'd have to blow my nose. Only, there was no place to put the tissues. I think it was just a mind game — he was proving how superior he was by making me sit there with a handful of snotty Kleenex." He remembered that office so well, the bookshelf in the corner that had a lot of pop philosophy books, Rollo May and Erich Fromm, and even some novels, and then, on the very top shelf some thick, scary medical books about drugs and neurophysiology. He went on, almost as if talking to himself, "He had a couch in one corner, you know, for his patients in analysis, and I remember thinking to myself, the whole time, Please God don't make me have to lie on that. I don't know why. Maybe I thought it would mean that I was really crazy." He could hear Dr. Sanders's voice, pressing him always to be more personal: You're the star of your own memories, John, you can't remember anything except from your own point of view. Sanders thought he needed more self-esteem. Jack looked at Timothy, who was watching his face. "He kept prompting me with questions — he'd make all these connections, like I'd tell him how I was feeling about jerking off and he'd ask me what I thought my sister would think if she knew. The trouble was, he kept making all the wrong connections. He didn't really under-stand, he kept trying to draw me out. I knew where I wanted to go, but he kept leading me in the wrong direction."

"Why didn't you —"

"Tell him?"

"Or at least" — Timothy shrugged — "take a little control. Lead him."

"Hey, I made him happy, he thought he was helping me be-cause things kept turning out the way he wanted them to. Besides, I was only sixteen." Jack coughed. "What about your guy?"

"Actually, I was seeing a woman. She was great. She really helped me a lot."

Jack tried to imagine this. "I don't know about a woman. At least when I was sixteen, seventeen, I don't know how I would've felt about telling a woman some of that stuff."

"I was a junior in college, and it didn't bother me too much."

"Even about your father?"

"You don't believe me." Timothy scratched his ear. "It's true, though. That really is the way I used to picture him. It wasn't helped by the fact that I was a late bloomer — I didn't, y'know, mature, until I was almost fifteen. It was kind of rough. Puberty, and all that —" For almost the first time, he sounded a little tentative.

They were interrupted by a discreet cough behind them. "Good evening, Timothy."

Timothy stood up, and Jack followed suit. "Jack, this is Mrs. Prescott. Mrs. Prescott, this is my friend Mr. John Newland."

"How do you do, Mr. Newland."

She was what he'd pictured, a trim elderly lady, with neat unfashionable clothes and the kind of lines on her face that he associated with people who had done the same task for a long time (Don't make faces, Johnny, his mother had told him, it might get stuck that way). He realized that she was sizing him up too, probably wondering how much he would eat. She addressed herself to Timothy. "I have a nice steak for your dinner. It's five o'clock now. When would you like to eat?"

"Oh, around six, I guess. Is that all right?"

"If you like." She was noncommittal. "Where would you like to eat?"

"In the dining room, please."

She raised an eyebrow at this but said nothing.

"I'll take care of the wine," Timothy went on. "All right?"

"Oh yes." She seemed ruffled by something. "Perfectly all right." She went off toward the kitchen.

"Eccentric servants," Jack murmured, thinking of something Kate had said to him once.

"We've disturbed her routine. She didn't know we were coming."

"I didn't know we were coming," Jack reminded him.

"Yes, well. Let's get some wine." He led the way to a pantry off the kitchen, then down a flight of stairs to the basement. It was dry and well swept. The brand-new oil burner in one corner looked anachronistic, the house having so much the feel of another era. A lone pair of cross-country skis stood forlornly in a rack against one wall, and some folded-up cardboard boxes, the sort movers use, were piled nearby. A Ping-Pong table, with no net and no paddles apparent, looked freshly dusted. Mrs. Prescott's efficiency. But something about the room was wrong. Basements were like kitchens to him, they were the secret heart of a house, the warm secure retreats of his childhood. He'd gone to the kitchen, as a little boy, whenever something had frightened him; as an adolescent, when life overwhelmed him, he'd gone into the basement and perched among his family's detritus — before his parents' deaths had put an end to that collection. This neatness, the calculated look of it, disturbed him. He followed Timothy through a door and into a room where rows of bottles lay on racks. A stray shaft of light from somewhere touched the secret red heart of one of them.

"Some claret, I think," Timothy said. "Are you in the mood for greatness? A Petrus?"

"Thanks for the compliment, but I don't think —"

"No, perhaps you're right." He took a bottle down. "This'll do." They went back upstairs and deposited the bottle in the pantry, then Timothy led the way into a family room and made them a couple of drinks. He sat on the couch and Jack sat on the floor nearby. "Cheers," Timothy said. "Where were we?"

"Your father," Jack said again.

"Always my father. He designs the most beautiful buildings in the world, you know. Have you seen his design for the new wing of the Pendleton Art Gallery? I look at it and I think, that's a perfect form, it's exactly balanced, it needs nothing to complete itself, it's absolutely still."

Jack quoted quietly, "Beholding beauty with the eye of the mind, he will be able to bring forth, not images of beauty, but reality, for he has not hold of an image but of reality." There was so much pain in his voice that Timothy sat up, startled, spilling a little of his drink.

"What's the matter, Jack?"

"I once read the *Symposium* with a friend, when I was in school.

We used to walk in the woods and study it. Near here actually. We thought we could live it — more fools we." He could hear Ripley's voice, over the cracking of twigs as they walked, or over the running of the stream in the little hollow where they would sit, reading. Jack had memorized whole sections of it then, which still came back to him like tattered pennants in a bitter wind. Ugly, wise Ripley and beautiful, dissolute Jack — Socrates and Alcibiades, as Ripley had inevitably liked to think of them. He didn't want to talk about Ripley, or about love and beauty. He looked up at Timothy. "I'm sorry," he said impatiently, being deliberately harsh to distract Timothy. "I don't understand all this. It sounds to me like you have the usual kinds of feelings people have about their fathers — I mean, it's not that uncommon. Why all the angst?"

Timothy stared back at him. All right, he seemed to be thinking, if you want to change the subject; but don't think I don't know you're doing it. "I'll tell you a story that might help you understand." He lay back down on the couch, his face toward Jack. During the whole of his recitation, his voice had a very trustful quality to it, as if he counted on Jack to understand without a lot of explanation. "When I was fifteen, my father got an offer from a firm in London. It was a big breakthrough for him and he couldn't turn it down. My sister was in college already, and I wanted to stay in New York and finish at Fieldston — I had this idea that I could do very well in the apartment with just me and the housekeeper. But my father said that I could go to any school I wanted, and the idea of being a public-school boy with an old school tie and all that seemed pretty exciting to me. I ended up going to Winchester." He shrugged a little to himself, and burrowed down further into the cushions. "I don't know why. Probably because it was supposed to be the most academically demanding of all the schools, and that was the one thing I was sure I was good at. I had to take all kinds of tests, which I passed with flying colors, and I guess maybe someone pulled some strings to get me in, and I thought, so far so good."

He brushed some hair off his forehead and went on. "It wasn't until I showed up for my first day that I started to think I'd made a big mistake. I suppose any institution has its own peculiarities, but Winchester, being older than most, has more of them. They have their own slang, and you have to know it all, we even call ourselves Wykehamists because the school was founded by William of Wykeham, who was Edward the Third's lord chancellor. So there I was, a new boy, not knowing any of this stuff, which wouldn't have been so bad because none of the new boys knew it, but on top of that, I didn't really understand the whole system. If I'd gone to an English prep school, it wouldn't have been so bad, but being from the States — it would be like taking an American baseball player and putting him on a cricket team. A few things seemed familiar but they weren't, really. I had an older boy to help me out, but still I was miserable, and that tended to make me cry a lot, which didn't help matters. And there was a general snobbery about America and Americans that was more or less pervasive — we were barbarians or at least, as Harold Macmillan put it, Romans to their Greeks." He swallowed, took another pull at his drink, and put the glass down on the floor. "Then there was one boy who hated me — I don't know why, perhaps he was just a natural bully, and God knows I felt like a natural victim. He used to trip me up in the courtyard, elbow me, you know, the usual petty things. At that point, I would rather have died than complain, and it just seemed like another piece of nastiness when he announced that someone had stolen fifty pounds from him and accused me."

This was so unexpected that Jack almost said something. But he didn't want to break Timothy's mood — he seemed almost to have hypnotized himself — so he took a furtive sip of his bourbon and waited.

"At first I thought it was some kind of a rag or something, but the kid had evidence — it was circumstantial, naturally, because I hadn't done it, but it was convincing. Like someone who'd seen me in the town spending a lot of money, which was true, I was buying my mother a birthday present. That kind of thing. So they sent for my father."

He stopped abruptly and got up and walked slowly across the room to the window. Jack kept expecting him to continue, but he didn't. Finally, Jack said, "It sounds like *The Winslow Boy*."

Timothy turned around. Even at the distance, Jack could see

his blue eyes blazing. "Oh no. Not quite like *The Winslow Boy*. Afterward, when it was over, I got a copy of the play and read it — very much the same, except for one detail, one minor detail."

Jack, who'd been stretched out on the floor, sat up straighter. "Do you —"

"There's a line from the play," Timothy went on, ignoring Jack, "that I copied down. About how everyone in the Winslow family is afraid of the father, even Ronnie, 'though he doesn't need to be,' his sister says. 'Father worships him,' she says. That's really what the play is about, a father's doing everything possible to clear his boy's name."

"Timothy," Jack said loudly, if only to slow him down. "Come on and sit down. Please."

Without looking at him, Timothy came back and sat on the couch. Jack waited for him to continue, feeling more and more uncomfortable. He measured the enormity of what would follow by Timothy's wholly uncharacteristic difficulty in getting it out. Finally, Timothy took a large swallow of his drink and went on. "My father came down and we met with the second master, who explained the situation to him. And my father said — he said, 'We'll pay the money back.' He didn't even ask me if I had done it. He just sentenced me right there. Even the school hadn't come to that conclusion yet, they said they were still investigating. But not my father. He couldn't wait to make it easy for them."

"Oh," Jack said, and then, "I'm sorry." He thought of his friends, the kids he'd known in boarding school. Their fathers had all seemed odd, inexplicable characters who veered in their sons' estimation from a kind of amiable irrelevance to an intolerable interference as the fortunes of adolescence changed. But he couldn't imagine any of them failing to stick up for his son against an accusation like that. He said, "Were you expelled?" In his world, expulsion from prep school, though not the badge of honor it was reputed to be in some circles, was at least not disgraceful: Boyd had been kicked out twice before finally graduating, a year late. But Jack somehow didn't want it to have happened to Timothy, and especially not in those circumstances.

"Nn-nn." Timothy shook his head. "There was this older boy, I told you, who had been assigned to be my, mentor, I guess.

He and a couple of other kids, and one of the dons who liked me, didn't believe the whole story. They found out that it had all been faked, and how. So the other kid got punished, and I was sort of a hero."

"Well, it makes sense to me now, that you hate your father."

"Oh no," Timothy said quickly. "No. I don't hate him. Really, I love him. He's a great person in a lot of ways. We can't seem to get along, is all, but I don't hate him. I don't want you to think that."

This was undiscovered country; Jack was unequipped to pursue the point. His own father hadn't lived long enough for him to have worked this sort of thing out.

Mrs. Prescott came in at that point and announced that dinner was ready. They went into the dining room, and while they ate, Timothy, his mood evidently restored, talked on about Winchester, what a beautiful place it was, what a good time he'd ended up having there after all. Jack watched as his enthusiasm played on his mobile face. The beauty of the soul, Jack thought, remembering Ripley and the *Symposium.*

"What do you want to do after dinner?" Timothy asked.

"I don't know." He hadn't been thinking beyond the moment. He hadn't felt that it mattered much, since Timothy seemed prepared to have him stay as long as he wanted. "What're the options?"

"Well, we have a bunch of movies on tape. Or we could go out. They're showing Japanese films every Saturday night this summer up at Westfield."

"No," Jack said, and he felt his whole face close up with denial. "I don't think I want to go up there right now." Too many memories.

They ended up lying at either end of the large couch in the family room, watching *To Have and Have Not.* By the end, Jack was half asleep. He felt very warm and unusually contented, and a sense of Timothy's physical presence had been growing on him all evening. When the movie ended, he yawned elaborately. "I'm pretty tired, even if I did sleep all day. I think I'll go upstairs."

Timothy barely moved. "Good night. See you in the morning. Sleep well."

Upstairs, he lay in the high bed in the darkness, feeling the comfortable roughness of the newly laundered sheets on his skin. He knew what he was waiting for, what experience had taught him would be the inevitable conclusion of the evening. Timothy would be quietly turning off the lights downstairs. He would pause in the entry hall a moment, the faint glow from upstairs gleaming whitely on his hair. He would climb the staircase, purposely walking in the center of its curve, and stand a moment on the landing. Then he'd go into his room and get undressed and put on a bathrobe. He'd walk down the hall and stand outside Jack's door (and even though it was foggy out, Jack imagined the whole scene flooded with moonlight) and raise his hand and knock.

The image was so real that he almost fooled himself into hearing the knock, but there was nothing. He replayed the fantasy over and over in his mind — the staircase, the hallway, the moonlight, the soft rapping at his door — thinking, I don't want it to happen that way, thinking, It always happens that way, waiting, until he fell asleep.

He awoke at nine-thirty — a little more respectable, he thought. The fog had disappeared and bright sunlight shone through the curtains. He showered and dressed and went downstairs. Mrs. Prescott, standing in the kitchen, looked at him balefully. "I suppose you'll want some breakfast."

He realized that ten o'clock was probably outside the breakfast window of opportunity, but he also knew a thing or two about women like Mrs. Prescott. "Oh, don't bother. I usually don't eat breakfast. Just a cup of coffee'll do."

"What? You need your breakfast. Most important meal of the day. Coffee's not enough. I'll fix you some eggs."

He smiled. "No thanks. No eggs. Maybe just some cereal. Cheerios?" he asked hopefully. He had a mania for Cheerios that caused Billy endless amusement.

Timothy came in as he was finishing. "Good morning. Did you sleep well?"

Jack nodded.

"Like to come outside and have a look around the place?"

Jack followed him out the back door. The house sat on a fairly steep rise, overlooking a pond. To one side was a swimming pool surrounded by blue slate with a pool house at the far end. On the other side was a series of gardens laid out on a succession of long ascending terraces: first a small Japanese fish pond, then a rose garden in full bloom, then a flower garden, and finally a wide allée of yews leading to a small summerhouse with a long veranda on which there were a couple of chairs and a cushioned bench. "It's beautiful, Timothy."

"My great-grandfather planted it nearly eighty years ago, before the First World War, my mother's grandfather. That's why my father hasn't changed anything — it doesn't exactly look good for a modernist architect to live in a hundred-year-old house, but my mother's sentimental about it."

All his talk was simply a background to Jack's enjoyment of the garden. Here and there, as they progressed up the slight incline, the hedge that surrounded the terraces was pierced to provide a view, of the pond below or of the mountains, the Berkshires, in the distance. He thought of all the time it had taken for the plants to mature, how very different it would have looked eighty years ago, all mud and seedlings. "Think of the certainty it must have taken."

Timothy nodded. "I knew you'd see that." They stood in the warm sunlight, warmer especially after the fog of the day before, the garden smelling a little of heated earth. Timothy said, "We have to drive up to Great Barrington to do some errands for Mrs. Prescott. It's her revenge for our showing up here unexpectedly."

"Oh. I don't know." The isolation of the day before, the enclosed feeling in the garden — he didn't want to be with people.

"Just some errands, Jack. Nobody's going to know you, or care if they do."

Listen, he felt like saying, who brought me here in the first place? He hadn't asked to come. "Sure. Let's go."

There was a shiny blue convertible in the garage, with the top down. As they drove off, Jack tried to remember where the house was in relation to the landmarks of his Westfield life. Once they'd driven down the long driveway and along a narrow lane to the main road, though, he knew exactly where he was. They passed the entrance to the nature conservancy, and then, a couple of miles later, pulled up at the intersection by the school. "The Westfield Academy for Boys," he said, looking at the brick buildings across the lawns. "Four years of my life."

Timothy drove on toward the little town of Westfield. "Did you like it? It's a great school."

"I guess." It had been a mixture of loneliness and friendship, victory and failure, popularity and disdain, what Ripley had called the adolescent cocktail, but spiked with an uncommon dose of tragedy. He wanted to look back and see only the good things — the medals he'd won for the swim team, the intense private moments of discovery when he finally understood a book he was studying, the hills in autumn. But everything was colored by what had happened alongside those years, and before and after. He said, "The first book I was assigned in my first English class was *A Tale of Two Cities*. It was the best of times, it was the worst of times. We thought they did it on purpose."

"At least it wasn't the *Inferno*," Timothy said.

"No." He hadn't had any hope to abandon. "It was just the usual stuff."

"Nothing as dramatic as being accused of stealing?"

Unless you count having your parents drive off a cliff as dramatic, Jack thought.

"Tell me about your time at Westfield," Timothy said, and there was something of the arrogant, masterful boy in his demand.

Jack looked over at him. His hair was blowing in the wind, and behind him a mountain rose. The road seemed deserted but for them. The air was hot and dry, filled with summer and all the promise of fulfillment. "I don't think I want to, right now," Jack said.

Timothy looked at him a moment and then back at the road. "You will, though. Eventually."

He thought about this, about Timothy's certainty. Most people he knew had no depth, were one-dimensional, like Boyd; or else they hid whatever profoundness they might have beneath layers of assumed behavior. But Timothy's depth was all on the surface. He said, knowing that they would come to it sooner or later, "I believe you."

Great Barrington was its usual Sunday noontime self — New

Yorkers buying food for picnics at Tanglewood, after-church families sauntering down the sidewalks, too many cars. The town always seemed abrupt to him — he usually approached it from back roads that cut through mountains and farms. He cringed a little at it that day, because it was so much the opposite of the cocoon he'd felt himself to be in at Timothy's house. They stopped at a few stores, then went into an antique shop, where Timothy became involved in a protracted negotiation with the proprietor. It had something to do with a painting his mother had ordered that hadn't been delivered. Jack wandered aimlessly, examining a gilt frame, looking at the face of a moon clock, touching the mahogany surface of a Queen Anne dinner table. His finger left a damp mark on the surface, which evaporated as he watched. He signaled to Timothy and went outside.

In a park across the street, a baseball game was going on. He wandered over, standing next to the low bleachers, which were full of the wives and children of the players. The men were all wearing T-shirts with the names of two local businesses stenciled on them. There was a hot dog smell in the air, from a barbecue over beside first base. A bat cracked and the ball described a perfect arc over the left fielder's head and into some bushes. The batter circled the bases. Jack remembered a home run he'd hit in Little League a few weeks before his eleventh birthday. A game-winner. The pitcher glared at the next batter and wasted a pitch low and away. In the bleachers, someone yelled encouragement — a pregnant woman in a flowery cotton shirt, with a two-year-old on her lap.

Jack thought about Billy, about a game the two of them had gone to a few weeks before — one of the few afternoon games the Yankees played anymore. It was a familiar ritual to Jack, one that reached back to his childhood. He'd told Billy about the very first time he'd come, with his father, he'd been maybe five or six. It had been a warm day in late spring, and they'd taken the subway uptown, through the dark tunnels before bursting out onto the el just before 161st Street. They'd joined the crowds milling around the old stadium, passing the lines outside the bleacher entry. He remembered feeling a little scared by all the people, by the loudness and the scale of everything, and by the impression, here in the Bronx, of being locked in the concrete of the buildings and the iron of the el. And then the magic, never-forgotten moment of astonishment when they stepped out of the portal, and the whole vast expanse of green spread out before him. He said to Billy, "It was the total improbability of seeing, all at once, all that grass. Up here in the middle of the Bronx." He looked around at the crowd that was slowly and in an unde-liberate way filling up the grandstand seats, at the umpires con-ferring behind the plate, at the empty Yankee dugout.

Billy, munching a hot dog, said, "The first time I came was with you and dad, in 'seventy-eight."

The legendary season. Jack remembered the day. Looking back, they seemed an ill-assorted trio, although anyone seeing them would have thought they were a father out with his two widely spaced sons, guessing David to be older than he was. It would have been a case of only slightly mistaken identity: the brother-in-law as surrogate father, the uncle as surrogate brother. Billy wiped some mustard off his face. "We saw Guidry pitch, remember."

"He has — had, the most beautiful delivery I've ever seen. Like a perfect circle coming over the top, leg, arm, leg, arm, it was like watching a pinwheel. And then, after he delivered, the way he'd practically jump off the mound and sort of crouch, ready to field the ball."

"You should be a baseball writer, instead," Billy teased.

They stood up for the National Anthem. Jack took the cap off Billy's head and handed it to him, and started to sing. Billy, a little embarrassed, held the cap awkwardly.

The game had gone on, distinguished here and there in itself, but seeming to Jack to be one more inning in a long game that he would be watching all his life. With only a few exceptions (the playoff game in '78, or Fisk's home run in '75, neither of which he'd seen in person), he didn't remember individual games, only the steady unfolding of a single game, baseball. A game where nothing really unexpected ever happened, a game fenced in by its own comfortable history embroidered in endless statistical ta-bles of hits and runs and errors. One could speculate endlessly about baseball because it was so unchanging in an elemental way.

Ten years from now, just as ten years before, he thought, he would be sitting here with Billy watching the same game.

Timothy walked up and said, "Who's winning?"

"I don't know." He'd been watching the game, not keeping score. "God, I love baseball."

Timothy laughed. "You're in a funny mood. Ready to go home?"

That afternoon, they went swimming in the pond behind the house. The land, planted with trees and shrubs and having a wild look to it, sloped down sharply from the house. A narrow path led to a small lawn at the water's edge, shaded by weeping willows and oaks. An Italianate landing, white marble, seemed to float on the water. They swam for a while and Jack said, "I love the way lake water always smells of earth: not dirty or salty or chloriney. It's the best kind of swimming there is."

They had nothing to do. That was the essence of the afternoon. He had, for months, for years, it seemed, hurried along at the force of other people's expectations — Elizabeth's, David's, Kate's — and now, hidden from even the most searching eye, he felt those expectations lift. He knew that the other life had merely withdrawn, was hovering somewhere near, that he would go back to it. But at least this afternoon he felt he could ignore it. Timothy was lying on a little bench in the shade of one of the willows. Jack sat on the edge of the landing, his feet in the lake, the marble beneath him warm, the air around him warm, the water swallowing his legs in a brown haze. A punt was tied to the marble railing nearby, and a long pole, but he didn't feel like even that much work. He untied it and climbed in, pushing off with a canoe paddle. Then he lay back against the cushions and half closed his eyes, letting the faint breeze blow him.

Floating aimlessly in the hot sun, with amorphous clouds creeping like amoebas across the sky, he remembered spending a whole afternoon like this with Kate at her parents' house in Palm Beach. They had a couple of air mattresses, and as the water circulator pushed them slowly around, they occasionally bumped together, and Kate would reach for his mouth, trying not to tip them over. Finally she put her hand on his stomach, her fingers just inside the waistband of his trunks, keeping the two of them together. And all afternoon he ordered more drinks to be brought to them, and Kate laughed. "You know, John, you're the first man I've ever brought here who knows how to handle servants."

She came into his room later, before dinner, while he was lying in the bathtub with the bubbles bursting against his sunburnt skin. Her hair was wrapped in a towel and she was wearing a yellow silk robe belted beneath her breasts. She was holding a hard plastic hairbrush and a black hexagonal bottle adorned with the initials of a famous hairstylist. "I've decided," she announced, "that you should do something different to your hair."

They were going out that night, to a party at the tennis club, and he didn't want to do anything different to his hair.

"Sit up," she said.

"What are you going to do?"

"Don't be so suspicious. I'm going to give you a shampoo, for starters."

"I don't know, Kate." He looked uneasily at the bottle she was holding, but he sat up in the tub. She took some of his usual shampoo and rubbed the lather up. He was starting to enjoy it, the feel of her fingers in his hair. "This is nice."

She took two handfuls of soap bubbles and put them on his chest, over his nipples. "Not fair," he said, in a strangled kind of voice.

She pushed back on his shoulders until he was lying in the tub again, his head under water and clouds of shampoo floating away from him. He felt totally vulnerable to anything she might do to him: if she pressed her hand down on his face he would lie there until he drowned. Then she tugged at him, and he sat up.

"Now we'll dry your hair." She did, with a large towel, pulling his head close to her chest. He kissed her while she opened the bottle she'd brought with her. "What's that?" he asked warily.

"Styling mousse. Trust me." She rubbed the goop into his hair, then very gently used her brush on it.

When she was done, he got out of the tub and looked at himself in the mirror. His hair looked sort of spiky, not punk exactly, but not its usual silky self either. The mousse made it look a different color, darker and more monochrome, subduing the streaks of red and gold. "I don't know."

She came over and kissed him hard, the silk of her robe cool against his skin. She put her hands behind his thighs, just touching him with her fingertips. "I love you, John."

It was the first time she'd said it, and he thought, The way it's supposed to turn out. She said, "I want to take you to bed, but we have to go to this party." And she slipped out of the room. He stood in front of the mirror again, calming himself down. He thought about combing his hair out, but didn't.

At the party he felt her watching him, his hair, the way another girl might constantly be aware of a new engagement ring. He didn't much like the way it felt — he kept wanting to put his hand up to see if it was as stiff as it seemed. He wondered whether everyone else was noticing it too. Her brother, her parents, some of her cousins — maybe they thought he was going to show up in a mohawk next. He would, probably, if it would make her happy. His hair the way she had arranged it.

That was her world. Men worked and women arranged. Even when women worked, they worked at jobs that were just another form of arranging, like Kate's job publishing art books, setting up gallery shows. Unlike the women Jack knew from college, who went out in the world and did more or less the same sorts of things men did, employed for their skills in law or business or scholarship, Kate was valued for her taste, which was just another way of saying her skill at arranging things. It wasn't an acquired taste, it was innate, the product of all those generations of women who could have anything and therefore had to choose only what was the most valuable. Faced with two jade pieces, Kate would infallibly choose the more exquisite, the more ancient, the more finely worked in ways that Jack himself couldn't even see; faced with a choice between mediocrities, she wouldn't even be interested.

He opened his eyes. Above him, the sky revolved slowly as the punt turned in the water. If it was Kate's world, it was his also, at least he had made it his in default of other, more dangerous possibilities. He had allowed her to rate him too, which at least had the advantage of removing any doubt about where he stood. Now, lying in a boat in the middle of a lake on this afternoon devoid of connections, surrounded by hills in all the colors of high summer, walled off from anything outside, he had to laugh at the thought that he stood anywhere.

There was a splash, and he looked around to see Timothy swimming toward him. He climbed into the punt rather expertly, tipping it only a little, and straddled the flat end facing Jack. "You look indecently relaxed," he said.

"I am. I feel like I'm incognito in paradise."

Timothy laughed. "Is that a Fitzgerald novel?"

"Or a Fellini movie. If I were you, I'd never leave here. Forget New York."

Timothy rocked the boat up and down a little. "I know what you mean. But you have to grow up sometime. I'm just glad I have it to come back to when I want." He picked up the pole, which was lying in the side of the boat. "I used to punt at Winchester." He stood up and experimentally dipped the pole in the water.

"I thought the water might be too deep," Jack said.

"In the middle maybe. But if we stay by the edges." He pushed off more confidently, and the punt leaped forward. "I had a good friend who was a great athlete, and we'd go out in the afternoons sometimes, and he taught me how to manage it properly." He sounded, for a moment, very English, that trace of foreignness Jack had noticed in him from the beginning.

"The last time I was in a punt," Jack said softly, but Timothy didn't hear him and went on.

"We used to hoard cookies and cakes and take them with us. The big treat was when we could have strawberries."

The last time I was in a punt, Jack thought, I ate strawberries. He had taken a year off after college and had gone to England, living in London in a small flat in Kensington. He was working for a film company that was owned by one of David's clients. It had all been David's idea, actually. "Take a year off, John, decide what you want to do. Go somewhere, live somewhere else. If you could live anywhere in the world, where would it be?" San Francisco, he'd thought, but Ripley was there, and the idea bothered him. Some African city, exotic and remote, a desert city out of the *Arabian Nights*, but he was afraid he'd lose himself altogether and forever if he went someplace that foreign. London, he'd said, and David had worked it out for him. At first it had been a blast. Friends from college and from Westfield kept stopping by for their summer abroad, crashing on his floor for a few days before moving on to Paris or Amsterdam or Rome. But as summer turned to winter, the visits became less frequent.

He was very much alone, then, on purpose. He remembered himself, with long hair and an oversized raincoat huddling against the weather on his way to the Tube, wearing old clothes to work because they seemed more arty (the film company having pretensions in that direction). The other people in the office were English, and they existed mostly to provide temporary refuge to screenwriters polishing scripts or directors holding conferences between location shootings in remote parts of Britain. Jack began cultivating a certain wildness that appealed to them, especially to one of them, a man named Richard. Prince Hal, Richard called him, after Jack quoted from *Henry IV* one day. Richard was about forty and divorced, with children in Swiss schools, and he had a nebulous job meeting unimportant visitors, overseeing the junior staff (of whom Jack was one), and taking long lunches at his club with played-out actors, insistent press agents, and minor Whitehall types who might hold the keys to dwindling government subsidies. With Richard leading the way, Jack cruised the odder reaches of London's nightlife. There was a pub in Brixton where time was called but the drinking went on surreptitiously, and his evening would end when a woman invited him home for a price. There was another pub, in the docklands, where the drinking was ferocious, and tough unemployed men, who had been Thatcherized out of England's great green lawn, would start fights in which he'd sometimes join, coming to work the next day with scraped knuckles that excited the secretaries. There was a bar under a church in Pimlico where a raucous transvestite floor show went on, completely ignored by the shaven-headed boys with sliced leather jackets who sat disdainfully on barstools while older men supplicated vainly, until bargains were struck and the odd couples disappeared up the steps into the night. There was a private club behind Shaftesbury Avenue where girls in black panties came and sat on his lap and ordered themselves champagne at thirty pounds a bottle while a naked couple made love on the floor under a blue spotlight. Richard leaned over one night and whispered to him, "I am corrupting you. I've always wanted a boy to corrupt."

Jack, drunk, looked at him and thought, He means it, he thinks of himself as an artist, when all he does is arrange the travel schedules of real artists. Jack was just material to him, apt perhaps, but still only a curiosity, a Yank who could quote Shakespeare. He whispered back, "I know thee not, old man."

It was Richard who introduced him to Marci, at a party at his mother's house, a big old heap in Surrey that Richard told everyone would go to pay the death taxes if his mother ever managed to finish dying. He said she was an invalid, but she looked perfectly healthy to Jack. Marci was an American woman who worked for Citicorp. She had a four-year-old, a tow-headed boy whose picture she showed Jack that first day at the party. She had a nanny to take care of the kid and a flat in Belgravia and no apparent husband, and the day after the party, she called Jack and asked him to go to the theater with her — she suddenly had two tickets for a performance the next evening. They had dinner a couple of times, and she called him her pirate, because he had gotten into a pub brawl that left him with a purple bruise on his cheekbone. After their fourth or fifth date, she took him home with her.

He woke up the next morning before she did and prowled around the room. He found a long T-shirt with a Greenpeace logo on it and put it on, leaving his suit from the night before lying on the floor. He went out into the living room and turned on the radio. It was a Sunday morning, and the classical station she listened to (that was something else they had in common) was playing the Schubert Mass in G, which he knew pretty well from a music theory class that Ripley had talked him into taking at Westfield. He half-hummed, half-sang along, walking around the room looking at things. He found a yo-yo on a table and started to play with it. It suddenly struck him as funny — standing in someone else's apartment, with almost no clothes on, playing with a yo-yo and singing *Deus Pater Omnipotens.* He laughed. Then he heard a noise and turned around.

A little boy was standing there, staring at him. He was wearing pajamas with a clown face on the shirt, and he was holding a brown bear that was half as big as he was. He looked at Jack and said, "You're not my daddy."

"No, buddy, I'm not." The boy reminded him of Billy and Hank. "I'm John."

The boy looked at him still. Then he said, "I'm Superman, and you can be Lex Luthor."

So they played Superman for a while, until Marci came in and rescued him. The boy and Jack became pretty good friends. They went to the zoo and to a circus, and one day the three of them drove out to Oxford and rented a punt. They had a bucket of strawberries and some cookies, and Jack poled the boat past the green fields behind Christ Church, watching the undergraduates go by much more expertly. That was the last time he'd been in a punt. It was something you could learn only in England, he decided, the way Timothy had.

Jack watched him for a while. He was bare-chested, his swimsuit damp around his thighs. There was something satisfying about the play of muscles in his chest and arms as he worked the punt. His body was compact, economical, willowy — that was a very British word. Is that what they had thought of him at Winchester? Jack wondered. He said, "What did you do after Winchester?"

Timothy bent to the work, his arms pushing hard against the bottom. "I went to Brown. I majored in history and German."

"Why German?"

He lifted the pole for a minute, and they coasted forward. "It's silly, isn't it, the way we choose things like that. One of the dons at Winchester taught German. For some reason I was quite attracted to him, I think it was because he had the most far-ranging mind I'd ever met. It wasn't just that he was incredibly bright and a fantastic teacher, it was the way he looked at things. The way an outsider can see some things better than an insider. He wasn't German, he was English, but looking at the world with German glasses on." He stood still for a moment, thinking, and then went back to poling the punt. "In any case, I started to study German with him. At Brown it was my second major. That's how I got to Columbia, studying German history." He brushed some hair away from his forehead. "That's really why I'm going to spend the summer here. I'm reading for my dissertation."

"What's it about?"

Timothy said, "The impact of the Napoleonic wars on three

minor German poets. They all happened to be living in Weimar during most of the period, so they naturally came under the influence of Goethe and Schiller, and there was a lot of correspondence among them all. The real thesis has to do with the collision of history and idealism — which is a very German sort of idea."

Jack trailed a finger in the water. "You must love it."

"I do, you know. Most people think I'm crazy, that it's so narrow. But it's perfect for me — history and German poetry, my two favorite things." He had guided them into the shade of the willows and now poled out again into the light. "Have you ever thought about going back and getting your degree?"

Jack shook his head. In college, and even more in graduate school, he'd wanted to be a scholar, to sit in the ethereal stillness of an old library so that forever afterward the world would know more than it had. But his mind didn't work that way, it defied system, and instead he'd left school and gone to work at the magazine, and lived a life as far removed from the contemplative as he could imagine. "I couldn't do it — I just don't have the ability."

"Do you have to sell yourself short all the time?" Timothy asked impatiently. He gave another great push with the pole and they shot toward the shore.

That evening Jack called Billy. He called late, not wanting to talk to David or Elizabeth, knowing the habits of the household. A sleepy voice answered. "Yeah. Who is it."

"Hey, sport, it's me. Sorry to wake you up."

"Oh. Hold on." He heard rustling noises as Billy sat up in bed. "OK. Wow. Uh, where've you been? It's getting to be a drag waiting for you every morning, if you're not going to show up."

"Sorry. Listen, I'm away. Visiting a friend." He heard Billy yawning. "I have to ask a favor of you. Billy. You with me, kiddo?"

"Yeah, yeah, I'm here. What is it?"

"I'm going to give you a number where I can be reached, but only in an emergency. I don't want it spread around."

"Why not?"

"Because I don't. I need a little time on my own."

"You don't want my parents to know, is that it?" Billy yawned again.

"Look. Don't get yourself in trouble or anything. Just be discreet."

"Shit. Let me get a pencil, hold on." The receiver clattered down on the night table, and Jack could picture him digging around on the cluttered desk. He came back on. "Go ahead."

Jack gave the number. "Thanks, Billy."

"That's up in Westfield. What are you doing up there?" When Jack didn't answer right away, Billy said, "OK, don't tell me. Your secret is safe with me."

"Thanks, pal, I really appreciate it. Sleep tight."

Jack woke up in the middle of the night, completely alert. This happened to him once or twice a week, more often lately. He'd begun by fighting it, but now he knew there were only two solutions — he could give up and read for an hour and then try again, or he could take a big slug of bourbon and knock himself out. Either way he would probably feel lousy in the morning. He went downstairs to the library, which had both books and booze.

He scanned the shelves, from old editions of eighteenth-century novels collected by Timothy's great-grandfather, to books on architecture and modern art. A little reluctantly, he took down a volume of Plato and opened to the *Symposium*, but he didn't read it. He didn't have to. "Ripley," he said softly, letting the book slip out of his hands onto his lap. He knew why he'd been thinking so much about Ripley in the last two days — it was Timothy, his presence and his influence. Not since he'd met Ripley had he had a friend quite like Timothy. He stood up, resigned, and poured out some whiskey.

The next morning, Timothy announced that he had some reading to do, and Jack volunteered to drive into Millerton and pick up some things for Mrs. Prescott. That accomplished, he drove around more or less aimlessly. After half an hour, he ended up where he'd known he would, in the little parking lot of the nature conservancy a couple of miles from Westfield. He got out and walked down the wide path that skirted the marsh, bordered on the one hand by a steep rocky hillside and on the other by a ruined stone wall. Red-winged blackbirds perched on the tall cattails, and a bullfrog croaked hopefully across the water. The trees were in full leaf, the track was damp but not muddy, and except for the sound of his sneakers breaking twigs, it was very quiet. Without looking at the markers, he found the trail he wanted, and even though it had been four years since his last visit, it was all horribly familiar. He could almost see Ripley's rounded shoulders and wide hips ahead of him as they penetrated the woods. He came to the top of a rise and stopped, looking down at a flinty formation of rock cracked as if by a thunderbolt, and heard the distant bubbling of the river ahead. Slowly now, he went on, and came to the bridge over the water: it was new since his time, the old bridge — their bridge — having been replaced. There had always been something wonderful about this next stretch, a flat path, almost like a track beneath the over-hanging intertwined birch branches — in the autumn it was a tunnel full of fluttering falling leaves — and it had always seemed very ancient, the sort of cart path that would have been used by the early settlers of this remote woodland. He hesitated for the first time, a little unsure of himself, then left the path, struggled through the underbrush, and came out into a small depression by the side of the stream. It was sheltered by a growth of ever-greens and by its own banks, and the river washed over a series of ledges in a pretty, tuneful cataract. It was here that he and Ripley had come so many times so many years ago. He sat down tentatively, then lay back, his head on his arm, looking up at the treetops brushed by breeze. Out of the past, like Roland's horn, high and clear as a lost cause, he heard a voice calling to him.

V

"JOHN. JOHN NEWLAND."

He was walking along a brick path with Jeff and Stephen in the early afternoon sunlight. They were laughing about a comment their English teacher had just made.

"I hate it when they try to be, like, one of us," Jeff, his roommate, said.

"All these old guys who went to Woodstock and all," Stephen said. "I think they smoked too much dope or something and it turned their brains into Swiss cheese."

He was fifteen years old, it was three months since his parents had died, and it was getting to be all right to laugh again. On a gorgeous October day, with the leaves all filled with color and the air pungent with early decay, and the gold light warm with almost the last warmth of the year, there didn't seem to be any reason not to laugh. It seemed possible for a moment to forget. And then he heard a voice calling to him: "John. John Newland."

The three boys stopped walking and looked around. Stephen pointed with his chin. "It's Lewis."

"What does he want?" Jeff asked, his tone mixing dislike with the grudging admiration they all felt toward Ripley Lewis.

"John. Come over here a minute."

Jeff poked him with his elbow. "Go ahead, Newland. See what he wants."

As he walked slowly toward Ripley, he could hear Stephen giggling behind him at something Jeff had said.

Ripley was standing in the middle of the sidewalk, parting the stream of boys released from afternoon classes. Conscious of his friends watching, he swaggered a little, holding his books on one hip, his head cocked a little to one side. "Yeah?" he asked.

"I want to talk to you. Let's go for a walk." Ripley turned on his heel and struck out in a purposeful way across the grass and down the hill, leaving him stranded for a moment. He thought of Jeff and Stephen, probably watching sarcastically — they'd rag him pretty bad if he chickened out now, and besides, he was curious. He hurried a little to catch up. "Listen, Lewis —"

"No," Ripley said. "Not Lewis. I detest jockiness, and I hate being called by my last name. Mr. Lewis won't do, at least not if we're going to be friends. You may call me Ripley. What shall I call you?"

"John, I guess." He could hear the sounds of the school receding behind them. He was supposed to be playing touch football with some of the guys from the swim team.

"I don't like that," Ripley said airily. "It's very formal, isn't it, and then it has unfortunate lavatory associations."

"Thanks a lot."

"We'll think of something. Nicknames. You don't have any nicknames, do you? No? And you probably have one of those forbidding family names as a middle name."

"White," he said shortly.

"John White Newland. Impressive. How about Whitey? Whitey is a kid who plays second base on a Little League team. Little Beaver Cleaver's friend. That's no good. Maybe I could call you Johnny."

"No." He stopped walking. It was what his parents had called him. "Not Johnny."

Ripley looked at him curiously from behind his round steel-frame glasses. "No? Too bad. Like all diminutives, it has a certain affectionate quality. Not if you don't like it, though." He was silent a moment, and this, after his usual way of thinking out loud, was a little unnerving. "I know," Ripley went on. "I shall call you Jack. Jack and Jill, Little Jack Horner, Jack Sprat. Jack and the Beanstalk."

"Jack be nimble," he muttered.

"Ah, are you a devotee of nursery rhymes?"

"I have a nephew who's three. He likes them." He had known who Ripley was, but this was the first time he'd spoken more than passing words with him. Everyone knew who Ripley was. He was the number one brain of their class, reputed to be a genius on the Richter scale, and so notoriously contemptuous of fools that some of the teachers seemed a little afraid of him. He was undisciplined, especially his tongue, and ungovernable — he said and did what he liked — and even his nonconformities failed to conform to acceptable limitations. He played no sports, had no friends, dated no girls, and in classroom discussions took no prisoners. Jack was fascinated by him but knew better than to tip his hand. "So, what do you want to talk about?"

Ripley, as if guided by an invisible divining rod, threw himself down on the ground, saying, "This will do." Jack was reminded of going to the beach with his mother — they would trek aimlessly across the sand, like Mormons in the wilderness, until some private portent told her this was the place. "Jack, sit down. Why do we have to talk about anything? Can't we just talk? Or are you one of those people who believe everything must have meaning? If so, you'll get along well with all of them." He jerked his head back, to indicate the school behind them.

Jack sat down next to him. Ripley, whatever the auspices, had picked out a perfect spot to sit. They could see over the lake to a steep mountain that was tufted, like a royal Persian rug, in red and gold. Next to them stood six Corinthian columns, etched against the blue and white sky. These surrounded a granite floor on which were carved the names of the Westfield boys who had fallen in the First World War. Between each pair of columns was a marble bench, and Jack sometimes came here to study when he wanted to be alone. He said, "What about all of them?"

"Seekers after meaning," Ripley said sarcastically. "Lab technicians of literature. Dissectors of text. Pluck out the heart of mystery — but then what's left if a book has no heart?"

"I don't know what you're talking about."

"Oh yes you do," Ripley contradicted. "You do it too. You were showing off in class just now —"

"I was not." He had been, but it was one accusation he was bound, reflexively, to contest. Having made up his mind to stick around for a while and talk to Ripley, he took off his school blazer and loosened his tie a little.

Ripley shrugged. "Why bother to deny it? It was a very nice analysis, tied Richard the Second up in a neat package with a bow on top, but didn't you miss something — all the beauty of the poetry, the heart's cry of a deposed king: 'For God's sake let us sit upon the ground and tell sad stories of the deaths of kings.' The meaning isn't in the meaning, it's in the poetry."

Jack had been sitting cross-legged on the ground, tearing at the grass. Now, he lay back with his head on his arm and said, "A poem should not mean, but be."

"At least you've read MacLeish. But do you believe it? Close your eyes," he said abruptly.

"Why?"

"Just close them."

Jack did so, reluctantly. Maybe he would be left alone, lying here like a jerk. Maybe, defenseless, he would be kicked in the head — he imagined the blow and then a vast explosion of light in his head. Ripley said, "Listen," and began to recite in a quiet voice.

> *"Season of mist and mellow fruitfulness,*
> *Close bosom-friend of the maturing sun;*
> *Conspiring with him how to load and bless*
> *With fruit the vines that round the thatch-eaves run."*

Jack listened as the words chimed out in Ripley's high, clear voice. The verses seemed to enter into him, to take possession of some inner core of self that he steadfastly had refused to visit for months now. The sunlight felt warmer through his shirt, and the air smelled of apples and leaves, and the grass was brittle under his hands. Serenity entered with the poetry, and a great stillness, as Ripley concluded: "And gathering swallows twitter in the skies." The last line lingered on and on like a note struck on a single silver bell, decaying into infinity. Jack sighed. "It's beautiful, Ripley. Did you write it?"

Ripley snorted. "Jesus, no. Where have you been? It's Keats, the ode 'To Autumn.' I'd give my life to write one poem like that."

Jack rolled over and propped his head on one bent arm. "Keats. We haven't studied Keats."

"We haven't studied MacLeish either," he said drily. "Thank God."

Jack, anxious to have his approval, said, "I don't know where that came from. It's something I picked up somewhere."

Ripley took off his glasses and held them up to the light before polishing them on his tie. "You don't need to be defensive about it. I happen to love Keats," he said, the way someone might say, I prefer dark meat. "I wonder what Keats would make of this place?"

"Westfield?"

"He once wrote that 'the imagination of a boy is healthy, and the mature imagination of a man is healthy.' If he'd come here, he wouldn't have said that. No healthy imaginations here. A swamp of lust and sticky sheets, don't you think."

Jack looked away from him at the hazy air that hung over the lake in the valley below. "Whatever gets you through the night."

Ripley stood up. "A pat answer. Unworthy of you. You can do better than that." He began to walk away.

"Hey," Jack said. He scrambled to his feet, picked up his books and his blazer, and chased after him. "Hey. What's the matter, someone choke off the blood supply to your brain?"

"No, Jack." Ripley turned on him. "No. Just don't pretend to be stupid and conventional with me, because you're not. I've watched you for over a year now, and I know a little bit about you. All these other people, all the boys and most of the teachers, have great brains, all right, they're all so terribly, terribly intelligent. But they don't think. They just repeat their comfortable clichés, but they don't think. You think. I know you do, even if for some reason you don't like to admit it. Don't lie to yourself, Jack, you'll never get anywhere that way."

I don't lie to myself, Jack thought. Even if I do lie to everyone else, I know the truth myself. He looked at Ripley, wondering what to say, wanting to say anything but that. He already had a strong enough sense of Ripley to know that if he once admitted there was a secret behind the façade, Ripley would have it out of him. He said, "I don't see what this has to do with literature."

"Of course you do. They all sit in class, and it's no different. Everyone trying to confine a poem or play within a neat little interpretation. God forbid they should just experience it. Literature isn't a game, you know," he went on impatiently. "It's not there to be examined under a microscope for meaning to be extracted."

"I know that," Jack answered, wondering if he should confess the truth.

But Ripley was on to him. "What are you thinking?"

"Literature isn't a game," he said reluctantly, "but school is."

Ripley swallowed what he'd been about to say. "You're good," he went on after a pause. "You even had me fooled."

"I play the game," Jack shrugged, "because it's easier. It makes people happy. You mouth off in class, Ripley, and antagonize everyone, maybe that gets you what you want, I don't know. But I do know, just as well as you, all about the poetry."

"Yes." Ripley nodded, as if accepting Jack as an equal for the first time. "Tell me, what is it that you think I want?"

Jack frowned. "How do I know? To be noticed, maybe. I just do what they want because I don't want to be noticed."

"Why not?" Ripley was looking at him, and it seemed to Jack that a current of understanding passed between them for a moment, then Ripley backed down. "It's all right, Jack. Never mind. I sometimes get these attacks, you don't have to pay any attention."

"Yeah, well." Jack shifted his weight from one foot to the other. "I guess I gotta go now."

"Off to some sweaty athletic endeavor, no doubt. You must explain the appeal to me someday. Goodbye." He turned and walked off.

Jeff was in their room when Jack got back, examining his face in the mirror. "So, what'd he want?"

Jack tossed his books onto his bed. "To talk."

"Talk." Jeff turned his head to view his other profile. "He sure can do a lot of talking." Jeff was from New Orleans, and he exaggerated his accent at times for emphasis.

"I guess." Jack felt confused — he didn't want to run Ripley down, but he didn't want to argue with Jeff.

"John, boy, you don't want to get messed up with this guy. Next thing, you'll be wearing a little plastic thing in your shirt pocket and picking at your asshole." Jeff, outdoorsy and, Jack supposed after Ripley's diatribe, totally without imagination, despised anything that smacked of the abnormal.

"Blow it out your ass," Jack said. "I never even talked to the guy before today. I'm not going to get messed up with him." But in the library that evening, Jack took down a volume of Keats and looked through it. He was a little disappointed the next afternoon when Ripley ignored him completely. But the following day, after class again, Ripley stopped him in the hall. "How do you like opera?"

"I don't know," he answered truthfully, looking around to see who else might have heard.

"Well, then come up to my room and hear some. Then you can decide." He led the way, Jack in tow, across the campus to his room. It was on the third floor, the top story of the building, with a view of the headmaster's house, and there was only one bed.

"You have a single," Jack said. He didn't know anyone who lived alone, he hadn't known there were singles.

"I had five roommates in the first six months last year," Ripley said proudly. "The school decided it was easier to give up on me."

"Are you that hard to live with?"

"When I want to be. I wanted to be. What I didn't want was some stupid hockey player with bad breath or a little mousy kid who cried because he was homesick, which were two of the more presentable candidates. Sit down." The room, in contrast to Ripley, was neat and sparse, almost monkish. There were no posters on the walls, the bed looked hard and tightly made, and the desk was clear. Relatively few of the books that crammed the shelves were school books, the rest being, as best Jack could tell, novels, volumes of poetry, and a stack of history books from the school library. On the floor next to the desk a modest cassette player sat between two speakers. There was a large box of tapes, through which Ripley was sorting. "Let's see. We can try the easy approach, forty famous melodies, but that's not really serious, or we can try total immersion. What do you say?"

Jack sat down on the floor. "Go for it."

He leaned back against the bed and listened. He had been raised with classical music; his parents had subscribed to the Philharmonic and the City Ballet, and they'd taken him to concerts at Tanglewood and Avery Fisher Hall, and he'd gone annually to

The Nutcracker with his aunt Clara until he was eight or nine. On the long drive from the city to the house here in the country, his father had listened to tapes of Beethoven and Mozart and Bach until the music had woven itself into the strange dreams Jack would have in the car. One of the last times he'd spent alone with his father had been on a Sunday afternoon the previous April. Jack was home from school for vacation, and they went to a concert at the Philharmonic. He couldn't remember the program, but he could remember the familiar dazed look on his father's face as he listened to the music. Jack, even though he knew it was hopelessly childish, had wanted his father to hold him for a moment, right there in the auditorium. Instead, he put his elbow on the armrest and, as if inadvertently, pressed it for a moment against his father's side. Afterward, as they walked across the plaza between the columned buildings, his father put his arm around Jack's shoulders and squeezed him close. But opera hadn't been part of his parents' repertory for some reason. Presumably they hadn't liked it.

Jack did, though, that afternoon, listening to it with Ripley. First Keats, he thought, now this. He was used to new experiences, it seemed that his life the last few years was nothing but new experiences. As the tedious, earnest books on adolescence his parents had given him never tired of pointing out, this was the time of life for new experiences. His body had gone through all the changes depicted in the books by clinical line drawings of boys with their skin cut away to reveal inner organs, their scrotums dangling to unnatural lengths. And all the accompanying emotional swings as well. Dr. Sanders kept saying, like some demented refugee from the collapse of flower power, Let it all hang out, when all Jack wanted was to stuff it all back in. But Ripley was introducing him to a whole new set of experiences, intellectual experiences. Jack knew he had a body and feelings, he'd been told so over and over, and he wasn't sure he liked either. Now he was being told he had a mind. Ripley, he thought, is someone who knows exactly what he thinks, precisely where he is going, and all Jack would have to do was follow along.

"Well, did you like that?" Ripley asked after an hour or so.

Jack nodded. "I did. Especially the one by Beethoven. Play that one again."

Ripley smiled. "You picked my favorite. One of my favorites, anyway." He ran the tape again, and against its background said, "You know, if I'd asked anyone else in this school to come listen to this they would have laughed or made a snide comment or looked at me like I wanted them to eat shit or something. They're all so close-minded."

"That's not true." In the best Westfield tradition, argument was always required in response to generalization. "There are plenty of guys who must like this kind of thing. What about the choir? — they sing music like this all the time."

Ripley switched off the tape. "Not the point, Jack. I'm not talking about people who are predisposed. I'm talking about how willing people are to be exposed to new things. Your friend Jeff, for example. He may be great with the backstroke and a whiz kid at first base, but can you see him even considering this for a minute?"

Jack didn't want to defend Jeff to Ripley any more than he'd wanted to defend Ripley to Jeff. "What about you? Suppose I asked you to play touch football with us. Would you come?"

He'd surprised Ripley, who for once didn't have a snap answer. Finally he said, "You wouldn't ask me."

"But if I did."

"You wouldn't."

"Well," Jack said stubbornly, "I'm asking you now."

"It's different," Ripley mumbled dangerously. He got up and popped the tape out of the machine. "Everyone's supposed to play football, it doesn't take any guts."

"Oh," Jack jeered, "and this takes guts?"

"Yes, it does. Do you think it's easy being me? Being different. Believing in what you are because you believe it and not just because everyone else does. That takes more guts than some stupid football game."

He was standing at the window, looking out, his back to the room. Jack watched him, wondering at the outburst. "Cool your jets. I just don't want to be like some experiment you're studying."

"Never mind. I'll see you later."

Jack waited a moment, then got up from the floor. "Yeah, sure."

And that, it seemed, was the end of that. Jack made himself

as available as possible, stood around in the hall outside class, sat in the dining hall where Ripley could see him, but nothing happened. He waited for Ripley to say something — it never occurred to him to speak first. Meanwhile, swim practice had started and he spent most afternoons in the pool or the weight room. There was something normal and comfortable about being surrounded by all these bodies, about the physical endeavor, the horsing around in the locker room. He thought, standing under the shower one afternoon, half watching Jeff soap himself, how normal this was, almost as if his life hadn't suffered the great discontinuity of his parents' deaths. But at other times he found himself looking at everything and seeing how much the same it all was, applying what he imagined were Ripley's standards and feeling a vague discontent.

And then, as abruptly as he'd gone, Ripley came back, sitting down next to Jack at breakfast one morning. "I'm sorry. I lost my temper. Someday I'll explain. I tried to — I couldn't just leave it where it was, I wanted to talk to you again."

"Banish Jack and banish all the world," Jack said, their Shakespeare studies having progressed. He had come across the line in his reading a couple of nights before and had lingered over it. There was something weird in the idea that he could be banished by another boy (what from? and why?). It implied all kinds of things that went beyond the usual bounds of friendship, but with Ripley he'd felt right away uncommon possibilities. He didn't have a name for those possibilities, or even a vision of where they might lead, just an inchoate longing for the depth of feeling and approval Ripley had promised and then withdrawn. He didn't know whether it was smart even to say the words now, but he did, wondering if Ripley would laugh or just be pissed off.

Ripley looked back at him through his glasses, and said, "Banish plump Jack, I think, but we'll let it go." And he picked up the conversation as if it had been broken for a moment instead of a month. Over the course of that next winter, woven in among discussions of Thomas Hardy and the Volstead Act, conic sections and the place of man in the universe, all given an odd tinge by Ripley's offbeat opinions, Jack pieced together a little of Ripley's life history. He was from Los Angeles. This was ordinarily the first thing that Jack found out about people — where they'd grown up, what their parents did, what schools they'd gone to before Westfield — but Ripley had no interest in small talk, so Jack had to fish the information out slowly, sitting by the stream of Ripley's talk. His father was an executive at one of the television studios. "He works all the time, really hard, just so we can have a nice house and a swimming pool and a hot tub. It makes me wonder what's inside him, what he really lives for. He does everything for me, but what I want to know is, what does he get out of it for himself? You have to believe in something, don't you?" As a child, Ripley had played the violin and been good at it, he said. Then, about two years before, he'd developed a kind of tendinitis in his elbow and had to give it up. His parents were Jewish, and he'd been raised going to temple, had had a bar mitzvah. Now he said he wasn't sure what he was. "I don't like the weight of all this Jewish history, thirty centuries of old men with long beards and funny eating habits standing on my shoulders. All this guilt, do this, don't do that — guilt is the one unifying principle of Judaism."

Jack, who knew more about guilt than Ripley, said, "That's the most unoriginal thing I've ever heard you say."

"You're right. Pure Philip Roth. I take it back. But you can't prove to me that God exists." And they were back on familiar ground again. Jack, who knew that God existed, constructed elaborate proofs, which Ripley just as elaborately knocked down. It seemed very important to them.

Through all of this, Jack maintained his other life, his normal life he called it, with Jeff and Stephen and all his other friends. He went to swim practice — he was still only a sophomore, so he didn't compete much, but the coach was encouraging and he did get to swim a leg of a relay now and then, when the meet was already won or lost. He went to dances at their sister school across the border in New York, something Ripley refused to do even though it was almost an informal requirement. At Christmas, he went sailing in the Virgin Islands with Jeff and Jeff's father and brother. Elizabeth wanted him to spend Christmas with her and David and the boys at the house in Westfield, but Jack didn't want to, and for once Dr. Sanders came through, backing him up. Like everyone else, he spent January and February in the kind of oxygenless stupor that inflicts closed communities of boys in the winter months. Even Ripley seemed to lose some of his verve.

In the spring they all recovered, and Ripley carried him off for long walks in the woods. They discovered the nature preserve and explored its trails, coming finally to the little hollow by the side of the river, which became their accustomed destination. One afternoon, as Jack lay on his back looking up at the treetops in their first leaf, Ripley said, "What about sex?"

Jack, whose reverie had been deep, took a moment to respond. Then he said, cautiously, "What? Here, now?"

Ripley giggled. "You're depraved. That's not what I meant at all. What do you think about it?"

Jack tried to recover some of his lost dignity. "I'm all for it."

"So I've heard."

He sat up. "What does that mean?"

"Oh, just that you developed a little reputation last year for certain — goings-on, shall we say."

Jack lay back down. "Oh, that. That was nothing." He had been asked by an older boy one afternoon. They'd gone down to the basement of one of the buildings, through a corridor hung with steam pipes, to a little room reserved by long association for carnal experiments. It had been groping, by unspoken consent there had been no feeling in it, just release with perhaps an undefined sense of rehearsal about it. He'd done it again with others, just a few times. Jack couldn't imagine how Ripley had heard about it. But then Ripley had a tendency to find out what he wanted to know.

"Well, I'm glad you're not ashamed of it."

"Why should I be?" He turned his head.

"No reason." Ripley stood up and began kicking pebbles into the river. "I'm sure it was all innocent and totally passionless."

It had been, but Jack didn't see any reason to say so. He thought idly of the dampish smell of the small room, the feel of another boy's hands on him. "Why are you so interested?" he asked.

Ripley put his hands in his jacket pockets. His shirttail hung down below his blazer. "Why did you do it?"

"Because they asked me."

Ripley snorted. He seemed about to say something but didn't. He squatted by the side of the stream and poked at the bottom with a stick. "Do you always do what people ask?"

Jack thought about this for a while. It seemed to him that the world was opening up after a long confinement; there was warmth underneath the chill of the April air and a mist of early green in the woods, and he could see himself opening up again, could imagine a life in which he did what everyone wanted and no one got hurt. "If you do what people ask, you make them happy. You don't hurt them."

"And if Jeff asked," Ripley's tone gave something a little nasty to the last word, "if your best friend asked you. Would you do it? What if someone who wasn't passionless or innocent, someone who desired you or even loved you, asked. What would you do then?"

Jack was annoyed, his mood broken by the twist Ripley was putting on it. "I don't know, Ripley. You're making this out to be more of a thing than it was."

"Don't dodge the question." Ripley walked over until he was standing next to Jack, looking down at him. "What would you do then?"

"You're talking about something —" Jack gestured with his hand, taking in the whole forest around them, "— totally different. You're talking about love." Although, in the end, that wouldn't really make any difference. If you wanted to make people happy, motivation didn't matter. Ripley, who had noticed his hesitation, was waiting, like an entomologist with a mounting pin. "Look," Jack said desperately, "if anybody cared about me, the way you said, then yes, if they asked me."

Ripley lifted his head and pushed his glasses up on his nose, then walked away. He stood looking down at his reflection in the water. "And if I asked you? On those terms?"

Jack sighed. He felt lost, and a little sick, as if he weren't really there. "I wish you wouldn't."

"But if I did."

Jack was silent, his answer having been given. Finally Ripley turned to him. "Don't worry, Jack. I wouldn't do that to you. I just wanted you to think a little."

"Thanks a lot."

That summer, Jack got long letters from Ripley, who was working at a Taco Bell in L.A. The letters were full of minute descriptions of his days, from what he saw on waking up to what he thought on going to bed. Jack had the feeling that Ripley was trying to involve him in his life, as if he were afraid somehow of losing contact. Jack received these letters at various hotels in Europe, where he was touring with David and Elizabeth, Billy and Hank, and a nanny. They went to London, where Elizabeth didn't like all the tourists, and to Paris, where she didn't like the French, and to the Villa d'Este, where she didn't like the rooms they were given, and to St. Moritz. His own letters were mostly travelogues of the today-I-went-to-Greenwich-and-saw-the-prime-meridian genre. He didn't write about the quiet hour he spent alone reading Keats in the flowery cloister at Westminster Abbey, or about being in the British Museum and seeing a manuscript in the poet's handwriting, or of standing alone on the terrace of the Palais de Chaillot at midnight looking across the river at the Eiffel Tower, or of his boredom amid the beauties of Lake Como. He had his sixteenth birthday in London, and his feeling of being unmoored was only strengthened in the foreign surroundings. In a rare burst of poetic scribbling, he wrote of foreign streets "whose names I know, whose faces I know not."

He didn't tell any of this to Ripley, who would have jumped at the information as an occasion for a discourse on something. The only incident he described in more than a flat overview was the discovery, immediately after their arrival at St. Moritz, that the nanny was stealing from them. This gave rise to much discussion between David and Elizabeth on the proper way to dismiss a servant three thousand miles from home. As she lived with them in New York, they couldn't very well send her back without allowing her access to the apartment, which they didn't want to do. If they didn't fire her immediately, Elizabeth said (in what Jack thought was major hysteria), she was likely to do something terrible, but undefined, to the boys. Jack's only interest in these

proceedings was his determination not to get stuck with the responsibility for watching Billy and Hank. He had more important
things with which to occupy his time. An American girl his age
was staying in the hotel.

She sat down next to him one morning while he was waiting
for David to come downstairs. "What a drag," she said to him.

"Really."

She had short brown hair and wore enormous earrings in her
small ears, was smoking a cigarette and wearing faded blue jeans.
She was everything he didn't like in a girl, and he was immediately
taken with her. "You here with your parents?" she asked.

"No, my sister and her husband. And their two little boys."

"Sounds like a barrel of laughs. Where you from?"

He had been seriously slouching on the chair, and now he sat
up marginally. "New York. But I go to Westfield."

"Hot shit." She blew out a big cloud of smoke. There was a
lipstick ring around her cigarette. "I go to Middlesex."

"Hot shit."

They sat silently for a while. Jack felt that something more was
required of him, so he finally said, "You here with your parents?"

"Yeah. We come here every year so my father can see a foot
doctor."

That sounded interesting. He sat up a little further. "Yeah?"

"Yeah. The guy's a specialist. He's famous. We always stay in
this hotel. All we do all day is climb mountains and go shopping.
I hate it."

Again there was a pause as she put out her cigarette, and Jack
bit his nail. He said, "So what's your name?"

"Missy Reardon. What's yours?"

"Uh, John Newland." He'd been about to say Jack, but that
was Ripley's name for him.

"So, you want to get high?"

He shook his head. "Can't. I have to go do stuff with my
brother-in-law and my nephew."

"Too bad. How about tonight, after dinner."

He calculated the present state of the great nanny debate and
decided it was, for the moment at least, unimpeding. " 'K."

"I'll meet you here at nine." She stood up and walked away as David came down the stairs with Billy. Jack scowled.

That night they walked around the town and found a secluded spot under some trees. Missy had a joint, which they smoked, comparing notes on prep school life. She was, as he'd suspected, an artsy-fartsy type, and said "shit" and "fuck" a lot more than most of the girls he knew. But she was easy to be with, and they went out most evenings, walking around the town, getting high sometimes (her stash was getting low). One night she kissed him, under the trees and out of sight of the world, and after his first surprise, he found himself kissing her back, thinking how strange it was to have her tongue in his mouth, not at all what he had expected. The next morning his lips felt all swollen. David and Elizabeth began to take notice, with Elizabeth teasing him a little until David came to his rescue.

On another night, the evening before she was to go back to New York, they were lying on the ground on a hillside behind the town and she leaned down to kiss him, and it all felt different. She pressed her body closer to his, put her hand on his chest, and then unbuttoned his shirt and touched his skin, which seemed very warm. Tentatively, he put his hand on her breast and then pulled away, not having expected it to feel so soft. Then, more confidently, he opened her blouse. He was getting a hardon and wondered if she knew it, and then she slipped her hand down over his stomach to his crotch and stroked him through his pants. They were both breathing hard and moving their legs together, and after a while he came. "Oh wow," he said with a stuttering kind of sigh.

"Feel good?" He felt her breath on his cheek.

"Mmm."

"Want to do more?"

He lay looking up at the stars, while her fingers played a little with the bulge in his pants, and he could feel the warm stickiness inside his undershorts. He looked up at the stars, feeling a little scared. "I dunno."

In the end they just kissed a lot more, and he put his hand down between her legs, trying and not really succeeding to make sense of what he was feeling through her underwear, and then she made him come again.

They walked back to the hotel. As they came down into the lights, she said, "Uh oh," and looked pointedly at him.

He still had on the gray light-wool slacks he had worn with a blazer at dinner, and now there was a big damp stain on the front of them. "Oh Jesus," he said, lowering his hands. He looked around quickly but didn't, for the moment, see anyone.

Missy looked at him critically. "You can't walk inside with your hands like that, it's too obvious."

He stepped back into a shadow. "Oh shit."

"My father'll kill me if he finds out," she said, a slight tone of satisfaction in her voice.

"Look," he said chivalrously, "you go ahead. No point in your getting into trouble."

She laughed. "It won't take them long to figure it out. Come on, I'll walk right in front of you." So, in procession, they walked up toward the hotel. "How're you going to dispose of the evidence?" she asked.

"I don't know. I'll see what it looks like in the morning."

They were just passing the fountain in front of the hotel when a large crowd of people came out from the restaurant and stood on the steps, waiting for their cars. "Christ," Jack said, nearly stepping on Missy's heels.

But she veered off and led the way to the fountain, where they sat on the edge and waited for the traffic to clear. "I hope this doesn't, like, spoil everything for you," he said.

"No." She looked down at her hands. "You're nice, John. I like you." She leaned over and kissed his cheek, and he blushed because it was the first time a girl had ever kissed him in public. "Maybe we could, you know, get together sometime. Back in New York."

"Sure."

She stood up. "All clear." She tipped her head to one side. "I do have another idea. About how to get inside. It's pretty radical, but —"

"What is it?"

"Let me try." She leaned down and put her hand on his chest

and then, without his realizing what was happening, she pushed him hard, and he went tumbling backward into the pool that surrounded the fountain. He came up sputtering, coughing from a snootful of water. He stood up, shaking himself. "What the hell'd you do that for?"

"Look," she said, not quite pointing.

His pants, which were thoroughly soaked, now told no tale. They both started to laugh.

When he got back to Westfield, he told the story, omitting the last part, to Jeff, who was his mentor in such things. "Congratulations, Newland," was his comment. "But next time work a little harder at getting all those clothes off. Comin' in your pants is OK as far as it goes." Jeff claimed to have visited a whorehouse with his older brother during the summer. "A hundred bucks," he said, grinning, "and she didn't hold back nothin'."

Ripley came back from California full of his usual imprecations on every aspect of life at Westfield. He wanted the most minute account of Jack's impressions of Europe, where he had never been. "My father says it's a waste of money. I'd kill to go, though. I've studied literature and history all my life, I feel like I know London better than I do New York, but I've never been there."

"There is something familiar about it. London — England — especially. And Paris. Nôtre-Dame is beautiful, but it wasn't, I guess, surprising. As if I'd seen it before."

"Victor Hugo."

"Maybe," Jack said dubiously. "Or television."

"I don't watch television. At least not that junk my father produces. And since he watches it all the time —" Ripley had some grievance against his father, something he talked around without coming to the point. Jack didn't press him, not wanting to know if it was trouble. Ripley also had a secret, something that he hinted at but wasn't willing to talk about until, one afternoon, they went for a walk in the woods, to their spot by the river. He said, "I read something incredible this summer."

"Yeah? What?" Jack was sucking on a broken sassafras twig, lying on the ground in his customary position.

"The *Symposium*. It's a dialogue. By Plato. The philosopher."

"I've heard of him."

"Sorry." Ripley pulled a book out of his pocket. "Here it is. Actually, this is a collection of the dialogues, the *Symposium* is only about forty pages." He sounded as if length would deter Jack. "Do you want to read it?"

Jack was feeling very content, happy to lie back and let the day wash over him. He was glad to see Ripley again, he'd felt all summer a kind of pang of absence. Now he looked up and said, "Why don't you read it? Aloud, I mean."

Ripley blinked and pushed his glasses up on his nose. "Do you mean that?"

"Sure. Why not?"

"Oh, Jack —" He stopped. "I'd love to." He sat down on the ground and took a deep breath. "The beginning isn't important, it just sets the scene. It's a party — that's what *symposium* means in Greek, a drinking party. Socrates is there, and Aristophanes, and Agathon the tragic poet, and some others. They play a sort of game — each guest has to make a speech praising Love. The first speeches just lay the groundwork for Socrates. I'll skip parts of it now and then, if you don't mind." And he began to read.

That afternoon, hearing the words for the first time, it was enough for Jack simply to listen. He had the sense of being in the presence of something great, and Ripley, whom he trusted as his guide, was obviously very moved. They read it again and again later on and discussed it endlessly, but from that first hearing he did remember a few things: the tone of Ripley's voice as it rose and fell with the dialogue; the surprising beauty of the language, almost poetic in translation (he had expected it to be stuffy); and certain passages that he felt he recognized although he hadn't heard them before. "And if there were some way of contriving that a state or an army should be made up only of lovers and their beloved, they would have found the best way to live, refraining from dishonor and emulating one another in beautiful things." He imagined himself standing shoulder to shoulder in battle with his best friend, bloodied but triumphant, the light of victory in their eyes. "Such is the power of love, great and mighty and omnipotent." Jack needed no philosophy to teach him that, he had seen the destructive power of love, great and mighty, omnipotent. "Love is the everlasting possession of the good." That would be nice to believe, to believe in good at all after what had happened. He believed only in evil, to which was opposed not good but retribution, and the chance at temporary shelter in the shadow of someone's brief approval. Ripley came to the great conclusion of Socrates' speech: "And the true order of going or being led by another to Love is this: beginning from beautiful things, to mount ever upward for the sake of that beauty, as by a heavenly ladder, going from one to two to all beautiful bodies, and from beautiful bodies to beautiful actions, and from actions to ideas, until from beautiful ideas he comes at last to the idea of absolute beauty, and at last understands the essence of beauty."

Ripley stopped reading. In the quiet, the river rushed over the rocks and a breeze felled some early-loosened leaves. Jack felt full of himself, as if he'd had a glimpse of a possibility denied him, and he had a moment's resentment at Ripley for forcing him to confront this. But he knew what Ripley would say: that he wanted him to think.

In fact, Ripley said, "There's more. Alcibiades, the beautiful young aristocrat, comes in and tells the story of how he tried to seduce Socrates one night and even climbed into the bed with him, but got up as untouched as if he'd slept with his father or brother. It's to prove the integrity of Socrates, I think, that he practices what he preaches."

"Platonic love," Jack said.

"This is where it comes from. Did you like it?"

"Yes." Jack sat up a little, leaning on his elbows. "Do you think it's true?"

"What? That people can live their lives for the pursuit of beauty and truth, can strive to love only the good and right actions?" Ripley seemed exhilarated — he had obviously thought all this out ahead of time. At the best of times he couldn't sit still, but now he was practically dancing around with excitement. "Jack, that's why I wanted you to read it. I want to live like that, I think we can do it. I think we should make the experiment, you and me together."

"Ripley —" But it was no use. Ripley carried him away with the force of his enthusiasm, as he always did. They spent the winter pursuing the good, making fine judgments about the beauty of their world — the school, the books they read, the actions of their classmates — it was all very rarefied and exalting. It was the kind of conversation that went on all the time at Westfield, debates couched in Manichaean terms of black and white: whether Shakespeare was really a great writer or just a hack who got lucky (as one of their teachers, annoyingly, liked to claim); whether Charlie Daniels or Jerry Jeff Walker was the better musician (Jeff once said that if God could play the guitar and sing he would be Jerry Jeff Walker); whether growing cynical was an inevitable part of becoming an adult, or whether you could still be an idealist at the age of thirty (none of them was old enough to remember John Kennedy, but they all referred to him vaguely, an inheritance from their parents). For Jack, the *Symposium* was just another term in the balancing of the equation — whether one could live for beauty and the good, as Socrates taught, or whether life was ultimately corrupt, as the world demonstrated — but for Ripley it had a life of its own. Sometimes Jack felt tempted to tease him about it, to tell him to lighten up, but Ripley said, "I have to know, I have to be right about this. How else could I live, if I didn't know for sure?"

Jack made the swim team that year. He won some medals in freestyle, and Jeff was winning even more in backstroke. For a while the two of them took up boxing, putting on gloves and helmets and climbing into a makeshift ring in the gym to swing away at each other under the watchful eye of a coach, comparing bruises later on. He loved being with Jeff, who was direct, uncomplicated — all the things that Ripley wasn't. He sometimes wondered what Jeff would think of the conversations he had with Ripley — the unreality of them. But then, when he was with Ripley, the only thing that seemed real was his talk of beauty or the good, it was Jeff with his stolid, unthinking approach who seemed unreal. Still, he thought, there was nothing better than coming out of the locker room with Jeff into the cold darkness, racing each other up to their room before ice could form in their hair, and in the wild rush forgetting Ripley and his questions.

One afternoon, just after their spring break, he was sitting in Ripley's room in the early gloom of a rainy day. Ripley reached into a dresser drawer and brought out a thin pint bottle of vodka. "Want to try some?"

"Sure."

"I did a lot of drinking this vacation. I wanted to see what it felt like." He unscrewed the top and handed the bottle to Jack.

Jack tipped his head back and tasted cautiously. The vodka was warm and then burning in his mouth and stomach. He'd never had a real drink before — David didn't approve of anything stronger than an infrequent glass of wine with dinner for him — and after a minute he felt it burst into his head. After a few more minutes the surface of his skin started to tingle with numbness.

Ripley said, "I believe in trying new things, at least to see what they're like. I think I'd try anything once."

Jack, feeling cocooned, rested his head back against the bed. The rough gray blanket was tucked in with hospital corners—it was the kind of blanket that Jack had taken to camp with him and that now resided, he supposed, in a trunk in the attic of the house here in Westfield. He felt the coarseness of its wool against his neck. "I got high a few times this summer. With this girl in St. Moritz." Somehow, he'd never told Ripley about Missy — he'd met her in New York a couple of times during school vacations, they'd gone to a show, and he really liked her. He was trying to figure out a way to visit her at Middlesex.

"Everybody gets high," Ripley said.

"Everybody drinks." Jack took another swallow from the bottle. The vodka smelled like the alcohol his mother had rubbed on him when he'd had fevers — he could still feel her hands on his back, the damp and then the dryness as the alcohol coolly evaporated, the fumes seeming part of his fevered dreams. He sat and watched the rain run down the windows, glad he was inside, glad he was here.

"What about girls," Ripley said. It was his favorite conversational gambit, to say "what about" something and then proceed to cross-examine Jack on the subject, all with the purpose of stating his own ideas.

"What about 'em?"

"Did you ever sleep with a girl?"

"No," Jack said dubiously. "Not exactly." Then he told Ripley the story of St. Moritz, including the part about the fountain.

Ripley thought it was hilarious. "I can picture it now. You standing there soaking wet, water running out of your hair, no idea of what had happened. How'd it go over?"

"Well," he said indistinctly and then repeated it more clearly, "well, we both caught some heat — David was especially bummed that we made a spectacle of ourselves trying to swim in the fountain, which is what we told them we were doing. But it went off OK."

Ripley took some more vodka. "Tell me one thing, though. How come you didn't have sex with her?"

"We did have sex. I did, anyway." He slid down until he was lying on the floor.

"You know what I mean. You didn't have intercourse."

Jack tried to feel his feet. He guessed he was getting drunk. "I dunno. I didn't feel like it. I guess I was a little afraid, or nervous or something."

"Didn't she ask you?"

"What's that supposed to mean?" he said angrily, knowing that they were both thinking of their conversation in the woods the year before. "Look, I'm only sixteen, remember. I don't feel all this pressure to get laid or anything. I had a nice time," he added with some dignity. "I think she did too."

"Just asking," Ripley said. A gust of wind shook the window, making the rain sound hard and nasty.

That summer, Jack worked as a lifeguard and instructor at the swim club at the lake. He had a curious reluctance to leave Westfield. Dr. Sanders questioned him endlessly about this, and Jack finally said that it had to do with being a senior the next year and going to college the year after that. Sanders thought that was great material, and they talked about his future and what college he might choose and why. The truth was, he was comfortable at Westfield, he fit in, people liked him, his place was clear. At Yale, his first choice, he knew he would be adrift — alone, unknown, undefined. He talked a little about this with Ripley, who seemed unable to understand his predicament.

In November there was a late warm spell, and they went for

a walk at the nature conservancy. The trails were deep with leaves, obscuring the path in some places. Occasionally they came to fallen trees, sawn flat on top, bridging what would in other seasons be muddy places, covered with chicken wire for easier footing. At the bridge, Ripley stopped and looked down into the river. A branch, an inch or two in diameter, had gotten stuck against a rock, making a little backwater with brown foam in it. Ripley leaned over to move it, and Jack, without thinking, said, "Don't."

Ripley looked at him. "How come?"

"The consequences —" he started to say.

"There won't be any consequences," Ripley said shortly.

There are always consequences. "It belongs there. It was put there by nature."

Ripley adopted his philosophical tone. "But it's man's nature to move it." And he shoved the branch free with his foot.

They came to the avenue of birches, denuded now, and pushed through the bushes to their spot by the river. Ripley was being unusually quiet, and Jack kept looking at him, wondering what was coming. The silence had something preparatory, almost ominous about it. Jack sat on the damp ground and poked around in the leaves aimlessly.

"What about your parents," Ripley finally said.

Jack sighed. "They're dead."

"I know. Do you want to tell me about it?"

Jack concentrated on digging a small rock out of the ground. "Do you want to hear about it?"

"Yes."

He picked the rock out of the earth and threw it into the stream. "My parents were killed in a car accident, two summers ago, right after my fifteenth birthday." He pushed with his finger at another rock, getting some gritty dirt beneath his nail. "They were at a dinner party at the Westfield Country Club. They were driving home on the Upper Mountain Road and, you know the place where the road has those two sharp bends — the car went out of control and smashed through the guard rail — it was just made out of wood then — and down the side of the mountain." He tossed the second stone into the stream, then drew his knees up to his chest and hugged them. "My mother was killed right away, but Daddy was still alive when they found the car, and they took him to the hospital. He had" — he stopped talking for a moment and then went on — "you know, internal injuries and broken bones, and he was bleeding badly. They didn't have enough blood of his type in the hospital. They didn't know about me, that I was the same blood type, and even if they'd called the house, I was out. He died." He put his head down on his knees and shut his eyes.

Ripley stood over him helplessly. Jack thought, Please let him touch me, just hold me a little, something. But Ripley had never touched him, and didn't now. "I'm sorry, Jack. I guess that's a useless thing to say." He sat down a little way away. "That's why you feel so guilty, isn't it."

He nodded, and sniffled. "Yes. I guess so." It was the story he'd made up for Dr. Sanders, it would do for Ripley.

"Don't," Ripley said in his most definitive voice. "You can't blame yourself like this. It's not your fault."

Blah blah blah, Jack thought. It was what everybody said. But he couldn't blame them, it was what he wanted them to say. Now it was his turn to say what everyone wanted him to say. "I know, Ripley. He would have died anyway. Most likely."

At Christmas, he had another fight with Elizabeth. He wanted to spend the vacation in New York, while she as always wanted him with her in Westfield. They had long discussions, all of which revolved, for him, around the question of whether he could be trusted alone in her apartment. He was seventeen and a half, he kept saying, if she didn't trust him now, when would she? Finally he agreed to be in Westfield for Christmas weekend and then to spend the rest of the vacation in New York with his aunt Clara. He didn't care where he stayed, he just wanted to be able to spend his time with Missy.

They hung out together most of the time. Sometimes they walked up and down Fifth Avenue, watching the hordes of shoppers returning gifts, talking about how materialistic Christmas was. They went to the Guggenheim and progressed slowly down its ramp as Missy talked on and on about the paintings and he thought how much she knew about art. They went to Staten Island on the ferry, standing in the bow for as long as they could while the cold harbor air blew around them. She invited him to have dinner with her one evening, when her parents were going to be out. She giggled a lot as she cooked, saying she'd never had a dinner party before, and afterward she took him into her bedroom, and they made love. At first, when he realized what was going to happen, he wondered if it would work, if he would work properly, but then he lost himself in her and in his own feelings, and thought, I'm in love.

Back at school, Jeff's comment was, " 'bout time, Newland." Ripley didn't ask, so Jack didn't tell him, at least not until Jack started disappearing on weekends. He would find excuses, as often as he could, to get permission to go home to New York, or to the house in Westfield, would borrow David's station wagon and drive to Middlesex to pick up Missy. They'd drive around, find a lonely spot, and make love in the car. Jack always worried that they'd make a mess or leave stains and that David would find out what was going on, but he never did. To Jack, it suddenly seemed that sex was everywhere, not just with Missy, but in the way girls at dances looked at him. He had the feeling that they knew he wasn't a virgin anymore, just as they'd known when he was. It changed all the relationships, it made sex possible with everyone.

In April, Jack persuaded Ripley to go to a dance. It wasn't much of a success. Jack danced a lot with different girls, while Ripley, who was pretty drunk, sat on the sidelines and made sarcastic remarks. Jack finally got a girl he knew to ask Ripley to dance, and Ripley, cornered, went with her. Jack watched them awhile — Ripley was jerking his arms in a generally uncoordinated way, but Jack told himself that most kids didn't know how to dance, that it didn't matter. The next day, Ripley was uncharacteristically quiet, while Jack tried to cheer him up. They were sitting at a table in the corner of the library, hidden behind rows of bookshelves. Jack was reading an economics text, highlighting passages with different color markers, although he could never remember later what the various colors were supposed to signify. He gave up after a while and tilted the chair back, trying to balance it on two legs. Ripley, next to him, was supposed to be reading history, but he'd brought his copy of the *Symposium* instead. "You know," Ripley said eventually, "what my favorite part of this is?"

"No, what?" Jack overbalanced and had to kick his legs up under the table to avoid falling backward.

"This: 'He must believe that beauty of the mind is more precious than beauty of the body.'"

Jack had succeeded in balancing his chair. Now he cautiously raised his hands over his head the way kids did on a roller coaster. "Look. No net." When Ripley didn't laugh, Jack brought his hands down onto the table. "OK. I'll bite. Why is that your favorite part?"

"Because I'm ugly. It's hard enough to study beauty, to want to live by it, when you're not beautiful in yourself. It would be unbearable if it weren't for this."

Jack frowned. "You're not ugly. What makes you think you're ugly?" He considered the round face behind the glasses, the slightly rounded shoulders, the brown hair. "I don't think you're ugly."

"Don't let's kid ourselves. Why do you think I had a lousy time at the dance, why I don't go to dances in the first place, why no one asked me to dance, except once, the whole evening?"

"You didn't try very hard," Jack said cautiously.

"Which is the point, isn't it. How hard did you try? You didn't have to try at all, did you?"

Jack, who had gone to the dance for a good time, hadn't thought one way or the other about trying. "What do you mean?"

"Oh, Jack. Don't you realize." He took a deep breath. "You're the most beautiful person I've ever known."

They had been talking quietly, in deference to the library, but now Jack looked around to see if anyone might have heard. Ripley caught him at it. "Don't be so conventional." He shook his head. "You are beautiful, and you nobly take it for granted. Well, I don't take it for granted. I know you better, probably, even than you know yourself. I can close my eyes and still see you." He shut his eyes. "Soft tangled hair, the color of cognac held up to a candle, brown and red and deep inside a flame of gold. Small ears, tight against your head. Eyes — I was in a jewelry store with my mother this summer and there was an emerald necklace in a case — a huge stone set in diamonds — and I thought of your eyes, not just green but emerald green and surrounded by diamonds. And your swimmer's body, long with long muscles, and almost no hair, and your skin as if it were polished. You have a scar on your left hand, just below the thumb." He was speaking very gently, as if not conscious of speaking at all.

Jack interrupted him. "Ripley, please stop." He had always known in an informal sort of way that he was good-looking, his family had all told him so, but he assumed everyone's family told them that. This was different. He'd never seen Ripley so close, and it made him want to look away.

"Are you afraid of being beautiful, Jack?"

He took refuge in flippancy. "Knock it off. I thought we were supposed to be looking for the beauty of the soul, anyway. Isn't that what Socrates said? Physical things don't matter."

"Socrates was notoriously ugly."

"Not half as ugly as you say you are. I'm surprised the mirror doesn't crack if you're as ugly as all that."

Ripley left it there, but he'd scared Jack badly, and it put a constraint between them for a while. He was left with more questions than he wanted to face. If Ripley thought Jack was good-looking, it didn't have to be anything more than the kind of objective judgment he would make about a Keats ode or the quartet from *Rigoletto*. But the comment had been different — perhaps in the dreamy way he had spoken or in the glimpse Jack had had for a moment, as if Ripley were showing his soul. He brooded about it and then let it go. He didn't have time for much of anything then other than the fact of their approaching graduation. He felt as if he were rushing down a hill, always accelerating, as the familiar things in life became blurred fixtures slipping past.

A couple of weeks before graduation, he and Jeff and Stephen, and Ripley, were down at the lake at eleven o'clock one night, which was one infraction of the rules, and they had a few bottles of assorted kinds of booze, which was another. The school had a small beach on the lake, behind the ninth hole of the golf course, which was used a lot by faculty families, and a small playground area had been built nearby. In four years at Westfield Jack had never been there — he'd done all his swimming in the pool.

Jeff was hanging upside down from his knees on the monkey bars. Jack was lying on the ground underneath him. They were passing a bottle of vodka back and forth. Stephen was perched on a bench nearby in a stupor. Ripley, who usually kept his distance from Jack's swim-team friends, was somewhere around.

"Hey, Newland," Jeff said.

"Yeah."

"You think they do stuff like this at Princeton?"

Jack looked up. From his own slightly distorted perspective Jeff seemed to be suspended from the starry sky. "I dunno."

"I love Westfield. These are the best years of my life." It was a rare burst of sentiment, coming from him. "Hey. Try this. Open your mouth."

Jack obediently opened his mouth. Jeff reached down and poured vodka into him, gradually lifting the bottle. Jack choked a little and moved his head, and the vodka splashed over his face and into his hair. They were both laughing.

Jeff swung down to the ground. "You smell like a distillery."

"Great." He reached out a hand and Jeff pulled him up.

"Let's go swimming."

"Now?" Jack looked down at the lake. "It'll be cold."

"Pussy. Come on."

They walked over to the beach and took off their clothes, and stood shivering in the shallows for a moment as their feet adjusted to the cold. Jack turned around, hugging himself. Ripley was watching them, the light glinting off the frames of his glasses. He won't come in, Jack thought — it'd just embarrass him to ask him. He looked a little lonely, staring at them, and Jack wanted to include him somehow. He said, "Watch our clothes for me?" and gave a sort of a shy smile, which Ripley didn't acknowledge.

Jeff drew in a deep breath and then ran into the water, diving under and coming up spluttering. "Christ, it's cold."

Jack went in more slowly, waiting for the moment when the water reached his groin before diving under. He came up next to Jeff. Back on shore, Stephen had revived and was hopping around on one foot, pulling his underwear off. A minute later he joined them. "Fuckin' cold," he said, his teeth chattering.

Jack looked across the lake. "That's the swim club where I worked last summer."

"Let's swim over there," Jeff said. "I'll race you."

They headed out. Jack got into a slow rhythm, the stroke he used for long-distance practices. He was enjoying the feel of the water — it was amazing what a difference there was between skinny-dipping and wearing even a swimmer's brief bathing suit. About three-quarters of the way across, he stopped, treading water. He could hear Jeff splashing along a few yards behind him, but there was no sign of Stephen. He reached out a hand and stopped Jeff.

"What?"

"I can't see Stephen." They listened for a moment, and then heard some splashing and what sounded like choking. "Shit. He's drowning."

They headed back, trying to locate the sound in the darkness. The water was suddenly much colder and blacker, and Jack was getting tired. He thought, All three of us, what a stupid thing to do. Then Jeff called to him. "He's over here." Jack swam over and found them, Stephen still gamely trying but tired out. Jeff and Jack supported him under his armpits and dragged him along toward the swim club. "Kick, you bastard," Jeff said.

When they got to shore, Stephen staggered out of the water and immediately threw up. "That's disgusting," Jeff said. They all sat down on the grass to catch their breath.

"What d'we do now?" Jeff said.

"I don't know. Go back, I guess."

Jeff nodded in Stephen's direction. "He can't swim back. And we can't carry him."

"He'll have to walk."

They contemplated this for a minute. The object of their discussion, lying on his back, white in the darkness, began to move. "I can't walk back. I don't have any clothes."

"Tough shit," Jeff said.

"Listen, Stephen. If you walk along the edge of the lake here, you'll get to the bridge. Then cross the bridge and walk up the hill a hundred yards or so. There's a path on your right that'll get you back." Jack was pretty sure that was right.

"But what if a car comes?"

"Just hide in the woods," Jeff said. "The only time you have to worry is when you're on the bridge. Come on, John, let's go."

When they were most of the way back, they stopped and looked around. "There he is," Jack said.

Stephen was climbing the embankment by the bridge. He got up on the roadway and started across. And then, with a sweep of headlights, a car came by. Stephen leaned over and covered himself, and all they could see for a moment was his bare ass shining. He got halfway across before the second car came, from the other direction this time, and the same thing happened. Jeff was laughing so hard he swallowed some water and Jack had to hit him on the back. The third car, which came by just as Stephen reached the end of the bridge, was a police car.

They wound up the next morning in the headmaster's office. Stephen had tried to cover for them, but Jeff wouldn't let him, so they all stood together to take the punishment. Ripley, who had gotten tired of waiting for them, had left before the fun began and so escaped. Jack was sure they were going to be expelled.

"We're not going to get expelled," Jeff kept telling him. "We're graduating in two weeks. All we have to do is tell the truth and take it like men. He likes us, Newland."

"I don't know."

"Shit, John, you think you're going to be expelled every time you have an overdue library book. Don't worry."

In the end, after a hellfire lecture, they were let off. They graduated on a sparkling June day. Jeff would be going to Princeton, Stephen to Trinity, Ripley to Berkeley. When he didn't get into Yale with Jack, he picked Berkeley because, he said, it was the last place his father wanted him to go.

Jack went to visit him in California later in the summer. Ripley was all of a sudden fascinated by drugs, and they spent a lot of time driving around Los Angeles dropping in on people he knew who supplied pills and powders for which Jack paid in large bills. They had an ever-replenished cache of coke, which they drew out into lines of elaborate patterns: their names in script, a spiral that seemed as if it were three feet long when Jack tried to do it up in one breath, once Ripley drew a heart with their initials inside. They went to a Dodgers game that lasted about eight days because Ripley had given him some major downers. They got some things that looked like downers but weren't, as Jack discovered when he realized he was driving at about ninety miles an hour along the Pacific Coast Highway up past Santa Barbara. Another time, Ripley heard about a guy who supposedly had something great to sell, so they went driving around a neighborhood of low stucco houses with Moorish arches and blank front windows and tropical-type plants in the yards, looking for the right address. When they got there, Jack had to stay in the car — the guy was paranoid about strangers or something — so he sat low down in the seat, hoping that any narcs in the area might overlook him if they picked that moment to stage a raid. There was no action anywhere, no kids playing in the yards, no cars passing, not even any water sprinklers turned on, like one of those episodes of "The Twilight Zone" where someone wakes up and finds he's the only person left in the world. Just the still heat, he thought, and an eighteen-year-old boy hiding behind sunglasses in the front seat of someone else's car.

Ripley finally came back. "Let's go," he said. "You wouldn't believe what's in there."

Jack stayed slumped down, just able to see over the dash.

"The whole place is painted black, walls, ceilings, even the floor. Except for some wild designs you can only see when he turns on a UV light." Jack felt Ripley looking at him, but he was busy holding his breath, waiting to see if there were any other people left in the world. "Anyway, I got some acid. He makes it himself in the basement, that's why he's so paranoid."

Jack sat up finally. "Not for me."

"What?"

"Tripping. It's not on my list. I don't want to fuck with my mind."

"It's not fucking with your mind. It's opening it up." There was a pause while they got onto the freeway, which was always a scary moment when Ripley was driving. Jack shut his eyes every time, ready to die but not if he could see it coming. Safely on, Ripley said argumentatively, "How do you know if you've never tried it?"

You've never tried jumping off a building, either, he heard his mother saying to him. "Forget it, Ripley."

"Jack —"

Jack looked at him, turning his head deliberately, putting the wall of his dark glasses between them. "If you're so hot for it, do it yourself," he said, which pissed Ripley off. It occurred to Jack that Ripley never seemed to get very high, and he wondered if Ripley had even taken any of the things he was giving to Jack.

They drove down to the beach, stopping to buy a bottle of bourbon with a fake ID Ripley had, and then they sat in the car watching the water, drinking out of the bottle. Jack still had his sunglasses on; the glass was thicker than normal, dark purple, and very round and small, and he felt safe again behind them — nobody would recognize him. He took a swig from the bottle and looked at two girls go roller-skating by. Come back, he thought. Ripley wasn't watching them. Jack passed the bottle to him, but Ripley shook his head. A black guy walked by with a muscle shirt and shorts cut off so high the bottoms of the pockets showed raggedly. Jack put his tongue inside the bottle and licked it for a moment.

Ripley said, "We got invited to a party at my friend Mark's. Tomorrow night. Some of his parties are great, and some of them are just a drag."

Jack thought a minute, trying to evaluate what Ripley might think was a great party. " 't's up to you. What's he like?"

"Mark?"

"No, George Washington."

Ripley put his hands on the steering wheel, unnecessarily. "Remember I told you once I thought you were beautiful."

"You're drunk," Jack said, putting the bottle back into his mouth.

"Well, Mark is almost as good-looking as you are. I used to think, before I met you — never mind. He's gay, though."

"Yeah." Jack took a big swallow and put the bottle down. A boy on a bicycle, wearing a black bathing suit and no shirt, rode slowly past, licking green ice cream from a cone, the white drawstring hanging between his legs as he pedaled. "Does that make him any less good-looking?"

Ripley watched the boy go by. "He's a junior at Stanford and he has all these wild friends, really smart, really creative. He's very charming, so he gets them all to pay attention to him. You'd like them. But sometimes he just invites this leather crowd and everyone postures for two hours before disappearing on motorcycles."

"I don't care. If you don't want to go."

Ripley started the car and drove along slowly. "I'll tell you what. We'll go, and if it's no fun, we'll leave and see a movie or something." The kid on the bicycle crossed the street in front of them, and then Ripley gunned the engine and they took off for home.

Instead of the acid, they smoked some hash before dinner ("hashish," Ripley kept saying with a fake Middle Eastern accent) and then went out to a Chinese restaurant. Before the appetizers came, Jack excused himself and went into the men's room and threw up. He felt as if the whole stall were spinning around him, and he put his hand on a wall to steady himself. When that didn't work, he leaned against the wall, then gradually slid down until he was sitting on the floor next to the toilet. I'm going to die, he thought. The men's room door opened and he heard Ripley say, "Jack? You OK?" Jack reached up and unlatched the stall door. "What are you doing, you all right?"

For an answer, Jack turned his head to the toilet and threw up again. Ripley helped him stand up, and they went over to a sink. He splashed some cold water on his face, and then he threw up in the sink. "Jesus Christ," Ripley said.

"I'm going to die."

"No, you're not. You're probably just allergic to hash." He was running water in the sink, and he sounded almost clinical, a doctor observing a specimen for the expected reaction. "Come on, let's go home. Can you make it to the car?"

Jack nodded his head. His whole body was sweaty under his clothes and his nose felt like it was full of vomit. There was a bad moment while they waited for the valet to get the car, and then he was sitting in the car with his head down between his knees and his hands on the dash to steady himself. After a couple of blocks, Ripley pulled over and made him sit up. He opened the glove compartment and cut some coke. "Here, do this. It'll make you feel better."

"No, I don't want any more."

"Come on, Jack. It'll settle your stomach."

He leaned forward and did the first line. As he inhaled, a piece of something came unstuck from his nose and went into his throat, and he gagged a little. But Ripley was right, he did feel better. He woke up the next morning and swore he'd give it all up. Drugs were just a distraction anyway, they took his mind off other things, but he wasn't addicted or anything. So he did one line to get himself going and decided he'd quit after that.

They sat out in the back yard all day by the swimming pool. Ripley, who had decided to major in philosophy, was ostentatiously reading Plato. Every so often he would get up and walk around the pool, or stand at the fence looking down at the smoggy L.A. basin spread out behind the trees, and make a sarcastic comment. Then he would sit down again and pick up his book. Jack was reading a novel about Alexander the Great and dreaming dreams of glory; he knew Ripley's moods by then and let him be. Later, he went for a swim, and when he came out, Ripley had gone into the house. Jack stood, letting the air dry him, being careful not to drip on his book. He had caught Ripley's restlessness, and he wandered around the pool deck, past the potted plants, the hot tub, a small glass table with condensation rings on its surface. Ripley had left his book lying on the chaise, face down, open to the page he'd been reading. Jack picked it up: there were marginal notations in Ripley's neat, indecipherable handwriting, and one passage had been underlined: "Love can neither do nor suffer any wrong." Jack put it down abruptly and went into the house. In the kitchen, he stood still, letting the air conditioning chill him a little. He started to make a sandwich and was spreading the peanut butter, concentrating for some reason on applying it as neatly and smoothly as possible, no imperfections, when Ripley came in.

"Jesus Christ," he said. "What are you doing, watching your weight?"

"Huh?" Jack lifted the knife very carefully, trying not to leave one of those little swirls you usually get when you spread peanut butter.

"Making a sandwich with only one piece of bread. Women always do that, they say they don't want to eat too much. But they always have another one anyway, so what's the point? It's phony."

"Hey, chill out, take it easy —"

"You take it easy. I hate it when people do that."

Jack put the knife down. "There was only one piece of bread left, Ripley."

They looked at each other, and Ripley opened the freezer and got out another loaf. Then he leaned against the counter next to the range. Jack went back to applying the jelly, surreptitiously looking at Ripley every now and then. He was tracing the coil of one burner with his forefinger. Jack picked up the sandwich and ate it. "Is it all right if I have some beer?"

Ripley shrugged. "Cooler's next to the hot tub."

Jack suddenly thought, Ripley resents me. He didn't know where the thought had come from — the way the two of them were standing, the way Ripley wasn't looking at him, the way the kitchen felt like a set from a sixties sitcom, cramped and full of appliances that looked out of date, as if Jack were the main character and Ripley his marginal friend from next door — but he felt sure of it. He felt embarrassed, wondering if he'd done or said something wrong, or if he'd just stayed too long. "Ripley?"

Ripley pushed his glasses up on the bridge of his nose. Then he turned around and left the room.

Jack went outside and put on a tape before climbing into the hot tub. He opened the cooler and drank the first bottle really quickly, then a second. He put his head back and looked up at the air, which was especially dirty that day. He wondered if anyone could see through that haze. An alien in a spaceship, looking down from outer space, what would he see? Just a boy sitting in a hot tub, and a cooler with about a million bottles of

Mexican beer, listening to Lou Reed sing "Heroin" and "Walk on the Wild Side" while an invisible snow of toxic waste fell on him. All alone behind his sunglasses because his best friend resented him. If Ripley doesn't like me anymore — he's my best friend and now I'm alone. He wondered, if he sat in the hot tub long enough, would he melt, disappear down the drain, trickle out into the cement trench they called a river here in angel city. He was getting drunk, he realized, but it wasn't helping.

Ripley gave him the silent treatment in the car, and he was feeling even more alone when they got to the party, which turned out to be pretty dull. After Ripley's buildup, he had expected movie stars or fashion models, Hell's Angels, or at least some Valley Girls and surfer boys. He'd thought there would be wild dancing or wild costumes or lots of drugs. But these kids looked basically the way his friends in New York would at a party, there was nothing California about it. A couple of girls drifted by and asked him the conventional questions and he gave the conventional answers. A man in his thirties came over, but all he wanted to talk about, after he found out that Jack had gone to Westfield, was the preppy life. A couple of boys nearby were arguing about Congress and the economy, but they didn't seem to know anything special about either subject. Jack wasn't helped by the fact that Ripley was pointedly ignoring him. Once, when Jack went to get another beer, he had to interrupt Ripley, who was talking to a really pretty girl in a really tight tank top, and Ripley didn't even bother to introduce him. Jack put his sunglasses on so that no one would be able to see him. He was ready to leave. And then a boy in a Rolling Stones T-shirt sat down next to him. He had very straight ash-blond hair and dark eyes, disconcerting by contrast. "Hi. I'm Mark."

Jack shook his hand. "Hi. I'm John."

"Not Jack?"

"That's what Ripley calls me." But not anyone else, he wanted to add.

"How do you like Los Angeles?" Mark lit a cigarette and then reached very deliberately over Jack's knees for an ashtray.

He shrugged. "It's OK."

"I hear you're going to Yale."

Jack nodded. The conversation was boring already. "How long have you known Ripley?"

"Since he was twelve. We went to the same school." Mark brushed the end of his cigarette on the glass ashtray, and a minute amount of ash fell off. "Small talk is a drag, don't you think?"

"So, what do you want to talk about?"

He smiled and tossed his head back, clearing the hair from his forehead. The red tongue on his T-shirt lolled toward Jack. "There are only two topics of conceivable interest — you or me."

"I don't want to talk about me," Jack said. He wasn't sure if he liked Mark or not.

"Then I'll talk about myself." And he did, about Stanford, about his family, about his plans to go to law school. He seemed to take it for granted that the two of them had known each other forever, and after a few minutes, Jack found himself forgetting everyone else in the room. Mark created a kind of special space that was only big enough for the two of them. He was talking very quietly, making small, intimate comments about his friends, assuming that Jack was interested. Ripley had said he was charming, and he was. This is for you, he seemed to be saying, I've made this for you; while, not quite hidden, Jack could see the conjurer's tricks, the mirrors and smoke, that made it all possible, the fascination of the magician.

Mark, as if sensing Jack's appreciation, said, "If you want to see what I'm really like, why don't you come to my room."

"What for?" Jack said.

"Well, you can always tell a lot about a person by what their bedroom looks like." He stood up. "I'd like you to."

Jack wavered for a moment, knowing what was coming and feeling unable either to go forward or back, frozen in the moment between wanting and not wanting. He looked across the room, at Ripley's back. Then Mark stretched out one hand and said, "I want you. To come with me." And Jack took his hand and let himself be pulled to his feet.

"Sit down," Mark said, closing the door and indicating the bed. Jack sat down and Mark sat next to him. "Are you always this tense?"

No. Yes. "I don't know."

"I could get you a 'lude." Jack shook his head, and Mark said, "How about a drink?" He got up and went back to the party, saying, "Don't move, be right back."

Jack stood up. The room didn't, in fact, tell him much about Mark. It looked like any other room. He thought about going back to the party, getting Ripley and leaving. He thought about Mark. He saw a picture on the desk and went to look more closely. It was a photo Ripley had taken of Jack after a big swim meet where he'd finished second. He hadn't realized before how exposed he looked in the picture, just the brief bathing suit and the hard silver medallion at his chest.

Mark came back. "Ripley sent me that. He writes me long letters about you. Didn't you know? Come sit down." And Jack, dutifully, sat down on the bed and gulped at the drink. Mark reached up and took off Jack's sunglasses. "Ripley was right, you have the most amazing eyes. It's a sin to hide them."

Jack thought, Ripley doesn't want me. He resents me, and he's probably right.

"You with me, baby?" Mark asked very softly, taking the glass out of his hand.

Jack turned his head and looked at Mark. He saw, for the first time, cold desire in another person's face, directed at him. I want you, Mark had said. Jack nodded. He felt one of Mark's hands on the back of his neck, the other one unbuttoning his jeans and tugging his shirt out of his pants, and he closed his eyes, thinking, This isn't happening.

When they came back to the party a little while later, there was no sign of Ripley. Mark offered to drive him home. "He's just in a snit," Mark said. "He gets like this." They were driving through crowded streets, and Mark's hand was resting on Jack's thigh. "You won't let it worry you, will you?"

Everything worries me, he thought. Here he was in a car, being fondled by another boy, in whose mouth he'd had an orgasm less then an hour ago, and he didn't feel anything about any of it. Only, perhaps, a certain reassurance that Mark wanted him at all; the rest was the price he had to pay for that. I let him seduce me, he thought. "Ripley's my best friend."

"Yeah, well, I don't envy you that." He moved his hand to

change gears, then put it behind Jack's neck, caressing his hair. "Did you have fun tonight?"

"Sure." He sensed that something more was called for. "You're pretty fantastic."

Mark laughed. "Heartbreaker." They pulled up in front of Ripley's house. "He'll be furious. Do you want me to come in with you?"

That would just make everything worse. "No. Thanks. Thanks for the ride. And all."

"Goodnight. I'll call you in the morning."

Don't, Jack thought. The house was dark, but the front door was unlocked and the lights were on in the back. He went out to the pool. The underwater lights, reflecting off the house and the fence and the bottoms of the tree leaves, made everything look wavy and surreal. "Ripley?"

"Welcome home. A little earlier than I expected." He was sitting on a chaise in a dark corner. Jack went over and sat next to him.

"What's the matter," Ripley said. "You couldn't score?"

"Cut it out."

"What am I supposed to think, that he showed you his stamp collection? That you discussed 'The Wasteland' with him?" He took a swig from a bottle of vodka that Jack hadn't noticed at first. "I'm not stupid, you know. Did he put his hands all over you? Did he stick his prick up your ass?"

"Oh go to hell." He stood up. "I don't have to listen to this."

"Yes you do. That's the one thing you owe me — to listen to this. Have a drink, if you want." He held out the bottle, but Jack shook his head. Ripley shrugged. "I thought you understood. All that talk about beauty and goodness — I meant it, Jack. Platonic love — it was everything to me. I thought, at least it's something to Jack, at least he understands, he sympathizes. Now I find out you're just like everyone else. It didn't mean anything to you. Did it?"

Jack shook his head. "You're getting carried away."

"That is a ridiculous thing to say. Think with your head at least, not with your penis."

Jack had been prepared to take a little punishment, maybe he hadn't been exactly fair to Ripley, but now he was angry. "Stop telling me to think all the time. I don't want to be intellectual about everything."

Ripley laughed. "As if you, of all people, could escape it. You're not a lump like your friend Jeff, or a pretty face like Mark. You're a thinker, Jack, whether you like it or not. You believe in things."

"I don't. At least I don't believe in Beauty and Truth. I don't believe in Love. Things happen to you, is all."

"So you just go along."

"Yes." He clenched his fist, not caring what he said. "Yes. You knew that about me, why are you so shocked? I went along with you, didn't I, I sat at your feet these last three years while you played Socrates. It's all I can do. I'm not like you, you're sure of yourself, you believe in yourself. Sometimes I'm not sure I even exist."

Ripley got up and stood next to him. "You exist, all right," he said almost maliciously. "And you'd be a lot more sure of your existence if you did what you wanted for a change instead of what people ask you to do."

"Bull-shit," Jack said. "You're the one who does what he wants, you don't care who gets hurt. Well, I know better. The only way to avoid hurting people is to do what they want. It doesn't matter if it's beautiful or true or good, I just don't want anybody else to get hurt."

He could feel Ripley standing next to him, he could hear the sound of his own breathing. "And what about you, Jack? What about your getting hurt?"

"It doesn't matter."

"Why? Why doesn't it matter? Because you feel guilty? Because you think you killed your father."

Jack turned around quickly and shouted, "I did not kill my father."

Ripley half-fell, half-sat on the end of the chaise. Jack looked down at him, at the greenish light reflecting off his glasses, and thought, Jesus, I hit him. He said, "I'm sorry, Ripley. I didn't mean — it's just that —" His voice trailed off. Ripley, of all people to hit.

For the first time there was sympathy in Ripley's voice. "I shouldn't have said that."

They looked at each other. Ripley's face was damp, as if he'd been sweating, and Jack was breathing the way he did after finishing a swimming race. Ripley reached down and took a swig of the vodka. Then he gave the bottle to Jack. Their hands touched — on purpose, Jack thought. Ripley said, "Still friends?"

"'Course." Jack sat down next to him. "Besides. What does it matter so much. It's just something that happened. I'm not gay or anything."

"I know you're not." He paused and then said, "I am."

"What?"

"Don't make me repeat it, will you. It's hard enough to say once." He leaned back in the chair. "Cat got your tongue?"

For all his flippancy, Jack could tell that he was really worried about his reaction. "I didn't know. I mean, how long —"

"Since I was twelve. All my friends were drooling over girls. All I could do was fantasize about other boys. It never entered my mind that it could be different. For me. I just knew I would never love women."

"But why didn't you tell me?"

Ripley sighed. "Will you understand it if I say I wanted to protect you? I didn't want to influence you, not about that, anyway. I knew that if I asked you, you would say yes, and then I'd never know if I'd done the right thing for you. That's why —"

"What?"

"Why tonight was so difficult for me. I'd watched you for four years, and then to see someone else step in at the last minute, and Mark especially — do you understand any of this?"

Jack had been taking it all in, and now he puzzled it through. "It's kind of a big thing to learn about your best friend, all at once."

"Still friends, though."

"I said you were my best friend." He shook his head. "I'll tell you this, Ripley. The last place I'd ever expect to find you, with your big mouth and your arrogance, is in a closet."

And they both laughed.

Six years later, Jack got a letter that had been written weeks before it was sent. It was the last of all the letters he and Ripley exchanged:

I used to tell myself, when a special thing happened, that I wanted never to forget it, that I wanted to remember this or that moment for the rest of my life. What is the old proverb? — be careful what you wish for, it may be granted you. Well, mine was granted. I'm going to die before I have a chance to forget, senility forestalled. I wanted you to know that you were what I most wanted not to forget. The way you'd look up at me with those wide green eyes from under a fringe of hair, so beautiful and innocent. And then you'd come out with a stunner — do you remember what you said to me the first time we talked? — that school was a game. You'd taken me in completely, the way you do everyone, pretending to be naive but always playing along with anybody's game, knowing it was a game. Or when you asked me to read Plato aloud to you. Did you know that my greatest fantasy was to lie with you beside our stream and read of love, were you playing my game then? — I don't think so. I think that was a true response, from Jack Newland's heart, it was what you wanted. I nearly burst with love that day.

Did you ever love me? I've known all along that you aren't gay, that my sexuality isn't something you would ever share, even though sometimes I let my heart fool my head about that. (Did your ears ever burn? — some of the fantasies I had — here you may imagine me grinning wickedly.) I remember the first time I saw you after your parents died. It was at a barbecue, right after school started. You were wearing a bright big shirt, all untucked, and you were bending over to pick something up, and your beautiful hair was falling down over your face, and I had the strongest sense of your body beneath your clothes, thin and unfinished, the touchable ribs and the hard muscles. It made me dizzy for hours afterwards. That's why I called out to you the first time, I couldn't help myself. And then, that day I played you the opera tapes, I realized I was falling in love with you, and I knew it was the wrong thing, so I went away and I stayed away until I had mastered my feelings. Mark kept telling me to go ahead and seduce you, that I had nothing to lose, but I couldn't do that. I felt as if I held your soul in my two hands, and one false move would break you, and my love for you. That was why your little episode with Mark hurt me so much. It was as if you (and he, he knew what he was doing, and I'll never forgive him for it) were flaunting in front of me everything that I'd denied myself for so long. I know it meant nothing to you — less than nothing.

But I like to think that you did love me, in some basic way. Can there be love without sex? Aristotle teaches that things exist to fulfill their function, that everything has its appointed purpose or end in the world. What then is the end of love, if not sex? Plato thought there could be love of the mind, without a physical dimension, and maybe we proved it. I want to believe that it was more than a school-boy crush. But perhaps that is only the distortion of Death, a need to see things as other than they were.

This, then, is my valedictory to you: love. Do you remember, during our senior year at Westfield, they gave us Plato to read — not the *Symposium*, too many references to boy-love, but the *Phaedo*, the death of Socrates. Do you remember my telling you that I wanted to take my epitaph from it: "Will you not allow that I have as much of the spirit of prophecy in me as the swans? For they, when they perceive that they must die, having sung all their life long, do then sing more lustily than ever, rejoicing in the thought that they are going to the god they serve." I have tried to serve love, as best I could. Now you must carry on.

Jack received this letter in January during his first year in graduate school. He booked the next flight he could to San Francisco and went to the hospital. Over the past few months, he had read what was available about AIDS, but he wasn't prepared for Ripley. He was lying back in the bed, nearly swallowed up in the pillows. Jack had always thought of him as being a little plump, but now he was wasted, almost a caricature of the emaciated children one saw in pictures of African famines. He had an IV tube stuck into his arm, and he had some distorting reddish-purplish blotches on his face, and he had a lump under his right ear. Mostly, though, he had a hole cut in his throat — to help him breathe, a helpful nurse explained. He was unconscious most of the time, but once he opened his eyes and smiled at Jack.

He was in a room with two other men: one older, with a bandage around the top of his head, one younger, with yellowish skin.

They both stared at Jack angrily while he sat by Ripley's bed. Jack got up and arranged for Ripley to have a private room. "His insurance doesn't cover it," the hospital administrator said dubiously. "I will," Jack answered, and gave David as a bank reference. He visited the hospital every day for a week, and in between sat in his hotel drinking room-service bourbon and watching TV. He thought about calling Mark, who was in a law practice in San Francisco, but he didn't. He thought about calling Ripley's parents. He was afraid, almost, to use the phone, it was as if the whole city were infected with disease.

One afternoon, Ripley opened his eyes, which now seemed to fill his face. Jack looked at him and saw only what he himself was feeling: yearning and regret. He answered what he saw there, not caring if it was the truth or not: "I love you, Ripley." And Ripley seemed, feebly but definitely, to nod.

He died that night. He was cremated, and Jack brought his ashes back to Westfield and scattered them over the little hollow in the woods where they'd spent so much time, where he was lying now, with his memories.

VI

THE SPELL OF MEMORY was so strong that Timothy asked whether something had happened when Jack returned from the spot by the river late in the afternoon, empty and hungry, overrun by the past. Timothy wanted to know, but Jack put him off. Tomorrow, he said, I'll tell you tomorrow. He wanted to sustain his illusion at least that long.

But the next morning they sat out on the terrace at a wrought iron table under the yellow-and-white-striped awning, and while they ate breakfast, and on into the morning as they drank pots of coffee, he told Timothy about Westfield and Ripley, all the pent-up memories of the day before. It was a clear, warm day, and the sun shone all around them, on the pond below, on the opposing hillside, but in front of him Jack could see the snows of a Westfield winter, or the thick smog of Los Angeles. Timothy listened quietly, getting up only to refill their coffee cups, effacing himself. At the end he said only, "I'd like to have known him."

Jack, feeling drained, said, "I think he would have liked you." He toyed with his coffee cup. "The worst part is —"

Timothy looked up at him but said nothing.

"— is how completely gone he is. How irrecoverable it is."

"What is?"

Jack frowned. "You'll probably hate me for this." He stopped. If Timothy thought it was bad enough, maybe he wouldn't ask. That's what Boyd would do — Hey, Newland, don't tell me if you don't want to, do another line instead. But Timothy wasn't Boyd, of course. "I lied to him. I told him I loved him."

"And you didn't?"

"I don't know if I did or not. I said it because he was dying, and it was what he wanted to hear. What I thought he wanted to hear. But sometimes I think that's a terrible thing to have done, to lie to someone when there's no possible chance of setting it right."

"You had a choice, you did what you thought was best. Do you have to keep beating yourself up about it?"

Yes, Jack thought unhappily. Being here in this almost hidden valley, with the pond below and the mountains across the way, and Timothy with him, he'd felt disconnected from his past, from all the ghosts. But there were some ghosts even Timothy couldn't exorcise.

He heard a series of popping noises from somewhere far away, as if to prove the point that even here he wasn't entirely disconnected from the world. Timothy said, "Firecrackers. It's the Fourth of July."

"Oh, yeah. I forgot." He forced some animation into his voice. "We should celebrate. Do something special."

"Later, maybe. If you want." Timothy obviously wanted to finish the conversation.

"No, seriously. We should at least hang out the flag. You must have a flag around somewhere."

Timothy nodded. "Sure. Only I don't know where it is."

Jack stood up. "Well, if you were a flag, where would you be?"

"In the attic?"

"Let's go."

The attic stretched the length of the house and was divided into rooms. Timothy stood at the top of the stairs and looked around. "I'd forgotten how much stuff there was."

The first room they came to was filled with sports equipment — skis and boots, a toboggan, old wooden tennis rackets in presses, an archery target full of holes and an unbent bow. "That's my father's bow," Timothy said. "He told me I could use it if I was strong enough to string it. I never could." He looked at it a moment and then went over and, holding one end between his bare feet, bent the bow and slipped the string into the notch. "Ta-da."

"Congratulations," Jack said. "You just saved yourself three years of analysis."

The next room was piled with trunks. "Check this out," Timothy said, opening one of them. Very carefully, he lifted out a blue uniform coat with gold ornaments — stripes and braids and buttons. "Look."

Jack reached out to touch. It had a heavy feel, from another time. "Civil War?"

"It was my great-great-grandfather's uniform. He was a captain in a New York infantry regiment. There are some letters of his down in the library."

Jack was thinking of the age of the thing, the fact that it had survived. He'd had the same feeling in the rare book library at Yale, handling three-hundred-year-old volumes with crisp imprinted type, their pages grainy and mottled like an old person's skin, this sense of handling history. "I'm always amazed," he began.

"By what?" Timothy was kneeling down, carefully packing away the coat.

"The way the Civil War touched this part of the country so deeply. You drive through New England towns, and every one of them has a monument on its town green, there's something enduring in the memory of all those men who died for the Union."

Timothy stood up and brushed some dirt off his bare knees. "They believed in what they were fighting for."

"But so did the southerners."

"Did they? There's nothing noble about fighting to preserve a way of life that's wrong, just because it's comfortable."

Timothy led the way into the last room of this wing. A louvered vent let in blocks of sunlight, which hung in the air, illuminating a surreal miscellany of objects. A doorless cupboard was filled with large stuffed birds in an advanced state of decay. A plaster statue stood in one corner. Something about it bothered Jack, until he realized that it was a copy of the Venus de Milo to which arms had been grafted. Timothy had picked up a walking stick with a lion's head handle and was poking around with it. "I had a great-uncle who was an ornithologist." He rapped the Venus on her behind. "This is an unfortunate legacy of one of my aunts, who had a mania for displaying classical statues as they might once have appeared to their creators."

Jack touched one of the restored arms.

Timothy went across to another corner of the room and pushed aside a group of carpets that had been rolled, tied with string, and stood on end. Behind them was a sort of bookcase with glass doors. He sneezed. "Now this is truly bizarre. One of my cousins, actually, my great-grandfather's cousin, was a victim of that peculiarly Victorian disease, the inventing of new religions. This was his altar." Timothy hit one of the rolled rugs with the walking stick, releasing a cloud of dust and a brown moth. "It didn't make any sense. But he believed in it."

"What do you believe?" Jack asked absently, staring into the glassy eye of an owl.

"Oh, I believe in God. Of course. Don't you?"

"I don't know." One of the owl's ear tufts had been eaten away by moths. "I believe in half a God, I guess. The God of retribution but not of redemption."

"That makes you a Republican," Timothy said, laughing.

"Right." He looked around the room again. "Was everyone in your family so —"

"Eccentric?"

"No, that's not what I mean. I don't know. Science and art and religion — didn't you have any businessmen?"

Timothy shook his head. "Not really. Most of my family was from Boston, and even the ones who lived in New York saw themselves as essentially Bostonian. The American Athens and all that. It runs in the family, more on my mother's side than my father's. They'd find him a little too practical, I think." He stuck his cane into a pile of books, like an explorer planting a flag. "Come on, let's see what else we can find."

Timothy led the way back through the rooms they'd visited and over into the other wing. He found a box with Christmas ornaments and said, "This looks more promising. Let's see." He began rooting through boxes, finding more tree ornaments and then, unexpectedly, a box of books. "These are from when I was a kid. *Peter's Long Walk. The Golden Book of Pirates.* That was my favorite — there's a story in it about a boy who sailed away from his home and found an island, all for himself. He had great adventures, with pirates and buried treasure, but the next summer, when he sailed out, he couldn't find the island ever again. It fascinated me, I remember. You're awfully quiet."

"Oh." Jack shook his head. "I was thinking about a time when

I went up into the attic of our house. My mother was looking through a pile of my baby clothes and crying."

He had been fourteen. It was the last Christmas before his parents died. That afternoon he and his father had gone out into the woods and cut down a tree — or rather, Jack had cut it and his father had watched. It was another stage in the continuing role reversal in which they were engaged. In previous years it had been his father who had done the sawing, then lately they had each held an end, pretending to be lumberjacks. Now, his father stood off to one side, leaning against a tree. The sky was very low and scalloped, and snow flurried intermittently. Jack had the feeling winter always gave him, of being enclosed by a small box in which no sounds echoed. He was wearing the regulation dress of that time — blue jeans and L. L. Bean boots, a cotton oxford shirt, and over that a hooded sweatshirt, and over that a heavy plaid shirt, and he got warmer and warmer, yanking the saw through the knotty, twisted trunk, his hands sticky with sap. But he finished it himself, determined not to ask for help. When the tree came down, his father said, "Good job, Johnny." His breath, scented with scotch from before lunch, hung in the air between them. "Put your hood up, you don't want to catch cold."

They set the tree up in the corner of the living room. He showered and put on some old clothes, the soft kind that he saved for times when he wanted reassurance, and went downstairs and played cribbage with his father. That was another change they were marking — in the past, his father had usually been able to win at least half the time, but now Jack was beating him regularly. While they played, his father had a drink, and his mother put on a record of Christmas carols and sat on a couch by the fire and read a magazine. She hummed along occasionally, and when the record got to "Jeannette Isabella," Jack looked over and gave her a private kind of smile, because that was her favorite Christmas song. Everything was more or less the way it was supposed to be, the way it had always been. Elizabeth had been getting all the attention in the family lately, along with Billy, who was nearly three, and Hank, who was just one. He was finding out that happy grandparents weren't great parents, at least not to him when the babies were around. But Elizabeth and company had all gone to David's parents', and that, Jack thought, was a lot nicer.

When his father got up for another drink, his mother said, "Let's decorate the tree. I'll go up and get the ornaments."

He looked at his father's back, and then at his mother. "You don't need any help, do you?"

"No, dear. You can get the next batch."

They played another three or four hands, and then his father said, "Where's your mother? She's been up there a long time. I'd better see if she's all right."

Jack finished moving his pegs on the cribbage board. "It's OK, Daddy. I'll go. Maybe I can give her a hand. Be right back." He ran up the front staircase and stopped at the top to catch his breath. More quietly, he slipped up the attic stairs. His mother was kneeling on the floor with her back to him. In front of her was an open trunk. "Mommy?"

She turned around. She was holding some clothes in her hands — a little shirt with bears stenciled on it, corduroy pants with a polka-dot flannel lining, and some tiny underpants. "These were your favorites," she said, "when you were a baby." A pile of other clothes, his baby clothes, lay on the floor next to her. She was crying.

He stared at her helplessly. "Mommy?" he asked again, wondering if he should put his arm around her shoulders, not wanting to.

"Why was she crying?" Timothy asked.

"I don't know. I think she wanted me not to grow up. Not really, not forever, but maybe just for that moment, she wanted me to be a little boy again." He picked up a Christmas ornament from the box next to him, a glass ball with an alpine scene. "I think she was right. It would be better, wouldn't it, not to grow up, to be nine years old and ignorant again, to un-know everything."

"Feeling sorry for yourself today?" Timothy said flippantly. "This wouldn't just be an emotional hangover from what you told me this morning. Is there more?"

Jack shook the ornament he held, releasing a snowstorm. "Yes. There's more. Of course there's more. I keep thinking, maybe if I'd loved him the way he wanted me to, he wouldn't have died.

Maybe he wouldn't have been driven to do whatever it was that made him ill. To live that kind of life, I mean. He was essentially chaste — maybe I could have kept him that way if I'd given him what he wanted." Timothy was kneeling on the floor, sitting on his feet. One curl of blond hair hung limply on his forehead in the heat, and his eyes were again that penetrating blue. Jack thought what a right-thinking person Timothy was, straight-thinking. Come on, he thought, condemn me; confirm me.

But Timothy wouldn't. "You want absolution, Jack. For something that no one but you blames you for. I can't give you that. I won't tell you not to blame yourself — you don't need me to tell you that. But I can't forgive you, and I can't punish you."

Don't say that, he thought; it wasn't what he wanted to hear. He almost stamped his foot on the floor, he wanted to smash the glass ball that he held. He had never shown anyone, not even Ripley, one-tenth of his heart as he had shown it to Timothy — he had hidden himself all these years, fearing the things that would crawl out if anyone ever lifted the rock. And now, having lifted it himself, no bolts fell from the sky, no sentence was passed, Timothy refused even to sit in judgment. Perhaps Jack had been wrong all that time. But then, perhaps not: at least since Ripley, no one else had died.

Timothy said, "Here's the flag." They went downstairs and hung it by the front door. After lunch, they carried a load of paraphernalia out to the pool — books and towels and glasses and tubes of lotion. Timothy had on white swimming trunks with a slash of red across them, and his skin was very fair and smooth. He put a lot of sun block on. "The doctor told me I have this kind of skin that'll get cancer really easily, so I have to use all this goop."

"I have really dry skin, and after swim practice I used to have to put all this lotion on. You can imagine what kind of comments I got for that."

They got settled in a pair of chairs, their backs to the pond below, facing the pool, and Timothy said, "How do you like it? This is the only part of the property that my father was allowed to touch. The old pool was falling apart, so they put in a new one."

It was a classic statement of the Archer/MacNeill credo —
natural materials, sharp uncompromising lines, no ornamentation.
The pool was set into a shelf that had been smoothed in the side
of the hill. A fieldstone retaining wall had been built to hold back
the slope, shorter at the end nearest the house, but rising gradually along the length of the pool until it merged with the pool
house. The pool house was set at an oblique angle to the flagstone
terrace that surrounded the pool, and one corner thrust itself out
aggressively toward a sheer drop down to the pond. The roof of
the pool house floated on glass walls, seemingly supported only
by the retaining wall and a single steel pillar at the end, and the
tall fireplace that was visible inside. He thought what a great place
it would be on a wintry night, with a fire going and the view of
the valley filled with falling snow. "Do you think," Jack said, "that
your father would let me interview him for the magazine?"

Timothy turned over on his stomach. "I don't know if I'll let
you." He handed Jack the sun block. "Do my back, will you?"

Jack squirted some lotion onto his back and spread it around.
"Why not?"

"There are some parts of my life I like to keep to myself. To
keep away from my father anyway." He turned his head to look
away over the pond. "You could meet my sister Ellen instead."

"Sure," he said, not really paying attention.

"She'd like you." Timothy rested his chin on his crossed hands.
"She'll be here on Friday."

"Oh?" He still wasn't sure whether he wanted to see anyone
else. Timothy's sister, he supposed, was better than most.

"She's coming up here for a couple weeks for vacation." He
paused, waiting for a reaction, and then went on. "I love being
with her," he said seriously. "I hope you will too."

It was a nice way of extending the invitation, Jack thought. He
would wait and see, right then it didn't seem very important. He
was concentrating on what he was doing, spreading the sun block
evenly, feeling the softness of Timothy's back, the play of the
muscles beneath the skin, the almost boyish feel of his bones. He
absentmindedly traced the line of his spine, and said, "You have
really nice skin." It was the kind of remark he made to himself
about people all the time, part of the summing up he did in his

role as observer, but almost never aloud. As soon as he spoke, he saw the blood come to the surface all over Timothy's back. He couldn't see his face.

"Thanks," Timothy mumbled.

Jack snapped the top of the lotion shut loudly and then opened it again with his thumbnail. What he desired from people was usually determined by what they offered him. Now, with nothing on offer, he wondered what he wanted. "Oh, God, I hate —"

"What?"

"Nothing. I don't know. Being confused."

Timothy laughed. "Oh, that, that's the human condition. What else would we need psychiatrists for? You shouldn't waste your hate on that." He twisted around a little and looked at Jack. "You know, we used to play this game in college, the hate game. It was supposed to reveal the deep inner core of your being or something." Jack giggled, and Timothy went on. "Like, I hate the way the poles in the subway always feel greasy." And Jack shuddered a little, knowing exactly what he meant. "Now it's your turn."

He thought a minute and said, "I hate cucumbers."

"Oh, come on, you can do better than that." Timothy elbowed him. "Try again."

"I hate driving in New Jersey."

"OK. I hate dreams where the only thing that happens is what happens in real life."

"That's convoluted," Jack said. "I hate those guys on TV news shows who always ask the mother of some girl who's been raped how she feels about it."

"Good. I hate people who hate things."

"A paradox," Jack said. Timothy, having played the game before, obviously had a whole store of answers. Jack had to think a minute. "I hate almost any character in Dickens who you're supposed to like."

Timothy thought a minute. "Like Copperfield?"

"Well," Jack admitted, "not like Copperfield. He's the only one I do like. But Pip, for instance, or Pickwick. Don't stall, it's your turn."

"OK. I hate girls who flirt."

"Really?"

"Yes, don't you?"

Jack laughed. "I don't know any who don't. Every girl who comes within ten feet of me seems to flirt. It must be the same for you."

"What would you do if you met one who didn't?"

"I don't know. I think I'd be so shocked I'd have to marry her." He thought guiltily for a moment of Kate — he was going to marry her, he reminded himself.

Meanwhile Timothy, having tired of the game, had picked up his book. It was a largish volume, in German, and he rested it on his knees. Jack could see the unfamiliar squiggles of the German typeface. He thought again of that old collection of junk in the attic, the ornithologist uncle and the arty aunt and the mad religious cousin. He knew there were such families, where a line of distinguished predecessors stretched back through the Social Register, or at least he had read about such families, the Jameses and the Lowells, in which each generation seemed to produce another giant of the cultural scene. His own family was from a different tradition, New York merchants, businessmen who moved ships and railroads the way Henry James moved commas. His father had been a lawyer, and his father before him had been a banker. Deeper back in the family mists was a younger son, a slippery trader in the opium ports of the south China coast. Jack liked to imagine him skippering a lone bark among the shoals of the Pearl River, fending off pirates and jealous Brits, kowtowing where necessary to get the sticky drug ashore. His grandmother still had four tapestries that dated to the Ming, ransom collected from one of Commissioner Lin's enforcers under the threat of the ship's cannon before the first Opium War. Kate's family was the same, only more so. The Wellands had dabbled in tea and tobacco in the Far East, and in cotton and sugar in this hemisphere, before turning to railroads. The North River Trust was the product of the union of the two families, founded in 1910 by his great-grandfather and Kate's. They had seen the collapse of China coming and had used the bank to shelter their personal fortunes from the fall, and now that union of interest was about to be ratified by a more personal union, his marriage to Kate. It all fit together so nicely that it might almost have been arranged, which in his role as spectator (even of his own life) he appreciated. Kate would never make a false move, never be unexpected and, more importantly, would never believe that he could be unexpected. She had position and personality and purpose; as long as he was with her, he would appear to be like everyone else in her world. And that guaranteed his anonymity: you couldn't hide in a crowd of strangers any more than you could hide a blackbird in a crowd of cardinals.

With Timothy, Jack had no idea. It wasn't just that their families were so different, except in the sense that they were both products of their history. With Timothy anything was possible, and that meant that nothing was certain. He looked speculatively at Timothy, who was concentrating on the text, the tip of his tongue just showing between his lips. I like him, Jack thought, more than anyone I know, because he's what I might have been if — if all the things that had happened hadn't, a foolish speculation. Timothy reached for things not caring if he failed. He went at life pell-mell, while Jack's life had been a series of failed trajectories.

He stood up, and Timothy looked at him from beneath a shading hand. "I think I'll take a swim."

"OK."

He did laps, trying not think about Ripley or Timothy or anything, settling at last on Kate. He knew what she would be doing now. It would be about nine in St. Moritz, she would be sitting at a table in a restaurant with her mother and sister. There would be men in the room, men from the hotel, and they would know her, because she was the kind of woman men wanted to know. She was so beautiful (that's what he clung to in his mind for a couple of laps, how beautiful she was), and she would flirt with them. After dinner, they would go to a bar, one of those Swiss chalet bars with flickering sconces and wagon-wheel chandeliers, and drink kirsch, and the men would gather around her. She would encourage them, wanting to know that she could have them. It didn't occur to him that she would be unfaithful (even if he had been prepared to make that kind of claim on her) because for her it was the comfort of possession that counted, and with the confidence of generations she knew that the ability to have was the same as having. She might even go for a ride in a car with one of them, park under the fir trees and watch the lights of the town below, and she would only view it as more proof of how suited Jack was for her, that she could dally with someone else while loving him. Their world, that was how it worked, and he, damn it (he said to himself, not quite sure why he needed to be so vehement), was comfortable in it.

He pulled himself out of the pool. In the interim, Timothy had gotten a tray with an ice bucket and a bottle of bourbon and a bottle of vodka and some mixers. "Want a drink?"

"Just some ginger ale," Jack said, breathing hard from his workout. He sat back down in his chair and took a glass from Timothy.

"Don't drip on the book," Timothy said. "I had to mortgage my firstborn to borrow it."

"What is it?"

"A critique of Goethe by one of his deservedly little-known contemporaries. This is the only copy in the United States."

Jack leaned back in the chair and sipped his soda. "I don't know any German except 'Das Lied von der Unzulanglichkeit Menschlichen Strebens.'" He felt like showing off.

Timothy looked surprised. "What's that? 'The Song about —' How did it go again?"

"Ah. Got you." He grinned. "When I was in college, the theater people were gaga about Brecht and Weill. We put on *The Happy End* one semester and *The Threepenny Opera* the next (I learned how to say that, too: *Die Dreigroschenoper*). I had some friends in the cast, and I helped a little with lighting and stuff, so I learned a lot of the words. Through osmosis." He said the song title again, trying to fake a broad German accent. "Das Lied von der Unzulanglichkeit Menschlichen Strebens."

Timothy thought a moment. "Song about the Inadequacy of Human Aspiration?"

"It's totally cynical, don't you think?"

"Charming." Timothy held up his book a little. "It's a long way from Goethe. I didn't know you were in the theater."

Jack shook his head. "Definitely not in the theater. Just a groupie. I was dating a girl who was an actress." He didn't want to talk about that. "I think I'll have a drink now," he said, pouring out some bourbon. "What did you do in college?"

"It was almost embarrassing." Timothy laughed. "I was totally impossible, at least my freshman year. I was quite the little Wykehamist."

"Wykehamist?" Jack asked vaguely, drinking his bourbon.

"Graduate of Winchester College. That's what we call ourselves, I told you."

"Oh, right."

"I'd just spent two years in England," Timothy went on. "I played the part to the hilt. I gave sherry parties in my room at Brown. I lounged around in a silk smoking jacket. I drawled my way through seminars. I cultivated cigars. I was insufferable."

Jack could picture it all. "It sounds like fun."

"At first it was. I got a lot of attention for it. But then I had to keep it up, because it was what people expected. I'd built this whole identity around being the perfect English gentleman, and after a while it wasn't what I wanted anymore. It was just camouflage. That's when I started seeing my shrink." He went on more speculatively, "It's funny about Winchester — it's so old, has so much history in it, that you get an absolutely perfect sense of being. It doesn't make any compromises at all, because it doesn't have to. What I took away, beneath all the superficial mannerisms, was a sense that what's important is not to compromise your essential self. Does that make any sense to you?"

Jack sipped at his drink and didn't answer.

A couple of hours and a lot of bourbon later, he was standing on the diving board, playing air guitar along with an old Who tape they'd found in the pool house. They'd cranked the volume, and Jack was singing "Behind Blue Eyes." He tried a couple of Townshend air-guitar whirls and nearly lost his balance. Timothy was watching, laughing. "Let me see you dive," he called out.

"What?"

"Do a dive."

Obligingly, Jack dove off the board, trying for some extra elevation and not getting much. He swam to the side and pulled himself up next to Timothy. "Why the dive?"

"Oh." Timothy blushed again. "You'll think it's silly."

Jack reached for his glass. "I'm getting really 'faced here. You can trust me when I'm drunk."

"Well, when I was a kid, one day, I watched you diving at the swim club, all those gainers and pikes, I don't know what they're called. I tried all summer to be — to dive like you, but I couldn't. Why are you looking at me like that?"

"I remember that day. I hated it. I thought I was terrible."

"You would think that," Timothy said drily. "But you weren't. In fact, for years, the idea of the perfect dive was one of my most persistent fantasies." He looked at the pool, at the diving board, and Jack could feel him imagining some ideal dive, the kind that went on, in dreams, for eternities of fall. Timothy went on, matter-of-factly, "What's your most persistent fantasy?"

He was about to say something flippant, something blatant and sexual. Instead, he blurted out the truth. "That my parents hadn't died."

Timothy looked at him and nodded. "I knew that, I think. I wish it were something else. I wish it were something I could make happen."

It was in Jack's head, then, to ask a question he'd wanted answered ever since he'd awakened for the first time in Timothy's guest room. But he didn't ask it, not until later. Timothy made them hamburgers on the grill, and then they showered, and now they were sitting, back on the pool deck, with their chairs drawn up to the edge where the hill fell steeply away. The first burst of scarlet came, above the opposite hill, from the Westfield town fireworks display, lighting up the sky, and then the concussion, strangely delayed and muffled by the distance. Jack watched Timothy's face, rapt and half-smiling like a little child's, lit red and silver and blue. Softly, Jack said, "Why are you doing all this for me?"

He didn't turn away from the fireworks. "I know what you've been thinking," he said confidently. "But I've never had sex with a man and I can't imagine ever wanting to."

"Then what is it?"

At that, Timothy did look at him. "Don't you know?"

PART THREE

Bilbao

Moon

~~~~~~

VII

ON FRIDAY EVENING, Jack drove Timothy's convertible up to a restaurant in Cornwall and parked it under a tree. Then he sat for a moment, gathering his courage.

An hour or so before, Timothy had gotten a phone call. "I have to go out," he announced. "There's a problem with the goddamn cows."

"What cows?" Jack asked.

"Oh — look, I'll explain later. It's just that I was supposed to meet my sister Ellen for dinner. At a restaurant in Cornwall. She's getting a ride up from the city, and I said I'd meet her in an hour." He ran a hand distractedly through his hair, which immediately fell back down over his forehead. "I'll leave a message at the restaurant. If she calls, tell her I'll be there eventually."

Jack, on the spur of the moment and with as much nonchalance as he could muster, said, "Why don't I go meet her. You can join us later."

"That's nice of you, but —"

"What?"

"Well," Timothy said dubiously, "I know how much you've wanted to be alone. I don't want to stick you with anything."

"It's OK." He went on more forcefully, "I really mean it. I'd like to." And he meant it, or halfway, anyway. He felt as if a glacial change that had long been under way in him was now making itself felt, provoked perhaps by the events of his birthday and the succeeding week. It was improbable that the structure he'd so meticulously made of his life over the last thirteen years, which had protected him so well for so long, should now, and without any discernible attack, be crumbling. All because of a twenty-five-year-old boy who didn't seem to play by the same rules, and perhaps not even in the same game. Timothy was, in Jack's new consciousness, like one of those magic Chinese castles

that appear and disappear in the tales of the *Arabian Nights* —
he had arrived in Jack's life with the same kind of solidity, oc-
cupying the same kind of volume, as a palace in a paradise. What
the effect of this visitation might be, even what its intent was,
remained to be seen, but Jack was holding stubbornly to his sense
of change and to Timothy's role as herald, or talisman, or agent
of the transformation.

Now, sitting in the parked car, he began to have his doubts.
If he had, after a week in Westfield, shed a part of his old self,
the only thing that had appeared to replace it was Timothy's
conviction that anything could happen, that the world was a place
of infinite possibilities. The thought made Jack nervous, and he
toyed with the idea of just driving off and pretending — something, he would make up an excuse. But then his new determination reasserted itself. All right, he thought as he switched off
the car, let anything happen. He got out and straightened his tie.

It was a Westfield Academy tie, which Timothy had dug out of
some neglected closet, and as he approached the restaurant Jack
felt disconcertingly like a seventeen-year-old being taken out by
his roommate's parents. He had, he remembered unpleasantly,
come here once with Jeff's parents, who had been in from New Orleans for a school function — parents' weekend or the Groton football game or something. The restaurant had once been an inn, or so
it claimed, and at the time of Jack's last visit (admittedly ten or
twelve years before), it still clung, desperately and with all the effort modern technology could muster, to a devious rusticity. Floor-
boards tilted noticeably but nontortiously away from one another,
bits and pieces of ostensibly colonial ironware decorated the walls,
and the dowels in the chair backs obtruded. The waitresses, wearing starched aprons and gingham dresses, looked out sullenly from
under idiotically frilled mobcaps. The dining room was dominated
by the carved figure of an outsized woman, and Jack had embarrassed himself completely and for all time by referring to it as a
maidenhead. Jeff had laughed so hard he'd choked on his soup.
Such were his memories of the Traveller's Inn. He couldn't imagine why Timothy, of all people, had chosen it.

The first sign of change was in the name — it was now simply
Travellers — and the inside was similarly transformed. The floor-

boards had been evened and in places replaced with a cool orange tile, the furnishings were distinctly modern, and the only maid-enhead in sight was a leggy blonde at the bar. Most promising of all was the faint scent in the air of garlic, a tuber unknown to ye olde Traveller's Inn because it could not be boiled. He went over to the maitresse d', an Oriental woman in a short leather skirt and a burlappy blouse open to her navel. "I have a reservation. It's in the name of Archer."

"Yes sir. Right this way."

He followed her, appreciatively, between tables and then out through a wide archway to a wooden deck, which was also new since his last visit. The deck overlooked a pond with a dam at one end — it had probably been a mill pond once. Two or three oak trees had been left growing through the deck to shade the tables. A solitary swan occupied the middle distance, and, across the pond, a cluster of willows hung down into the water. Beyond all, a huge orange moon hung on the horizon. The hostess led him to a table at the edge of the deck, where a young woman in a white dress with black polka dots sat reading the menu, a glass with something fizzy in it on the table in front of her.

"Hello," he said. "I'm Jack Newland. Timothy's been delayed, so I came instead."

She looked up very coolly, unsurprised, with the same blue eyes her brother had. "Hello. I'm Ellen Archer." She held out a hand for him to shake. "Please sit down."

"Thanks." She looked like Timothy, not just in the eyes, but in the shape of her ears and the fullness of her lips — aspects of Timothy that hadn't registered before, he now saw recapi-tulated in Ellen. He heard himself saying, You have really nice skin, and stopped himself from repeating it out loud. Where Timothy's hair was gold, Ellen's was black, setting off even more the blue of her eyes. He saw her begin to smile and realized he'd been staring. "You look like your brother," he said by way of apology.

"I'll take that as a compliment."

"I meant it as a compliment to him." He turned a little in his chair and signaled for a waiter. "Would you like a refill?"

"Just a glass of wine, please."

"And I'll have a Wild Turkey on the rocks." He leaned back and crossed his legs. She was sitting against the background of the pond and the willows, with the moon rising above her head, and he could pretend to be observing the view. "Timothy was held up at the last minute. He got a telephone call from someone — I think his name was Fred? He and Mr. Prescott tore off in the car. It had something to do with cows," he ended lamely. When she laughed, he felt a little foolish. "It didn't sound right to me either. I guess I got it wrong."

"No, no." She laughed again. "My father owns a farm in Canaan. He likes the idea of being a gentleman farmer. Fred manages it for him. What's funny is the idea that anyone would think Timothy would know anything about it."

"No, he's not the farmboy type." When she laughed, she tilted her head back a little. It wasn't an extreme movement, and her laugh was not the kind that reverberated elegantly at deadly dinner parties in New York.

"Although," she went on, "it would appeal to him. He picked up a distinct lord-of-the-manor air at Winchester. He doesn't get a chance to display it very often, but he's very cute when he does."

"He'd hate it if he heard you say that."

"He would. Every summer, at least once, the cows get loose and we all have to rush over to Canaan and shoo them back where they belong. Last year we had them all back except one, and Timothy was missing. We finally found them, the cow grazing happily on a little hill and Timothy sitting with his back against a tree declaiming at it in German. Schiller, I think. He said it was a Holstein, so it should understand German, and it clearly hadn't understood English. He made it sound perfectly reasonable." Their drinks came, and Ellen held hers up. "Cheers."

"To the beginning of a friendship," he said, clinking his glass against hers, wondering where he'd gotten the courage to say that.

"A beautiful friendship," she corrected. "Isn't that how the movie ends?"

He swallowed some of his bourbon and nodded. "But it's not a very satisfactory ending."

"Why do you say that? And why do you look so serious?"

He wasn't prepared for that, so he smiled a little self-consciously. "I'm writing an article about the Bogart movies."

"Hasn't that been done?"

"You sound like my editor," he said combatively. "It's revisionist criticism. I think *The Big Sleep* and *To Have and Have Not* are better films than *Casablanca* and *Key Largo*."

"The Bacall factor. Although she was in *Key Largo*." Ellen leaned back and looked off over his shoulder. "I can just imagine them, making *To Have and Have Not*. She was what? Nineteen. That whole movie crackles with what's between them."

"Sex," he said, making an uncharacteristic advance.

"That she was as tough as he was."

"Passion."

"Love." She laughed again. "You won't convince me."

"I don't want to," he conceded. "I agree with you, actually. He's too coy in *Casablanca*, too much of a tease. He is as tough as Bacall in *To Have and Have Not*. And vice versa."

She picked up her wine goblet again and sipped, considering him, and he wondered if they were going to get stuck in a conversation about film criticism. But she changed the tone. "What's your favorite Bogart movie?"

"Well," he said didactically, "the best one —"

"No," she interrupted, putting her glass down again. "Your favorite."

He gave in. "My favorite is *Sabrina*. It was the first Bogart movie I ever saw." The first time is always the best, he thought irrelevantly. "My mother was a real fan of old movies, and I used to watch them with her when I was a kid. One night, when I was about ten or eleven, they went out to dinner, and left me alone. *Sabrina* was on TV, and I watched it. I thought it was the greatest movie I'd ever seen, the most sophisticated, the most romantic. When I told my mother, she took me to see *Sierra Madre* and *Maltese Falcon*, because she said *Sabrina* wasn't at all a typical Bogart film. But I still like it."

"Why? Because it was your first one?" she asked, echoing his thoughts.

"No. Because it has everything. Bogart and Audrey Hepburn, William Holden and 'La Vie en Rose' and —" He swallowed hard, and then said, "and 'Isn't It Romantic.' "

"Let's order," she said abruptly. "I'm starving, and if we wait for my brother we may be here all night."

"What's good?" He didn't open the menu.

"Well, what do you feel like eating?" she answered, looking down at hers.

"Lobsters and champagne."

"Jack." It was the first time she'd said his name. "Are you flirting with me?"

"I would," he admitted, "if I knew how."

"That's not what I've heard."

"I'll let that pass."

After they ordered, he excused himself and went to the men's room. He stood looking in the mirror, inhaling the pinkish scent of the disinfectant cakes in the urinals, wondering what he was doing. He was engaged to another woman and here he was — he didn't even know if he had a name for what he was doing. Well, anything is possible. "Go for it, Newland," he said grinning at himself in the mirror. Then he checked the stalls to make sure no one had heard.

"What do you do?" he asked after their appetizers came.

She frowned, twisting her fork to get at a recalcitrant snail. "I collect tolls at the Lincoln Tunnel."

"Funny, I've never seen you there. But then, I try not to go to New Jersey very often."

"The truth is far more unbelievable."

He finished a snail, and licked a little garlic off his lips. "A CIA operative? A riveter? A Rockette?"

She smiled. "I like that idea."

"Let me see your legs," he said, lifting the edge of the table-cloth.

"And we barely introduced."

"A tugboat captain," he pursued. "A schoolteacher. A movie star."

"A physicist," she said with finality. "I work for Consolidated Technologies."

"You're kidding." He had never met a physicist before, other than a table full of aspirants in a dining hall at Yale — the same six eating together every night and glorying in the stereotypes of their nerdy status: unkempt hair, unhealthy complexions, and an affinity for the sort of peas-and-gravy dining hall food no one else would eat. "I didn't know there were any women physicists since Madame Curie nuked herself."

"Damn few." She rested her elbow lightly on the table. "What are you thinking?"

"I've always loved the idea of physics," he said. "It seems so pure and theoretical, platonic almost."

"Platonic?"

"Well, the notion that there are ideal forms of things, fundamental correspondences among all things." He thought fleetingly of Ripley. "Plato believed that everything on earth was an imperfect image of an ideal, heavenly form. That all forks," he picked up a salad fork from the table, "are images of the one ideal fork. Physics always seemed to have that same quality to it, that we're all made up of the same essential, invisible particles."

She thought for a moment. "I've never thought about it before like that."

"Oh, don't give me any credit. I don't really understand the first thing about it. When we did physics labs in school I was always messing up. All those protons and photons and quarks, I can't keep them straight."

She laughed. "Well, at least you know something about it. Most people I talk to think a quark is either an Australian animal or a Chinese dynasty."

"That's about the extent of my knowledge." He paused. "But seriously, I love it that you're a scientist. I know a lot of investment bankers and lawyers, and even actors and musicians, but I don't know any physicists."

She looked at him speculatively. "A lot of men find it intimidating." Before he could follow this up, she said, "Here's Timothy."

Jack twisted around in his seat and looked across the deck.

Timothy was walking toward them. He was wearing white pants with a razor crease, a very soft-looking pink shirt, a white-and-pale-blue-striped tie, and a blue blazer. He was topped off by a straw boater with a red and navy blue band. He looked very fresh and a little outrageous. "Hello, children," he said. "Sorry I'm late."

"You've managed to arrive in time for dessert," Ellen said.

He swept off his hat and leaned down to kiss her cheek. "It's great to see you. I didn't suppose you would have waited for me," he added a little wistfully.

"You can have what's left of mine," Jack said, indicating a single scrap of veal sitting in a congealing pool of sauce next to a mound of pilaf.

"Ah, greater love hath no man than this, that he lay down his rice for a friend."

"Sit down, Timothy. Unless you're deliberately trying to attract attention."

"Always, you know me. The exhibitionist." He sat down. "I have a problem of etiquette. When one dines al fresco, is it proper to remove one's hat? What do you think, Jack?"

"I'll defer to you. You're the one with the exquisite manners."

"A touch, a touch, I do confess. I shall leave the hat off." He put it on the table in front of him, upended like an empty fruit basket, and looked around the deck. "I could really use a drink." He waved for the waiter and ordered a vodka and tonic. "Fred called this afternoon," he said to Ellen, "something about a new milking machine. He wanted Dad, of course, but he took Mr. Prescott and me instead. What I know about milking machines you could write on the head of a pin and still have plenty of room left over for Part One of *Faust*. But we looked at it, and Mr. Prescott and Fred talked very knowledgeably about feeder some-things, and I cleared my throat a lot, and Fred seemed happy. I went home with the sense of a duty well done and the pleasing aroma of cow dung clinging to my boots. And here I am." He drank a little of his vodka.

"It reminds me of that weekend the time I visited you in England."

Timothy explained to Jack. "One of my friends from Winchester invited us to spend a weekend with him at his ancestral estate. He liked you, Ellen, you should have married him. You'd be a duchess now."

"No I shouldn't have. Are you going to eat any dinner, Timothy? They'll close the kitchen while you talk."

"All right, all right."

Jack sat and listened to them, looking cautiously from time to time at Ellen's face. No matter where he looked — at the pond, now still in the evening, at the sky emptying of light, at Timothy's happy grin, at the moon which was fading as it rose in the sky — he found himself drawn to look at her. There were movie stars who did that to him — Garbo was one, Dietrich another. When they were on screen the rest of the scene might as well be empty, he couldn't look at anything else, his eyes refused to take in the surroundings. But Ellen was the first woman he'd ever known in person who did that to him.

"How do you like my dress, Timothy?"

"It looks great."

"He bought it for me in Paris," Ellen said. "I had to go to a conference over there, and I brought Timothy along, courtesy of Con Tech. One afternoon, while I was listening to a paper, he went and bought me this dress. Do you like it?"

Jack nodded. He could see the two of them, Timothy and Ellen, sitting in the window of their hotel room, overlooking a courtyard hung with vines, sipping cocktails as the purple Paris night descended. La vie en rose. He didn't know why he pictured them like that, they might have stayed at the Hilton, not the kind of Old World hotel he was imagining, maybe it was the moonlight shining down on them, warm and bright (the moon did not, in his experience, shine on Hiltons). And of course, it was just like Timothy to buy his sister the perfect dress. It was, somehow, another mark of the difference between their families. Here they were, and in ten minutes had talked about their vacation in England, their trip to Paris, things they had done together. It wasn't that he didn't or wouldn't go to Europe with Elizabeth. It was that the Newlands went to Europe as tourists, or at best as visitors, and always had (he thought of his grandmother, installing herself every winter in Monte Carlo) while the Archers went as guests. A Venus de Milo, even one with arms, was irreconcilably different from a postcard, a tinted reproduction suitable for framing. He shook his head. "It's nice that you two are such good friends. My sister's ten years older than me — somehow it's not the same." My surrogate mother, he thought.

"Oh," Ellen said, putting her arm around Timothy's shoulders. "He's adorable, don't you think?"

As they were walking down the stairs that led from the deck toward the parking lot, Ellen linked her arm through Timothy's and then looked back for a moment, up at Jack. He thought, I'm going to marry this woman, and the idea was so sudden and complete, he was so sure of himself, that he stood still a moment, almost as if to take stock of himself, to make sure that he was all still there and still himself, had not been transmogrified. Be careful, he thought reflexively. He didn't want to hurt anyone, least of all himself, and this was the kind of feeling, the sudden rush of emotion, that he'd learned to distrust.

He was still pondering all of this that night in his bedroom when he heard voices outside. He went to the window and looked out. Below him and to the side, on the first terrace of the garden, he could see them walking. Timothy, with his white pants and pink shirt and blond hair, shone in the moonlight. Ellen was more a dark blur next to him. They walked around and around the fish pond, talking, their heads close together. Only an occasional indistinct word reached him.

And later, when he was lying in the four-poster bed reading, there was a knock on his door. "Come in," he said, gathering his robe more closely around his legs.

It was Ellen. "I saw your light on. I hope you don't mind."

"No," he said, his mouth a little dry. "Not at all."

"We were talking about *The Big Sleep* before, and I wondered if you'd ever read any Chandler, so I brought up *Farewell, My Lovely*. It's one of my favorites."

"Thanks, I haven't read it." He took it from her. "Physics and mysteries?"

She laughed, the laugh he'd noticed at the restaurant. "Detective fiction is the highest recreation of the overeducated."

"Then I'm sure to like it."

She stood a moment, her hair falling softly around her face. "Well, goodnight." And she was gone.

At breakfast, he said, "Have you ever been to Chesterwood?"

Ellen shook her head. "No, what is it?"

"I have," Timothy interjected. "It's the studio of Daniel Chester French, the sculptor who did the Lincoln Memorial and the Minuteman at Concord."

"It's a museum," Jack said, "up in Stockbridge. It's very pretty. I was thinking of driving up there today. Would anybody like to come?"

"I would," Ellen said.

"Not me, I have some reading I should do." Timothy sounded disappointed. "I'll get Mrs. Prescott to pack you a picnic lunch if you want." He went off to find her.

In the car, he was very aware of her presence. She seemed to be content to sit back and watch the scenery; she didn't seem compelled to fill the silence. Jack had the opposite feeling, though, and when they pulled up to the intersection by the school, he said, "I went to school at Westfield."

"Oh. And your family has a house in town, don't they?"

"Mm-hm." He pointed across the lawn. "That was my dormitory. See the big double window on the corner on the third floor — that was our room."

"Our?" She looked where he was pointing.

"My roommate Jeff and me. He's from New Orleans."

"Did you like Westfield?"

The same question Timothy had asked, the obvious question, he guessed. "Pretty much. It wasn't the best time in my life."

"No, I suppose not, with your parents dying."

She said it so matter-of-factly, as if it were a long-established fact between them. None of his friends would have done that, they all treated his tragedy as if it were still fresh, not to be talked about unless he himself brought it up. But she even pursued the subject. "I remember when it happened — I must have been about seventeen and I read about it in the local papers. I remember seeing you later that summer, at the general store. You looked so normal, just the way you'd always looked — you were wearing shorts and a T-shirt, and old Mrs. Bailey was yelling at you for being barefoot in the store, silly what we remember — and I thought how strange it was that you would be the same. I thought it would have marked you somehow for everyone to see: orphan."

He stiffened a little. "I never liked that word much."

"I'm sorry. I remember it all so clearly. I felt so sorry for you, I thought you were being so brave."

"Oh, I was brave all right," he said bitterly.

"You don't like to talk about it, do you?"

"I don't even like to think about it, to tell you the truth." He found he was holding tight to the wheel, and relaxed a little. "I'm sorry. That was rude."

She didn't make any comment on this. He was grateful to her for abstaining from all the normal responses: Oh, how awful for you, or, It must have been terrible, or even, How did you feel about that. He hated that one most of all, the question TV reporters always insisted on asking the survivors of lurid disasters, and he heard it over and over, as if most of his acquaintances got their conversation from the six o'clock news. He wasn't a charity case, the orphan boy, and the world wasn't entitled to his feelings as a kind of payback for its sympathy. Even if he had known what his feelings were.

"Why did you say, last night, that most men are intimidated by you?"

She looked at him a moment, and then back at the road. "It's not what nice girls do, physics. I learned that when I got my Ph.D. at Columbia, and even more since. I'm supposed to be one of the boys, safe inside a lab coat with my hair in a bun and a pencil stuck behind my ear. They're not sexist in a conventional way, the men I work with. It's as if they've never seen a woman before and don't know how to react. Especially at first it seemed that the only way I would fit in was if I played a role I didn't like."

A tractor was driving slowly on the road in front of them, the farmer bouncing up and down on its exposed seat. The tractor turned off into a field, leaving a smell of fresh dirt in the air. Jack said, "It sounds lonely."

She nodded. "It was at first. And my social life wasn't so wonderful either. I had a boyfriend while I was at Columbia. His name was Michael, he was a lawyer with a small firm in midtown, and he had an apartment in a small building on the East Side. I'd known him in college, but not very well. He's the kind of person who would do the most romantic things — flowers and champagne, dancing and jewelry, he took me to the Empire State Building on our first date — but there was always a distance. I could be with him and still feel that he was a hundred miles away in his own mind." They came to a humpbacked bridge over a small stream, and he dawdled over it, giving them time to look down at the water. Ellen seemed in no hurry to continue, and he wondered if that was all she would tell him, and then she said, "He never slept in my apartment. We went out for almost three years, and he never once slept in my bed — it always had to be in his apartment. He told me he couldn't explain it, so, like a fool, I never pressed him about it. Then, when we broke up, he blamed me for not being forceful enough with him, for letting him push me around."

"Why did you break up?" It seemed so natural to him, to be here, to be talking to her like this. Without any intermediate stage, they seemed to have gotten to a level of intimacy that in his previous experience he had taken months to reach, if he ever had. I've changed, he thought fleetingly. Timothy changed me.

"Oh, he wanted to get married, or he said he did. And I didn't. Not that I have anything against marriage, but it seemed too sudden. I had just gotten my doctorate, I didn't know what was going to happen to me next. His proposal came out of the blue, I couldn't understand why it had to be right at that moment for him. He got impatient and we broke up." She laughed a little harshly. "I saw him recently, at the Harvard Club. He has a wife and a kid now."

"He sounds like kind of a jerk." He squinted as they came out of the shadow of some trees and into the sunlight.

"Well, I'm making him sound like that. It really turned out to be the best thing that could have happened to me. For one thing, it made me much friendlier with my mother."

Jack was surprised. "What do you mean?"

"Well, it always seemed to me that Timothy was Mom's favorite, her special child, the same way I was my father's. Timothy and Mom are sort of dreamy types, literary and intellectual, and Dad and I are both very technical, scientific types. But at that point, I didn't want to have anything to do with men, so I relied on my mother a lot more." He looked at her as she talked, as she leaned back against the door, her head resting on one bent arm, her eyes hidden behind black sunglasses. "It was a silly kind of shock to receive at the age of twenty-eight, but it turned out that my mother is a real human being. I told her all about Michael, and about how lonely it was to be a woman where women weren't wanted. And she told me about how lonely it feels to be the wife of Archer/MacNeill. She's really upset about how badly Dad and Timothy get along. It's something Timothy never understood. He doesn't like it that Mom won't back him up with Dad. Or, if he understands it, he can't quite forgive her for it. Somewhere deep inside he's still a little boy, and he wants to think that he comes first with her even though he knows he doesn't. What do you think?"

He wanted to say to her that he understood, at some deep level of imagination, how she felt about her mother. Because, in the realm of fantasy which was all that was left to him, he had a mother with whom he shared confidences, who loved him, who was his best friend. He started to say something, but couldn't find the words.

Ellen, sensing his difficulty, went on. "It did change my attitude toward work, though. I decided that I'm a woman, whatever my profession, so I was going to act like a woman. I started wearing nice dresses and makeup and perfume — all the things I'd do if I were in a normal job. All that's gotten me is a reputation — Dr. Archer, *femme fatale* — but I don't care. It makes me feel good." She laughed. "That's why I said men are intimidated. Sort of a long-winded answer."

All this time they had been driving through the Berkshires. He had avoided Route 7, with its strip malls and traffic lights, and had found instead the unmarked roads of his childhood. The hillsides were covered with trees, or in pastures that tilted at crazy angles, with patches of gray stone showing through grass clipped close by cows. The roads followed the valleys, dipping down suddenly into the coolness of a riverbed or emerging into

wide waterfields. They passed barns built snugly against the road-
side, survivals of an unmotorized age when every extra yard of
driveway had to be fought for. Stone walls lined the roads, some
surmounted by old barbed wire strung between posts as gray and
carved as driftwood, to keep indifferent cattle in or nonexistent
rustlers out. He didn't hurry, he drove almost cautiously (for him),
as if this drive would go on forever. There was nowhere he needed
to get to, no deadline, only the road running out to the promise
of a future that was a repetition of this: he could spend his life
simply being with her. And she hadn't asked him for anything,
didn't even seem to expect anything from him.

At Chesterwood, they wandered the grounds aimlessly. Ellen
said, "I don't know why I've told you all this." They were standing
in the garden in front of the studio, in a little enclosed space. "I
don't think most men would understand."

He broke off a flower from a bush and gave it to her. "Why
most men?"

"It seemed to me that one of us was being unreasonable —
either Michael or me. I couldn't help feeling that maybe that was
just the way men are. He wanted some kind of conclusion, something definite. Marriage or nothing, and it almost didn't seem to
matter which. Do you think that's the way men are?"

"I don't know." He stood very still, feeling the sun through his
shirt and hearing a bee in the rosebush: summer heat, summer
sound. "I don't think I'm the best person in the world to talk to
about what men feel." It was hard to concentrate in the warm
garden, and with half his mind he was weighing the effect on her
of anything he might say. He looked at her holding his rose and
was dazzled by the way the sunlight fell around her. Perhaps he'd
been stung and didn't know it, the poison seeping through his
blood. Gardens. He would write an article on the effect of gardens,
insularity and the myth of Eden, unicorn tapestries and the perfection of earthly love. And the memory of a day he'd spent here
with his mother. "I'm sorry, but I'm feeling kind of — out of it."

"Shall we go inside?" she said mildly. The path led between
bushes with a profusion of large flowers, and then into the studio.
"Do you feel better?" she asked in the interior dimness.

The studio was a large outbuilding, with a huge window filling the upper stories of one wall and a skylight above that. At one end, iron tracks led out through barnlike doors for the transit of marble blocks. I don't know what came over me, he thought. Love.

Ellen walked slowly around the room, occasionally turning on her heel as something struck her — a sketch, a bust, a table with sculptor's tools. She stopped in front of a large carved sculpture, which depicted a young woman, nude, lying on a rock. "Andromeda," she read from the thin metal plaque at its base.

He walked over and stood next to her. The Andromeda was lying on her back, like the sacrifice she was. One leg was bent at the knee with the foot drawn in close to her body, the other hung down from the rock. She might have been sunbathing, but for the hint of chains at her wrist and the tight grip of her fist. At once erotic and helpless, pathetic and innocent, she was mute.

"I've forgotten my mythology," Ellen said. "It's a constellation, of course."

"Cassiopeia, the queen of Ethiopia, boasted that she was more beautiful than the sea nymphs, so Poseidon sent a sea serpent to ravage the country. Only by sacrificing their daughter, Andromeda, could the king and queen appease the god. So Andromeda was chained to the rock to await the monster. At the last minute, Perseus appeared, killed the monster, and rescued the princess." It was one of his favorite stories — as a child he'd seen himself as Perseus, flying through the air with his magic sandals, rescuing the beautiful princess. Now, looking down at her, all he could see was a child, laid out for anyone who would come and take her.

"And they all lived happily ever after?" Ellen prompted.

"Not quite. This is a Greek myth, remember. First he had to deal with the man who'd been engaged to Andromeda. He did that by turning him to stone with the Gorgon's head. Then he killed his grandfather —"

"Why?"

"It was an accident, and according to a prophecy. His grandfather had tried to avoid it by putting him and his mother in a trunk and throwing it into the sea. But in the end, yes, they did live happily ever after."

"It's a beautiful sculpture," she said. "I read that he was eighty-one when he carved it, and he left it unfinished when he died."

"He must have been a spry old goat," Jack said and giggled. "Let's go have lunch."

They got back into the car and drove a little distance to a place where a narrow river neared the road. He parked, and they carried the picnic things across a small field to the water's edge. He spread the blanket and they munched the sandwiches that Mrs. Prescott had made. "Where do you live?" he said, wiping mayonnaise off his fingers.

"I have an apartment on Seventy-fifth Street, between Second and Third."

"Oh? My sister and her family live at Seventy-seventh and Park." And, he thought guiltily, my fiancée lives on Seventy-ninth between Park and Madison.

"Your sister's name is Elizabeth. I remember her too, from when we were all kids. But she's a lot older than you, didn't you say?"

"Ten years. It used to seem like a lifetime. I have a nephew who's sixteen."

She brushed crumbs off her dress and began to peel an apple. "Would you like some? I don't know if I'll ever have nephews. Does Timothy strike you as the marrying type?"

"Why not?" Jack shifted a little, uncomfortable. She wasn't asking him if Timothy was gay — Jack had known all along (even if he hadn't admitted it to himself) that he wasn't. "I've never had sex with a man and I can't imagine ever wanting to," Timothy had said. And "I know what you've been thinking." It was what Jack had been thinking. Not because he particularly wanted to have sex with men, but because it was what most people, men and women, seemed to want from him. He felt a little embarrassed that he had, that first night, imagined Timothy coming to his room in the moonlight, and not even Timothy, just some guy who would want him. It wasn't sex that Timothy wanted from him — in fact, it seemed that Timothy was one of the few people who didn't want anything at all from him. Impulsively, he said, "You know, I really like him. He's a lot different from most of the people I know, you both are. Special."

"Good," she said decisively. "He could use a good friend. Did he tell you about Winchester, and my father and all that?"

Jack nodded.

"Sometimes I think he exaggerates it. That it was really just part of growing up. He did some very strange things."

"Oh? Do tell."

"He'll never forgive me. He used to run around the house naked — he'd come home from swimming and drop his bathing suit in the laundry room and run around without any clothes on. He did it until he was twelve or thirteen. It was his revenge, I think, for maturing so late — he told me once, when he was much older, that the worst thing that ever happened to him was having to change in the locker room with other kids and being the only one with a boy's body." She paused, concentrating on the apple peel, which fell around her wrist in a long ringlet before she cut it off. "It's strange to think of one's brother —"

"What?" He picked up the long peel and chewed on it.

"Growing up. Becoming a man. Having sex." She looked up. "He does?" she asked hopefully.

"As far as I know," Jack answered, not really knowing anything, not sure what she was getting at. Elizabeth would have asked that kind of question as part of her eternal quest for information, which she used to fine-tune her arrangement of all their lives. He thought for a minute of what an extraordinary balancing act that was, all the little pieces — David, Billy, Hank, Jack, the bank, their friends, their families — all of them wanting to move in different and unpredictable directions. All of the pieces rubbing against one another, pushing or shoving or threatening to burst out of the press altogether, but the whole kept in order by Elizabeth's ceaseless vigilance. He had never before quite appreciated the scope of her efforts, where a single wrong move could bring the whole structure into peril. But Ellen's question, by contrast, had been natural, the product of her curiosity rather than her system.

She cut a wedge from the apple. "He's always been secretive about his girlfriends, even with me. I don't know why."

"He said there were parts of his life he liked to keep to himself. To keep away from your father."

She said impatiently, "I wish he'd get over that. It's a stage all kids have to go through, I think, hating their parents, but in his case it's gone on too long."

He thought of Timothy, and then of Hank. And then of himself: if they're around to hate. He lay back on the blanket and looked up at the treetops. There was a soft breeze, and the leaves were in constant motion. He heard Ellen get up and walk away, but he didn't feel any need to follow or even to look where she was going. He rolled onto his side and took out his little notepad from his hip pocket. Under the message he had scrawled in Central Park on his birthday the week before, he wrote: "There is something majestic about the crowns of trees whether they be storm-tossed or still. You may have the stars, if you leave me the tree-tops." It was corny, fakely Emersonian. He put the pad back into his pocket and lay down again, closing his eyes. He could see her next to him, still, the apple in her hand. The curve of her shoulder as it emerged from her dress. The softness of her skin, and how it would feel to touch her. A day, he thought. He'd known her less than a day and already he could imagine her, how it would be to stroke her hair, to hold her in his arms with his chest against hers, to kiss her.

In the car on the way home, he said, "Did you really want to marry him? Michael, I mean." He had thought about this a lot while he lay on the picnic blanket and she explored the shore of the stream. She had told him the story very deliberately, as if there was some meaning beyond the obvious encoded within it — meaning for her, of course, but also, he sensed, for him. Like her brother, she was direct, but this outpouring of romantic history had been more than directness. He wanted to know what she had intended by it.

She thought for a while and then said, "When I was a girl, twelve or so, we all waited to get our period for the first time. It was such a milestone, we thought, but we couldn't control it. We could buy bras we didn't really need, and we could shave our armpits more than we had to, but this was something that just happened by itself. Or didn't. We waited, on the edge of something that we knew we didn't understand, no matter how carefully our mothers and gym teachers explained it. And I remember feeling that it couldn't come soon enough but also thinking that I didn't want it to come at all." She paused and said, "Is it like that for boys?"

He thought of himself at that age, and all he could see was a mass of impatience. Nothing had happened fast enough for him, he'd wanted all the changes at once, he and Dougie had talked about everything, especially when Dougie started having dreams and Jack didn't. He kept reading the part in the book where it said that kids grow up differently; besides, Dougie was three months older than he was (which helped, but only until three months had passed). It had finally happened in a sleeping bag in a tent on a mountain in New Hampshire; he'd awakened to the memory of a girl he couldn't name and the fierce jetting of semen against his belly. After a moment's surprise at how damp it felt, how much there seemed to be, he felt an overwhelming outrage that it had happened while he was asleep. It wasn't until later that he learned how to make it happen while he was awake.

She hadn't answered his question, or maybe she had in an oblique way. Men gave hard answers, he thought. Women unfolded their lives.

"Look," she said. "There's a tag sale. Let's stop."

In the front yard of a farmhouse, old scratched wooden tables had been set up, and on them was piled the accumulated junk of a family. There were boxes with books, broken-spined paperbacks of the romance genre with luridly lighted pictures on the covers, children's books, and a whole library of marketing textbooks. Another table held kitchen implements, broad-bladed knives with tired wooden handles, an aluminum orange juicer, a rusted wire whisk, and one of those all-purpose machines that are advertised on late-night television — "It slices and dices and chops and cuts and if you act now we'll include at no extra cost this genuine —" He laughed, and Ellen looked at him from across the yard. A pile of old board games was on the next table, and he looked, wondering if there might be a vintage Monopoly set or an original Scrabble board. Then he saw a shoebox full of baseball cards. They were from the early seventies, the high time of his own baseball consciousness, meticulously arranged by team, and he browsed through them happily, remembering Boog Powell and Andy Etchebarren, Yastrzemski and Lonborg, Clemente and Steve Blass, and most of all the Yankees: Munson and White and Blomberg and Michael, and his hero, Bobby Murcer. He thought of summer camp, trading baseball cards or flipping them, and he tried to remember what had happened to his collection. Maybe Billy had them. Maybe they'd been lost in the general purging that proceeded under David's methodical direction after his parents died.

"Let's go inside," Ellen said, and he looked up from his shoebox. "There's a quilt for sale."

They went in through the screen door and found themselves in a large room, part kitchen, part sitting room, part family room. "I love old farmhouses," she said, standing in the middle of the floor and looking around. "Someday I'm going to move out of the city for good and live on a farm, in a house like this."

He grinned. "I can't see you riding a tractor around and chasing cows that got away. Not forever."

"I will, though," she said, an edge in her voice, the same kind of stubbornness that Timothy sometimes showed. "I've always wanted to do that someday."

"Let's make an offer, then," he said nonchalantly. "What do you think they'd want for this place?"

The lady of the house came in and took Ellen off to look at the quilt (which she didn't buy) and Jack was left to contemplate life in a farmhouse. No more job with the magazine, no more film reviews, no more benefit balls, no more nights with Boyd and Amy. No more Elizabeth. Who would he be without all of that, he wondered.

As they drove away, he yawned, and she said, "Am I keeping you awake?"

"Sorry. I stayed up late and read *Farewell, My Lovely*."

"You read the whole thing?"

"Yes," he said, looking straight ahead at the road, listening to the wind rushing past them. And then, by way of explanation, even though he assumed that somehow she understood him, he added, "It was the first thing you gave me."

VIII

WHEN THEY GOT BACK to the house, Timothy was waiting for them, practically hopping up and down on the doorstep. "Where the hell have you been?"

"Why?" Ellen asked. "What is it?"

"Lois called. She invited herself over for dinner. I tried to talk her out of it, but you know Lois."

Ellen walked into the big front hall, shaking her hair, which was tangled from the wind. "She's not so bad."

"Not for you, she's your friend." He appealed to Jack. "This friend of Ellen's who has this thing for me. No matter what I do, she keeps trying."

He looked almost comical, and Jack grinned. "Let's dust her. Go out for burgers or something."

"What a great idea," Timothy groaned. "I wish I'd thought of it before."

"Why?" Ellen put her sunglasses down on a side table. She moved very deliberately, he thought, as if she were still lingering over their day together. She was living (for him anyway) on a different plane, untouched by all of Timothy's dismay.

"After she called, Andrew phoned, he has some drawings he wants to drop off for Dad. So I invited him and Tony for dinner." When Ellen wrinkled her nose, Timothy said, "Well, I needed some air cover and Andrew is always good for that. He never stops talking. And by the way, Andrew's cousin is staying with them —"

"Man or woman?"

"Woman, and she's coming too." He ran down like an unwound watch.

"Well, I hope Mrs. Prescott is ready for them. And we were having such a nice day." She smiled at Jack. "Andrew Toller is a decorator —"

Jack said, "I've heard of him."

"Well, he's done a lot of work with my father. Tony is his lover. I don't know anything about the cousin. Would you like to bow out and go for hamburgers?"

More than anything, he thought, he didn't want to meet these people, to have the almost perfect privacy of the last week invaded. But more even than that, he wanted to be with her. He said teasingly, "I'll gallantly squire the cousin, leaving Timothy to your friend."

"I won't even sit next to her at the table, she, like —" Timothy shuddered. "I told you I hate women who flirt."

Ellen walked over and took him by the shoulders. "Don't worry. She's not so terrible." She reached up and kissed his cheek. "Jack and I will protect you."

"Well, they'll be here in half an hour, so you'd better get ready."

She had said "Jack and I" as if they were a unit, Jack thought. He hadn't known that he wanted her to say that, and he didn't think she meant anything by it, but to him it was full of import. He was collecting these moments, these firsts, with the confidence that he would be looking back on them with her years later. Tell our grandchildren. He watched her as she drifted up the staircase, lit by the window on the landing. He said, "Timothy."

"What?"

"Well, I didn't bring a lot of stuff with me. I wore my only good shirt to dinner last night. I wouldn't exactly feel comfortable in a tennis shirt."

"'s OK. I'll bring some stuff to your room. We're about the same size."

"Thanks." He went upstairs to shower. He was dreading the evening, like a convalescent after a breakdown making his first foray into society, wondering if the mental connections would stand the test, wondering if anyone would notice if his hands shook a little or if he laughed too loudly. What he really wanted, what he liked to do before going to parties, was to have a bath, lie sleepily in hot water while steam rose around him. But there wasn't enough time for that, so instead he stood directly under the stream of hot water, letting it hit hard on the top of his skull, running down over his face with a kind of mesmerizing effect.

He came out of the bathroom and put on a pair of boxer shorts, and then Timothy came in with a pile of clothes. He handed them to Jack and went to the window and looked out. Jack said, "Have the guests arrived? Or perhaps I should say, your guest."

"Don't tease me, OK?"

"Sorry." He sat down on the bed. "Are you OK?"

Timothy nodded.

"Well, could you turn around and look at me, then. Just so I know for sure."

Timothy turned, then went and sat in the rocking chair. He rested one ankle on his knee and began picking at the sole of his shoe. Jack, shirtless still, said, "Do you want to tell me what's up?"

"It's Lois. A few years ago we were at a wedding in New York, one of Ellen's roommates from Harvard. I asked Lois to dance — I was asking all the women, you know." Jack could imagine him politely inviting each of them in turn, doing his best to make sure no one was left out, it was what he did at Val's. "I didn't realize that she was kind of drunk, and while we were dancing, she kept letting her hands slide down over my ass and all, and then when we went back to the table, she put her arm around me and started — caressing me, I guess, in a very sexual way. I felt like a complete jerk."

"Well?"

"I don't know." He looked away from Jack. The stretched-out light of the late sun touched his face and he squinted a little. "The thing is, all the time she was — fondling me like that, I didn't feel anything, except totally uncomfortable. I never know how to act around her. I always think she's going to do it again, embarrass me in front of people."

"Embarrass you?" Jack snorted. "It's more likely to embarrass her. If she can be embarrassed."

"I just didn't like the feeling that she thought I was there to be — women talk about being sex objects, that's exactly how I felt."

Yes, well, Jack thought. He knew a little about that himself. Stock in trade. "If I were you, I'd think about what kind of person would do that to another person. After all, it's not the victim's fault." Unless the victim volunteered, put himself out to be caught. "What should I wear here?"

Timothy got up and they looked through the pile. "I'm not sure if my shirts'll fit you."

Jack put one on, and they surveyed the result. "I don't know."

Timothy sorted through the pile. "Here, this'll hide the problem." He picked up a cotton sweater with thin blue stripes, and Jack put it on. "Your collar's not straight," Timothy said. "Let me fix it for you." He reached up and straightened it, his hand brushing the back of Jack's neck, the fringe of his hair. They stood for a minute, very close, looking into each other's faces. Jack thought, with another person, in a previous life, this would dissolve into a bout of meaningless sex. It was a measure for him of how far he'd come in the last week, even in the last day, that that possibility now seemed so remote as to be almost indistinguishable. Timothy first, and then Ellen, had seemed to offer him another world, a country such as Sinbad might have found, full of treasure and danger — now, for a moment, he had a view of what he would be leaving behind. He turned away from Timothy and pulled a brush roughly through his hair. "Once more unto the breach, dear friends."

When they got down to the library, he paused in the doorway, letting Timothy go in first. Ellen was standing at the tray in the corner, mixing a couple of drinks. The couch was in the possession of a small, square woman in black pants and a red blouse. "Timothy," she said loudly, "how wonderful to see you. Thanks so much for the invitation."

"Hello, Lois. I'm glad you could make it."

"But where's your friend, I'm dying to meet him. Such an interesting person, don't you think?"

Jack had started into the room already, so he had to make his entrance on that ridiculous note. After what Timothy had told him, it didn't make him think any more kindly of her.

"Jack," Timothy said. "Come meet Lois Winters."

"How do you do." He held out his hand.

"Well, I'm thrilled to meet you. Timothy never told me he knew the famous John Newland. I read your pieces in the magazine faithfully. Come sit down next to me." She patted the couch, and for Timothy's sake he sat. He knew how this game played out — she would compliment him on his writing, wonder "what it was like" to be a writer, comment that she wrote poetry or had a theory of film criticism or found nightclubs too boring. He decided to head her off at the pass. "Oh, let's talk about you. I'm sure you're much more interesting."

"Me?" She gave a contradicting laugh, daring him to take it back. "Why do you think I'm interesting?"

"Well, didn't Timothy tell me that you're an anthropologist?"

She was taken aback. "I don't know what Timothy told you, but I'm not an anthropologist."

"Well, an archaeologist then. I always get these 'ologists mixed up." Behind him he heard Timothy strangle a laugh. "I once wanted to be an archaeologist — digging through layers of history to find some unravished bride of quietness. Do you know that there's a Venus de Milo upstairs in the attic? An Attic shape, in fact."

"But —"

"That's right," Ellen said, handing Lois a glass. "How do you know that, Jack?"

"Timothy and I were up there looking for something the other day. It's a fascinating story. You should tell it, Ellen." And in the way he said her name, he hinted at more complicity than could be accounted for by the joke they were playing on poor Lois.

"But —"

"Listen," Ellen said, and she began telling the story of the armed Venus.

Timothy perched on the sofa arm next to him. "Do you give lessons?"

"I made it up as I went along. Pure stream of consciousness. It was a little rude, I'll have to make it up to her somehow. What does a guy have to do to get a drink around here?"

"Stand up, walk over to the tray, and pour."

As he got up, he heard the second group of guests arriving. Feeling he'd done enough for the moment, he decided to make himself a vodka martini. He didn't drink martinis often (he used to say that he liked them too much for a regular drink), but sometimes he treated himself. It had the added advantage that it took longer to mix than straight bourbon, and he kept his back resolutely turned until he'd finished shaking the cocktail and had taken a swallow. Behind him, Timothy said, "Jack, meet Tony Michaels."

Tony was a very thin, short man, a little older than Jack, with bleached blond hair (it looked tatty, Jack thought, next to Timothy's) and a willowy air about him. "And this is Andrew Toller." He and Jack shook hands. "And this — where?" Timothy looked around for a moment. "Oh. Come meet Andrew's cousin. God, I've forgotten her name," he said softly, indicating the young woman standing next to Ellen.

"Susan Howell," Jack supplied, and she looked up. "Hey, Howell."

"Hey, Newland."

"You know each other?"

"We went to college together."

"A reunion," Andrew announced. "I've never been to a reunion — they don't have them at the school I went to, and then, I never graduated. What are you two going to do — sing 'Boola Boola'? Or is there some special college cheer? Do we wave banners?" He was probably six or seven years older than Tony, and better looking, dark with dark eyes, and obviously in command of the situation — any situation. Jack could see why Timothy wanted him for cover. "Cousin Susan," he went on, "I gain new respect for you every day."

"That," she said, giving it back to him, "implies you had very little to begin with. Or else that you overrate John's importance."

"Oh, not his importance," Tony said, appearing at Andrew's elbow and looking Jack over. "Surely not his importance."

"Don't be bitchy, Tony. Timothy, be a good boy and get us something to drink. Tony's on this odd diet and will only drink clear things — aquavit, poire William, slivovitz — I forget what else. You'd better get him a vodka. And I'll have a Perrier, I want to keep my wits about me tonight. Cousin Susan —?"

"You used to drink bourbon," Jack said.

"And so did you." She looked quizzically at his martini glass. "I still do."

"I'll get it," Jack said. When he came back with it, he looked over at Ellen, who was sitting next to Lois on the couch. Her eyes caught his, and she smiled deprecatingly, as if dismissing the importance of all these people. He took a deep breath and gave the glass to Susan.

Andrew had pounced on Lois as the most likely target. "Well, Lois. Tell us how you know Ellen."

"We went to college together." Lois was looking at Andrew suspiciously, wondering perhaps, after her earlier encounter with Jack, why she had again been singled out.

"Another reunion. Fair Harvard. On the banks of the Charles. I've often wondered who Charles was. Is it a first name or a last? A king? Perhaps we should call it the Chuck in honor of our more informal society. And speaking of kings, Ellen, what does your father think of Prince Charles and his rantings about architecture? I rather liked that business about 'a carbuncle on the face of an old friend.' It has a sort of putridness that one somehow doesn't expect from royalty. Or does one? Timothy, you're our expert on British nobility, what about that friend of yours, the earl or the duke or whatever. Are they all so subtly disgusting?"

Jack was enjoying the show — he knew the type. Wind him up and set him talking, and he would touch on every subject of fashion in turn, waiting indifferently for someone to take him up on some topic, pausing, as he had now, only for a feed line.

"Viscount," Timothy said, playing along. "There is nothing subtle about the aristocracy when they want to be disgusting. They have that typical English fascination with excrement, for example. Carbuncle probably came from a speech writer."

"He probably would have said puss-filled." Andrew reached for his drink and then, in a transition that Jack scored as a perfect ten, said, "And so, Lois, what do you do?"

Jack felt Timothy nudge him, so he said, "Lois is an anthropologist." He saw Ellen shake her head at him.

"But —"

"Now that's fascinating," Andrew pursued. "I'm very interested in the primitive — I'm always telling Tony that Native American is the coming thing in design. Although I don't see Archer/MacNeill building tepees. Or perhaps you prefer to follow Margaret Mead, observing the Maoris in their nuclear-free zone of bizarre sexual practices. Incest, isn't it? Funny how the child molesters of our world go to prison for behavior that would be considered perfectly normal in Papua New Guinea. Or do you make a study of African society? I was in Africa once — have I ever told you —"

Mrs. Prescott interrupted him at that moment to announce dinner, and they trooped into the dining room. Ellen placed Lois between Tony and Andrew, and Jack next to Susan. Andrew, taking the change of scene in stride, went on with his story.

"I was in Paris — it was ages ago, I was this innocent boy with my hair much too long, all agog in the City of Light, living in a tiny attic room in Montmartre — too first act of *Bohème* —" here he looked at Jack, who nodded, "and peddling my —"

"Careful, Andrew," Tony said.

"— my designs to anyone who would look. I had this grand dream that some sickeningly rich Frenchman, a sort of Yves Montand with a title and race cars, would hire me to redecorate his chateau and then throw a huge party. I saw myself standing at the top of the grand staircase with a glass of champagne and an outrageous suit on with all Paris admiring my work. That was my great dream." For a moment he sounded almost wistful about it, the mask slipping. He looked at Jack again. "What's your dream, John?"

But if he'd been hoping to catch him off guard, it didn't work. Jack was too practiced at this social game, he'd sat through too many dinners in sleek apartments above Park Avenue to get caught. It didn't matter what he said as long as he didn't reveal anything about himself. "I want to win the Nobel Prize for Advertising."

"A worthy ambition." Ellen was talking to Tony, and Timothy was talking to Susan, but Andrew went on, relying on them to return to him when their own conversations flagged, and not really caring if they did. He would talk to the wind, Jack thought, to distract the clouds.

"One day I met a man who owned a coffee plantation in the Ivory Coast and he invited me to visit him. I had to go to the most tiny little consulate you've ever seen for a visa, and they kept me waiting all day. I sometimes think a country's bureaucracy is in inverse proportion to its importance — although what that says about this country, where it can take three months to get a permit to move a wall — and then I had to get some kind of injection, I had a lump the size of a walnut on my arm from the swelling. Then I flew to Morocco and got on this tiny airplane that was full of crates with Oxfam stencils all over them — I half expected some Arab with a pig to get on with me. Only Moslems don't eat pork, do they?"

They were well into their meal by now. Nobody seemed the least bit perturbed at the length to which Andrew ran on. He had a very plastic face, all part of his act, and the others seemed content to be entertained while they solved the carving problems presented by a game hen. Only Lois, the putative cause of this torrent of African lore (and he had only just reached Africa), seemed uneasy.

Jack stopped paying attention. He was beginning to sense something slipping a little in Andrew's performance — either Andrew was getting bored, or Jack was. He listened a moment to Ellen and Tony, who were talking politics. "My only point," Ellen was saying, "is that SDI will have tremendous theoretical and technological value, even if it's not a success."

"And fund your research, too," Tony said.

"My research is funded anyway, Tony." She lifted her wine goblet and held it in midair a moment, her bare arm and wrist and hand making a nice curve.

Jack smiled to himself. He turned to Susan, who was sitting next to him. "It's nice to see you again."

She looked at him, amused. "Is that the best you can do?"

"Pretty weak, I admit it." He wasn't sure how she would feel about him after all this time, what she might say about the past they had shared. "What would you like me to say? Something witty yet profound? trenchant yet humorous?"

"Sounds like you're auditioning to be David Brinkley."

He shook his head. "I don't have the jowls for it."

She laughed. "Maybe we'll find a quiet corner somewhere, later, and catch up on old times."

The plates having been cleared, Andrew reclaimed everyone's attention. "So there I was, on this plantation, the hottest place on earth, just a clearing in the forest, these enormous trees. I would lie on a cot in my bungalow with my arms and legs spread out, totally naked, and still I'd sweat like a pig — do pigs sweat, really? —"

Tony interrupted him. "That's the second extraneous pig you've introduced into this story. Is it becoming a thing with you?"

"Only since I met you, Tony." And he went on without missing a beat. "There was no running water, and the only shower was a sort of a spigot attached to a tree, and a ring with a curtain around it. I went out there the first morning and got under it. Well, I must have brushed against the curtain, because all of a sudden a spider the size of New Jersey fell out on the floor next to me. All I could imagine was it crawling up my leg and biting my weenie, and then where would I be? So I got out of there as quickly as I could. Of course, it was time for a shift change or something and the whole place was full of these huge black men going out to the fields to pick coffee or whatever they do, and here's this one little white boy running bare-assed, grabbing his crotch, the spider chasing me the whole way — it was neck and neck, so to speak, until I got to the bungalow and slammed the door. I could hear it prowling around for hours afterwards."

They all laughed, except Tony, and Ellen said, "Let's go into the living room and have coffee."

Jack let the women precede him, then made the mistake of sitting down too quickly, and immediately Lois sat next to him. "Now, John, I want to ask you something." She had an intense look, and he steeled himself for the usual questions — he would be civil, at least, it was the penance he owed for teasing her before. She said, "I read your review of the Gamble premiere. It was devastating. Did you see it, Ellen? It had the most vicious first sentence, do you remember, John?"

He quoted for her, something he hated to do, it was show-offy and self-indulgent, but it was another part of his punishment: "It was the premiere of John David Gamble's 'Hymn to the Outer Planets' and the crowds were flocking from the hall in record numbers." He heard Timothy laugh from across the room.

"Yes, it is very amusing," Lois said tightly. "What I wanted to ask you is — do you know John Gamble?"

"Not from Adam."

"Well, he happens to be a good friend of mine. And he was crushed by your review."

Oh Jesus, he thought, a groupie. "No he wasn't. Or at least, if he was, he shouldn't be presenting his work to the public."

"I agree with that," Andrew said, joining the conversation from out of nowhere.

"It wasn't that you didn't like the music," Lois went on doggedly. "It was that you didn't take it seriously."

This, he thought, was the time to sidestep the whole discussion with a well-aimed impertinence, something that would make everyone laugh and divert attention. He was reaching into his quiver for the *mot juste* when he suddenly thought, rebelliously, I don't have to hide from this person, and I don't have to defend myself. He had meant what he'd said about the music. "Yes, Lois, that's exactly right. It didn't deserve to be taken seriously."

"Oh come on, John. Gamble slaved over that piece. Don't you have any idea of what he's trying to do? He has a whole new concept of music, and because of people like you his ideas are being stifled."

"Ideas." He shook his head and frowned. "What is he, a composer or an ideologue?"

"All great artists embody a theory about art," Lois said sententiously. "Beethoven, for example, and Romanticism."

"No. The theory came after. Beethoven wasn't a Romantic until some critic called him one." He looked up at the warmly lit room, with its deep-cushioned furniture and the paintings on the wall and the smell of coffee from the silver service in front of Ellen. He thought, this is the sort of room for this kind of conversation — remembering Timothy's eccentric ancestors with their collections embalmed in the attic. Not the kind of conversation he ordinarily had after the dinner parties he and Kate attended. He realized that they were waiting for him to go on. He amended, weighing his words, "Or, if he had a theory, it wasn't the master of his music. His artistic conception was the master, not some ideology. The music mattered, and that's why it's sublime. With Gamble, with a lot of modern composers, the ideology matters and not the music, and so we get rhythm instead of melody and repetition instead of structure, without the least concern for whether anyone can listen to the stuff. Beauty and harmony — artistic harmony — are totally lost."

"Well," she said huffily, "if it's beauty and harmony you want."

"Of course it is. What else is any art about if not about beauty and harmony?" Lois had obviously assumed that he hadn't thought about this before he wrote the review, that he had just been flippant and sarcastic. Well, a lot of people thought that about him, and he didn't exactly discourage them. He saw Andrew watching him closely, and said, "Take interior design. There's a whole history of beautiful work that one can draw on — walk through the period rooms at the Metropolitan some day. Would you jettison all that in favor of some theoretical construct?"

Timothy, sitting cross-legged on the floor, tipped his head up and frowned. "Are you saying that you reject modernism?"

Ellen laughed. "Not in this house, I hope. My father would have a stroke."

He kept his gaze on her hands as she quietly poured out the coffee into demitasse cups, and laid a little shell-shaped spoon on each saucer. He had a moment of intense longing — to get rid of all these people and be alone on that soft couch with her. Not yet, he thought, but soon. "I don't reject modernism at all, Timothy. Not in the sense that Eliot, for example, embodied it. Modernism was a reaction, it denied traditional forms and even meanings, but at least it was cognizant of tradition. Who was more steeped in cultural icons than Eliot, iconoclast that he was?"

"So what are you saying?" Lois made one last attempt. "On the one hand you're a modernist, on the other you make fun of John Gamble. Which is it?"

"Gamble isn't a modernist, he's an ideologue, an egotist with a theory, is all. If he wants to be a composer, then he should be willing to be judged by musical standards, including beauty and harmony, and not by the standards he sets for himself. But for him, the theory is more important. He might just as well have written an essay about metronomic dissonance — you see, I do understand what he's trying to do. Music, any art, is essentially human and personal, and ideologues don't believe in anything human. They don't believe in anything larger than themselves, only in their theories. The primacy of the idea."

"The Nazis tried that," Timothy said.

"And the communists."

"What do you believe in, John?" Andrew said.

It was a question he didn't want to answer, not ever, but he deserved it for being so emphatic. Ellen, sensing his discomfort, or perhaps simply having decided that the conversation had gone far enough, said, "The communists. Isn't it incredible what's happening in Poland?"

He saw Andrew watching him still, but Ellen had effectively changed the subject. There followed, as Ellen refilled coffee cups and Timothy passed after-dinner drinks (Jack didn't want one then), a general rearranging of groupings, and Jack was left standing next to Susan. "Still laying down the law, John?"

"You could have helped me out a little." They had had conversations like that at Yale, about the Nature of Art and the Purpose of Aesthetics.

"It's nice out," she said. "Shall we go for a walk?"

He looked over at Ellen, and Susan caught the glance. "Do you have to ask permission?"

"No."

She said, "I'm going to the bathroom. I'll meet you outside in a minute."

He went out through the French doors and onto the flagstone terrace and stood for a moment, inhaling the night air, which was damp and tinged with mist. Then he stepped down onto the lawn.

IX

THE WHOLE VALLEY in front of him waited like an empty amphitheater, the opposing hills blackly overlooking the little lake, which gleamed in the moonlight like a hard surface, awaiting a titanic actor who would step forth from the shadows and declaim the opening lines of some great play: "I am Dionysos, son of Zeus," or more bluntly, "Who's there?" He had waited for her once before in a theater, also empty except for the corrupt sonorities of Kurt Weill from the stage band, rehearsing the music from *The Happy End*.

He heard her step on the terrace and turned. "Hey, Howell," he said softly.

"Hey, Newland. It's good to see you. We've lost touch."

"You didn't answer my letters. I thought you were still angry with me."

"After all these years? How long has it been?"

"Shall we take a walk in the garden?" He gestured toward the fish pond, and they walked together over the grass. "Six years."

"I'm a lousy correspondent."

The garden stretched out in front of them, blotched with black moonshadows. He thought of a night with Kate and Boyd and Amy at some club with a strobe light, dancers seeming to move in the black-and-white light like figures in a Mack Sennett comedy, and Boyd saying over and over in a bored voice, "This is bush, let's go somewhere else." This black and white moonlight was the original of that copy. "Are you still angry with me?"

"It was six years ago, John."

"We seem to be going around in circles." The petals of the flowers were bleached of all color in that light.

"Does it matter to you so much?" she asked.

"You said some nasty things to me."

"Oh," she said mockingly. "Who's angry with whom?"

"I didn't mean for anybody to get hurt."

"Someone did, though."

She means Harriet Singer, he thought, her roommate at Yale.

It was during their junior year. He'd been sitting early one morning in the nearly empty dining hall, a very cold-looking sun streaming across the common room from the windows that looked out into the Berkeley courtyard. Harriet had come in, wearing her mink coat, which was the subject of endless gossip among the other women of the college, and looking as best she could, that semester, like Tallulah Bankhead. Ignoring the empty tables, she walked, carrying a coffee cup, the length of the dining hall and sat down next to him. She lit a cigarette and blew the smoke into the space above his head. "I have a terrible hangover," she said.

She looked perfect and she knew it. He didn't say anything, he had a hangover too.

She dropped her cigarette into her coffee. "I have a rehearsal to go to. Come with me?"

He stood up, feeling lost in his parka and scarf. He had hardly spoken to her before. Now he was following her to a rehearsal. Of what? he wondered. They walked out of the college and across the street. The campus seemed empty, even for a Saturday morning, and a nasty wind blew a newspaper up against the iron fence of the Old Campus. "What are you rehearsing?"

"*Romeo and Juliet.*"

They turned up Library Street, the flagstone walk between the moats and gothic walls of Branford and Jonathan Edwards, which always made him think of a lane in a medieval town. "What do you want me for?"

"If you have to ask, I'm wasting my time."

At the Dramat, she was greeted with a flurry of kisses by a variety of people in various states of Saturday morning dishabille, her fur coat standing out, as she wanted it to. She stripped it off and handed it to Jack. "Watch this for me, will you."

The crowd on the stage sorted itself out, leaving him standing awkwardly to one side. He went down the steps and sat in the darkened auditorium. A tall boy with an enormous sweatshirt took charge and began the rehearsal. It wasn't *Romeo and Juliet* at all, it was some play Jack didn't know. At one point the director called out, "Peter, where's Peter? He's always late, what are we going to do? We have to be out of here by noon — where is he?"

A voice called lazily from the back of the auditorium, "No need to mess in your pants, Josh, I'm right here. Just give me a minute to wake up." The boy sauntered to the front, and Jack recognized him: Peter Callahan. He and Harriet had been paired in a couple of college productions — Jack had seen them in one — and the reviewer in the *Daily News*, striving for either esoterica or credibility, had referred to them as "our Lunts, perfectly matched on stage."

After the rehearsal, Harriet retrieved Jack and her coat. He said, "How's your hangover?"

"It's your fault that I have it at all," she said, banging through the swinging doors and out into the freezing brightness of the street.

"My fault?" He was fumbling with the zipper of his parka and trying to keep up with her.

"I tried to make myself as available as possible last night, but you hardly looked. So I got drunk instead."

"I didn't know."

They stopped at a corner for a light. She buried her chin in the collar of her coat and with one finger pushed back a lock of hair from her face. "Is that an act you have? Sitting in the corner, looking devastating, staring out at everyone with those green eyes of yours — God, what I wouldn't do with eyes like that, careers have been made with less. What were you waiting for?"

"It's not an act," he said, answering what seemed to be the easiest of her questions. "It's the way I am."

"Oh, the way you are." She led the way across the street, past the Art Gallery. "I'm starving. Will you buy me lunch?"

"Sure."

They went across Chapel Street and into a bookstore that had tiny round tables squeezed in among the bookshelves, where sandwiches of brie or curried chicken salad on thick slices of French bread could be had along with exotic and aromatic coffee. Harriet settled down with much show, spreading her coat lavishly over the back of her bentwood chair. "It's my prop," she said, indicating the coat.

"So I've noticed."

She put one elbow on the table, rested her chin on her open palm. "And what's your prop?"

"Don't have one. I don't even smoke."

She looked at his face. "Except those eyes."

"What? A prop? Or smoking?"

"Either. Both." She shrugged, and opened her purse, taking out a box of Dunhill cigarettes. "I once read one of those books on teenagers, you know, one of those books your parents have that tells them what's happening to their kids. It was hopeless. But I remember something from it —" he lit her cigarette from the matchbook on the table, and she screwed up her eyes against the smoke "— that teenagers find aloofness very attractive, that the most popular kids are the ones who are the most elusive."

"Is that a paradox? Or just the law of supply and demand?"

She had, it seemed, constructed a thin veil of smoke between them, and now she looked at him through it. "Is that your game?"

"I don't have a game."

"I could pretend to accept that, anyway." And then, as if that part of their conversation had never taken place, she said, "I woke up with a hangover this morning and the feeling that my availability hadn't registered with you. So I decided to see if you were available. It comes to the same thing in the end. Are you?"

"Available for what?" he hedged.

"Dinner. A movie?"

"I guess so."

He had gone out with other women at Yale — when he wrote to Ripley that he was involved in a "relationship," Ripley wrote back angrily that of course he was in a "relationship," but what kind of relationship was it? The next time it happened, Jack used the word "affair," which had a mendaciously grown-up sound. Those other girls, he now thought, had been playing house. One of them loved to sit around at night in the living room of his suite in her nightgown and bathrobe, her hair wet from the shower and bound up in a towel, laughing with his roommates. Another carried him off to the Cross Campus Library, key undergraduate hangout, where they could study together and everyone could see them. She especially liked it when he spent the night in her room, so that they could have breakfast with her friends (it wasn't to show him off, he thought, but rather to make him part of the normality of her life). Another borrowed the master's kitchen and dragged him along to cook meals, instructing him from the depths of a cookbook, and laughingly kissed confectioner's sugar off his nose. One of his roommates during his sophomore and junior years was a very cute, very shy boy, and each of Jack's girlfriends in turn had adopted him as a kind of mascot, a third wheel who went everywhere with them as if he were their child.

Harriet, the great actress, would have none of this, wanted nothing mundane, held nothing back. Everything they did together was charged with immediacy and abandon. He compared her to Cleopatra, whom they were studying in their Shakespeare class: not treacherous or fickle, fleeing on a whim from the battle, but a blazing lover, caring nothing for convention or life, who would shake the very foundations of the world with the perfection of her love. That was how she infected him, with a kind of feverish excitement, which showed itself at least partly in rhetoric that seemed even at the time overheated.

"You are like Cleopatra," he murmured to her one night in bed.

She sat up immediately. "What do you mean? That I'm poison for any man?"

He shook his head, full of his own dream. "That you would do anything for love and not care what the consequences were."

She loved that. It was the way she saw herself. She got up from the bed, and naked, crossed the room to her desk. She came back with her copy of the play. Her hair was tangled around her face, and he smiled wildly as he watched her. She read: "If it be love indeed, tell me how much."

He had picked the lines out on first reading them, and now he recited from memory. "There's beggary in the love that can be reckon'd."

She appreciated that too, knowing why he had learned them. "I'll set a bourn how far to be beloved."

He reached for her, and finished the exchange: "Then must thou needs find out new heaven, new earth." With her, sometimes, even that extravagance seemed possible.

She was uninhibited in bed, well instructed in a way that the other girls he'd known hadn't been. She knew what she liked and didn't hesitate to tell him, assuming that he wanted to learn what he didn't already know (and in fact, aside from the general concepts he had picked up from books, he didn't know very much, other than the basic act itself). For Harriet, sex was a kind of prolonged performance, taking up whole blocks of time with multiple variations on the theme. He would come away from her bed dazed, punch-drunk almost, and reel through the campus feeling weak. But he loved it — he had never thought of these things as real, only as stories to be swapped with other boys who, he'd half-suspected, had mostly been lying to him. Now they took on a reality that he held to himself like a secret.

That summer, between his junior and senior years, he commuted from Manhattan, where he was working at his father's old law firm and hating it, to a small town in upstate New York, where she was working in summer stock at a community college. The weeks were dull, the city was hot, and he was staying with David while Elizabeth and the boys were in Westfield. It was strange, sleeping in Billy's bed, surrounded by the remembered life of a nine-year-old, and dreaming of Harriet. Even stranger was David's presence — he had never seemed more impossibly older, and there was no way Jack could explain to him this experience that had utterly, he thought, transformed his life. David was as stolid and certain as always, full of the slow days at the bank, summer time, when all of the clients and most of the senior managers went to Newport or the Hamptons, while David with his exaggerated sense of duty remained behind, always willing to mind Thomas Welland's fort for him. Jack and David watched ball games together on TV, they talked awkwardly about politics, he tried desperately to find some point of contact, but there wasn't one. He listened while David talked, but all the time he was thinking, I want to be with Harriet, if I leave now I can be there by midnight, spend a few hours with her and then be back in time for work; but he didn't go. David, he suspected, disapproved of Harriet, whom he'd never met and knew only through Jack's theatrical weekend absences, David never having been theatrical in anything. When the summer ended, Jack went back early to

New Haven and was waiting for her on the train platform when she arrived. They rushed off to his new room, a single, high up under the roof at Berkeley.

As much time as they spent together, they were often not alone. She was a star, he told himself, she needed a firmament in which to glitter. They were part of a group — Harriet's roommate Susan; Peter Callahan and his latest girlfriend; a pair of identical twin brothers, Marco and Nicco, who had a juggling and magic act they performed from time to time at the Cabaret; people's girlfriends and boyfriends and roommates who tagged along. They would all meet for dinner in one or another of the college dining rooms, or go to movies, or cluster together at parties that other people gave. There seemed to be a demarcation between the theater people and all the others, but Jack, for some reason, crossed the line. The company — actors, directors, techies, most majoring in drama — at first ignored him as Harriet's shadow, the boy who held her coat during rehearsals, who sat tongue-tied and stationary while they, privileged by the abandon with which they did everything, moved magically around him. Later, as he became more of a fixture, they gave him little jobs to do — organizing costumes, running errands, hanging lights, even assisting at the light board for *The Happy End*, their major production during the fall of his senior year. He didn't mind that most of this made him little more than an inglorious gofer, he felt only exhilaration in the possession of arcane knowledge. He took everything in, he watched silently, insinuating himself, an unnoticed machine recording every aspect of their mystery. In this house of roles it was the part for which he was fitted: to observe and then, in the silence of the night, to process the observations, drawing his own conclusions.

One of those conclusions was that Harriet's acting was for real. He had that snobbery of intellectual patricians which equates overeager marketing with shabby goods, and he'd thought at first that her renown, even her notoriety, was due as much to her habit of self-promotion as to any real talent. But in Harriet's case the one was merely an extension of the other. It was only gradually that he began to realize that Peter Callahan was an even better actor than Harriet.

He was a tall boy with hair the color of cornsilk, which hung in straight bangs over his forehead. His hands, with long fingers, and his face were very pale, his skin having an almost translucent quality that bordered on waxiness. Peter was as unlike Jack's other friends as Harriet was unlike his old girlfriends. Peter knew nothing about life in New York or boarding schools or the world that Jack's parents had inhabited. He was from Kansas, his father was a mailman in Abilene, and his mother taught elementary school. He was all-American and innocent, a farmboy of the plains, or at least he liked to pretend to be. He walked lazily, affecting a disdain for effort that extended to an unregional drawl and a habit of pretending to fall asleep whenever he was the least bit bored. This proved to be a devastating weapon at parties, where insufficiently interesting girls would sometimes find themselves prattling away at his closed eyes: from this there was no graceful retreat, and Jack noticed that they never came back. But then, when he was acting, the languor disappeared, as if all the energy he hadn't spent offstage was now coiled within him, waiting its moment to strike, keeping the audience wondering when he would release it. He and Harriet were well matched onstage, and Jack sometimes wondered why she had chosen him over Peter, why Peter seemed to involve himself casually with a string of women, why they weren't equally well matched offstage.

Peter was single-minded about acting. "You live for it," Jack said to him, "even more than Harriet does."

"She doesn't live for acting. She lives to be an actress. I live for acting."

He made Jack into a kind of disciple, someone with whom he discussed technique and directors, plays and playwrights. He would drag Jack away on long walks and try out on him different interpretations of whatever he was preparing for acting class. Gradually it occurred to Jack that Peter was trying to fix in his own mind, with words, the lessons he was learning in class or in rehearsals. "I have all these instincts," he said. "But I'm afraid they'll go away. You have to know stuff, not just produce it out of thin air."

"You do know," Jack said definitely, comparing Peter with Ripley. Ripley was always sure of everything, and it never took him any time to become sure. Peter sat, as if fishing patiently by a stream, waiting until his thought came to the surface to be taken. He would do something on stage and then, perhaps days later, come to Jack and explain what he'd done. Intellect working on instinct, Jack wrote in a letter to Ripley, but the instinct came first.

"I can't talk to anyone else about this," Peter said. "I don't know why, but you're the only person who — And you're not even a theater person. Only by marriage. Nobody else would get it."

Harriet hated it when Jack and Peter got into these long discussions. She didn't like to talk shop, as she put it, and she used to break them up whenever she could. One night, they were all in a bar in the basement of a hotel on Chapel Street, and she interrupted their conversation to gossip. "Look at these people, think how involved we all are with one another." She nodded in the direction of Peter's roommate. "Neil, for example. Last year he went out with Toni Phillips, but they broke up."

"Now she's going out with Marco," Peter said. "He used to be involved with that grad student, what's her name."

"And Nicco," Harriet went on, "went out with Susan for a while, but now he's got a thing for that freshman boy everyone's talking about, the one who's smoking that blue cigarette —" She pointed with her chin. "We saw him in a rehearsal of *Dream*, he's an adorable Puck."

"Marco and Nicco are performing at the Cabaret next weekend," Peter said. "They previewed a little for me. They're getting better."

"I'll say," Harriet said appreciatively.

Peter looked at her. "What do you mean by that? You have that tone in your voice."

"Why," she said, all innocence now, "what tone is that?"

"Never mind the Scarlett O'Hara routine." Peter seemed unaccountably short with her. "What about our twins?"

"Well." She lowered her voice and looked at Jack, as if to say he shouldn't worry. "It was a long time ago. I once slept with them. Both of them at once."

Jack pictured this in his mind. There was something a little indecent about it, as if it violated some biblical taboo, brothers naked in the same bed, the English Reformation. There was something missing, he couldn't really grasp what she was saying.

"And," she added, "only one of them is circumcised."

"Skip the details," Peter said distastefully. He looked at Jack, as if to send some kind of message, but Jack couldn't decipher it.

The next afternoon, Jack was alone in the theater. He was standing on top of a very long ladder, which wobbled a little, adjusting the focus of a spot that hung from a pipe on the left side of the stage. The ladder was almost too short, and he was standing on the narrow platform at the top and still having to stretch to reach the lamp. He heard footsteps below and looked down to see Peter watching him. "Hi," Jack said awkwardly.

Peter said nothing, he simply walked in a tight circle around the base of the ladder, his hands clasped behind him and pressed tightly against the seat of his pants, looking down intently at the floor. His hair hung down around his face, straight and fine and parted in the center in a neat white line. Occasionally he tossed his head to clear the bangs away from his eyes. Then he started to speak, in that slow drawl. "You know the story about John Barrymore, playing Hamlet? One night a cat walked onstage in the middle of one of the soliloquies. Enough to make anybody fumble a few lines, right?" There was something feline in the way Peter moved, just up on the balls of his feet. Jack watched him, fascinated, the distance between them seeming huge, and he thought for a moment that he might fall. He looked away, out at the dark, empty auditorium, the rows of worn plush seats. If he blinked, the rows seemed to rearrange themselves along a diagonal — blink, straight; blink, diagonal — op art. He felt dizzy and looked down again. Peter was looking up at him now, walking around and around the ladder. "Barrymore picked up the cat and stroked it, using it as part of the scene as if he'd rehearsed it for weeks." Jack, reaching up to tighten a nut, felt very exposed. He was wearing an old T-shirt and baggy pants that sagged around his hips, and he could almost see with Peter's eyes the warm darkness in the space between his shirt and his ribs, the way his muscles forked down into his pants. Peter, after a long circling silence, said, "But what I want to know is, what did the cat think?"

And then he abruptly stopped his pacing and wandered off into the wings.

One evening two weeks later, Jack stopped by Harriet's room. They were all going to a party in the law school, given by a cousin of Peter's. He found Marco in the room with Harriet, leaning over a mirror, cutting up some cocaine. "Hi, John," Marco said. "Just in time."

"Hi," he said. Harriet was on the couch next to Marco, so Jack went and sat on a chair across the room.

"Nicco and Peter are going to meet us at the law school." Harriet sniffled a little, and he knew they had been doing coke before he'd arrived, probably for a long time. "You didn't give me a kiss — don't I rate?"

He walked over and kissed her on the cheek, but she turned his head to get at his mouth. Then he went back and sat down.

She bent over the mirror with a straw in her nose. "Oh God. My hair's going to get all over. Hold it back for me, Marco, will you."

Jack looked at the closed door of the bedroom. "Where's Susan?"

"She's changing." She handed him the mirror, tilting it carefully to keep the straw from rolling over the lines. "She doesn't approve of this sort of thing."

He did a line, then sat back and lost himself. He spread out his knees and tapped his foot silently on the floor. He looked out the window at the deserted grass on the Cross Campus. When he'd first come to Yale, his favorite sight every day was to see, as he walked to dinner in Commons, the way these foundations of Gothic stone seemed to spring directly from the grass. Now, in the failing light of late autumn, it seemed impossible to recapture the sharpness of those feelings.

Marco began to draw more lines, and Jack watched him. He had a nice kind of skillfulness at it, moving the razor with economical movements of his wrist, like a violinist's bowing — the moment when direction changed was almost imperceptible. His hair, Jack noticed, looked damp and sleek, as if he'd just come out of the shower.

They did more coke. Susan came out of her room. "Hey, Newland."

"Hey, Howell."

She didn't say hello to Marco. After a few minutes, Harriet stood up and said it was time to go. She went into the bedroom for something. Jack watched her go, then stood up and followed her. He kicked the bedroom door closed.

"Hello, sweetheart." She smiled back at him from the mirror.

"I don't want to go to this party." He stood behind her, his hands on her shoulders.

"I know. It's a bore. But I promised Peter." She paused to apply some lipstick. "We don't have to stay long."

He slid his hand down over her belly, and put his lips against her cheek. "Let's stay here."

She leaned back into him. "No. We can't. I promised Peter."

He let her go. "OK."

"Don't sulk, John. You're too gorgeous when you sulk."

But he did sulk when they got to the law dorms. He stood against a wall with a large glass of bourbon. Susan sat on a chair next to him. "Hey, Newland. You still there?"

"I'm still here."

"Can I ask you a serious question?" She stood up so that she could talk more softly.

"No," he said obstinately, and took another swallow of his bourbon.

"Do you think Harriet's the type of woman for you?"

He scowled at her. "You're her roommate. Don't you know? Or are you just her messenger?"

"Take it easy. Would it help any if I told you I was your friend?"

That got to him. He stopped frowning. "Yeah. Thanks. Are you telling me she's going to dump me?"

"I just think that you don't seem very happy lately. Maybe you could let her down easy."

"Is she letting me down easy?"

They both looked over at the bed where Harriet was sitting next to Marco. Or maybe, Jack thought, it isn't Marco at all. Maybe it's his brother, Nicco. Stand up and drop your pants, he thought — but that wouldn't help because Harriet hadn't told him which of them was circumcised. Or maybe she had just made that up.

"She's just Harriet. That's the way she is."

Jack looked at her, with a clutch at clarity. "What about you?"

"What about me?" She put her hand up to her mouth and began biting on a nail.

"What makes you such a creature of the shadows? Tagging along behind her. I mean, I know about the way ugly girls are s'posed to attach themselves to beauties, but you're not ugly."

"She's my friend," Susan said. He could tell she was unprepared for this conversation, but she had started it.

"Do you think Harriet's the type of person for you?" he mimicked. "To be your friend, I mean."

"That's kind of a rotten thing to say."

"It's a rotten world."

He felt great, having said that. It was a great line. He wasn't sure what it was from, but it should have been from a black-and-white forties detective film, a Bogart movie in which he's thrown over by a woman and takes his revenge on the rest of the world. Disillusion overpowered him, and he reveled in it, an attitude he could adopt for himself. He laughed, trying to sound bitter.

But Susan didn't see the humor. "If you believe that, maybe she is for you. You deserve what you get."

"I deserve what gets me," he said as she walked away. He got another highball glass full of bourbon and drank it. What was left of the cocaine seemed to have melted and was dripping down the inside of his skull. He looked around the room and didn't see Harriet — she'd left without him. Marco left, giving Susan a big kiss on the way out. Jack slid, gracefully he hoped, down the wall, to land with a bump on the floor, his legs sticking straight out in front of him. Here he drank some more bourbon that someone gave him, some of which he managed to spill on himself.

He awoke the next morning in a strange bed. The room was full of a yellow light that hurt his eyes, and he still smelled faintly of bourbon. He sat up and looked around. Peter was lying in the bed next to him, asleep. He looked very angelic, his light hair all mussed on the pillow, one arm resting on his hip, the sheet pulled carelessly up almost to his waist, but he'd hardly been angelic the night before.

Oh God, Jack thought. He wanted to think that he'd been too

drunk to remember, but he hadn't been. He remembered Peter leaning over him at the party, helping him to stand up and then, in that weary voice of his, volunteering to make sure he got back to his room all right. And walking through the quadrangle at the law school, where all the bushes looked blurred in the moonlight. Jack asked where they were going, and Peter laughed, and they staggered together through the gate of Peter's college and up a winding stair to his room. Jack felt sober all of a sudden, as Peter reached out to unbutton his shirt, and he knew at that moment that he could get up and walk out. But Harriet clearly didn't want him, he had failed her in some way, which was only to be expected. Peter, on the other hand, clearly did want him: he'd slipped out of his clothes and was looking at Jack's face, and he said, "Don't go, John." And Jack had stayed.

Now, Jack ran one hand through his hair and sighed. "Good morning," he heard Peter say.

"I'm sorry I woke you," he said dully.

"Could you get me a cigarette?"

Jack looked at the pack on the desk next to him. "No, I don't — I don't want to get involved."

Peter laughed. "I don't want to get involved either. I just want a cigarette."

Jack handed him the pack and his lighter.

"Although," Peter said, blowing out smoke, "you're kind of nice to wake up to."

"I gotta go."

Peter reached out and touched his shoulder. "Don't take it so hard, John. It's just a fun thing to do." He sat up in the bed, his hands resting lightly at Jack's waist. "Tell me you didn't have fun last night and you can go."

"Peter —"

Peter started tickling him, and Jack began to laugh, and they both fell over in the bed, Peter's arms still around him, their faces close together. "It was fun," Jack said. He could feel their day-old beards scraping together.

"Good." They lay quietly for a while. Then Peter said, sleepily, "I didn't plan it this way, y' know. It just happened."

Maybe not, but you wanted me, Jack kept thinking, after Peter had fallen asleep again, his even breathing brushing Jack's shoulder. You wanted me, and Harriet didn't. Two hours later, when he left Peter asleep in the bed, the thought had been turned around a little: it was OK, boys are fun, but girls are better.

He was in his room that afternoon, writing a letter to Ripley, when the phone rang. It was Peter. "You want to get coffee or something?"

Jack frowned. "I don't know, Peter. I've got stuff to do."

"Don't get all excited. I just want to talk to you."

He thought, fun is fun, but I don't want to make a thing out of this. "I don't think so. Maybe some other time."

"John —"

"Take care." He hung up. Ten minutes later there was a knock on the door. "Who is it?" he called, not getting up.

"The Big Bad Wolf, who do you think it is?"

"OK, OK." He opened the door and Peter came in.

"What's with you?" He took off the tweed sport coat he was wearing and tossed it on the bed and lit a cigarette.

"Look, I had a good time with you. I enjoyed it — you enjoyed it. But that doesn't mean —"

"What?" He sat down on the bed and swung his legs up. "Oh. Is it OK if I sit here or is that too suggestive?"

"It's OK."

"Maybe next time I'll come in disguise so I won't embarrass you. I could wear a turban and stain my skin brown. Or maybe just a false mustache — I've always wanted to wear a false mustache. Would that make you feel better?"

"Look. It's just that I'm not gay."

"Well, I'm not gay either. So there. Nyeh, nyeh." He stuck out his tongue.

Jack laughed at that. "OK. I surrender."

"Could I just be your friend, maybe?"

He thought of Susan the night before, saying almost the same thing. "Everybody wants to be my friend."

"Lucky guy," Peter said, blowing out a cloud of smoke. "No one wants to be mine."

Jack shook his head. "Don't be ridiculous. Everybody likes you."

Peter got out another cigarette. "I'm easy to like. A kind of easy charm, it's what I trade on. But I don't really have any friends."

Jack counted them on his fingers: "Harriet. Marco. Nicco. Susan."

"But not you?"

"I was getting to that. Of course I am. Is that why you wanted to talk to me, to see if I was your friend?"

Peter sat up on the edge of the bed. "No, actually. I just thought it would be better if we cleared the air between us. I promise to keep my hands off in the future." And they went out for a cup of coffee, talking about acting as if nothing had happened.

Two days later, he was eating lunch in the dining hall at Berkeley when Susan came over and said she had to talk to him. She had a class to get to, so they arranged to meet at the theater at four. She seemed strange to him, stilted, and he wondered what had happened. She usually wasn't so secretive. He went to the theater to work on some changes to the lighting cues and then sat at the back of the auditorium waiting for her and listening to the stage band practice, the words in his head from hearing them at so many rehearsals:

> That old Bilbao moon, love never laid me low,
> That old Bilbao moon, why does it haunt me so.

On the empty stage, Bill's Beerhall in Bilbao leered emptily down at him. He loved its cheap look, down at the heels. Maybe he would run away and join the merchant marine and spend his life on oily tramp ships or in dirty bars on foreign waterfronts. It was the kind of fantasy that appealed to him — not much of a life for a guy who gets seasick easily.

Susan sat down next to him. "Hey, Howell. What's up?"

"Harriet knows."

He looked back blankly. "Knows what?"

"You tell me. What is there to know?"

He had a lot of secrets and one big one. It wasn't possible that Harriet could know anything about his parents. "What are you talking about?"

"Based on what I've heard lately," she was trying to be withering, "you could have any number of nasty little skeletons in your closet."

He was annoyed. "Hey, look. Enough of this bullshit. Just tell me what you think is so important, 'cause I'm not gonna play twenty questions with my life here. Everybody has secrets. So what. What does Harriet know?"

She pulled her head back, so that she was at a distance. "Are you having an affair with Peter Callahan?"

He looked away, at the set on the stage. The band had stopped and he could hear the director giving some instructions. "No."

"Harriet thinks you are. She has proof, she says."

"She's wrong. What difference does it make?" He looked down at the seat in front of him, at the little plaque with the seat number, at a dirty word someone had scrawled next to it.

"What is it with you? You seem like such a nice person, but scratch the surface and it's like there's nothing there."

"Suppose I don't like to have my surface scratched. Suppose I say it doesn't matter to me what I do. Why should it matter to you?"

She stood up and walked to the back of the room, then turned and came back. "You have no self-respect, do you? You're just a pathetic person who doesn't care what he does to himself, is that it? Why would you throw everything away? Why would you have sex with another guy?"

"Because he asked me," Jack said loudly. "Just like Harriet asked me. And what about her, you think she doesn't sleep with other guys? What was she doing with Marco that afternoon — you were there, what were they doing? Playing tiddlywinks? Discussing dramaturgy? You tell me."

"It's different. She's Harriet. That's the way she is."

"Yeah, right," he said bitterly, knowing that he had no right to feel bitter. At the time, it had seemed simple: he did what Peter wanted. Now it didn't seem so simple, and maybe he shouldn't have done it. Either way, it seemed, he would have disappointed someone. At least he hadn't made the choice himself, it had been made for him. He looked at Susan, wondering why she was suddenly so quiet. "What is it?"

"She's in love with Peter. She has been since freshman year.

She's crazy about him, it's like an obsession. He won't even look at her. Not that way."

Most people find aloofness attractive, she'd said. "I didn't know."

"Well, now you do. She's furious. I've never seen her so angry, and depressed. I just wanted you to know."

"Thanks."

She stood up again. "I don't know why you do this kind of thing. Why you abuse yourself, why you think the world is rotten, why you hate yourself. I think it's sick."

"Thanks a lot." She walked away, leaving him listening to the band.

Hours later, he was sitting on the cold stone floor of a little alcove outside the door to Peter's room, his back against the cut stone wall. Above him a window was open a crack; he'd tried and it didn't close properly, and he was cold — he hadn't taken a jacket with him to the theater that afternoon, and he hadn't been back to his room since. When he'd left the theater, he'd gone to Peter's room. Peter was out, and Jack spent a moment trying to think where he might be. Then he went down the stairs and stood in the courtyard, his hands stuck in the pockets of his pants, wondering what to do. Behind him the sun was going down, and the carillon in Harkness Tower was ringing a Bach fugue. He didn't want to go back to his room, he didn't want to go anywhere he might see Harriet. I've messed up everything, he thought.

He started to walk, out of Saybrook and across the Old Campus, through Phelps Gate and onto the Green. He said all these names to himself as he passed, in a deliberate effort to keep his mind in the present tense, because he didn't want to keep thinking that he'd messed everything up.

The little plaza at the corner of Church and Chapel was filled with pigeons, and an elderly man in a brown suit and brown shoes and an old brown hat was feeding them popcorn out of a small square bag, and suddenly the pigeons all took flight at once, filling the air around Jack with a cracking of wings so that he flinched — stay away from me — until they disappeared in the dark sky. Chapel Street was where Yalies never went, where black people shopped, where stores open to the sidewalk advertised cheap stereos with blasting disco music, where fried chicken was sold from narrow windows, and shop signs were bilingual. An old woman was clearing out the display window of a jewelry store, taking the two-hundred-dollar diamond rings and the ten-carat gold-plated zodiac charms out of the reach of brick-wielding night-walkers. He didn't know where he was going, only that he wanted to walk, away from campus, from all the hurt he'd caused and the mistakes he'd made.

The street humped over the railroad tracks, black-and-white high voltage signs, and he thought he would just touch a trans-former and fry himself, sizzle away, but the thought of dying only reminded him how little he'd be leaving behind, so he hurried on, past the brick army induction center, toward the restored barrenness of Wooster Square. He found a pay phone and called Peter, letting it ring and ring, hitting the side of the phone with his open palm. Just as he was hanging up, he thought he heard someone answer, so he quickly dialed again but no one was there.

He was walking under a high overpass — 95, 91, 34 — he wasn't sure which road, he was all disoriented. He was standing on a vast pool of asphalt that stretched out in all directions. He was sure that it must be a parking lot, but no lines were painted on it; that roads must lead across it, but there were no signs. It might have been a storage yard for a factory, but there was no fence and no factory. At the base of one of the massive piers that held up the roadway above, he saw a metal garbage can with a fire burning in it and a group of men standing around. He could join them, he thought, he could make himself disappear, just go over and sit down with them, ignore their smell and their bad teeth and their unshaven faces, he could piss with them in the night against the sides of buildings while his clothes disintegrated around him. They'd welcome him or they wouldn't, but they'd never ask him, he'd never again be asked, to do anything, and no one would ever get hurt again. He walked away from them. Above him the roadway rumbled and chattered as the trucks rolled by. Behind him an empty bottle smashed into bits.

He was now in an open space of high grass, with no buildings in sight and only a large darkness ahead, the air full of the muddy smell of a salt marsh at low tide. He pushed through the grass, waist high or higher, until he came to the edge of the harbor. Across the way, a freighter was tied up at a dock, arc lights outlining the crane that was poised like a poking finger over her deck. The light at the top of the stack of the power plant blinked whitely. The water lapped at the rocks at his feet and he nearly kept walking, wondering, would his body come washing up beneath the cyclops eye of the power plant, naked and bloated, oil-slicked and anonymous. The Cyclops in the Odyssey had cried, I die and No-man gives the blow. No-man: I'm so alone, I want to be alone, I can't be trusted with people, I hate being alone. He started to cry.

It was a good cry, big warm tears that he couldn't stop. He made choking noises to stifle the sounds, instinctively, even though there was no one to hear. He clenched his fists and looked up at the sky, and the tears ran down his face, behind his ears, and over his neck. "Oh God," he kept saying, "please help me, I didn't mean it."

It wore itself out in time. He would stop crying and then start all over again, but his jag finally stopped. He shivered. I need to see Peter, he thought, otherwise something else bad will happen. He didn't name to himself what that would be. He went out through the weeds and discovered that he was much nearer campus than he'd thought. He walked back and found Peter still out, so he sat down outside his door and waited, feeling colder and worn out and empty. He closed his eyes, hugging his knees to his chest.

Later he woke up from a dream in which a huge moon had smiled at him singing the music from *The Happy End*, to hear someone come up the stairs, whistling the same music (That old Bilbao moon, love never laid me low — the whistling broke into singing).

"Peter," he said thickly.

"Jesus. You scared the shit out of me." He waited while Jack got groggily to his feet. "What are you doing here? Come on in." He unlocked the door and switched on the light. "This is unexpected — hey, you're shivering."

Jack stood in the middle of the room, his teeth chattering, his arms crossed tightly over his chest, his eyes blinking in the sudden light. "I gotta tell you something."

"Don't you have a coat or something? Here, sit down, take this." He picked up a neatly folded blanket and wrapped it around Jack and made him sit down on the bed.

"It's OK. I was just sitting outside for a while. I didn't realize how chilly it'd gotten."

Peter brushed his bangs out of his eyes and sat down on the desk chair. "You look like you're in shock. What happened?"

Jack told him the story just as he'd heard it from Susan.

"I had no idea," he said when Jack finished.

"Really, Peter?"

"Yes." He lit a cigarette. "I mean, I knew she had a thing for me when we were freshmen. But I didn't — she was too good an actress, that was obvious from the start. I wanted to work with her. I didn't want to screw it up with — pardon the pun." He added, "I just wasn't attracted to her. That's the real reason."

Jack was lying on the bed, the blanket around him. His head was on the pillow, which smelled faintly of Peter. He said suddenly, "I hate sex."

Peter laughed. "No you don't. But I see your point."

Jack turned a little toward the wall. "Do you think that men always end up hurting women?"

"You might as well say that women always hurt men."

Or that people always end up hurting each other, no matter what they do. Harriet had wanted him. Peter had wanted him. "I thought if I did what everyone wanted, everyone would be happy."

"You're not responsible for everything that happens, you know."

"Only for the consequences."

"I'll see Harriet tomorrow, I'll fix everything up." He stubbed out his cigarette. "You want to sleep here tonight? I could go over to your room."

"No," he said into the pillow. What he really wanted was not to be alone, to feel someone's arms around him, Peter's would do as well as anyone else's. He toyed with the idea a minute — just to be held. "I can get home all right. Don't worry."

Peter reported back the next day. "It's all fixed. You're forgiven, but your romance is dead — her words, I swear, total acting-class delivery. I'm the bad guy, but I don't give a shit because she has to act with me and that's all I care about. As long as —"

"What?"

"I know I sound like a twelve-year-old with a terminal crush, but I like you a lot, and I'd hate it if —"

Jack looked at him for a minute. He said, "Call me Jack."

"Jack?"

"It's sort of a special thing. It's what my best friend calls me." It was the only thing he had to give.

And they remained friends. With Susan he maintained a nodding acquaintance, which thawed as they neared graduation, and one afternoon when they met by accident in the courtyard, they had a long conversation. Harriet, on the other hand, didn't even nod.

And now Susan came out of the past, trailing all these memories, to tell him that someone had gotten hurt. He kicked his foot against the grass, smelling Mr. Prescott's roses in the air. He said, "Harriet wasn't the only one, you know. I got hurt too."

"It was you I was thinking about," she said simply.

They had reached the last terrace of the garden, and something told him not to go up any farther, to the summerhouse with its cushioned benches and its air of privacy. He turned, and they headed back to the house. "Me?"

She walked more quickly, ahead of him on the raked pebble path. "Everyone else ended up happy. You obviously were unhappy."

"Was I?" He wondered how much she'd known, how much he had shown during that next empty time.

"Oh, you were. I used to watch you. In class, in the dining hall. Once I sat across the reading room at Sterling a whole evening, watching you. Of course you didn't notice." She kept walking while he stopped and watched her, her pale dress showing white around her legs. She looked back, and he hurried to catch up, while she said, "I don't blame you, your mind was on other things. Still, it would have been nice."

"I didn't know." She'd been in love with him and he hadn't

known it. Harriet had been in love with Peter, and Peter hadn't known it. He was in love with Ellen, and she didn't know it. "I'm sorry."

"I got over it," she said drily. "Don't worry, I won't interfere in your romance with Ellen Archer. Speaking of which, we'd better go back in. They'll start to talk. Andrew especially, and my God can he talk."

"I'll say." Jack wasn't sure he wanted their conversation to end like this, he felt something else should be said. They strolled down past the fish pond.

"John, you can't imagine what goes on. Timothy invited us to dinner. At first Andrew wanted to say no, I think he thinks Tony has a thing for Timothy."

"He won't get anywhere with that."

"Then Timothy told Andrew that you were here, and Andrew all of a sudden changed his mind. So then Tony didn't want to come. I finally told them that I was an old friend of yours and wanted to come and then they had no choice. John —" her voice faltered a little.

"What?"

"You and Peter, you weren't like that, like Andrew and Tony?"

He shook his head. "No. Peter and I are just good friends who happened to spend a night together. That's all. We're still good friends, he's married with a baby girl — you haven't asked me about him."

"You haven't asked me about Harriet."

"No," he said. He didn't want to know any more than he could find out in the alumni directory.

When they got back to the house, Andrew was sitting on the patio at a white wrought iron table, smoking a cigarette. "Ah, cousin Susan, you're wanted inside. Some kind of argument they seem to think only you can settle. Not you," he said as Jack started to follow her into the house. "I want to talk to you myself."

Jack looked in through the open doors to the living room. Tony was at the piano, and idle music, slow jazz improvisations, floated out to them. Ellen was sitting on the couch, the coffee service in front of her, the others gathered around her. She looked up and smiled at him across the distance. He pulled out a metal chair and deliberately scraped it on the stones. Then he sat down at an angle to the table, crossed his legs, and put his elbow on the table. He had nothing to say to Andrew, and all this was just stage business to fill the silence.

Andrew reached out and held Jack's wrist. "That's a cute little watch. Star Trek, isn't it?"

"Star Wars," he corrected. "It was a birthday present. From Timothy."

"How charming." He touched Jack's sleeve. "What a nice sweater. I love stripes. Especially this time of year."

"I just borrowed it for tonight. It's Timothy's."

"I know. It was a birthday present. I gave it to him."

Jack wished he were wearing another sweater.

"You two must be very close. You have his watch. You wear his clothes."

"And I sleep in his guest room. Alone."

"How direct you are." He puffed on his cigarette. "Would you like to sleep in my guest room?"

"No." He was annoyed at the whole transaction, with himself for bringing it up simply because it was on his mind. He was annoyed with Andrew, with the way he held the cigarette loosely over the edge of the table, with the way his predator's eyes watched Jack for any sign of irresolution, and with the game they were playing, in which "No" could mean "Yes — but only if you try harder."

"No? You weren't captivated by my African tale?"

"Is that why you told it, to captivate me?"

Andrew leaned back languorously in the chair, which Jack thought made a good effect but looked uncomfortable. "Well, I believe the best way to seduce someone is to tell him everything."

No, Jack thought. The best way to seduce someone is to get him to tell you everything. Like a long interrogation in an underground cell, the inquisitor coy and aloof, the victim offering more and more in his effort to please until he offers up his ultimate treasure, whatever it is that the inquisitor most wants. Unless the victim was willing, in which case no one needed to say anything. He said, "I wasn't captivated."

Andrew shrugged. "*Tant pis.* I had to ask, you know. This

house simply reeks of lust tonight, and I thought, as long as the atmospheric conditions were favorable — what were you talking about so avidly with cousin Susan?"

"Old times. The little dramas of teenage life that grow up to be daytime soap operas."

Andrew laughed. "That sounds like a line from one of your magazine columns."

"It probably will be."

"I'll look for it."

Another conversational dead end. Jack wished Andrew would get on with whatever it was he wanted to talk about. Jack could have asked him, point blank, but he wasn't about to give Andrew that advantage. Instead, he stared up at the moon, which hung unobscured above the valley, looking old and hard now where before, lower on the horizon, it had been large and yellow. That old Bilbao moon, love never laid me low —

"What are you humming?" Andrew said.

"Sorry. It's from *The Happy End*."

"I never heard of it."

"Kurt Weill and Bertolt Brecht. The story of a Salvation Army girl and a gang of crooks. Like *Guys and Dolls*."

"Musical comedy," Andrew said shortly. "Tony thinks life is a musical comedy. Do you think that's true?" Jack let that pass, so Andrew said nastily, "I think it's a typical faggot's view of the world, myself." He dragged deeply at his cigarette, and then put it out, twisting it into the ashtray. Then, sounding very businesslike, he said, "Did you mean what you said inside, before?"

Jack considered. "I meant most of it. What in particular?"

"About interior design being an art, that it needs a vision, has to refer to the past."

"To account for the past, anyway. Yes, I meant that. More to the point, though, what do you think?"

Andrew clapped his hands softly once. "I knew it. The minute I heard you talking inside, I knew. John, listen, will you write an article about this? I'll take you to see all my favorite spots in New York. I'll show you my latest work and then we can write about it, just as you said inside. It would be wonderful."

Jack thought of what Val had said to him, making almost the

same request: a little bit of the right kind of publicity never hurt. In an age when interior decorators had replaced painters or liberal politicians as the celebrities of choice, it was a natural. "I don't think you could show me your latest work. And besides, I've already seen it."

"What do you mean?" Now it was Andrew's turn to be suspicious.

"Your latest work is Blanche Morgan's apartment, isn't it. I don't really see her letting you bring me tramping through with a photographer to do a glossy layout full of pointed comments about art and nouvelle decorating. And besides, I was at her apartment two weeks ago, right after you finished." He smiled at the look on Andrew's face. "She's an old family friend. Her daughter Anne grew up with my mother. Blanche wanted my opinion on your work. I told her I liked it."

"I can't believe it."

"Oh, come on, you can do better than that."

"No, I mean, that you were there at all. I got the impression that she doesn't have many visitors."

Jack grinned, feeling a kind of foolish pleasure at the thought that he had bested Andrew. "It's part of my mission in life."

"To boldly go where no man has gone before?"

Behind them, Tony interrupted loudly, "Where no man has gone before, Andrew? Deflowering virgins again?"

"Oh, don't be disgusting."

"Pot calling the kettle black?" Tony looked down his nose at Jack. "Or won't Johnny play?"

Jack looked up and said evenly, "It's John."

"Oh, excuse me. Andrew, I'm ready to go home."

Jack and Timothy saw them to the front door. Jack felt like a character in a banal nightmare: all evening he had been attempting nothing more difficult than to return home, to get back to Ellen and be alone with her (Timothy almost didn't count), and now, as he stepped into the living room he thought, At last, no more Andrew, no more Susan, no more memories of Harriet or Peter — no more obstacles. He had forgotten Lois.

She was sitting in the middle of the couch, and she was obviously drunk. It was a stupid prejudice, he knew, especially given the kind of life he'd been living, but he hated it when people got drunk, and women especially. Intoxication was one thing, he made that distinction, because it had an aura of gaiety and even exuberance to it. But drunkenness was different, it was tied with ropes to the ground, a Gulliver in Lilliput. Drunks couldn't be roused, and they couldn't rise to the occasion either. Lois was lolling on the couch, her mouth open slightly, listening to Ellen talk about Tony. Jack felt sorry for her. After what Timothy had said about her, it had been easy to pretend that the two of them were in a sort of conspiracy against her, and that was what had prompted Jack's teasing, a kind of male solidarity in the presence of an unwanted woman. He wondered whether women did that kind of thing to men, whether Ellen and Lois had ever conspired to keep at bay some unsuspecting boy. Jack wondered what kind of man Ellen would find especially unappealing: a chunky rugby player who liked to dance even though he couldn't, who had a beer can in his hand all the time, who worked in an investment bank on Wall Street and was beginning to show the little veins around his nose and eyes from too much drinking — or was that too stereotyped? How about a twenty-eight-year-old magazine writer with green eyes and a hard dark labyrinth in his heart where Theseus and the Minotaur wrestled each other to a perfect balance. "Lois," he said, "I'm sorry I teased you before. About being an archaeologist."

Her eyes came back into focus, and she closed her mouth. "I couldn't understand that at all. I write manuals for a software company."

He decided to be gallant. "I apologize abjectly. It's one of my worst faults. You see, I'm terribly shy when I first meet people, and sometimes I hide it by clowning around."

"I can't believe you're ever shy about anything."

"Oh, it's true," Ellen said. "When I first met him, he was practically tongue-tied."

Jack tried to remember, until he realized that now he was being teased.

"I think I'd better go home," Lois said.

"You shouldn't drive," Ellen said brusquely. "It's been a very festive evening."

"Oh, I'm not drunk."

"Well, even so —"

Lois started to protest, then changed her mind. She fished her keys out of her purse and held them up, jingling them a little the way one would before an infant. "Timothy. Would you drive me home then?"

Jack almost laughed, but didn't. Behind him, he could practically feel Timothy start to panic. Chivalrous to the last, he thought, and said, "Timothy's had too much, too. He's one of those cheap dates, give him two drinks and he's out cold. I'll drive you." He stood up and took the keys from her before she could protest. "Where do you live?"

Timothy said, "Drive up to the school, but instead of going on into town, make a right. About a mile up there's a road on your left. It's the third house on the right."

Not too drunk to give accurate directions, Jack thought, but Lois didn't notice.

They didn't say much in the car. Jack was thinking what a change this was — that he should be the sober one after a party. Two weeks ago he'd been running around with Boyd and Amy, drinking bourbon after bourbon, snorting whatever was handed to him on a silver mirror, waking up with blood in his eyes and blood in his nose, and now he was feeling clear-headed and clean. I've taken a cure, he thought.

He walked Lois to the door and then drove back. She really wasn't so bad, he thought. Timothy had been exaggerating. It was funny the way these things got blown out of proportion, the way he had blown his relationship with Harriet out of proportion. He could barely believe, looking back on it now, that he had been so shaken by it. Everything had counted for more then. He came to the traffic light and, instead of turning, went straight on and pulled over next to the school. He got out of the car, leaving the door open, resting one foot on the bumper, bar-rail fashion. There were lights on in the headmaster's house, but the dorms were dark, eerily silent. They had seemed, in his day, always to be full of sound, and never more than at night, when they'd echoed with the inflammable dreams of teenage boys. Even now, during summer session, with only fifty in residence — the raging dreams of fifty boys should be enough to ignite the world. Ripley had said to him one night when they'd sneaked out to meet by the First World War memorial on the hill overlooking the lake, "The place is breathing, dreaming. That's the secret that housemasters know — to keep those dreams in bottles. If they ever get out, the place will explode. That's what I would do if it were up to me — release the dreams and let them wander over the world. We'll come back in ten years, Jack, and see if the dreams have lasted." And here he was, ten years later; his only dream had been not to dream, his only care not to let that genie out of the bottle — dreams only enslaved, or died. And then he thought of Ellen, and his dream seemed suddenly real.

He got into the car and drove quickly back to the house. The front hall was very quiet, and the lights were off, except for a dim wall sconce. From the library Ellen said, "Jack, I'm in here."

He went in. She was sitting on a leather couch. One lamp burned in a corner beneath a yellow shade.

"Timothy's gone to bed," she said.

Jack sat down next to her. Every woman he'd kissed, every woman he'd touched, had wanted him, he had awaited their lips, their fingers. He had known their want and had given in to it, those were the rules. But now he didn't know, knew only his own wanting. That was against the rules. He leaned forward and kissed her, softly on her lips.

She put her hand up to his face. "I've been wondering when you would do that."

But he hardly heard her. He put his arms around her and held her to him, kissing her again, feeling her hair on his face, the warmth of her body fitting against him, as if holding her was all there was in the world for him, and the soft bruising of her lips and the almost tentative touchings of their tongues. He turned his face aside and leaned his cheek against hers. "Oh, Ellen," he said sighing her name, feeling emotion like a geyser inside of him, trembling with it. "Ellen," and he found her mouth again.

She lay in his arms, her hand warm in his. The top of her head nestled under his chin, and he was almost idly stroking her back. He moved a little, trying to hold her more closely, but she said, "I have to go to bed."

I could lie here like this forever, he thought. "I could lie here like this forever."

"Mmm," she said. "I feel wonderful. But sleepy."

"But —" She pushed a little away from him and then kissed his forehead. She stood up, and he caught at her hand, holding it. "I don't want to let go of you."

"I'll still be here in the morning. I won't go anywhere."

He stood up and kissed her again. "Well —" After she'd gone, he stood at the window, still shaking a little, looking out at the moon setting behind the hills across the valley.

He went upstairs and paused at Timothy's door. He knocked softly and, getting no answer, went in. The moonlight lay around the room in white blocks — on the desk, which was scattered with papers, on a patch of the pale brown carpet, on the bed. Timothy was lying on his back. His skin looked bloodless in the light, like the polished marble of an antique sculpture, Eros Asleep. Jack could hear him breathing softly. He said his name.

"Mmm."

"Timothy. Wake up."

He opened his eyes, and Jack could see, even in the half-light, how blue they were. "Timothy. I'm in love with your sister."

And Timothy, yawning, still half-asleep, said, "Silly. Why do you think I brought you here?"

PART FOUR

Isn't It
Romantic

~~~~~~

X

HE SLEPT UNEASILY. His dreams were tangled. In one, he was
the star halfback of the Westfield football team, playing in a night
game at Harvard Stadium, which had miraculously sprouted
lights. In another, he was in a classroom at Yale listening to a
lecture, Peter Callahan sitting next to him taking notes. Jack
couldn't hear the professor very clearly and kept looking over
Peter's shoulder, thinking, I'm going to fail the test and I need
this class to graduate; and then he was outside the lecture hall,
looking for a men's room because he felt sick to his stomach.

He woke up. The clock next to the bed read six-thirty, and he
really did feel sick. He could feel dampness on his forehead and
that metallic, bloody taste in his mouth — he got out of bed and
ran for the bathroom, standing a moment looking down over what
seemed an immense distance to the water in the toilet, and then
he threw up. He stood with his head down, retching, and then,
after the third or fourth time, stood up and took a drink of water
from the glass. He blew his nose and stood, shaking, wondering
if that were all, then flushed the toilet and went back to bed. He
thought, I must be sick, I didn't have anything much to drink
last night. He tried feeling his forehead, but he couldn't tell. He
dozed a little, but a half-hour later he was vomiting again. He
had a headache too.

As he crawled back into bed, there was a knock on the door,
and Timothy came in. "Are you all right?"

Jack lay back in the pillows. "No."

"I didn't think so. What's the matter?"

He closed his eyes. "I don't know. Probably just a virus. Every
time I get sick, I throw up."

"Well." Timothy grinned. "If this is what being in love does
to you —"

"Oh God," he groaned.

"Would you like some ginger ale or something?"

"Please. Maybe some Tylenol. I'll be all right. It sounds worse than it is."

"It sounded awful." Timothy went out, shutting the door. Jack rolled over on his side. Not exactly the romantic day he'd hoped to have — he'd pictured something more like the day before, a long drive around the mountains, lunch at a little restaurant where they could sit outside and no one would know that he was in love with her, and maybe later they would go up to Westfield and borrow a rowboat, alumni could do that, and go out on the lake, which would be flattened in the late afternoon.

When he woke up again, he felt a little better. It was after eleven. Timothy was sitting in the rocking chair, reading.

"Hi," Jack said.

"Hi. How do you feel?"

"Better." His head throbbed, and he amended, "Getting there."

"I called the doctor. He said there's a twenty-four-hour bug going around and that you should stay in bed." He stood up, dropping the book on the foot of the bed. "Here's a thermometer. Want to take your temperature? I'll get you something to drink."

He lay back on the pillows, the thermometer in his mouth. When he was a kid, he and Dougie had had a whole catalogue of ways you could fake having a fever if you didn't want to go to school. One required you to put a penny in your mouth — they hadn't been sure how it worked, but according to legend it did. He took the thermometer out of his mouth. "A hundred and one point two," he said when Timothy came back into the room. "God, I'm sorry."

"Sure. It's all your fault. Take this." He gave him a glass of ginger ale with crushed ice, and some Tylenol.

"Thanks. Where's Ellen?"

"She went to return Lois's car. She'll be back in a couple of hours. You want to play cards or something?"

"Sure." It was like being a kid all over again, having one of those mysterious fevers that come and go. Every year in January, he had gotten strep throat and missed a week of school. He would lie in bed in a fevered state, half dozing, imagining the microbes inside him, all paisley-shaped and buzzing, like things seen through a microscope in biology class. His pulse would bang in his earlobes, against the pillow, louder than the intermittent sounds that reached him from the world outside: the taxi horns, the doorman's whistle, the elevator door shutting, the bubbling of ginger ale on the nightstand next to him. In the afternoons, Dougie would come by to give him his homework and play the piano to cheer Jack up, or just stand in the doorway (not being allowed to get too close) and try to carry on a normal conversation while Jack's mother hovered in the background. He had done the same for Dougie when he was sick. Once, Jack remembered, he'd smuggled a cheeseburger up to Dougie's room without his mother finding out, which they thought was pretty amusing until Dougie had to throw up.

But mostly his mother was there with him. She never seemed to run out of things to do with him when he was sick. They would play cards together, gin or casino (but never cribbage, that he played with his father). She would read to him from C. S. Lewis or Jack London or Lewis Carroll — he was her beamish boy, she'd say — or her favorite, Robert Frost, "Stopping by Woods" or "Mending Wall," and then discuss with him whether good fences in fact make good neighbors. She would play tapes of Broadway musicals, *Gypsy* and *Guys and Dolls* and *My Fair Lady* and *Camelot* and sing along with them, tell him about the night she had first seen this or that show, what boy had taken her to see Brando in *Streetcar* before she met his father. And they would always do a jigsaw puzzle on a bed tray — always the same puzzle, a bowl of hydrangeas on a table in front of a picture window that looked out on sailboats and the sea. He could still see the shape of her hand, the way the tendons moved beneath the skin as she arranged a piece of the puzzle in place. He'd once been tempted to make fun of it because after all those years the puzzle was barely a challenge, but he didn't say anything. Knowing how much she liked it, he didn't want to hurt her feelings, and even now hydrangeas made him think of her. That was how he remembered her, caught on the spikes of her favorite things, a presence in his life.

He felt tired all of a sudden, and said to Timothy, "Is it OK if we stop for a while?"

"Sure. Do you want to rest?"

"Yeah. Listen, don't go." He added, "If you don't want to."

"Sure." Timothy took up his book and sat in the rocking chair. Jack watched him, thinking dreamily that he'd always wanted to have a brother. A lot of his friends had brothers — Jeff's brother George had been three years ahead of them at Westfield and had won all the athletic prizes in his year; there had been a reflected glory in sitting on a cold autumn day at the football field, watching George beat Andover or Groton. Peter Callahan had two brothers, one older, one younger. Jack and Dougie had been almost like brothers, they'd spent most of their time together after school for years, but Dougie had a real brother, a lot older.

Of course, Jack had a brother-in-law instead, which wasn't quite the same.

Jack had been eleven when David married Elizabeth. Old enough to sense something not quite right in his parents' reaction to the engagement. He would come home from school during that period before the wedding, full mostly of himself. At dinner, he would tell his parents about his day, or they would talk about current events — politics or the war, endlessly replayed, which seemed never to conclude. It was his father's idea that they should talk about important things. He would mostly stop listening when his parents talked about Elizabeth, but he had the hazy idea that they thought her too young to get married, or that David was unsuitable in unspecified ways. From this, or from David, or from somewhere else, had come a constraint between David and Jack, and then his parents' deaths had shifted the relationship permanently.

Only once had Jack and David approached any real sympathy. It had been about two months after his breakup with Harriet, during the last days of the semester, when the whole university took on an air of convivial grimness. Everyone had work to catch up on, and the libraries became crowded, the dining halls subdued, and people vied for the honor of most hours studying to make up for earlier records set for most hours partying. Jack, seemingly alone, avoided the camaraderie. He felt his own suffering was real, the inescapable vision of the wreck he had made of his love for Harriet and of hers for him (it hadn't been love,

he knew that, but it might as well have been, he told himself —
he wouldn't have acted any differently). Action or inaction, loving
or ignoring, lust or chastity, all seemed to lead to one result,
someone's broken heart. So he retreated to his room, emerging
only when it was absolutely necessary to get food or library books,
both of which he took back to his room to consume in solitude.
He would venture out sometimes to the pizza place over by Sil-
liman, calling ahead first. One night, as he waited to pay, he saw
a group of underclassmen sitting at a round table in the corner.
They had collected the hollow plastic swizzle sticks from their
sodas and from surrounding tables and were building an airy castle
on the checkered tablecloth. They were full of what seemed, with
a nod to his own sadness, to be perishable exuberance, and he
thought, They should remember this night. No matter how many
times they return to this place, no matter how many times they
recall the magic endeavor, they will never be able to recapture
it. The conjunction of events, of time and mood and moment,
will never recur. They would have to come back on as many nights
as there are nights in the history of the universe before that would
happen again.

But mostly, he hardly moved from his room. He would wake
up in the morning and stagger out to the bathroom to brush his
teeth, furiously hoping not to meet anyone in the process. He
would spend the day in the sweatpants and flannel shirt he'd slept
in, enjoying the familiar feeling. He had never sweated very
much, even after hot exercise (it had been almost a joke with Jeff,
who told him that in New Orleans it was a mark of virility to have
damp circles on your shirts), it didn't seem to be part of his
metabolism. Now, he felt a permanent dampness in his armpits
and in his socks which, when he touched himself, wasn't really
there. He kept looking for stains in his sweats but couldn't find
any — it became almost an obsession to see how long he could
go without showering or shaving, existing on pizza and bourbon,
avoiding the outside world by unplugging his phone.

In the midst of this blue period there was, late one afternoon,
a knock on his door. He looked up groggily from the book he was
reading and realized how dark it had become. Outside, it had
begun to snow in New Haven's peculiar way — three parts rain

to one part sleet — and beyond the pool of light from his desk lamp the room was shadowy. He switched on the overhead light, blinking a little, and opened the door. "David?" he said, still blinking.

"Hello, John. I tried to call but I couldn't get an answer."

"Uh. Come in."

He watched as David, in a Burberry over a three-piece suit, looked around the room. At the gaping pizza boxes with dried cheese encrusted on the tops; at the half-empty bourbon bottle — even worse, at the fact that there were two or three half-empty bottles; at the unmade bed, the sheets accusingly dirty-looking and the pillow crammed drunkenly in a corner against the walls; at Jack himself, his hair unkempt and no doubt looking dirty, his face unshaven, his clothes wrinkled, his green eyes looking out from the wreck waiting for judgment.

"I had an appointment in Middletown, and I thought I'd come by and take you to dinner."

But now that he's seen me, Jack thought, he wishes he hadn't. He's going to tell me to snap out of it, to put on a tie and fly straight — whatever it is that fathers say to wayward boys. He'll give me the standard lecture on taking charge of my life, the old college try. He'll tell me what to do.

"We could go someplace casual — I wouldn't mind taking off my tie and jacket. Or we could just order pizza if you want. Whatever you say."

He meant it, too. He could have made it sound like a reproach (Elizabeth would have done that), but he didn't. Jack had never seen David in public without a tie on, but he was, for whatever reason, willing to do it for Jack. "Thanks, David. I'll tell you what. Give me a few minutes to shower and all, and we'll go to Mory's."

"You sure?" David said mildly, looking around again. "You seem pretty engrossed."

"No, it'll be great to get out for a while."

"If we go to Mory's, you'll have to pay, I'm not a member. I wanted this to be my treat."

The more gallant he was about it, the more grateful Jack was for the effort, and the more determined he was not to involve

David in the self-imposed consequences of his own nasty actions. "I'll send you the bill."

When he came back, showered and shaved, already regretting a little the badges of his solitude, which he'd washed down the drain, David said, "I plugged in your phone. I wanted to call Elizabeth."

"I was studying pretty hard, I just didn't want to be disturbed."

"Why don't you call some of your friends and ask them to join us. What about Harriet?"

Jack was at that moment balanced on one foot, hopping to get his pants on. "We broke up," he said, losing his balance and sitting down on the bed.

"Someone else, then."

"Oh, I don't know —"

"Well, I'm getting old, I'd like to see how the younger set lives."

Jack called Peter, who unexpectedly agreed to come. Jack was mildly annoyed at him — he'd been counting on Peter to say no — so he sat back and let Peter make conversation, which he seemed perfectly happy to do, discussing college life with David and blithely ignoring Jack's silence.

"You have it lucky," David said at one point. "Things you take for granted, we had to fight for. No dress code. No course requirements. Coed dorms. Women at all in some cases."

"At least you fought," Peter mused. "When we got here, there was nothing left to fight for. What's a college student without something to fight for?"

"Premed," Jack said, and they all laughed.

After dinner, David said, "I started college in 1964, a year after Kennedy was killed. I remember how inspiring he was, even to a kid in high school, how he made us feel challenged, personally challenged. Then he was dead, and all the idealism he'd stirred up was let loose on the world without a leader, without control." He slowly took a sip of his brandy. Jack, on his best behavior, was drinking soda water, which had visibly shocked Peter. "The idealism seeped away, dissipating itself in drugs or rock concerts or meaningless political aberrations. Everything that came after that — Vietnam, Watergate, the whole dismal seventies — just made for cynicism. People stopped believing in anything except their own gratification."

"I've never heard you so philosophical, David."

Peter said, "I think that's really interesting."

"He's studying you, David, watch out. Someday you'll see yourself on stage." The conversation was making Jack uncomfortable. He changed the subject. "How's your father?"

David shook his head. "Not good." He explained to Peter, "My father's in a nursing home. He has —" he made a helpless gesture, "old age, I guess. He's dying. Maybe that's why I'm so philosophical, John. I've been thinking more and more what it means to be head of the family. When one's father has always been there, it's odd to think of him gone."

Jack looked down at the table, in which the initials of undergraduates were, according to strict tradition, elaborately carved. How dare he, he thought, who does he think he's talking to? He had a moment of overwhelming anger, but all he did was trace the letters on the tabletop with his index finger.

They walked David back to his car and watched him drive off. Peter said, "He seems like a pretty nice guy."

Jack hunched down in his raincoat. "For a brother-in-law, I guess."

"Come on." Peter started walking down the sidewalk, avoiding the puddles. Headlights gleamed on the wet pavement. A drop of water fell from a tree branch onto Jack's neck. Peter was walking a little ahead, wearing an old tweed topcoat that he'd bought in a thrift shop on the edge of campus. Jack, idling along behind, watched him studiously — the coiled energy in his walk, the almost delicate lightness with which he moved around the puddles. He turned around and faced Jack. "Let's go to the library. It's the place to be, where the elite meet."

Jack shrugged. "Sure. I need to get a magazine article for anthro."

Peter wrinkled his nose. "I hate that class. I thought it would be like one of those African movies, Farley Granger and Deborah Kerr, and rioting natives with bones in their noses. It's just dull. Why are we taking it?"

"Distribution requirement."

"I tried calling you yesterday. You didn't answer."

"Yeah, well. I've been studying pretty hard."

They turned into the small forecourt of the library and Peter looked up. "My cousin, in the law school? When he first came to Yale he thought this was the university chapel. He couldn't find the library." He had lit a cigarette and now he exhaled, and in the damp drizzly air his head seemed to be enveloped in a ball of smoke. "I saw you in here the other day. You looked like hell."

Jack didn't answer, there was nothing to say; he scuffed at the wet flagstones with the toe of his loafer.

"Are you still beating yourself up about Harriet?"

Jack looked up. "Yes."

"You don't have to, you know. It wasn't your fault."

"It was someone's fault." He drew in a deep breath. "I'm getting cold. Can't we just go inside? Or something."

Peter held open the big heavy door, and Jack went into the warm quiet hum of the big central hall, which did look like the nave of a vast cathedral. He said, "I have to go to the Periodical Reading Room."

"OK. I'll meet you downstairs at the machines. What time?"

Jack looked at his watch. "I don't know. Midnight?"

"See you then."

Jack was a little late, on the off chance that Peter would have given up. The machines were in the basement, in a tiled, white, antiseptic space that reminded him unpleasantly of a hospital. The central core of this area was lined with vending machines, dispensers of coffee and candy bars, miniature TV dinners and thick orange soups, and nameless, unspeakable foods that could be heated in a nearby microwave, even limp hamburgers on damp buns that steamed when they came out of the oven and infected the air with their smell. He got a cup of coffee, leaning tiredly on the creamer button. He usually drank it black, but this coffee required camouflage. He carried it over to one of the booths that lined the wall and looked around. Nearby, a couple of football players were scarfing down the odious burgers, and behind them a couple of women talked softly, their heads close together. A study group debated some point at a corner table unnecessarily cluttered with papers. He'd been in a study group once in a course on English history; they had even, once, met down here. One of the others had argued forcefully that the only English kings who were deposed were homosexuals. Jack had quit the group after that. He saw Peter come up the ramp from the Cross Campus Library.

He had taken off his tie and had his overcoat and blazer stuffed under one arm and a stack of books under the other. His hair looked white under the overhead lamps, and a little disheveled. He dumped his stuff next to Jack and went to get some coffee. "I had to stand in line for fifteen minutes to check out. Half the books in that library are on overnight reserve."

"I hate it down there," Jack said. An underground library was a contradiction to him, lightless and airless. It gave him the uncomfortable feeling that he was breathing in what other people had just finished breathing out.

Peter pushed his hair back. "Shakespearean criticism. I don't think I'm going to learn anything about acting from all this." He shoved the pile of books aside.

"The critic is the actor's better half," Jack said pedantically.

Peter ignored him. "The one thing about Shakespeare that I've never understood —"

"Only one thing?"

"— is the way his characters fall in love at the slightest provocation. One minute Romeo's in love with Rosalind, the next it's Juliet. Orsino spends the whole play swooning over Olivia, and then at the drop of a hat marries Viola. I mean, how can you possibly play that so it's believable?"

"I think it's supposed to mean that when love is right, it's right." This was a sore subject with him, of course. He said, changing the subject, "Did you know that Viola and Olivia are practically anagrams?"

But Peter didn't want to be deterred. It was the old discussion, not what a play meant so much as how one would perform it. Jack let him run on, knowing that Peter didn't really want Jack's opinions, not yet anyway, he was just trying out ideas. His whole manner became animated, he dropped his lethargic pose and found his own words when he talked about acting. Jack watched him, appreciating the transformation.

"What are you staring at?" Peter said eventually.

"Huh?"

"I asked you a question and you didn't answer, you're just staring at me."

"I was thinking —"

"What?"

"I was just noticing — that you wear an undershirt." Most of the people he knew didn't wear undershirts. It was the kind of thing Jack thought of as being very midwestern for some reason, and he'd been watching the undershirt between the wings of Peter's collar. Jack felt warm and a little drowsy, it was late and he'd had a big dinner. He said, "I think it's very sexy."

Peter frowned and shook his head. "Careful, Jack."

"That's not what I meant." He felt very sad suddenly.

Peter got out a cigarette, and Jack watched his hands while he lit it. "Is this all because your brother-in-law came to visit?"

Jack shook his head. "No." Then he said, angry again, "I can't believe he sat there and talked about his father dying, about his father not being there anymore. Insensitive clod." Peter coughed at that point, and Jack said glumly, "You shouldn't smoke so much."

"Jack, he's entitled to his feelings, isn't he?"

"Yeah, but not to mine."

"He probably wasn't even thinking about you. Hard as that is to believe."

"Oh shut up." He leaned against the wall and swung his legs up on the fake leather bench. "What are your brothers like?"

"My older brother lives in California, he went to MIT and now he works for a computer company. I really miss him. The only good thing about his being in California is I have someone to call at two in the morning if I'm bummed out. My little brother is really great, though. He'll be up visiting in a few weeks, we should do something. He's sixteen, and he's the sweetest kid. Did you ever know anyone who has perfect instincts?"

Jack looked into the paper cup with the handles like two misshapen ears, wondering what the residue was — machine coffee, powdered milk, that indefinable something, like fuel oil — that floated on the top. "You."

"Wrong-o. About acting maybe —"

"About me, maybe."

"No. It doesn't matter. I mean perfect instincts about life. My little brother is like that. You'll meet him."

As they walked out of the library later, Peter said, "By the way, Jack, this solitary confinement number you're doing isn't exactly cute. Are you going to give it up, or what?"

"I guess so," he agreed, reluctantly. And after that he'd gone back to his life. He felt changed, more brittle, tougher on top, like snow after a hard frost, but he gave up his willful seclusion. Sometime later he realized that as usual he had done exactly what David wanted, he'd snapped out of his isolation. David's method — dinner out, a friend — wasn't what Jack had expected, but he'd accomplished what he wanted just the same. Jack found out later, by accident, that David hadn't just dropped by, that Elizabeth, hearing reports through her shadowy network and unable to reach him by phone, had sent David on a reconnaissance mission. Somehow, that wasn't what he thought of when he imagined having a brother. Someone more like Timothy.

Looking at him in the rocking chair now, Jack was enveloped in a kind of haze, midway between sickness and health, between waking and sleeping, as if he were dozing with his eyes open. In this state, sounds came to him with great clarity, the turning of the pages in Timothy's book, the cry of a bird outside, the slamming of a car door.

"Ellen's home," Timothy said.

She came into the room a minute later. "How do you feel?" She sat down on the bed next to him and put her hand on his forehead. "Any better?"

"I'm getting there. Be careful, I don't want you to catch it."

"If I didn't get it from you last night, I never will." She brushed the hair back from his forehead and he thought, She loves me.

"I see you have everything you need," she said, and he thought, Now I have everything I want. "You're not usually so efficient about things, Timothy."

Timothy put his hand to his chest, pretending to be wounded. "Oh, come on. It's what I like best about myself, how efficient I can be when I want to."

She shifted her position on the bed to get more comfortable, and Jack leaned his head against her shoulder. Her skin felt very cool to him. "Seriously," she said, "what do you like best about yourself?"

Timothy considered. "I don't know. Kind of a tough question to answer, isn't it." They waited while he thought. "What do you think I should say?"

"Wimping out?" Ellen said. "I think that what you should like best about yourself is your honesty. What do you think, Jack?"

He thought of that night at Val's, his birthday, when he'd been so candid with Timothy — that's what had started all of this, he thought. Timothy was honest, both in himself and in the way he inspired honesty in Jack. But there was something else about him, that sense that he held nothing back, that he didn't seem to know that exposing himself so completely could only lead in the end to his getting hurt. Or, if he knew, he went ahead anyway and didn't count the cost. He said, "His innocence."

Timothy groaned. "Great. Mothers can trust their daughters to me — what an awful thought."

Jack said, "I didn't say you were trustworthy. I wouldn't know about that. Just that you were innocent." He was thinking of himself: neither trustworthy, if that meant the ability to say no, nor innocent.

Ellen said, "What I like best about myself is the way my mind works. The ability to analyze, to nail down facts, to be precise and orderly —"

"The scientific method," Jack said.

"Exactly."

He pictured her at work. His acquaintance with labs had terminated with his last biology class at Westfield, but he had an image of her sitting in front of huge machines that hurled minute particles at each other while she watched, her face lit orange by the glow of their decay; or did she even go to the labs? Perhaps the experiments were conducted in faraway places, out in the desert or under the Alps, and the data were relayed to her by satellite, appearing as numbers on a computer screen (the glow on her face turned from orange to green). He could picture her standing before a blackboard on which complicated hieroglyphs were written, her fingers yellow with chalk, solving equations full of Greek letters, the calculus of creation. How easily he could envision that, her hair in a dark cloud around her face, the clicking of her high heels disturbing the reverential hush with which her colleagues (all old men with straying white hair and lab coats) approached their sacred task, her crimson dress lighting up their darkness. Their eyes would be fixed on the beauty of worlds in collision, the catherine-wheel release of subatomic particles, or the delicate trail of bubbles in a chamber, and all the while her beauty, whole and intact, would be standing amid them, unseen. I love her, he thought.

"What about you, Jack?" she said.

"Hmm?"

"What do you like best about yourself?"

"Oh," Timothy interrupted, "Jack doesn't like anything about himself. You'll see. He thinks he's a terrible person, he needs absolution."

"Timothy —" his sister said.

"No, really," he went on blithely, making light of it. "I don't know what it is, but Jack seems to think he's done something awful."

Damn him, Jack thought. He paraphrased *Casablanca:* "I absconded with the church funds, or ran off with a senator's wife."

"How romantic," Ellen said. "But what do you like best about yourself?"

"The same as you. My mind. But for opposite reasons. The way it makes connections between things that have no other connection. The way it jumps, totally unsystematically, from one idea to another, from one subject to another." He yawned. "I couldn't master physics, or anything else that required an intense focus. I can barely concentrate on three things at a time, let alone one."

Timothy stood up. "Fish and fowl. Will you excuse me? I think I'm going to take a swim."

After he'd gone, Ellen said, "Are you tired?"

"I'm all right." His head was starting to hurt again, but he said, "Tell me about physics."

She laughed. "Physics 101? Quantum mechanics? What?"

"Archer physics. What do you do?"

"I'm with Con Tech's pure research group, working on particle research. Mostly mathematical derivations of experimental data." He watched as she talked. She appeared so relaxed, so calm. He was used to people who, being simple in themselves, were aimed at complicated purposes, who were all sound and fury. Her aim was simple, or direct anyway, it was her personality that seemed complicated. He wondered if this were just a feverish paradox or a real truth. "Do you follow any of this?" she concluded.

"A little. Matter-antimatter asymmetry — it's the stuff that Nobel Prizes are made of."

"Someday," she said matter-of-factly.

"Is that why you do it?"

She stood up and walked to the window, looking down at the garden. "I do it because it's right for me," she said, and again he had the impression of great simplicity. "I've never done anything else that gives me that same feeling, as if something important in me is coming to the surface."

"The scientific method," he said. "I envy you your sense of purpose."

She turned around and leaned against the windowsill, smoothing her dress on her thighs with her hands. "But you must feel that too. You say you can't concentrate on any one thing, but I have the feeling that all of that intelligence, your ability to talk so beautifully and knowledgeably about anything under the sun, all that modern art and southern rock, is just a mask, a kind of patter to distract people from the real you. You're good at it. I imagine it fools most people."

But not you, he thought. Or Timothy. He didn't answer her.

"Is that what you're doing? Fooling people?"

He pushed his back into the pillows. He could tell her that his head was hurting, that he felt sick again, and she'd leave it. He said, "I used to think, in college, when it was the thing to do to sit around all night and analyze people, that a person is like an onion. You can peel away layer after layer, like stripping away all the ornamentation of a personality, the patina that we like to say hides the so-called real self. But when you do that, when you cut away the last layer of the onion, you have nothing left. The onion is all layers, one after another. What makes the center one any more real than any of the others?"

She thought about this, and he could see that she was giving it the kind of studious attention she would give a problem in her work. She said, "What if you looked at it, though, the other way around? It's not the taking away of layers but the accretion of them that shows the whole person. It's not that the inside is more valid, it's the way the layers are revealed, their order, that's important." She waited for him to answer, and when he didn't, she said, "Is Timothy right about you? Is there something you're hiding?"

Of course there was. A great gaping hole in the center of his personality, a literal void, like a well that had no bottom. You could drop a rock into that blackness and sit by it all your life waiting for the sound of its downfall, but you would never hear, and if you fell in, you would never come to the bottom, because there would be no one to catch you. He had looked, from a distance, through a complicated series of distorting mirrors, into the hole, and he had some idea of what was in it, but he wouldn't get close enough for a good look, wouldn't invite disaster — vertigo, a false step, the endless falling. Now she was pushing him right to its edge. "Ellen," he said, his voice sounding impossibly distant even to him.

"Oh, Jack, I'm sorry." She came and sat next to him on the bed. "I didn't mean —" She put her arm around him.

"The scientific method." He made his voice as light as he could.

She laughed. "Oh, I'm sorry. But you make me laugh. I should let you sleep or you'll get sicker."

"Couldn't we just stay like this?" He snuggled down into her arms, and she stayed with him until he fell asleep.

He woke up hours later, alone in the room and feeling a lot better. He stretched lazily, and got up and took a bath. Then, feeling almost well again, he dressed and went downstairs.

The big house was quiet and cool, full of long banners of light from the afternoon sun. He heard voices from the back and walked toward the kitchen.

"You always take his side," he heard Timothy say petulantly.

"Oh, poor baby," Ellen answered. "I didn't know this was a contest."

"Well, it is. I found that out a long time ago."

"If it's a contest, tell me what the object is — how you know if you've won or not."

Jack, in the hall outside, leaned against a wall and listened.

"I win if I can manage to get away, to feel good about myself occasionally without always having him lecture me on all my weak points. Otherwise he wins."

"Well, then," Jack heard her take a bite of something before she went on, "then it seems to me you're doomed to lose."

"Why?" Timothy asked combatively. "Because his standards are so high for me. Because he'll never be satisfied, because I can never live up to them. Or because I'm really not good enough."

"You're being a little melodramatic aren't you?"

"That's what Jack says." His voice sounded sulky. "What if I am? I'm entitled to, sometimes."

There was a long silence. Jack wondered if he should go in, but he didn't want to interrupt them, and besides, he wanted to hear the end of it.

Timothy finally said, "Then what did you mean, I'm doomed to lose."

"I'll tell you. You're letting him set the rules. Not even him, but your image of him. You're unhappy because of what you think he thinks about you, when the only thing I can see being important is what you think."

"That's easy for you to say —"

"All I'm saying is that you're twenty-five years old. You graduated summa from one of the best schools in the world, you were Phi Beta Kappa in your junior year, you're about to get a doctorate. Don't you think it's time to take responsibility for your own life? What if he was the worst father in the world, what if he'd beaten you and abused you and hated you — at some point it stops being his fault and starts becoming your responsibility. It's your life, after all."

There was another long pause, and Jack, who was beginning to feel a little wobbly again, decided to interrupt. Timothy was saying, "You're right, of course, but —" when Jack came in, and he broke off. It was like a tableau, the two of them turning to look at him, but otherwise not moving. Timothy was wearing his bathing suit, and over it a long gray sweatshirt with the sleeves pushed up, his hair damp and dark from the pool. Ellen was sitting on a stool, leaning easily back against the counter, holding a glass of lemonade. He felt as if he'd intruded into something very private, a child in an adult world. The moment seemed oddly prolonged, and then Timothy broke it. "How're you feeling? You were supposed to stay in bed." He looked at his sister, as if to say, We'll finish this later.

"I'm feeling a lot better, actually. My fever's down to ninety-nine point eight. Practically normal."

"For a hot-blooded soul like you," Timothy said. He seemed a little uneasy, the hangover perhaps of his conversation with Ellen. "Let's go into the family room. You can lie down there."

Jack got settled on the couch, still feeling a little hazy, but lying down helped. Ellen sat near him on a chair. Timothy, his legs sticking out from the bottom of his sweatshirt, was wandering around the room, picking up things and putting them down, a magazine, an ashtray, a framed picture of his parents in evening clothes. "By the way," he said, "Andrew called before. He wanted to thank us for a wonderful evening. He was especially impressed with you, Jack. He wants to know if we'll join him for the dance at the country club Saturday night. The annual hoopla." He knelt down and opened the door of a cabinet that was built in under some shelves.

Jack hadn't been to the club dance in years, since he was twenty-two, and Elizabeth had fixed him up with some girl she'd thought suitable. Timothy snorted when Jack told them. "God, I remember her. She played the cello and talked about Bach a lot. Very wholesome. I wouldn't have thought she was your type." He sat back on his heels, looking into the cupboard.

"She was Elizabeth's type. It was her idea. She didn't much like my type in those days. I think we should go." His first real date with Ellen.

"Well, then," Ellen said, "we'll go. You'll have to wear your tuxedo, Timothy."

Timothy mumbled something. He was reaching into the cabinet, trying to get something that appeared to be just out of reach.

"What?"

"I said, three's a crowd."

"Then get a date."

"Where?" He finally got whatever it was he was reaching for — a box of some kind. He seemed deliberately out of sorts, and Jack wondered for the first time how Timothy really felt about all of this. Jack was his friend, after all, he'd brought Jack here, and now Ellen had come along and — what? taken Jack away from him. But he'd said the night before that that was why he'd brought Jack here in the first place. Jack said, "Why don't you call Susan Howell, Andrew's cousin. She's staying with them all week, I'll bet she'd like to go."

Timothy bit his lip, thinking. Then he shrugged and held up the box he'd found in the cupboard. "Here's our old Monopoly set. Anybody want to play?"

The next afternoon a tornado swept over them. Jack, feeling better but still tired, had taken a nap. When he woke up, the room was very dark and he wondered at first whether he'd slept through supper. He got up and looked outside.

The sky was black, with huge clouds that towered upward, and he could see them boiling within themselves. There was a dangerous green tint in the sky and the air smelled of ozone. The trees were showing the white undersides of their leaves, and the wind gusted up and then, almost more alarmingly, fell still. He put on his shoes and went downstairs, looking for Ellen and Timothy.

The thunder started without warning — no early rumbles but a full-fledged crash that shook the house, and then another, banging as if something vital were being cracked open, a large oak, perhaps, or the vault of heaven. The lights in the house went out.

Across the valley he could see the trees on the hillside bending to the gusts, and then the water in the pond whipped up, and then the grass in front, before the wind slammed against the windows. A porch chair, out on the terrace, blew over, and he opened a sliding door and went outside to retrieve it. In front of him (it seemed almost close enough to touch) lightning forked down into the lake. Above his head, the yellow-and-white-striped porch awning cracked as the wind tore at it and he looked up at its metal frame, a perfect lightning rod. The thunder rang again, even closer, if that were possible, and he shook his head in all the wildness. His shirt was blowing around his body and his hair was tossing in the wind. Either he would reach out, touch the crank, and wheel the awning in, or it would get blown to shreds, like a sail he'd once seen at the Cape that hadn't been furled properly against the boom. There was more lightning, and with the feeling that he was daring fate, he took the metal crank in his hand and began turning it as hard as he could, reeling in the cloth. The wind kicked up even harder, and another chair blew over and scraped across the flagstone. Shit, he thought, this is not good. He had to lean against the wind to stay upright, and the first rain came. Within a few seconds, he was soaked. Where the hell is Timothy, he thought, and tried calling for him, but the storm tore the words away. There was another flash of lightning, so close now that he almost heard the buzzing of its static field, and for an instant he thought he felt it in the now nearly completely exposed awning frame. He gave one last turn to the crank, tightening it, and then leaned against the wall.

He knew that he would never forget what he was seeing. Across the lake, barely visible through the rain, trees were collapsing on the opposite hillside, an invisible foot was stomping out of the sky and breaking the trunks off. He couldn't hear the sound, but he could imagine the wrenching, tearing noise it was making. Hail began to fall around him, bouncing off the terrace, and he wondered if the killing wind would cross the lake and walk up to the house. It would rip the roof off, he thought, there's nowhere to hide.

He ducked back inside the house. He couldn't see the tornado across the pond anymore, the valley was full of blackness, either mist or rain, hail or dust. As he stood in the dark, breathing hard, water running out of his hair and down the sides of his face, he held on hard to the feeling that he'd been in a confrontation with something far removed from the cloistered world of words and wit that he usually inhabited, and that he'd won.

By the next afternoon, Jack was over his bug and Timothy had a date for Saturday night.

"I called Susan Howell," he said after lunch. "She wants to go with me."

He and Jack were walking in the garden, which had come through its ordeal of wind and water relatively unscathed. Some tall spiked flowers were broken off, and one of the stems of a rose bush had broken free from a trellis and was hanging down onto the grass, but otherwise, things looked more or less as usual.

"Actually, I had a long talk with her when she was here the other night. She seems like a really nice person."

"She is, at least she was when I knew her in college." He hadn't thought very carefully about the implications of all of this. How Susan would view his intervention in light of what she had told him on Saturday night, what she might tell Timothy or even Ellen about his past. What the hell, he thought impatiently, they're my friends. So what if they find out things about me. He said, "I went out with her roommate. It ended — well, badly, I guess, and I sort of lost touch with Susan after we graduated."

They had reached the end of the garden and turned to look back. The terraces of grass fell neatly, one after another, the lawns clipped as close as moss. Beauty and harmony, he thought, looking down the arranged ranks of flowers, over the valley and the pond. He noticed a stand of trees planted nearby, arranged as carefully as a centerpiece for a table, and the way the cypress spiked the sky. Nothing was unintentional, yet everything looked unplanned, so that the eye was fooled and, still more, the mind was lulled. "Timothy. Is this the most beautiful place in the world, or what? I've been here, oh, ten days and I feel like I've never been anywhere else. That whole life in New York seems so far away, so crazy. I can barely imagine going back. To Boyd and Amy, to Val's and all those places."

"To Kate," Timothy ventured.

Jack nodded slowly. He was engaged to her, secret or not, and here he was in love with another woman. But he wasn't ready to discuss that with Timothy. Not until he was ready to discuss it with Ellen first. "She's still in Switzerland for another two weeks."

"Well, I'm going to be here all summer. Most of it anyway. You can stay as long as you want." He paused, and then added a little mischievously, "Ellen has to go back after next week. Her vacation's over on the twenty-fourth."

"Mine's over at the end of the month. But I just might have to go back sooner."

"For a movie opening or something?"

"Or something." Jack laughed. They sat down on the grass and waited while Ellen walked up the garden to them.

"Have you read the paper?" she said.

"About the storm?" Timothy nodded. "From here to New Haven. It sounded terrible."

"It was," Jack said, remembering the storm stomping the trees. He lay on his side, his head propped up on his bent arm, listening to them, feeling the sun through his tennis shirt, thinking that maybe, after all, he really did deserve this. At least for a change, at least for a little while. Mr. Prescott was on his knees in a bed nearby weeding, and a crew of three or four shirtless young men, with tattoos and ponytails, were busy at a variety of purposeful tasks — wheeling barrows of dirt, mixing powders in watering cans, barbering the grass at the edges of the beds. The flowers were in full bloom, although in this garden, he thought, there would always be flowers in full bloom, it would have been made that way, and the bees hummed about undisturbed. The week stretched out in front of him, empty hours to spend with Ellen, and a dance at the end of it. Love, it seemed, was a series of moments irregularly spaced and of varying significance, the time between them taken up by the meaningless transaction of daily life.

XI

IT WAS ELLEN who raised the problem of a tuxedo. Timothy was going to be wearing his to the dance, so he couldn't lend it to Jack, and their father's would be too short for him. "You could always rent one," she suggested.

"No way. I hate the idea of used clothes. You have no idea who had it on before you. It's gross."

"Well, then —?"

He thought a moment, staring up at the treetops, at the way their branches came together, the way the leaves were fluttering in the gentle breeze — losing himself for a moment to avoid answering. "Well, there is one possibility."

"What?"

He went on, a little reluctantly. "We could go over to my house and see if there's one there. I think I remember seeing one in some closet or other." He knew, in fact, exactly where he had seen it, but he wasn't ready yet to be definite. He wanted to see how it felt, first, to be in that house, before he made any commitments.

"Would you like me to go with you?" Ellen asked. "I have to mail some letters in town."

Relieved, he said yes.

When they reached the main road, instead of heading left, toward the school, he turned right. The road ran along the crest of a gentle rounded ridge between acres planted with corn. He turned onto a narrow road that wound through a cornfield and then petered out into a dirt track before entering a small wood. Through the trees they came to pavement again, and the road swooped down beside a tumbling brook. He stopped the car. "Do you feel that?"

"What?"

"That dampness — the sort of dark muddy dampness. From the river. First the hot sun, then the cool smell of the river."

"I never even knew this was here." She looked at the little stream that twisted down between the rocks. A bird flashed across the open space and lost itself in the woods.

"I learned all these roads when I was a teenager," Jack said. "During the summers — I lived with my sister and my nephews, my brother-in-law would stay in town and come up on the week-ends — I would drive all over the place. So I know all the shortcuts and all the scenic routes. This one takes us around to the other side of town without the traffic lights and all on Main Street. It was always the cool thing to find ways of avoiding traffic lights. My nephew Billy is sixteen, he'll probably find all the same short-cuts we found." He began driving again, idling along the narrow lane. "When I was eighteen and Boyd was sixteen — do you know Boyd?" She shook her head, but he went on without explanation. "I'd pick him up and we'd just tool around, going no place. Some-times I'd let him drive, even though he didn't have a license, we'd drive for hours it seemed, with the windows open and the summer night air blowing through the car, feeling hot and damp, just like this. Usually we'd end up parking over near Merriam's Glen, where the river comes out of the reservoir through that gorge? Sitting in the car, with the tape deck cranked, getting high. I still feel stoned sometimes, just listening to "Ramblin' Man" or "L.A. Freeway" or any song on the "Nightrider" album." He knew she wasn't following him, but he went on anyway. "Then we'd go skinny-dipping in the gorge — you know where that pool is, just below the first waterfall? There's a little cliff you can climb, all knobby and — I don't know, it always felt so real, somehow, under my bare feet, so solid, still warm from the hot day. It had a ledge at the bottom that stuck out a couple of feet, but under water, so if you didn't jump far enough out, you'd land on it. Everybody jumped anyway, though, that's how Chip Thomas broke his leg one summer. Boyd used to dare me to dive off it. No one ever did. But I did, once." The starry sky, the gorge thick with mist. Boyd's naked body, white in the black water, his legs moving slowly beneath the surface, his voice calling up, jeering Jack on. And Jack all alone on top of the rock, feeling the cool air surrounding his body, his toes curled around the edge of the rock, defying the vision that was in his head, until the vision won out and he cut head first through the air and cleanly into the water beyond the ledge. "The gorge was full of fireflies, thousands of them, all around me as I dove."

Ellen put her hand on his. "Why are you so nervous, Jack?"

He slowed the car down and turned into a driveway. "That. I guess." He pointed at the house.

"But there's nobody home, is there?"

"No." Still, he felt like an intruder. He wasn't supposed to be here. He had run away from New York, from Elizabeth and David, he hadn't told anyone where he was. He was falling in love with a woman who had no place in the usual order of his life, he was leaving behind another woman who occupied, by contrast, very nearly the most central place in that life. He had broken all the rules. Coming here was flaunting his transgression. "They're not coming up for another couple of weeks. Elizabeth has some committee she's on that had the bad taste to schedule meetings in July."

He parked in the front drive and they looked up at the house. "My grandfather built it. My father's father. He gave it to my parents as a wedding present."

"We don't have to go in if you don't want to."

"Oh, I'm all right. Don't you ever feel strange coming home after a long time?" He switched off the car and got out. "I used to go back to Yale and stand in the dining room at Berkeley College, where I'd eaten every meal, just about, for three years, and just feel out of place. I didn't quite know what I was doing there, how to fit in."

Ellen's sneakers crunched on the gravel as they walked up to the front door. "I used to feel that way at Harvard. But then I went back one day after three or four years, and I didn't feel strange at all. I told myself that was the moment I became an alumna. I just had a new role to fill."

"Writing checks," he said, taking out his keys. "Well, I fit in here. I own this house, or half of it anyway."

"Which half?"

"It's an undivided interest." He opened the door and they stepped inside.

The air was very close and hot, and all the curtains were closed over the windows. On a mahogany side table in the front hall was a white porcelain bowl with figures painted on it, deep blue and pale orange and thin green — an emperor receiving an envoy, while off near the edge two women hid behind a fan. He dropped his keys loudly into the bowl. Ellen laughed and reached out for him, and kissed him.

"What's that for?"

"The way you put the keys in that bowl. It seemed so habitual — I just had this vision of you always doing that, every time you came in here. Of the way you do things."

He smiled a little shyly. "It's true. I've been doing that since I was eleven or twelve. My mother said it was a Chinese export bowl — two hundred years old. I said if it had lasted that long, it wouldn't break from my keys."

"And you always got your way. Did they spoil you?"

"In some things." He stepped away from her but kept hold of her hand. He imagined he could still hear the bowl ringing in the silence.

"It's stuffy in here," she said.

"At least we don't cover the furniture with sheets."

She giggled. "My grandmother used to do that every winter before she went to Palm Beach."

"Mine too." He led her up the stairs. "Let's look in my room first." He knew the tux wasn't there, but it was a place to start.

His room was as he'd left it at Christmas, the last time he'd been back, but it might as well have been as he'd left it the day he went to college ten years before, as if it had been caught in a time warp. There was the old armchair, recovered in honor of his twelfth birthday in a black-and-white houndstooth that he'd never liked — he'd never liked the chair, come to think of it, it was oddly constructed to be uncomfortable. There was the boyish bed, chastely narrow, with the zebra-striped spread. He remembered lying naked, face down, on that spread, which had smelled to him of salt, the rough feel of its nap on his body as he rolled around noiselessly in a frenzy of fantasy, dreaming a long-legged girl beneath him, unbearably imaginable and distant, feeling the rush building in him like a great long-held breath, until at the last moment he rolled over on his back and spurted over his chest and belly (imagining David, maybe, listening at the keyhole). And now here he was, in this room with a real woman, something he had never thought of in adolescent days. He thought she must see those desires shimmering in the air above the bed like the heat from a glassy desert.

But Ellen was looking at the bookshelf, which stood on a battered chest of drawers. Most of the books had been removed to his library in New York, the few that remained having only archaeological interest. He reached over her and pulled one from the shelf: *Great Baseball Heroes.* On the cover an orange-faced Babe swung mightily at a ball, the crack of his bat indicated by little blue lines radiating from its end. It was the sort of book in which Ruth visited sick boys in hospital beds, Grover Alexander was always sober, and Jackie Robinson owed his success to the generosity of organized baseball. He couldn't imagine that he'd ever believed all that, lying in bed with the pillows propped against the wall, his own arms feeling loose from an afternoon of swinging the bat, reading of unstained heroes. He hadn't, at the age of eight or ten, known that there were only men in the world, swaggering, angry, or drunk, but not heroes. He said, "Did girls have books like this? Lives of the saints?"

She sat on the edge of the bed, and the heart of his adolescent avatar jumped at the sight. "When I was a girl, I used to read biographies all the time. Florence Nightingale, Clara Barton, Edith Cavell — I obviously went through a nurse stage. Marie Curie, of course. They were all referred to by their first names, which always made them seem girlish — ever notice how women are always called by their first names, even if they do somehow win the Nobel Prize? As if their lives are essentially cozy and domestic, no different from any other mom's. 'The baby was named Eve, and Marie was very happy.' Of course she was — taking care of the kids wouldn't interfere with the Crimean War or the discovery of radium. Mom, apple pie, and the Nobel Prize. Talk about having it all."

"Is that what you want?" He leaned against the desk and crossed his arms.

"What I want?" She laughed, a little awkwardly, he thought, and stood up next to the desk, not looking at him. "I've given up thinking about what I want. I've decided to live in the present, not in the future."

Yes, he thought, and I'm drowning in my past. He opened the closet door, and looked in. Some trousers, a half-dozen shirts, an old blazer, and a business suit hung on the rods. "No tuxedo."

"What's this?" She picked up a battered volume with an accordion binding.

"Oh. My old photo album."

"Can I look?"

"Sure. I'm going to go check next door."

He went into the master bedroom and opened the closets. David's clothes hung neatly, but his evening suit must still be in New York. It wouldn't have fit Jack anyway. He knew where the one he wanted was — if he wanted it. He sat down on the little stool in front of the table on which Elizabeth kept her perfume and her powder, her hairbrush and lipstick, where their mother had kept her cosmetics. He put his hand out and held it tentatively over the jewelry box, a gilt wooden case with an imitation French baroque painting on the lid, shepherds and shepherdesses, or aristocrats in drag. His fingertips brushed the surface, and then he opened the lid a fraction of an inch. His mother's jewelry box.

It wasn't a music box, but he had always liked to lift the cover very slowly to look at the treasures inside. He would come in here with his hair wet from the bath, feeling the sunburn under his ribbed cotton pajamas, when the sky through the window was almost painfully blue right after sunset, when his mother was dressing to go out to a party, and he would open the box and play with her jewelry. She had a diamond bracelet, he remembered, and a necklace that he used to spread out on the table top — a chain of blue and white stones with a large pendant, a sapphire surrounded by diamonds. He had to be sure that it was all flat on the table, all untangled and displayed for her. A whole set of her emeralds — earrings, necklace, bracelet, pin — had been put away in a bank vault in Manhattan, for him when he had someone to give them to. Emeralds — the color of his eyes. He looked into the mirror on the dressing table, seeing his green eyes; behind him, in the room, reflected in the mirror, he could see his mother.

She was wearing a long blue dress, with big skirts spread out around her, and her shoulders were bare, and her sapphire necklace was around her neck. Her hair, the same reddish golden brown as his, was caught up at the back of her head before falling softly on her neck. A little boy, perhaps ten years old, stood in front of her, wearing short pajamas, his hair stuck damply to the top of his head, one stray lock plastered to his cheek, which she gently pushed back into place. "May I have this dance," she said, holding out her arms, and she began to hum "Isn't It Romantic," the song they always danced to. He reached up and took her hands and, as she had taught him, began to dance a kind of fox trot. He had his tongue clamped firmly between his lips and his head down, watching his feet, and she kept saying, "Not so stiff, Johnny, look at me." When he finally looked at her, she smiled and leaned down in a cloud of perfume and taffeta rustlings and hugged him.

"How'd I do, Mommy?"

"Very good, darling," she said.

He hugged her back. "I love you, Mommy."

Dancing with her —

He was wearing a blue suit and a white shirt and a red striped tie. He was thirteen or so, and he was in a large room with forty other boys and girls, all similarly attired (Mary Henley was overdressed as usual, but Tommy Klein had nearly been refused entrance because he was wearing sneakers, being saved at the last minute by the foresight of his mother, who arrived with a pair of polished black shoes), in a hotel in New York. At one end of the room a small band was waiting, between numbers, and Mrs. Pauling, whose dance class (Academie de Danse) this was, was addressing a few words over the heads of her pupils to the parents gathered on chairs at the back of the room. The students had finished demonstrating their prowess through a series of waltzes, fox trots, rumbas, cha-chas, and even a generally unsuccessful tango. After Mrs. Pauling finished speaking (if she ever did, he thought, shifting his weight from one foot to the other), the exhibition would cease and more normal relations between the sexes would be established: the boys would stand on one side of the room, the girls sit on the other. At a signal, the boys were, in theory, to walk decorously across the room to ask the girl of their choice for the honor of a dance. In practice the signal always resulted in a mad rush across the floor, as each boy tried to be the first to ask the more desirable girls, and each girl tried to calculate the risk of turning down a firm offer in the speculation that someone better would come along. He had rather sarcastically described this scene to his mother, who hadn't seen the humor in it. "I hope," she said as she sat before her dressing table, "you don't participate in that."

"Why not?" He was rather proud of his technique in nearly always dancing with whomever he wanted: a wink, literally, was as good as a nod.

"Think of those poor girls who don't get asked. How do you think they feel?"

"Maybe they'd feel better if they got their teeth straightened or their noses fixed." He thought that a very sophisticated crack.

"John. I don't think that's funny, and I don't want to hear you talk like that. I remember a little boy, and not so long ago either, who refused to play football because he was always picked last. If you're going to be a man, act like one. And that means always including everyone you can, and certainly not hurting people's feelings."

Here he felt moved to defend himself, despite feeling that the position was not very defensible. "But I'm not hurting their feelings."

"Even so, you're allowing their feelings to be hurt. That's wrong, and it's ungentlemanly. Besides, you might find yourself liking it." She smiled back at him from her mirror. "I wasn't always the prettiest girl in my set."

After that, he made a point of always asking the gross girls, as they were called, to dance one or two of the five or six free dances that ended every class. Oddly enough, this seemed to increase his prestige. Blair Phillips told him she thought it was very mature of him.

Now, as Mrs. Pauling approached her peroration, he watched out of the corner of his eye as Blair tried to get his attention. He and Blair were the closest thing Mrs. Pauling allowed to a steady couple — he knew that if he looked at her, she would turn down anybody to wait for his invitation. But he didn't look, having another invitation in mind. Mrs. Pauling announced the dance and the rush began.

He stood up and, walking unconcernedly away from the line of girls opposite, pressed through the throng. He went over to his mother and said, "May I have the honor of this dance?" She, looking very pleased, held out her hand, and he led her to the floor, oblivious to the stares of his classmates and the appreciative stirring of the other parents. "Thank you, Johnny," she said.

"Wait," he said. For he had read Scott Fitzgerald by then and had had a few words with the bandleader before the dance, culminating in a pecuniary transaction, and when the band began, it played, "Isn't It Romantic."

"Johnny, this is perfect." They danced across the floor, and he felt as if he had done the most wonderful, adult thing of his life. And later, when he danced with Blair, she told him it was the most beautiful thing she'd ever seen, it had nearly made her cry. And looking into her eyes, her perfect blue eyes that he'd seen so many times, he thought that if he asked her, she would go out into the hall with him and kiss him (which she did). But the real reward, the best part of the evening, came when he led his mother off the dance floor, back toward her chair, and his father stood up, his eyes moist in his red face, hugging him and saying, "I'm so proud of you, Johnny."

His father's favorite song, "Isn't It Romantic." Played at all their parties, even the first one he remembered, here in this house.

He was lying on the bed, naked under a mound of mink coats, with his teddy bear, peeking out at the room. There was a party going on downstairs, some noise had awakened him, and he and his bear had gotten up to go to the bathroom. He had left his pajamas on the bathroom floor and had come in here to explore. The coats on the bed looked inviting, and he gradually burrowed his way under them until he could see out only a little, the fur prickling against his naked skin. Then he fell asleep until something woke him and he looked out.

His mother was sitting at the dressing table looking in the mirror, putting on some fresh lipstick. He could still hear the party, piano music from downstairs, but he felt far away from it here, and he thought it would be fun to jump up and surprise her. He was about to, when a man came into the room and shut the door. "I thought I'd find you here."

His mother turned her head, still holding the lipstick. "Hello, Ted. Were you looking for me?"

"You know I was." The man walked over and put his hands on his mother's shoulders. "This music is wonderful — 'Isn't It Romantic.' "

"It's my husband's favorite song," she said, turning back to the mirror.

He didn't like Ted much. That afternoon, they'd all gone out skating on the lake, and Ted had been too loud. His mother finished and closed down her lipstick. Then she stood up, freeing herself from Ted's hands. At first Ted let her go, but then he held her in his arms and kissed her.

"Ted," she said, "that's enough. Anne is my best friend, and I love my husband."

"So what." He tried to kiss her again, but she moved away. "I want you. Anne doesn't have to know. You know your husband will never notice. I can meet you in New York, next week, anytime."

"You're acting like a college boy," she said, looking at herself in the tall mirror, adjusting something on her dress. Then there was a knock, and the door opened. It was Anne. He liked her, she did a lot of fun things with him like going to the zoo or the toy store at Christmas and buying him a big train set. Anne said, "Here you are. Am I interrupting?"

"Your husband was making love to me." The two women laughed, and Ted looked angry and left the room.

"It's a good thing we're friends," his mother said.

"It's hopeless. I don't even know if I care anymore. With a stranger, I don't think I would. With you, though —"

He sneezed at that point, and they heard him. "Johnny," his mother said, "what are you doing here?"

"Hi, Mommy."

"Where are your pajamas?"

"In the bathroom."

They put his pajamas on and his mother said, "Back to bed, Johnny." But Anne picked him up and said, "He wants to go to the party, don't you, Johnny? Come downstairs." And she carried him down and sat him on the piano and sang a song to him, and then his father put him to bed, telling him they'd all live happily ever after.

And another memory, without a happy ending.

He was lying on the bed, sulking, while his mother finished dressing. He couldn't see himself very clearly: he was wearing a hooded sweatshirt and a pair of shorts, and his feet were dirty. His hair looked longer to him than he remembered it, and he was biting the index finger of his left hand. His face, though, was a blank, as if someone had sponged away all his features. He didn't want to know what his expression had been. His mother, standing in the little dressing area in front of her closet, called out, "I want you to go downstairs and apologize."

"You're being so unfair."

"You're being discourteous. I would have thought you were old enough now to behave properly." She came into the bedroom (and now he remembered again how beautiful she had been to him that night, even in his bad temper he had noticed her, standing still and angry in the middle of the room and had thought how beautiful she was) and then she went to the dressing table, to her jewelry box.

Petulant, he ignored the warning tone in her voice. "I am old enough. I'm fifteen. I can make my own plans."

"Well, you're not behaving very responsibly, considering that you are fifteen."

He sat cross-legged on the bed, watching her as she took out her emerald necklace. "Can I help you with that?" He wanted to make up with her — he knew he was wrong, but he was mad at his father.

"Yes, thank you."

He stood behind her and fastened the catch, not really feeling the skin on her neck or the softness of her hair. Then she looked at him in the mirror.

All along, without thinking, he'd been censoring his memory of that afternoon, selecting unconsciously, and now the censor

jumped up at him and said, No more. He looked down at the
jewelry box and let the lid fall shut with a click.

"Jack," he heard Ellen say, and he looked up at her reflection.
She was holding his photo album. "I don't know who half these
people are. Did you find the suit?"

"No." He shook his head.

"What is it?"

He smiled feebly. "I was thinking of my mother."

"Oh." She stepped into the room. "I remember her. She played
bridge with my mother a few times. I always thought she had the
most wonderful laugh. Is that silly? I always knew when your
mother was in our house, because of her laugh."

He thought of her laugh.

"I think we should go, Jack."

He nodded. "I remember where the tux is, in the attic. I'll get
it and then we'll go." She followed him up the staircase to the
attic, which was so hot it was hard to breathe. A cedar closet had
been built against one wall, and he opened it and took out a white
plastic garment bag. Inside was a tuxedo with a white dinner
jacket. His father's suit. He took the jacket off the hanger and
put it on.

Ellen looked at him critically. "It fits, pretty well. I like that
effect, with your shorts."

"Yeah, right. Maybe I'll wear this to the dance. 'Mr. John W.
Newland, in a white evening jacket and pleated khaki shorts,
accompanied Miss Ellen Archer, in a blue and yellow sundress.' "
He took the jacket off and they went downstairs. He retrieved
his keys from the bowl and they stepped outside into the air.

"It almost makes it feel cool out here," he said, tossing the bag
into the back of the car.

"I still have this album."

"We can go over here under the trees and look at it if you
want."

They sat down on the grass and began paging through the
album. "That one's when I was ten — my Little League team
won some kind of championship." The towers of Central Park
West in the background. "That's my friend Dougie Green, I grew
up with him. Here I am going to my first dance at Mrs. Pauling's."

"Oh God," she said. "Mrs. Pauling."

"You went to Mrs. Pauling?"

"Didn't everyone? I'll never forget those awful dances. I'd sit there, sweating under my white gloves, wondering who would ask me to dance, if anyone. It was so humiliating."

He stretched out, his head propped on one bent arm. Behind her head, little points of light fell through the leaves. A halo.

"Not like dances in school, when I was fourteen or fifteen," she went on. "The only people who danced at those were the kids who were going together. There was always some little drama going on — a determined boy who wouldn't leave a particular girl alone, or a girl who desperately wanted to be asked by a particular boy. I think they took the pressure off the rest of us, so we could stand around waiting to see what would happen. What are you smiling about?"

He lay back on the grass, his hands behind his head. "I was just thinking how different it all looked from the boys' side."

"How?"

"Well, there were always two or three boys who could sort of effortlessly walk over and ask a girl to dance. And there were a few guys who pretended to have no interest in dancing at all, the kind who would hang on the gym equipment or shove each other. And then there were the rest of us poor slobs. We'd stand around trying to decide which girl to ask, and if she would want to (they always said yes, so that was no criterion), and try to smell our breath to see if we'd sprayed enough. And wonder what went on in those endless caucuses that the girls always seemed to be having. What did you all talk about, anyway, while you turned your backs on us?"

"Who can remember? I can't imagine you ever at a loss for how to speak to a girl, though."

"Oh yes. Even me." He laughed. "It was easy at Mrs. Pauling's, everyone knew everyone else, we'd all grown up together. Once I got to Westfield, though, everything changed. No one knew anyone so it became impossible." He stopped and put a piece of grass in his mouth. "Four years of enforced celibacy in a community of teenaged boys didn't help much either."

She settled down into the crook of his arm, her head on his shoulder. "Those long winter nights."

"Cold and lonely."

"I always wondered what went on in those schools."

"I'm sworn not to tell. It's part of the graduation oath." He held her closely. "It wasn't where I learned to kiss."

A few minutes later he said dreamily, "Can I tell you a secret?"

"Mmm-hmm."

"I love to kiss. Sometimes I think it's the best thing in the world. But it's not something you can — I can really do with anybody. It has to be somebody really special. Someone I really care about." He swallowed. It had been an avowal, and he waited to see how she would take it.

"I love it that you would say that."

It was, on balance, a neutral sort of response, he thought as they drove away from his house. He didn't have a lot of practice telling people he loved them, so he didn't know how exactly to gauge her answer. But he thought it prudent, at least, to take some hope. They stopped in town, and while she went to the post office he wandered as unobtrusively as he could over to the pharmacy and bought a package of condoms. It made him feel a little strange. He'd bought them often enough in New York, there was a half-empty box in the night table next to his bed, but they had been purchased, as it were, on spec, and not with any specific occasion in mind. This seemed almost too calculating to him, scientific rather than romantic. He grinned at that, thinking Ellen would appreciate it. But he didn't tell her.

As they drove home, he said, "Would you like to go out on the lake?"

"The lake?"

"The school has a bunch of canoes and rowboats, or they used to. We could take one of them out."

"It sounds good to me. I'm hot."

He turned the car into the driveway, past the discreet sign that said "Westfield Academy for Boys," and drove slowly along the familiar way over the crest of the hill and down toward the lake. He parked near the little beach, where he and Jeff and Stephen had set out on their epic journey across the lake and their even more epic journey back. He told Ellen the story.

They walked across the grass, past the little playground, which was still there, and onto a small floating dock that rocked under their weight. Two rowboats and two canoes were tied up. He hadn't been rowing in — he couldn't remember how long. He recalled its being very satisfying, repetitive physical labor to a distinct purpose, a simple utilitarian act made magical by the fact that you couldn't see where you were going and had to set the course by looking at where you had been. "Would you like to row?" he asked.

She said, teasingly, "That's for men."

"Only because it's so much more fun than being rowed."

"You would say that. Most men I know would pretend it was an irksome duty while secretly enjoying it."

"If," he held out his hand to her, "you will step into the boat, I will enjoy it quite openly."

It was already late in the afternoon, and the air was still, and the lake flat and full of depth. He could hear clearly the rattling of the oarlocks and the bubbling of the whirlpools behind the blades as he pulled, and the little dribbling as he feathered the oars. The motion came back to him immediately — pull, down, twist, push, twist, up — and they were well out from the shore in a short time. Ellen was leaning back, her elbow on the gunwale, trailing her finger in the water.

"It's beautiful out here," she murmured. "I haven't been on this lake in years."

"I used to work at the swim club," he said, bending to the stroke.

"I remember seeing you there."

"It's funny how our paths always seem to have crossed without our really meeting. Mrs. Pauling's, here in Westfield."

"I'm two years older," she said, waving a mosquito away from her face. "That's a big difference when you're that age."

He shipped the oars, careful not to let them drip on her, and the boat rotated slowly, so he could see where they'd been headed. Across the lake a sharp pointed hill rose, houses clinging to its side. Behind it a larger, more rounded mountain blocked most of the view. Down beyond the end of the lake, hemmed in by the hills, great billows of clouds rose up, their edges lost in the yellow haze of the declining sun. He said, "I think we should do something nice for Timothy."

"Like what?" Her voice was distant.

"I'm happy," he said simply, "being here with you." It was another avowal, his second that day. He had a moment of wondering what had happened to him, that he would stray so far out of the prescribed channel he'd made of his life, in which other people measured out his feelings for him, or at least their public utterance. All he knew was that Timothy had made it happen. He said, "It was Timothy's idea, for me to come here. If I hadn't, I wouldn't have met you. He was the catalyst."

"Catalyst." She sat up a little straighter, and the boat rocked gently. "It's odd that you should say that."

"Just a figure of speech."

"Yes," she insisted, "but do you know what a catalyst is? In chemistry, I mean."

He shook his head. The sun, behind her, was shining in his face, and he watched her as she talked, hardly attending to what she was saying.

"A catalyst is a substance that changes the rate at which other substances react but that is unchanged by the reaction. For example, if you mix hydrogen and oxygen you get —?"

He realized she was waiting for an answer. "Water?"

"Right. But only very slowly. If you add a little platinum to the mixture, you get water much more quickly. And also —?"

"Platinum."

"Exactly." She nodded, just as a teacher would at a slow pupil, and he thought, how could he not love a woman who lectured him on chemistry in a rowboat in a lake. Lady of the lake. "So Timothy isn't, properly speaking, a catalyst at all. He didn't increase the rate of our reaction, he only brought us together," she concluded, smiling a little.

"You're being didactic."

"Yes. But I like exactness."

And I love ambiguity, he thought. In his life with Kate, in his relations with Elizabeth and David, in his role at the magazine, in his sexuality — it was the ambiguity that he coveted, more than the experiences themselves. He tugged at the oars, feeling in his arms the unaccustomed strain. "Well," he said, "catalyst or not, I think it would be nice to do something for him."

He turned the boat and headed back toward the dock. He could see all the way down the lake, which appeared to have lengthened in the late afternoon light. At the far end a little motorboat was racing, the noise muted by the distance. The clouds had spread and separated and were no longer massed above the mountain. Ellen put her hand in the water again. He thought she should have on a long white dress and carry a parasol. They should be drinking iced champagne and eating strawberries. Beside them, quite close, a fish jumped and left spreading circles on the water.

The church where his parents were buried was on a low hillock overlooking the green in the middle of town. It was a stone building with a square tower that rose modestly to a peak. The tower was pierced, two thirds of the way up, by a single arch on each face, through which the hanging bells could be seen. The arches were edged by white-painted woodwork, and he'd always liked the effect of the hard stones bound together by the light mortar, the white trim, the old bells, and the great wooden roof. He had gone to church on hot sunny days, and in autumn when the oak trees around it flamed, and in the winter when ice hung from its eaves, and always he thought it a building perfectly attuned to its place, spiritual and temporal, in the little town. He sat for a minute in the porch, looking at the town green spread out in front of him. In its center, where several paths came together, there was a small bandstand, where the first selectman addressed the crowds on Memorial Day, and where the town band played concerts on summer nights. At the far corner was a tall flagpole surmounted by a polished golden eagle, the flag hanging limply in the still air. And, at the near corner, just opposite where he was sitting, a statue of a very young-looking soldier, in a uniform like the one in Timothy's attic, looked bleakly out at the town he would never see again, a memorial to the Civil War dead. The name of his regiment was carved in the base of the pedestal. A wreath, left perhaps from the Fourth of July, leaned against it, wilting.

Behind the statue, two boys were playing catch. One of them, his Little League cap pulled down low over his eyes, the tip of his tongue sticking out in concentration, was pitching, rearing back for a full windup that was more theatrical than utilitarian. He was wearing running shorts, and the bottoms of his boxer shorts protruded in the current cool fashion. After a while, a third boy, on a bicycle, came by and stopped to talk. Jack had spent days like that, riding his bike into town, finding someone to hang out with, playing catch, picking up a game, or wandering through the fields or the woods on the mountains, or standing patiently by the side of a stream trying to catch frogs. Two girls in shorts and long T-shirts walked along one of the paths, then diverted themselves toward the boys. A conference followed, and they all walked off down Main Street, leaving the green empty.

He got up and walked around to the back of the church. The hill leveled out here, and the graveyard was ample. He opened the gate and walked between the plots to the corner under one of the oaks. He stood, looking down at the horizontal stone with the names and dates, automatically, as he always did, subtracting to calculate the ages. He brushed some grass clippings off the stone with his hand and wondered if the rector was around.

The rector was a tall, balding man who pretended to be part scholar, part social butterfly. Half of his flock were local residents, and half New Yorkers with summer homes, and Jack always thought he was playing both sides of the fence. Jack could almost hear his Church of England accents during communion: "Mumble-mumble-mumble-THIS IS MY BODY-mumble-mumble-mumble-THIS IS MY BLOOD-mumble-mumble." He had been at the house the night Jack's parents had died, along with the police chief. And he'd given the eulogy at the funeral.

"Those of us who were privileged to know them well," he'd said. The church was full, people Jack knew, people he didn't know. Later he wondered how many were simply tourists of tragedy, drawn by suddenness and violence, by the pathos of the orphan boy; at the time he had been merely dazed. The day was wet, with fitful downpours, and the church felt damp and enclosed, like a cabin at summer camp on a rainy day. There were sobs, and Elizabeth wept openly, but Jack sat with his head down, looking at his fingers, which he kept tightly laced together in his lap. He felt nothing, only a whistling emptiness that kept every-thing else at a distance, while his memories warred with the rector's homage to his mother.

Through it all, through the haze of that round voice, he only thought how she was the only mother that all his friends liked. Their apartment had been more of a gathering place than anybody else's because they could all tolerate having her around. When Dougie's parents were going through their divorce, Dougie had practically moved in with the Newlands. Jack remembered one afternoon coming home from school, where he'd stayed late for something. The apartment was unusually quiet; most of the time there were noises, and she liked to have music on when she was alone. He looked in the living room and in the library, but no one was around. Then he heard a noise from his parents' room, sort of a choking noise and someone saying "Shh." He went down the hall to investigate. Through the open door, he could see his mother sitting on the edge of the bed, holding Dougie in her arms; his face was against her shoulder and he was crying, and she was stroking his hair softly. She saw Jack and shook her head. A little while later Dougie came to find him, his face still tear-streaked. "Feeling better?" Jack asked, and Dougie nodded and went into the living room to practice the piano.

As Jack sat among the mourners, listening to the rector go on, talking about his father, he knew it was the moment in his life to which everything so far had led, from which everything after would lead. Later, thinking about it, that seemed obvious — Ripley would have said logically that every moment is the end of the past and the beginning of the future, but Jack felt afterward, and still felt, that on that day he had held for a moment all of the strands of his life in one hand. For some people, he imagined, that moment came with first love or a wedding, when a child is born or when a business deal closes. For him, death was at the node.

At the graveside, Dougie had stood next to him as the rector read the hopeless, familiar words, ashes and dust. He held Dougie's hand as the two coffins were lowered into the grave — later Dougie said that his hand had bruise marks on it, Jack had been holding so tightly. Jack didn't remember that, couldn't remember it now. Only the sight of his life in the squared-off hole.

Hidden now, beneath the flat stone. He wondered, if he lay down on it, if he put his ear to its hot surface, would he hear anything, would any message come to him from the self that lay beneath? What would that fifteen-year-old say to this twenty-eight-year-old? — it was foolish speculation. The only way those two could ever be united was in death, and he knew that if he once lay down on that grave for that reason, he wouldn't ever, not in this life, get up again. He turned away from the grave and went home.

"Do you want to see our fireflies?" Ellen asked him on Friday night.

He followed her out the back of the house and down a steep path. It was a dark evening, cloudy and warm, with gusts of breeze that blew up from nothing to rattle the treetops and then dissipate. It was a rise and fall of sound as much as of motion, a whooshing and then a silence, that gave him the recurring sense that something was about to happen. They came out by the edge of the pond, by the marble landing where Timothy and he had gone swimming, and the breeze felt more unrestrained, blowing at them from across the water. He stood with his hands in his pockets, waiting for it to subside.

When it did, the air in front of them was suddenly full of the blinking greenish lights of fireflies, seemingly hundreds of them. Jack tried to follow one as it made its way across the little cleft down which the path came, winking intermittently; but he soon lost it in the crowd. He put out his hand toward them, but the breeze came up again and their lights went out. He said, "The Japanese used to catch them and keep them in cages."

"How sad."

"Really? I would have said, how exquisite."

Gathering her skirt up a little, she walked out into the pond. He watched her go. His mood was contrary tonight, as something of what he was increasingly coming to think of as the old Jack reasserted itself. He had taken the lead all along, from the moment he'd first seen her, and now he wanted to crawl back a little into the shell of the old days, the warm riskless place where other people led him around, held his hand, and made him sure that, whatever happened, it wasn't his fault.

Put like that, it seemed almost foolish. But this reflection only increased his annoyance, because it made him think that now he could never go back to that kind of life. He tried to imagine himself in New York with Boyd and Amy, and Kate, dancing all night, drinking bourbon at Val's, blowing toot in the men's room: it seemed incredible to him that he had ever gotten to that point. But to give it up for this — this permanent uncertainty, in which he had to reach out his hand before he was sure of another's hand to grasp, was suddenly intolerable. He had not, he thought defiantly, spent the last ten years of his life learning how to protect himself and everyone for whom he cared, only to throw it all away now at a hazard. It wasn't in him to play games of chance, not if the end result was that someone might get hurt. To prevent that, he was willing to bet only on sure things and settle for the dullness of certainty. "Love stinks," he said softly. A man standing at the edge of a narrow, bottomless chasm that bisected his world — his brain told him he could easily jump across, it was no wider than a crack in a sidewalk, but his heart told him he would fall as surely as Lucifer, to bottomless perdition. "Man's first disobedience." His heart was broken, he said to himself, and answered, It's only a stress fracture.

"What did you say?" Ellen came splashing back toward him.

Nothing he would burden her with — the height of discourtesy. "I was just thinking about being in summer camp. We used to catch fireflies in glass jars and then study them. We caught butterflies too."

"What camp did you go to?" She was standing at the edge of the water. "Would you hand me my shoes, please."

He retrieved them for her. "Pemigewassett."

She laughed. "I should have known. It's so typical."

"Why?"

She stood first on one foot, then the other, and put her shoes on. There was something incredibly sexy in the way women put on shoes, he thought watching her, the way they lifted their feet off the ground a bit, the way they pointed their toes. She said, "Shall we go back up?"

What's the alternative, he thought helplessly as he followed her up the path: Kate. After this, after Ellen, knowing that I love her? Safe or unsafe, what choice did he have. At the top of the path, he said again, "What's so typical?"

"Oh," she said, turning into the garden. "Collegiate, Pemigewassett, Westfield Academy, Mrs. Pauling's, Yale. Everything that New York boys do if they're well brought up."

"I was well brought up," he said a little woodenly, willing to be made fun of, but only if he knew she wasn't serious.

"Of course you were. So what happened to you?"

"What do you mean? Have my manners slipped?"

She sat down on a curved white stone bench amidst the roses. "Your manners never slip. Nor your manner."

"A conundrum." He sat on the grass in front of her, looking away.

"I mean, why are you not like everybody else? You went to the same schools they did, the same camp, you have all the attributes, but something has slipped and it's not your manner. That's perfect, except when you let it go a little, as you have, I think, with me. But you're not like the rest of them, all those tame, channeled, obvious men my mother keeps shoving at me. Why do you care about things no one else cares about — you have ideas, when for most people ideas are just a kind of currency that's only good if everyone has the same ones. How many old Westfield boys do you see at the AIDS home? That's not exactly Social Register stuff. Your dissertation on modernism the other night, it would have been unusual even if it had been off-the-cuff party talk, but it wasn't, was it, it was something you'd thought a lot about. How many old boys have an aesthetic theory of modernism?"

He was leaning over his crossed legs, tearing at the grass. "Take it easy. You make me sound like — I don't want to be different."

"But you are different, and I want to know why."

The grass made a ripping sound as he tore out a clump, and it occurred to him that he would be leaving a hole in the otherwise perfect lawn. "Disorder and early sorrow."

"Your parents?" She shook her head. "Isn't that — I'm sorry, but — isn't that ancient history by now?"

"No."

"Aren't you entitled to let it fade away by now? It's been thirteen years, Jack. Almost half your life."

He looked at her and then away. "You're the physicist. You tell me what the half-life of tragedy is."

"That's just a play on words."

This is the scientific method, he thought. She would never let an evasion masquerade as fact. "It's not a play on words when you're living it. Don't think I do this for sympathy. Nobody even notices. People see that I'm — how shall I put it — good-looking? — and they think I must be stupid. Then, when they find out that I'm bright —"

"Brilliant."

"Bright," he insisted, knowing that she would see most what she most wanted to see, "and rich besides, they think my life must be perfect. They don't stop to ask."

"If they did ask — I'm asking — what would you tell them?"

He tossed away a small rock that he'd dislodged, hearing it land in the hedge across the garden. "Most people are so obvious. They only talk about one thing, they only want one thing. Always the same thing."

"And what's that?" she asked, a trace of humor in her voice.

He was angry, at himself for the strange mood he was in, at her for not taking him seriously. All right, he thought, if she wants to know. "Sex. Everyone only wants to go to bed with me. Sex," he added, "and money."

"That's two things."

"Not really. Sex and money are the same thing to most of these people."

"Now you're being obvious."

He drew in a deep breath and stretched out at the base of the bench, looking up at the moonlit clouds. "Things happen to me."

She sat, very still, thinking this over. "Has it ever occurred to you —" she began.

"What?"

"— that you could happen to things?"

His answer was forced out of him even as he tried not to say it. "Every time I happen to someone, as you put it, I fuck up their life."

Once more she waited, considering this. The breeze had come up again, and he could hear the rattling of the wind chimes in the summerhouse at the top of the garden. It had always seemed an ominous sign to him, and now he found it frightening.

"You happened to Timothy," she said finally. "He's OK."

"I think it's a lot more true to say that he happened to me."

"Maybe. And what about me? You very definitely have happened to me."

He stirred on the grass. He could deny it, or divert it, pretend that the opportunity wasn't there. Or he could throw caution to the wind — wasn't that what she was urging him to do? — and take whatever followed. "You're right. I have happened to you. I'd do anything for you. I'd throw myself at your feet —"

"You seem," she interrupted, looking down at him, "already to have done so."

He made a movement, as if to get up, and then subsided. "I want to give you romance, and you —"

"But it's not romance that I want."

She said this in a very hard voice, offering nothing. He rolled over on his stomach and pressed his cheek into the grass, looking away from her. She had given him no indication, only the assurance that she would give no indication. He heard her stand up, and he had a picture of her towering against the stars, and then, of the two of them, like a sculpture group in the warm night. Push, he thought, come to shove. She was asking for the denial of everything he'd made of himself. His memories stirred within him like dead leaves on a tile floor, but he pushed them back. I am here, with this grass against my face and these wind chimes ringing in my ear, this is all that matters. The pattern of his life was fully woven, and he could sit comfortably in the midst of its strands forever, not changing his position by so much as an inch lest he upset the balance and destroy. Go back to Kate, leave Ellen. Renounce love once and for all, as he had renounced it intermittently all along. Or reach out his hand and take what he wanted.

"I love you," he said inaudibly. And then, committed, he said aloud, "I love you, Ellen."

There was no response. He looked, and she was gone.

He stood up; there was no sign of her. He walked quickly back to the house and inside. It was very still, Timothy must have gone to bed. He turned off the light in the kitchen and walked through to the front hall. He stopped, taking in the large shadowy space, dark except for faint moonlight through the window on the landing. He climbed the staircase, stepping purposely in the center of its graceful curve, and walked down the hall to his room. He undressed and brushed his teeth and put on his robe. He slipped the package of condoms into his pocket and stepped out again into the hallway. He walked down the hall, across the landing again (looking out at the garden and the lake below, indistinct in the pale moonlight that shone through the clouds, overwhelmed by an imagined film in his eyes and the pounding of his heart) and down the other wing to Ellen's room. He raised his hand and knocked.

XII

IN THE MIDDLE of the next morning they were sitting, partially hidden, in the curve of a great bed of rhododendrons that was planted by the side of the driveway. It was a hot morning, the full glory of July, and Jack was lying on the grass looking up at Ellen. "I'd throw myself at your feet," he'd said to her the night before. What had seemed so complicated then had been reduced to simplicity by their night together. He said, "Thank you."

"For what?" She was looking through his photo album again.

"For last night."

She blinked. "Oh, Jack. I think I should be thanking you."

He reached out and rested his hand on her knee.

"When was this taken?"

He leaned over and looked at the photo. In it he was standing at the edge of a baseball diamond, on the grass beside third base. Behind him a great hill rose up, covered with fully leaved trees. He was wearing cut-off shorts and a white tennis shirt, and his hair was long, falling over his forehead to his eyes. He had a crooked smile, and his right arm was in a sling. "I was twelve. I was at Pemi, and I broke my arm."

"How?" She was leaning over the picture, squinting to see it better.

"We were out on a hike one day and we came to a place where there was a gorge between two cliffs — they weren't very high, maybe ten or twelve feet. Tommy Kramer dared me to jump across."

"And you did?"

"You bet. Tommy and I had a kind of rivalry going — one of those love-hate things kids get into." Jack batted third, Tommy hit cleanup. Tommy had the first leg in swimming relays, Jack was the anchor. They felt the kinship of the superior, able to outdo everyone else in their bunk, and unwilling to be outdone except by the other, which was barely tolerable. "I couldn't turn him down."

"I'll never understand boys," she sighed.

"Yes, you will, when you have one. My mother understood me." She had come up to New Hampshire from New York after he'd broken his arm, had taken the picture as a souvenir. She yelled at him a little, for jumping the gorge, but they both knew it was pro forma scolding. She understood that he was proving himself (his writer's mind caught at the word for a moment — to prove: to demonstrate or to test; he had been doing both, demonstrating his manhood by testing it, and she knew why he needed to do both) and she let him alone with his sense of accomplishment. To have fallen was nothing compared with the attempt, and the status of broken bones.

"Wasn't it strange?" she went on, following her own thoughts. "An all-boys prep school. An all-boys boarding school. An all-boys camp."

"It seemed normal. Almost a privilege. They made it seem like one, anyway."

"What did you think of girls?"

"It wouldn't be decent of me to repeat what we thought about girls." He laughed. "Though I will say we thought a lot about them."

"Seriously."

He put on a serious face. "Well. They were a different part of life. When I was little, they were just strangers, almost another species. When I got to be a teenager, they were very special, for dating and all." It was something he'd thought about, and now he paused, gathering his thoughts. "I have a good friend from Yale, Peter Callahan, who went to public school, and he has a lot of friends who are women. I don't. That's what it did to me, I guess, it made women people to go out with, to love, to marry. But not to be friends with."

"That's sad," she said, looking at him.

"Neither sad nor happy, I think," he said cautiously. "Just different."

"Would you want your son to grow up like that — separated from girls?"

He had only a vague image of what it would be like to have a child. "It would depend, wouldn't it, on who my son was."

She said definitely, "I can't see putting any son of mine through that. Think of all the sublimating."

He grinned. "There was a boxing ring in the gym, and my roommate Jeff and I'd go down and hit each other for half an hour. Talk about sublimating."

"Like I said, I'll never understand boys." She turned another page in the album, and he watched her, thinking that this was proof of love if any were needed, that she was willing, even eager, to look at the pictures of his past. Could the dreaded home movies be far behind?

"Who's this?"

He looked. "Ripley Lewis. My best friend from Westfield. That was taken at his parents' house in Los Angeles the summer after we graduated." He looked up at the broad green leaves of the rhododendron. "He died. He had AIDS."

She studied the picture. "Was he gay?"

"Yes."

She let the album rest flat on her crossed knees. "I had an argument with my father about AIDS a few months ago. He said he didn't see why AIDS patients deserved any special consideration, that they weren't any more deserving of help than leukemia victims, for example. I couldn't argue with him, but somehow I felt he was wrong, that they are. Or, if they're not more deserving of help, at least we sympathize more with them for some reason."

He thought of the AIDS home in New York. The faces of men who knew they were going to die, a roulette wheel of all zeros, with only the period of the ball's rotation in doubt. They lived with it, that was always the startling thing to him, how many of them lived with it. They didn't come there to die but to live out foreshortened lives. Most people thought the home was a place of death but, in this as in so many things, AIDS defied expectation. "It's because leukemia, brain tumors, Alzheimer's, whatever, come out of the blue. They're acts of God. In most cases, people didn't do anything to get sick. But AIDS is just the opposite. Most people get AIDS because of what they do. In a way, they bring it on themselves."

"But which way does that cut? Surely you're not saying that gay men deserve what they get."

"No, of course not." He thought of Ripley, dying with a hole in his throat. "But you can't judge God, can you? I mean, if you believe at all, it's just self-centered nonsense to believe that what God does is wrong." He shook his head. "I'm not saying this very well. I just feel a terrible sorrow for people who get caught by their own failure to act safely. We're all human, we all make mistakes. I think AIDS touches us in the place where we make mistakes, in a way that cancer, for example, doesn't. Nothing we do, or don't do, can help or hinder us in getting leukemia, it's totally random as far as we're concerned. But we can, any one of us, contract AIDS by a careless expression of love. And haven't we been taught to believe that love is essentially careless, joyful and spontaneous?"

"It certainly was for me last night."

He smiled. "That's a really nice thing to say."

She was still sitting over the album, not looking at it, staring ahead at the driveway. "Is that why — can I ask you a question?"

"Of course."

"Is that why you use condoms?" The night before, she had said that she didn't trust them and had put in her diaphragm, but he had used them anyway.

"No," he said, "not exactly." Like her brother, she seemed to have an innate capacity to wait, to not force the issue while he sorted out his thoughts. "My body and what I do with it are my responsibility. I guess I just believe that people are responsible for their own actions."

"A revolutionary idea these days."

"Maybe," he said dubiously. A bee flew down from the bush, and he brushed it away. "Besides, to be frank, I've had a sort of checkered past. I don't think you should have to take the risks of that." He relapsed into silence, while she continued to go through the album in a desultory way.

The night before. The night before. He said the words to himself as if they were a totem of the thing itself. Sex had, early on for him, become uncoupled from feeling — or perhaps it would be truer to say that feeling had become uncoupled from sex, as it had from the rest of his life. He thought of the first girl he had slept with, Missy Reardon — well, he hadn't expected love then, it had been more in the nature of an experiment, he had focused mostly on mechanics. Ripley's friend Mark, a quickie between drinks, over before it had a chance to make an impression. Harriet — she had set the terms there, but of course they had suited him perfectly. Peter: an almost forgotten detour by two friends who had taken a wrong turn one night before regaining the high road. Kate, an inevitability he had never questioned — but he didn't want to think about Kate. And the other women, he was almost ashamed to think of them so dismissively, but it was true, they had gone through him at their leisure, as if he were a kind of trophy, a notch in their guns. His body had been laid out in hot beds, a beautiful delusive object that men and women played with, thinking that they touched him, and all the while his feelings had wandered along lonely and distant paths on the cold shoulder of a high mountain, the body sentinel to the feelings. For thirteen years the arrangement had worked, until now it seemed that perhaps it would no longer be necessary. He had let the guard down and, like a thief in the night, love had crept in while the sentinel slept. Perhaps it was not a bad bargain after all.

He was lying with his eyes half shut, and he heard an odd noise, which seemed familiar but unplaceable, as if it were distorted by the heat. He heard Ellen turn another page of the album. Then she said, "My goodness. Who is this young Adonis?"

He opened his eyes, trying to remember the photos, wondering whom she would have classed as an Adonis. It was a dissonant thought, that on this morning she should find even the picture of another man attractive. He was about to make a joke of it when he realized that she wasn't looking in the album but down the driveway. A boy was jogging up it, his legs flashing in the sunlight, his shirt stuffed into the waistband of his bright red running shorts. "That's my nephew Billy."

"He's gorgeous."

He poked her softly with an elbow. "He's sixteen."

"So?"

"So. Pervert."

"What's he doing here?"

"Search me. They weren't going to come up for another week. He didn't even know where I was, just the phone number."

Billy was nearly level with them, but they were half hidden by the bushes and he hadn't seen them. "Billy," Jack called out. "Over here."

Billy swerved and ran over to them. He stopped and put his hands on his knees, breathing hard, his hair hanging down, his body gleaming. "That last hill was a killer," he said. He straightened up. "Hi, Uncle John. Nice to see you." He turned to Ellen and stuck out one large hand. "Hi. I'm Billy Lorburn."

She shook his hand. "I'm Ellen Archer. Pleased to meet you."

Jack, a little behind in all this, said, "I'm sorry. Billy's my nephew."

Ellen said admiringly, "Did you run all the way across town from your house?"

"No." He sat down on the grass and leaned back on his elbows. "My mom dropped me off at Westfield — I said I'd run around the track there and then jog home. It's only about five miles from here."

He's showing off, Jack thought.

"Well, you must be thirsty," Ellen said. "Would you like something to drink?"

"Yeah. Sure." He added, "Thanks."

"I'll go up to the house and get some lemonade. Or would you rather have soda?"

"Lemonade'd be great." He brushed away some of the hair that was sticking damply to his forehead.

As Ellen walked away, Billy said, "She's the friend you've been visiting?"

"Her brother. What are you doing here?"

"Hey. Lighten up. If you don't want me around —"

"No, no," Jack said hastily. "I'm just surprised to see you. How did you know where I was?"

Billy looked away and then, as if facing the music, looked back. "You can't be mad at me 'cause it wasn't my fault."

"What wasn't?"

"Well, after you called me? A couple of days later Mom asked me if I knew where you were. So I go, No, 'cause I didn't. But then she asked me if I'd talked to you and all, and finally I had to tell her. You know, about the phone call and all. The number you gave me."

So Elizabeth had put two and two together. She'd remembered that Jack had asked her about Timothy, or else she'd talked to Amy or Boyd, somehow she'd made the connection and looked up the Archers in the Westfield phone book.

Billy, sounding unhappy, said, "I'm sorry. But y'know I couldn't, like, lie to her."

"No, of course not. You did the right thing. But I thought you all weren't coming up here until next week."

"Yeah." Billy spread his knees, stretching after his run. The insides of his thighs were red from the sun shining through his shorts. "I don't know. I think it has to do with you."

"With me? What does she say?"

He tipped his head to one side and looked skeptical. "I don't listen to most of what she says. She and dad had a long talk the other night, about you and Kate Welland, and Amy Cornwell, and stuff. I didn't really listen. Then yesterday she came back from lunch and said we were going to drive up here right away."

Great, Jack thought. What does she want from me? He wasn't ready for a confrontation. He toyed with the idea of telling Billy about Ellen, about how great he felt, but that would be another secret — first his engagement to Kate, his telephone number, now this. Secrets weren't fair, nobody knew that better than Jack. He felt overcome with love, it seemed to be his natural habitat that day (and not inappropriately: before Ellen, he admitted to himself, Billy was the person he had chiefly loved). He said softly, "You should put your shirt on, you'll catch cold."

As they walked up the driveway, Jack put his arm on Billy's shoulder. "So five miles is nothing to you now? Up and down hills and all."

"I've been running every day. Alone."

"Sorry about that. One of my friends, Timothy, Ellen's brother, asked me to come up here unexpectedly. I didn't have any plans for my vacation —"

"We were going to go to some games at the Stadium, I thought."

"I'm sorry, pal. I just needed to get away for a little while."

"From me?"

Jack brushed Billy's damp hair with his fingertips. To be sixteen again, and the whole world revolving around one. "No, don't be a dork. Just a vacation."

"Boyd said you were pretty bummed out on your birthday."

"When did you talk to Boyd?"

"He called about a week ago, looking for you."

It seemed unlikely. Boyd hardly knew Billy, and it wasn't the kind of thing he would do. Boyd would just keep leaving messages on the answering machine and then go back to trading stripped Ginnies or doing really great cocaine until the next time it occurred to him to call. Unless Amy had put him up to it, which was the kind of thing she might do. Amy, who was on some benefit committee with Elizabeth. Jack suddenly felt as if the ghosts were creeping up on him.

"Hey, John. I got a favor to ask. Can you take me to Val's with you one night? It's the hottest place, and Boyd said you guys go there a lot."

"No," he said automatically. "I don't think so."

"How come? I run all the fuck the way over here to tell you we were here, and now you won't even take me —"

"Billy, I'll think about it," he said, to forestall what would be a half-hour debate. Besides, he didn't want to play Virgil to Billy's Dante, at least not in that particular underworld.

They sat by the pool with their lemonade. Ellen seemed impressed with Billy's athletic ability and engaged him in a long discussion of baseball. "I'm a big fan," she explained, "and I go to a lot of games with my father." The two of them avidly discussed the Yankees' current woes, Billy being very dogmatic and Ellen agreeing with him, feeding him a line every now and then to keep him going. But then, Jack thought, if Billy collected butterflies, she would discuss lepidopterology with him. That was what he loved about her. She was complicated. She had ramifications, like a house that had survived the successive renovations of generations, with odd corners and staircases where one least expected them. He had said to her that people were obvious, but there was, in the end, nothing obvious about her.

He reached out to touch her before he remembered Billy. He pulled his hand back.

"How's Hank?" he asked instead.

"My brother," Billy explained. "He's at camp."

"Pemigewassett," Ellen suggested, looking at Jack.

"No," Billy said. "I went there until last year. You know what, Uncle John? I hear they put hot showers in. Bunch of weenies."

"Horrors," Ellen said.

The look on Billy's face was comical. She might know a lot about baseball, but she was still, all said and done, a woman. "It was kind of a tradition," he said lamely.

Jack rescued him. "What about Hank?"

"He's at sailing camp, on Cape Cod. He hates it. He calls up every night to ask if he can come home."

Ellen said, "Why is he unhappy?"

"Well." Billy hesitated. "He told me, but he didn't want my dad to know, OK?" Another secret, Jack thought. "There's this kid. Who picks on him. I told him to deck the guy, but Hank's scared. He's kind of a wimp." Then he added, unexpectedly, "But he's not a bad guy."

Jack wondered whether Billy was beginning to appreciate having a brother, or if this was simply familial solidarity. Evidently David had driven up to the Cape to see what he could do. Hank wouldn't, Jack thought, get much sympathy there.

Billy was quiet in the car as Jack drove him home — almost obviously so. "What's up?" Jack finally asked.

"I thought you were going to marry Kate Welland."

"So did I," he said honestly.

"I don't get it at all."

Jack was about to say that sometimes these things just happen. But that wouldn't have been fair to Billy or to Ellen, or for that matter to himself. "I'm in love with Ellen."

"I thought you were in love with Kate."

"I did too. But — I don't know."

"Well." Billy frowned. "Mom's sure going to be pissed about this. She's counting on your marrying Kate."

Great, Jack thought. He let Billy out at the foot of the driveway and turned around. All he could think was that he had to tell Ellen.

When he got back to the house, though, Ellen had already left for the hairdresser, and Jack had to content himself with Timothy instead. Jack found him sitting on the veranda of the summer-house, a great mound of cushions around him and a huge volume, in the peculiar German print of the nineteenth century, balanced on his knees. There was a bowl of peaches next to him and his chin was sticky with juice. Jack told him about Billy's visit. "And so Elizabeth's here too."

Timothy snapped his fingers. "Oh, shit, I forgot."

"What?"

"On Thursday, when you were out, your sister called. I should have told you, but I just forgot." He looked down at the ground. "I'm sorry, Jack."

"It's all right. What did she say?"

"She asked if I knew where you were, and since I didn't, exactly, I said no. Then she asked if I expected you. And I'm afraid I said no." He took another peach to cover his confusion.

Jack thought of Billy: it was easier to lie over the telephone, to lie to someone who wasn't your mother. Of course, Jack hadn't wanted Elizabeth, or anyone else, to know where he'd been. But he couldn't remember ever discussing that with Timothy. It had been, all along, simply taken for granted between them. He'd had his reasons, and it hadn't occurred to him that Timothy might have had his own. "Why did you lie to her?"

Timothy sucked meditatively at his peach before answering. "You were falling in love with Ellen. That was obvious. And your sister wants you to marry Kate."

"Is that obvious too? You don't even know my sister."

"I know Kate," he said carelessly.

"What does knowing Kate have to do with Elizabeth?"

"Jack. All those nights when we all went out together. You know me. I'm honest and innocent, remember, women trust me, worse luck. Well, Kate talked to Amy about you. A lot. And I overheard them." He blushed. "I know it's rude to eavesdrop, but we were in clubs, they weren't exactly whispering. Some-times, Kate talked about Elizabeth. It was obvious to me that your sister, if she wasn't playing matchmaker, was certainly lead-ing the cheering section. You know that she and Kate are friends, have lunch together, that kind of thing."

"No," Jack said. "I didn't." He tried to remember. Kate had said, now and then, that she'd seen Elizabeth around. But it hadn't been, hadn't anyway seemed to be, the sort of thing Timothy was implying. He felt as if he were surrounded by conspiracy — Kate, Elizabeth, Boyd, Amy, all of them leading him on to the altar and a life of wedded bliss with the daughter of the North River Trust Company. Was that too cynical? After all, they were merely following the rules, his rules — if you put yourself out, wanting to be taken, you had to accept what came. One time you drew a Harriet Singer, another time a Kate Welland, and part of drawing Kate was that the stake, instead of a six-month affair, was marriage. Two weeks ago, it hadn't mattered to him except, and exactly to the same extent, as it had mattered to all of them.

"Besides," Timothy was saying, "women have these special antennas. They have ways of communicating we don't. They al-ways talk to each other about men and don't expect us to find out."

Jack got up from the bench and walked to the front of the porch. The garden was laid out in front of him, and from this slight elevation it took on a different look, more patterned, de-cipherable if one held the key. He had read somewhere that the gardener's art consisted of juxtaposition, and that in earlier times each flower had symbolic meaning ("There's rosemary, that's for remembrance," he thought), a garden could be read like a book. He wondered whether this garden concealed a greater purpose, a hidden meaning woven among the stems and stalks that held the blooms. "Timothy. I need you to explain all this to me."

"All what?"

Jack leaned against one of the posts that held up the roof. "Why you brought me here. It wasn't an accident."

"No?"

Jack turned around. "Then what?"

Timothy looked back at him. His blue eyes, normally so bright, seemed shadowed, as if he were attending to an inner debate over the wisdom of answering the question. Then he shut his book and put it down on the bench. "Sit down. It's a long story."

Jack sat down on the floor next to him. "Go on."

"Remember Ellen told you we went to Paris together, in April? She didn't tell you why, though."

"She said she had a conference to go to."

"Yeah, well, that's why she went. I went because her spouse was invited, and since she didn't have a spouse, she asked me." He sucked on a peach pit for a moment, then shifted it into his cheek. It made his voice sound funny to Jack. "All day long she attended sessions of the conference and I wandered around Paris. Alone. I saw all the sights you're supposed to, Beaubourg and the Cluny and stuff. But it was like a travelogue, none of it seemed real."

Jack looked up at him for a moment, at the bulge in his cheek, at his eyes, which were focused on a point somewhere out in the garden. "Why not?"

Timothy shrugged. "I don't know. I'd been in Paris before, I speak French well enough. I just felt dislocated, as if I didn't belong. Being alone always makes me feel illegitimate. I mean, everyone is supposed to have somebody, it's as if being alone is an admission of failure. Eating alone is the same way for me. Eating alone in Paris was the worst, it was as if everyone was watching me, thinking, Ah-ha, here's a man who has no friends."

"But you weren't alone," Jack protested. "You were with Ellen."

"That was the point, I especially didn't belong with Ellen. I told her so. We were walking back to our hotel one night from a restaurant, under the colonnade on the Rue de Rivoli. It was raining. There she was, the most intelligent, attractive woman in sight, what was she doing trailing her little brother around? She should have had a husband or a lover, at least a boyfriend. She didn't have anyone. Only that asshole, Michael, did she tell you about him? He was a jerk from the start, and even he had broken up with her. So she had no one."

He took the pit out of his mouth and threw it away. It landed in a flower bed, and Jack wondered if it would grow there, or if

Mr. Prescott and his minions would find it first. He said, "But why me? You hardly knew me."

Timothy stirred uncomfortably and uncrossed his legs. "I can't hope you'll understand this. I knew you enough. I heard about you, now and then, from my mother, from my friends who knew you, I saw you around. I remember one Fourth of July at the Westfield fireworks. I must have been fourteen. It was just getting dark, and we spread out our blanket on the lawn. You were standing nearby. You were juggling some tennis balls, and there were some other kids with you, Boyd probably, I don't remember. And then a little kid came running over, and you hugged him and picked him up and swung him onto your shoulders, and the first fireworks exploded. It seemed like a perfect moment to me." Jack remembered, vaguely. Timothy took a deep breath and turned very red. "I guess I was in love with you, with the idea of you, anyway — I had been ever since I'd seen you diving that day at the swim club. I don't usually idealize people, maybe that's why you made such an impression. Like a cliff falling on me. But it didn't work out. Not the way I thought it would."

Jack wondered about that. It seemed to him that it had worked out perfectly.

Timothy said, "Anyway, after the Paris trip, I started thinking about it and I decided you would be the perfect person for her. So I got to know you around the clubs, with Boyd and all. And I found out you weren't the ideal person I'd dreamed up, but a real person. It's easy to make plans for an ideal, but it's impossible to work them out when you're dealing with reality." He laughed, a little ruefully. "That's one thing I've learned from studying the Germans — the unbridgeable gap between imagining how people might act and trying to make them do it. People have to do things for themselves. Once I met you, got to know you, I had to treat you like a person and not something to be manipulated. So I gave up the idea of marrying you off to Ellen."

Jack was lying very still on his back, looking up at the beamed roof of the veranda. From far away, the noise of a motorcycle engine penetrated the garden, counterpoint to the silence. "That still doesn't answer the question. Why did you bring me here?"

"Because I cared about you. Because you were obviously hurting. I just did it. Why is that so hard for you to understand?" He sounded angry, and Jack wondered why. Timothy, answering his thought, went on, "You never think anybody will do anything nice for you, do you? Just because they love you?"

He didn't, but this wasn't the time for that. "And Ellen?"

Timothy sighed. "I won't deny that I still hoped, even though I wasn't going to make it happen. And I didn't. I had no idea you'd want to stay here as long as you have. I didn't even introduce you, remember, you introduced yourself. You went to the restaurant, you didn't have to. You took her to Chesterwood and to your parents' house. Listen, this is important to me. One thing I learned at college, when I was seeing a psychiatrist, was that I had a real identity, not a fake one that I could put on and off like a mask. That I couldn't treat myself as a character in a script and that I could never treat anyone else that way, either. So I don't want you to think that I manipulated this whole situation. I started to, but then I realized I couldn't, and I didn't." He stopped abruptly, as if he'd run out of breath.

Jack took it all in slowly. It seemed perfectly reasonable that Timothy would have begun, out of an impulse of love, to find a boyfriend for Ellen. If it had just been a matter of giving Jack her phone number, Timothy would have done it. But Jack wouldn't have called her, that would have been obvious to Timothy, and so it had come to manipulation, as he'd put it, and he'd drawn the line. With his honesty, his essential generosity, it seemed perfectly right that he had stopped. Which only made Jack's problem worse. "There's something you need to know," he said, almost involuntarily. "I'm engaged to Kate."

Timothy didn't look up, but he became absolutely still. "Oh?"

"Don't be so casual about it."

"What do you want me to do," Timothy said, angry again, "congratulate you? Punish you?"

"It was something that just happened. I love Ellen, I want to marry her."

"That's going to be hard if you're engaged to someone else."

He's entitled to be mad, Jack thought, I'm the one at fault, I should have said something to Timothy, to Ellen, sooner than this. "Look, I'm going to do what I can to make this come out right, for Ellen. I'm going to tell her as soon as she gets back."

Timothy softened. "I know. I don't blame you or anything. I thought you and Kate were about to get engaged. I didn't realize —"

"She wanted to keep it a secret, at least until she gets back from Europe." I should have said something, he kept thinking over and over as he sat at the edge of the porch and looked out at the garden, I shouldn't have waited, I made a mistake.

When Ellen came home, he met her in the house. "I need to talk to you," he said.

"Do you like my hair?"

"What?" He stared at her, then remembered. "Sorry. It looks great. I'm usually pretty good about that sort of thing."

"I'll bet you are." They were in the library, and she sat down on one of the leather sofas. "You look distracted."

"You said it. Listen, there's something I need to tell you. I meant all along to tell you, but it just never seemed important. I mean, it was always important, just not important to tell you right then. Before this, I mean."

"Well, if it's all that dramatic, maybe you should wait. I met your sister in town and asked her to stop by."

He looked at her, not understanding. "How could you do that?" he whispered. He couldn't make his voice work properly.

"Why not? What's the matter?"

Of course she couldn't know why not, because he hadn't told her. It seemed intolerable to him, he could imagine Elizabeth lurking around town waiting for a glimpse of Ellen and then forcing herself on them like this. "Ellen, I —" And the doorbell rang.

Timothy yelled from the kitchen that he would get it, and they listened to the muted voices at the front door. He tried to imagine Timothy's reaction, after their discussion in the garden. Elizabeth came into the room. "Hello," she said, her cheeriest smile on. "It was so nice running into you in town."

Ellen gave Jack a last, questioning look, and said, "Please sit down. You've met my brother, Timothy."

"Yes." She turned to Jack. "John, it's wonderful that you're up here. How unexpected."

He kissed her on the cheek. "Hello, Elizabeth." At least his voice was working again. He found himself trying to imagine their meeting in town — Ellen would have recognized her, said hello, mentioned that he was visiting her house. Elizabeth would have been surprised, breathlessly so, and Ellen would very naturally have invited her to stop by. He could even picture them, strolling slowly down Main Street, past the drugstore and the general store and the inn, two women discussing a man. Except that Ellen knew that she and Jack were in love, and Elizabeth didn't.

Elizabeth said, "It's been so long since I've been here — I haven't seen your mother in ages."

"They're in Alaska," Ellen said. "Would you like something to drink? Lemonade?"

"That would be lovely."

"I'll get it," Timothy said.

Elizabeth went on. "David, my husband, has always wanted to go to Alaska, but we never have. I hear the cruise up among the islands, where is it, the Yukon? —" She looked at Jack.

"British Columbia. Or the Alaskan panhandle. I don't remember which."

"Well, that's a first." She smiled. He had an odd impression that she was removing white gloves from her hands, the better to get at him, but of course she wasn't wearing any. "I certainly was surprised when Ellen told me you were here, John."

He didn't relieve her of her surprise. "How's David?"

"He went to visit Hank at camp. There's some problem or other. Hank's not very happy. I never much liked that camp, I don't know why. It isn't right for Hank. But he wanted to go. You must have encouraged him, John."

"Not me." He wasn't going to give her anything to work with, not until he'd figured out what she wanted. That she wanted something was obvious to him — he couldn't believe that the others didn't recognize the predatory look on her face. But then, no one knew her as well as he did, not even David, he thought. I have her blood in me, and she has mine in her, we would know each other instantly even in the thickest crowd on the darkest night from the slightest signs — even if neither of us understands the other.

Timothy came back with a tray and a pitcher of lemonade. As he distributed the glasses, Elizabeth kept up her chatter. "Hank is my youngest boy. He's fourteen. He's very fond of his uncle John, isn't he. I think it's nice he has someone to confide in."

This seemed to be intended as some sort of conversational gambit, but Jack didn't pursue it. Elizabeth tried again. "My older boy, Billy, is very different. I never would have thought two children of the same parents could be so different."

"How did you happen to run into Ellen?" Jack asked, thinking it was time to go on the offensive a little.

"Well, I was in the beauty parlor —"

"Why?" he interrupted. "I thought you always had your hair done in New York."

She looked at Ellen — one of those looks women give each other that excludes all men from some particularly feminine ritual — and smiled. "I'm very flattered that you're so up on my routine, John. Actually, I needed some shampoo." She said to Ellen, "This lemonade is wonderful."

"Thank you."

Women have special antennas, Timothy had said. Jack could practically see Ellen and Elizabeth waving theirs cautiously, each taking the measure of the other. It might have amused him if he hadn't felt himself to be the crumb over which they would soon come to grips. Absurdly, he giggled at this thought, making a fool of himself.

Elizabeth said, rather as if out of the blue, "And has John told you his big news?"

"What big news?" Now his own antenna went up.

"Well, I saw Kate on Thursday. She —"

He felt himself starting to panic. "But Kate's in Switzerland," he said, much too loudly.

"No. She came back early, her mother wasn't feeling well. It's not serious, but she thought she'd be more comfortable at home. Which," she pretended to scold him, "you'd know if you hadn't gone running off without telling anyone." She turned to Ellen, woman to woman again. "He's so irresponsible, leaving town and not letting anyone know where he was going. Men never think they might be needed in an emergency. Except a business emergency. My husband always tells his secretary exactly where he's going to be, but he'll go off for a day on the golf course without telling me."

"One of the differences," Ellen offered, "between being a secretary and merely a wife."

"Exactly." Elizabeth laughed. "Well, John, aren't you going to defend yourself?"

He would have said that he'd taken care that someone knew how to reach him, but that would have meant bringing Billy into it. He shrugged and looked chagrined. "I'm guilty. What was it you said to me on my birthday — I'm free as air."

"Not for much longer, though." She looked at him, her mouth set in a hard line.

"Why do you say that?" Ellen asked, as if on cue.

"Well," she said triumphantly, "that's just the big news I'm talking about. You haven't told Ellen and Timothy? Kate told me you'd decided to keep it a secret, but I'm sure she won't mind. John, I'm so happy for you." She put out her hand and covered his. "Congratulations. Can you imagine. My little brother getting married. It makes me feel old."

He heard Timothy groan softly, but his eyes were fixed on Ellen's face. She only looked surprised for a moment, almost a natural reaction. It was, he thought, one of the advantages of the scientific mind, the ability to look a fact in the face. He felt sick.

It was Timothy who saved them. He said, stretching the point a little, "We talked about John's being engaged — I have to confess that I can't imagine it either — for myself, I mean."

He even remembered to call me John, he thought. He was furiously trying to send Ellen a message, he could imagine what she must be thinking, that he had told even Timothy, but not her. He dragged his attention back to Elizabeth, who seemed clearly deflated that her bombshell had been old news. "Well, John," she said, "will you be staying with us tonight? I'll make up your bedroom."

"No," he said. "I'm staying here."

"Really?"

"Yes. I'm Timothy's guest. I've been staying with him for a couple of weeks."

Elizabeth looked curiously at Timothy. "When I called last week, Timothy told me he didn't know where you were."

Jack, clutching to save something from the general crash, said, "Well, I had told him that I didn't want anyone to know where I was — it was supposed to be a vacation, after all, I figured Rob Cone from the magazine would try to track me down and haul me back for something." He was running on, as lightly as he could, filling the space. "Obviously, if I'd known it was you, I would have called back, but Timothy forgot to give me the message until this afternoon."

"Forgot," Elizabeth said.

"Yes," Timothy offered brightly. "It's one of the differences between being a friend and being a secretary."

Ellen managed a laugh at that. "How long are you here for, Elizabeth?"

"We're here all summer, back and forth, of course, you know how it is, but here mostly. And you?"

"I'm only here for another few days — I've got to go back to work, but perhaps you'll come over for a drink one evening."

"Thank you so much." She stood up to go, and Jack found himself admiring her for it, knowing exactly how to play her hand without overplaying it: no big scenes, no breathless discussion of wedding plans, no needling, just the bare fact and the usual short visit of a casual acquaintance.

Jack walked her out to the car. He wanted to ask her why she had done it, but then he wasn't sure yet that he wanted the whole thing out in the open. Elizabeth evidently believed that she had scored a victory, even a knockout, and until he assessed the damage he didn't want to disturb her. Still, he couldn't resist leaving her with something to think about, and when she invited him to come by after dinner, he said, "No, I can't. We're going to the dance at the club."

He stood a moment on the gravel driveway. The heat hummed with insect noises and with the tight vibration of his own predicament. He had wandered once into a dark room at Westfield and heard an eerie, disembodied note in the air. It was a cello that had been left carelessly out of its case — some movement he made set off a sympathetic vibration in one of its strings, a nearly subaudible sound. Now he thought he heard that same bass buzzing in the stretched veins in his temples. It had gotten very hot — if he stood there long enough he could solve all their problems by incineration, disappear in a puff of black smoke, spontaneous human combustion. He turned on his heel and went back into the house.

"I wanted to tell you," he said.

"I know."

"It was what I was trying to tell you when she came."

"I know." She sat down.

"Do you want a drink?" She shook her head, looking down at her hands. He got a glass full of bourbon and sat next to her. "All I could think of, from the time I met you, was that I was in love with you. Nothing else seemed to matter."

"You told Timothy." She moved on the couch, not much, just a little twist of her shoulders, creating distance.

"I came back from dropping Billy off. You were out, so I talked to Timothy."

She went to the table in front of the window and picked up a glass ball. "I know you meant to tell me." She put the ball down. "That's not it at all."

"What then? Ellen, I'd give anything."

"Don't you see?" She rested her hands on the marble top of the table and leaned forward a little. "This is so humiliating. I know I told you I don't want to press love any further than it has to go. But I don't want to be someone's mistress, especially someone not even married yet."

"Oh God." He sat back heavily against the cushions. "Is that what you think?" It had been so clear to him all along, he'd skipped over her assumptions. "You think I'm going to marry Kate."

"You're engaged to her, aren't you? What was I supposed to be, your wild oats? Last fling before you settle down?"

He deserved that, and he took it, not looking away. It was what he would have expected from himself, he had no right to hope that she would think differently of him. "The first night we met, at the restaurant, I knew that I wanted to marry you. Not Kate or anyone else. I love you."

"But you're engaged to someone else."

He covered his eyes with one hand, holding his glass tightly in the other. He had put himself in such a false position that he couldn't think of anything to say — that he'd proposed to Kate out of the force of her expectations and the momentum of their world? that it had been one more move in the game? He was so finely tuned to the reactions of others (it was his curse) that he knew he would sound exactly as if he were making himself out to be the victim, when in fact Ellen was. "I love you. Nothing else matters to me."

She shook her head. "Don't you see, that's exactly what does matter. There is someone else."

"No," he said, adamantly.

"There is," she said. "I'm not blaming you, Jack. But if things had been different, if you'd said to me a week ago that you were engaged to another woman but you were in love with me, what would we have done?"

He felt defeated. He got another drink instead of answering.

"First," she said in her orderly fashion, "I would have told you to settle with Kate. One way or the other, and it would have to be your decision and your doing. Then I would have told you to come back afterwards, if that's what you still wanted and we'd see."

"I'll talk to her tonight. I'll leave now." He stood up. "Only —" His voice sounded very small to him, and far away.

"What?"

He stopped himself. He didn't have the right to ask. He wanted to be sure, before he left, that she knew he loved her, that he hadn't just been using her or playing with her. His sense of honor came to the front, now too late, and he couldn't ask that of her. Instead, he said, "It's Elizabeth. She's manipulating me, and I'm just going along with her. I hate that, and what she did to you." He had been a willing pawn for so long that he recognized the hand of the master when he saw it: she wanted him away from Ellen before any declarations had been made, she wanted him to go back to Kate, even with the message that their engagement was over. Away from Ellen, she could work on him, and she would.

Ellen thought a minute. "That's the irony, isn't it. That I invited her here — if I hadn't, you would have told me in your own way, and —" She almost laughed, and shook her head, looking down at her hands. "I feel like such a fool. There were other ways."

But none so crushingly successful. He burst out. "She's determined that I marry Kate. I don't know why it's so important to her. Because David works for Kate's father, maybe. Or maybe because she's always arranged my life for me, it's been her grand role ever since my parents died, and she can't stand the idea that I won't go along with her plans. Whatever it is, she won't give up, she never has."

Ellen was very definite. "That's why you have to go along with her, and do what she wants you to do, until you're ready to make a decision."

All along, his chief thought had been not to hurt her any more than he already had. Now, he looked at her face and realized what an effort she must be making. She had been so happy that morning, she hadn't had to tell him, it was obvious in every move she made, and now she was trying to be as calm as she could to spare him. That she wasn't furious with him for putting her in this position was remarkable enough, but more than that, she was even able to look at it from his side. He went over and hugged her, more in love than ever. He hazarded one last request. "Would you — would it be all right if we at least went to the dance tonight?" He stepped back a little.

She smiled, and brushed his cheek. "After all, you are still our house guest. And it would be a poke in the eye to Elizabeth, which she deserves."

I love you, he thought. But he didn't say it.

They arrived at the dance at around eight-thirty, as the sun was setting. The clubhouse was at the top of a hill with a view west toward New York, the Hudson Valley and the Catskills invisible but felt beyond. As they went inside, he wondered whether anyone else could sense, despite the brave front they put on, the damage Elizabeth had caused: it was as if, under their evening clothes, they were wearing bandages and splints and were streaked with iodine, applied in an attempt to save the patient; that it had survived long enough to come this far was, he thought, no guarantee that it would outlive the night. He wanted another drink.

The party, he could see at once, was going to be a dismal failure. They were sitting at a table with Timothy and Susan and Andrew and his date, a waiflike creature with thick blond hair clipped straight around at ear level. She was wearing an elastic-looking dress that encased her like a tube from just below her armpits to well above her knees. She looked either stupid or stoned but wasn't either. Andrew introduced her as Cleopatra, but she said her name was Lynn.

"Where's Tony tonight?" Ellen asked.

"He's being punished. He's done some naughty things lately, so I told him he couldn't come."

Jack got up and went to the bar for a drink and watched the band for a while. It produced a reliable stream of old favorites, Glenn Miller and Cole Porter, Rodgers and Hart, Sinatra, with an occasional detour into the already ancient world of sixties rock. This enabled the largest group of club members, now fortyish, to paint in artificially vivid tones their memories of what had in fact been colorless flirtations with the edge of the counterculture. It made Jack think of David. During one break, he went over and had a short talk with the bandleader, and some money changed hands. He went back to the table.

Timothy and Susan were up dancing. Andrew said, "The atmosphere is very thick tonight."

Jack deliberately misunderstood him. "It's been hot all day." He said to Lynn, "Do you live in New York?"

"Yeah. In Cobble Hill."

"That's Brooklyn," Andrew said. "Not New York." He seemed determined to be rude.

"Would you like to dance?" Jack asked, to get away.

As they danced, she told him that she worked for a printer and had met Andrew when he'd come in with a photograph he wanted handled a special way. She didn't like him much.

"Then why did you come?"

"He asked me." She looked over at the table where Ellen was talking to Andrew. "I thought I might meet people. Someone, anyway. Interesting, you know."

They went back to the table. The room was crowded now, a party in full swing, a scene Jack had always known. He had sometimes thought that he would one day be one of those men who sits at a table at a party watching his wife dance with other men, knowing that she would come back to him afterward. His fantasy had always been of a woman who gathered men around her, paying them due attention, extracting from them the details of their love affairs gone awry (which she would set straight), and their adoration, which they would give with no hope of return. It didn't matter that Ellen was not that sort of woman, that she wasn't a fantasy. She was real, and she was lost to him. Gone, he thought glumly, forever, at a breath from Elizabeth.

Andrew, sitting next to Jack, was telling another story, about an apartment he had decorated for an eccentric old lady (all Andrew's clients were either eccentric or social climbers but never both; evidently, eccentricity was affordable only by those who had already arrived). Jack didn't want to listen to Andrew. He kept watching Ellen. Her dark hair was pulled back and caught in a comb, leaving her ears and neck exposed. She was wearing a pair of diamond and sapphire earrings that cascaded down in the light, and a platinum and diamond necklace that he wished he'd given her. Her dress was a shimmering mass of dark green and black that changed color as she moved. He found himself admiring her clothing as she herself seemed to recede farther into the distance. She got up to dance with Timothy.

Andrew opened a gold cigarette case and began to smoke. He was behaving more elaborately than was usual even for him. "I have been thinking about you, John," he said, "all week. I've been imagining you in Venice, for some reason. Have you ever been to Venice? I think you should be surrounded with rich tapestries, with gold thread picked out by candlelight. I see you in a rotting palazzo, like an English lord in exile, living an almost corrupt life while dirty canal water flows beneath your window. I see you in a gondola with an older woman, perhaps you were on the Grand Tour when she trapped you — but that would mean you were innocent to begin with. Walking across San Marco in wintertime. Drinking at Harry's. At the Lido, with the sirocco blowing through your hair."

It was a neat cocktail, composed in equal parts of Mann and Waugh and Hemingway, having nothing of Andrew Toller in it except the arrangement. Jack had no patience for this sort of thing tonight, however entertaining it might have been under different circumstances. He thought a minute, searching for a quotation, and then said, "Venice is in the grip of the pestilence."

Andrew looked back at him blankly.

"Thomas Mann, *Death in Venice.*"

"Ah, yes. I saw that movie. That exquisite little boy in his striped bathing suit. How seductive." He inhaled some smoke.

Jack ignored this, keeping the advantage. "New York is in the grip of a pestilence, too. Why don't I ever see you at an AIDS benefit, Andrew?"

"My dear," he said patiently, "I deal with very wealthy, very careful people. People would wonder. I simply can't afford to be associated with AIDS."

"I would have said that you can't afford not to be. There but for the grace of God, and all."

Andrew rolled the end of his cigarette on the ashtray before stubbing it out. "I'm careful, John. Very careful."

"But you weren't always, I'll bet." He'd learned enough about the gay life to know what had gone on four or five years before. "You never went home with guys whose names you didn't know, had never seen before? You didn't pick up tricks on the beach at Fire Island? The baths. Glory holes."

Andrew looked around and lowered his voice. "You're being terribly vivid."

"It's a vivid disease," Jack said aggressively. "I want a contribution from you. For the home I work with. I'm on the board, so it's all legitimate. You can make it out to the West Side AIDS Home."

"You don't waste any time, do you?" Behind them the band was playing "New York, New York." Ellen was dancing with her brother, and Susan and Lynn were watching, talking about something. Andrew said, nastily, "What's your interest in all this?"

"My best friend died of AIDS about four years ago. Seeing someone you love with CMV and a hole cut in his throat so he can breathe really concentrates the mind. You mean to tell me you've avoided all that, all this time?" Andrew suddenly disgusted him, he was one of those people who lived on the edge of the plague but averted his eyes. "I think ten thousand dollars would be about right."

Andrew laughed. "What do you think I am, made of money? I'm not in your class, John, not nearly. Ten thousand dollars, I ask you."

Jack was feeling very cool. "I know what your fee was for designing Blanche Morgan's apartment. It's fully deductible, of course."

"Blanche Morgan," Andrew said slowly. Jack could see he was thinking about something new. He could imagine what was coming, a straight commercial transaction. Andrew would give him a check for the home in exchange for Jack's agreeing to write an article about Andrew and his work for Blanche. He could almost see the calculation in Andrew's eyes, and he was preparing to refuse the offer, when Andrew unexpectedly said, "I saw Mrs. Morgan this week."

"Really?" Jack said, a little nonplussed.

"Yes." He got out another cigarette, looking at Jack while he lit it. "I went up to her apartment about some final details — she's got her heart set on a perfectly awful fabric for some pillows, and I had a time convincing her she was wrong. You like the clients to believe they have some say in things — it keeps them happy — but not if they're going to do something gauche. I have my own reputation to think about. While I was there, her daughter came by."

"Anne?"

"Yes. And I happened to mention that I'd seen you." The band had switched to a jitterbug, and the usual assortment of incompetents were frantically whirling women around the dance floor, but Andrew kept his eyes on Jack's face. "Well, you know, you told me how close you were to Anne, your mother and all. So naturally I mentioned it, how well you looked, what a good time you were having with Timothy. And with Ellen. I think Anne likes me."

Think again. Jack knew Anne well enough to know that Andrew was the sort of man she would use to her advantage but whom she would never like, and his sexual preferences would have nothing to do with her judgment. He was too obviously on the make.

"So Anne carried me off to meet your aunt and your sister."

Jack sat up stiffly. "Elizabeth?"

"Yes." He took a sip of his drink, some syrupy-looking liqueur. "I must say, you have a lovely family."

That was how Elizabeth had found out. For all her snooping (as he imagined it), it had been Andrew who'd told her. That explained very nicely how Elizabeth had happened to meet Ellen that afternoon. He traced the steps in his mind: from Jack to Andrew to Blanche to Anne to Elizabeth to Jack again. All of them connected. Everyone he knew seemed part of the same web.

Andrew went on, "Mrs. Lorburn asked me to come look at her apartment, and I did. You'll never guess who I met there."

"The Easter Bunny."

"Ha ha." Andrew leaned forward, and if he had known that he was closing a loop he couldn't have done it any better. "Kate Welland. She's back from Europe. Didn't you know?"

"Oh yes, I know." *People are falling all over themselves to tell me.*

"I told her all about our dinner together. She was very interested, naturally, because apparently no one knew where you were. I hope I didn't give away any secrets. An illicit rendezvous in the shrubbery?" He got up. "And now I think I will dance. Come along, Lynn." As he walked away, he looked back over his shoulder and said, "I will send you that check, John. You've been so entertaining, you deserve something in return."

Fuck you, Jack thought. He had another drink, and looked around. Timothy was having a good time with Susan; they were involved in a very long and apparently deep conversation, from which they would surface periodically to dance. For once Timothy seemed to have forgotten his manners and wasn't obligating himself to dance with every woman in sight. Well, Jack thought, maybe some good will come out of this. Of all the people he knew,

Timothy deserved to be happy, and if that could be saved from the wreck, something would have been gained. He finished his drink with the same feeling of disaster he'd had the night he'd wandered New Haven waiting for Peter to reappear — the sound of the smash of a bum's bottle on empty pavement. He asked Ellen to dance.

The bandleader saw his signal. "This was my parents' song," Jack said. "The first dance they went to, my father paid the band to play it six times." He held her, smelling her perfume, feeling her move with him. He sang, in a whisper, " 'Isn't it romantic, merely to be young on such a night as this.' My father thought that was the most romantic line in any song ever written."

She turned her face toward his. "Jack. I love you."

He looked away, afraid to take so much in. He knew she loved him, just as he loved her, and he knew that it wasn't going to be enough.

"Do you want to leave?" Ellen asked.

"Yes, please."

He got the car from the valet and helped her in. She said, "Are you OK to drive?"

Sure, he thought carelessly. It was what he needed to clear his head.

Someday, he thought, as they swept out of the club driveway, I'd like to teach my son to drive. Not that it looked now as if he were ever going to have a son. He thought of himself learning to drive, had a very clear picture, as if he were watching home movies that had never been taken. His father saying, "Now just take your foot off the brake," and the car moving forward. His father's instructions — "A little more gas — turn the wheel harder — now the brake, easy — don't be afraid of it" — all in that same tone of loving patience he had always used in teaching Jack things. And then driving the car home: it was only two or three miles, but it seemed to him, perched on the edge of manhood, a distance greater than Columbus's, and at its end a world more new and wonderful than any America. He made it home and got out of the car and waited for his father to come around the car and hug him.

But of course, he realized with a start, it hadn't been his father at all. It hadn't been that loving voice, it had been David's nervous instruction. His father had been dead a year then, and Jack had manufactured memory out of desire.

"You like shortcuts," Ellen said. "Make a left turn."

He obeyed her automatically, having lost track of where they were, exactly, cruising on autopilot. His dream had been so real that it was a shock to wake up and find it gone.

"That was pretty gruesome," Ellen said. "I'm sorry I dragged you to it."

"Don't be silly. You couldn't have known. And it would have been fun."

"Do you think so?"

He nodded. "Timothy seemed to be having a good time."

"Isn't it romantic," she sang softly.

His father's song. The headlights lit up the winding road, penetrating into the woods, over decrepit stone walls, and down alleyways of birch as they rounded corners. He thought he would recognize the road in the light, but now it seemed only vaguely familiar. They had been slowly climbing the side of a small mountain, and now they burst out of the forest into the open. The hillside rose steeply on his left and fell sharply on his right, and the road twisted with the contours of the mountain. "Merely to be young on such a night as this," he whispered, realizing where they were, what road this was. His father's song. His father's tuxedo. His father's death.

He knew he was drunk. His father had been drunk that night. There hadn't been an autopsy, but Jack knew, had known from the minute the rector first told him what had happened, that his father had been drunk. The drinks in the living room before dinner, the drinks at the dance at the club. His parents dancing, "Isn't It Romantic." And more drinks. He would have gotten the car and driven off, seeing the road clearly at first (had he been thinking of Jack at all on that last ride?), turning onto the Upper Mountain Road, this road, humming "Isn't It Romantic." And at some point had the road seemed to divide in his sight, had the car drifted a little over the line and back again (Jack turned the wheel gingerly, experimentally, and the two lines he'd been seeing in the road merged back into one). His mother sitting quietly against the door, looking down at the valley below, at the houses lit like beacons eighty feet down (as Ellen was staring now). Did those beacons call to his trapped father, offering the chance of release: when there's no escape, there's still a way out. Or had he simply come too fast around a corner (Jack heard the rear wheels screech a little) and been confronted with another curve, a choice he didn't see until it was too late, the guard rail ahead (it had been wooden then, but Jack's headlights shone on bright metal) and no arrow, only a wide patch of sand and pebbles thrown up by cars that had more slowly made the turn. "Sweet symbols in the moonlight." He heard a crunching as his tires hit the sand, Ellen saying something, and the long fall ahead. He jammed on the brakes, and the car skidded on the ground, slewed around broadside to the guard rail, and stopped.

Ellen was talking to him, but he couldn't hear. He got out of the car and walked to the edge of the cliff. He saw for the first time the splintered ends of the broken rail, and below, the car nose down in the underbrush, the taillights reddening the air. The stretcher being brought up in a hurry and the ambulance rushing loudly, vainly, off. The other stretcher, and no hurry about this one.

Ellen was standing next to him. She put her arm around him. "Jack. What's the matter?"

He looked at her.

"What is it, Jack? You're shivering."

He thought, I killed my parents.

PART FIVE

The End
of Love

~~~~~~

XIII

JACK SWALLOWED some coffee from a Styrofoam cup and made a face. The coffee was cold — he'd been sitting longer than he had realized, looking vaguely at the computer screen in his office at the magazine. He opened his desk drawer, hoping for a candy bar but finding only the usual debris, augmented by two clear packages of sweet-and-sour sauce and one foil packet of ketchup. Evidently, in his absence, his office had been used as a lunchroom. He picked up a package of sauce, watching the air bubble inside float from one end to the other, then tossed it and its companions into the wastebasket. He thought about going to the bank to deposit his paycheck, but it was wet outside, a soft and gentle rain, barely enough to streak the grime on his one narrow window — he could go to an ATM later. He realized his mind was wandering, and he looked at his computer again. The last sentence on the screen read: "By the end of this erotic battle of wits and wills, it is entirely fitting that Slim and Steve sail away to battle the Nazis with only Walter Brennan to help: the world cannot stand against their passion." He wasn't very satisfied with this, but he could go back to it later. He reached for the coffee cup, remembered, and then started to type: "In *Key Largo*, by contrast, Bogart and Bacall are indistinct, overshadowed by Claire Trevor and Edward G. Robinson and Lionel Barrymore, but also by the insufferable nobility of their own characters. Even at the end, when Bacall opens her shutters and Bogie brings his boat to port in floods of light, they seem not so much transfigured as transfixed." Having gotten that far, he scrolled back to the top, read through what he had written, and pressed the Save key. Then he looked down at the copy of the latest issue of one of their competitors, which someone had left on his desk, opened to a picture of Kate and him at a party — the photo had been enclosed in red ink by a heart with an arrow through it.

His editor, Rob Cone, came in and perched on the corner of the desk. "Hey, Newland. What are you doing here?"

"Listen," Jack said. "Do you think the word 'perch' can apply to a guy with two hundred pounds of bagels inside him?"

"You call this perching?"

"The word occurred to me. It seemed inapt." He leaned back in his chair, which made an annoying creaking sound of which he was very protective. "You got any candy bars?"

"Seriously, Newland. I thought you were on vacation."

"I went up to the country," Jack said lightly. "It was a drag."

"Yeah? I went to the country once. I got stung by a horse and kicked by a bee. Or maybe the other way around. I think it was Van Cortland Park."

"The Bronx. That's what I call roughing it. Do you have any candy bars?"

"Fucking one-track mind, don't you." Rob reached into his shirt pocket and pulled out a flat chocolate bar. "I'll split this with you." He gave Jack half. "What are you working on?"

"An essay about the Bogart and Bacall movies."

"Been done," Rob said through a mouthful of chocolate.

"Revisionist criticism. Bogart for the nineties."

"Sounds like bullshit to me." Rob wiped his hands on his pants. "Listen, are you really back here to work? Because I have an idea that would be perfect for you."

Jack looked at him skeptically. "This wouldn't have anything to do with either a psychic or a leopard, would it?" he said, thinking of another of Rob's great ideas.

"No, but I still think that would have —"

"Forget it. Tell me."

"I want you to cover the mayoral race."

Jack turned his chair so that it emitted a loud creak. "No way. I don't know anything about politics. LaGuardia's running, right?"

"Hush, my son. The extent of your ignorance is well known to me." He settled himself again on the edge of the desk, knocking over a pile of books, which he ignored. "Our magazine is a cultural beacon in this city, far above —"

"If this is your lecture for J-school brats, spare me."

"Our initiation," Rob said, mustering his dignity. "The doctrine

by which we live. It does you youngsters good, now and then, to
be catechized. Remember, I have care of your journalistic soul."

"The creed by which we screed," Jack said, finishing his chocolate. "Cut to the chase, Rob."

"OK. If you want to know what the candidates are saying, you
can read the *Post*."

Jack pretended to shudder. "God forbid."

"If you want to know what to think about what the candidates
are saying, you can read the *Times*. But nobody's covering the
campaign. People don't want to know what the mayor thinks about
poverty. They want to know what his chi-chi friends wear to his
fund-raisers. Politics is supposed to be above that sort of thing,
but it's not really."

"In Verdi's day, opera was politics. You want to do politics as
opera." Jack grinned. "It could work."

"You'll do it?"

"I guess. It doesn't count toward my vacation, though, right?
I still have two weeks left."

"Greedy bastard." Rob stood up. "Make it as tongue in cheek
as you want. Be bitchy as hell."

"It's what I'm best at."

"There's one other thing," Rob said, standing in the doorway.
"A grand finale. Bush is coming to town for a Republican fund-
raiser next month. I want you to get an interview with him."

"Right. Me and five thousand other guys."

"No, I've got it figured. Thomas Welland is one of Bush's friends
— they did some oil deals, they hunt together, that sort of thing."

There was another screech from Jack's chair as he swiveled to
look out the window. Outside, in the little bit of sky he could
see, a pigeon circled in the rain. "Yeah. So?"

"So you're tight, you should pardon the expression, with his
daughter, Welland's, I mean. Get him to make the introduction."

Just what he needed at this point. If he was going to break up
with Kate, he couldn't exactly ask her father for a favor. He
temporized. "What would I ask him about? Bush, I mean."

Rob folded his hands underneath his belly and gaped at Jack.
"What are you, a writer or a lox that's been dead for three days?
This is the president of the United States we're talking about."

"I could ask him what he thinks of *Key Largo*."

Rob scowled. "He'll tell you the bonefishing is great. Come on, Newland, what's the matter with you?"

He thought of Kate's face, what it would look like when he told her: I'm in love with someone else. "I don't know if I can manage it, Rob."

"I thought you were our champion — always ready for one more time around the track."

"Maybe I've retired."

"That's perfect." Rob banged his hand on top of the computer monitor. "We'll put you out to stud. How about it?" When Jack didn't answer, he said, "That bad, huh? You want to go have a drink later?"

"I can't," Jack said. "Thanks anyway. I've got to meet some-one."

Kate, in fact, but he didn't want to think about Kate right then. He thought about Ellen instead, about their conversation the day before.

They'd been sitting, drinking coffee, on the terrace outside the kitchen. He'd looked out over the little valley, at the unruffled water in the pond, and then up to the broad expanse of the gardens. This is my last look, he thought. I have to leave here, this perfect place, and go to New York and —

"Treat her fairly," she'd said.

She couldn't know, of course, that she was giving back to him, admittedly in altered form and with a quite different intent, the dogma that had ruled his life: do what people want, don't hurt anyone. She and Timothy had for a brief time shown him an escape from the predicament into which that had put him, and now she was asking him to plunge into it once again. He rebelled a little. "It doesn't matter that much, does it? If I just ignore the way they feel and concentrate on how we feel? Why are you so worried about their feelings? Look at Elizabeth, she certainly isn't worried about us."

She pushed her hair back from her face. "It's us I am thinking about."

He stood up and pushed his hands into his pockets. There had been times, a couple anyway, when he'd wanted to go out with some girl he'd met, but hadn't because she was dating someone else. It seemed perfectly natural to him to give way to a man with a prior claim; it went against some sense of honor, some instinct of decency, even to try to take a woman away from another man. It seemed a little ill-natured that he would wonder at Ellen's willingness to do the same. But then, he thought, the underside of chivalry had always been the assumption that women couldn't be expected to behave honorably, so men had to do it for them. I love her, he thought dismissively, that's all that should matter.

She said from behind him, "How will you feel about yourself if you've treated Kate badly? What kind of foundation would that be for us?"

With a feeling of hopelessness, he gave in. "Let me call Elizabeth, then, and tell her I'm going back to New York."

Elizabeth's only comment was a request. "Will you do me a favor? Billy's bored up here."

"Is he?" After only two days, it seemed unlikely.

"That's what he says. He probably just doesn't want to be with his mother."

"He's sixteen," Jack said, keeping things impersonal.

"Exactly. You see, David's had to fly to Seattle for a meeting, and we don't know when he'll be home. Would you mind taking Billy back with you and putting him up? Or putting up with him, I should say." She laughed into the phone.

It was all, of course, a game, but Jack couldn't imagine what role Billy was cast to play. He looked at Ellen through the sliding doors and thought, She wants me to do what they want me to do. He shrugged. "Sure. I'll pick him up in an hour."

"You can take one of my cars, you don't have to inconvenience the Archers. David will drive it back."

When he related all this to Ellen, she said, "You'll know when you've done enough. Then you can decide."

But he'd already decided, he thought, as he and Billy drove among the farms on Route 22. It was a hot, clear day, and around each turn was another view — pastureland running up to the bottoms of steep hills, cows standing next to round water holes, a single puffy cloud in a gap between two mountains. Billy opened the sunroof and put his bare feet up on the dash, tapping them in time to the music — the Radiators again, a tape he'd brought, "Love takes a lot of raw nerve." Well, Jack felt himself clenching his teeth, raw nerve is what I've got, for once. He would call Kate, see her that evening, and tell her.

"Do you think my allowance is enough?" Billy asked.

"How much is it?" And they got into a discussion that seemed eerily familiar to Jack — hadn't he, at the age of sixteen, argued with David over the size of his allowance?

They stopped to get gas. Billy went off to the bathroom and came back hopping, the asphalt hot under his feet, looking taller in his running shorts. Jack said, "You want to drive?"

"You mean it?"

Jack tossed him the keys. "Why not?"

"Just that Dad doesn't —" He obviously saw where this would lead, and covered himself. "I mean, around Westfield and all, but not on 22. I can do it, though."

"Then get in." Another echo of his own past. Nothing in those days had been more important than driving, and never more so than when he'd been with David and Elizabeth. Watching Billy drive, watching him concentrate so hard, Jack almost felt himself to be sixteen again. New York was casting its wide net, and the closer he got the more reabsorbed he was in his old life, in the way he'd been before Timothy had scooped him up from the steps of the Metropolitan on his birthday, two weeks before.

They got to his apartment around four. Jack stood in the front hallway, uncertain, feeling almost too welcome, feeling familiarity overwhelm him. Billy barged in, swung his duffel bag down from his shoulder and dropped it on the floor, turned on the stereo and flopped down on the couch. Jack put his keys on the side table (shades of his parents' house, but no porcelain bowl) and went into the bedroom to call Kate.

"John," she said, and he shut his eyes at the excitement in her voice. "How are you? I missed you so much."

"I'm sorry," he said dully. Get a grip on yourself, he thought. "I mean, I'm sorry I wasn't here when you got home. Is your mother all right?"

"She's doing better. Nothing serious. Where've you been?"

He didn't answer her right away. Hearing her voice changed

everything, made it all real, somehow, in a way that it hadn't been during his drive that afternoon, imagining. "I need to see you. I'll come right over."

"I want to see you too, John. But I didn't know when you'd be back, so I told Daddy I'd go out with him tonight to some party. You're welcome to join us."

He shook his head. That would never work — he needed to see her alone. "I've got Billy with me. Maybe I could come by later."

"Oh, let's make it tomorrow. I don't know what time we'll be through and I'm still a little jet-lagged."

She talked about Europe, and he didn't listen. This wasn't the way it was supposed to go, the way he'd imagined it during the long sunlit ride in the car. He wanted to see her, to tell her, to get it over with. He wasn't sure what might happen if he didn't, he only knew that delay worked against him.

"I love you, John," she said.

"I want to see you," he answered dully.

"Tomorrow. I have something to do downtown in the afternoon. Let's have a drink in the Village — I'll meet you at Undine at five-thirty."

"Kate —"

"I've got to run. Love you. 'Bye."

The cab that took him downtown got stuck in traffic near Bleecker Street, and he looked at his watch, not wanting to be late. Finally, he dug into his trousers pocket and pulled out his money clip and paid the fare. "I'll get out here."

The rain had slowed to a drizzle, but the clouds were heavy, and the streets seemed tinted with an early-evening darkness. He stepped over blue puddles and around soggy pieces of newspaper glued to the sidewalk. With a big hop, he jumped over a drain and crossed the street. There were large dark spots on his light suit from the rain as he stepped into the restaurant.

It was a smoky, driftwood bar, with splintery floors and posters of Paris pasted to the walls. Above his head a long string of pin bulbs, like Christmas tree lights, was draped over and around the pipes and ductwork, bright points in the generally dim brown atmosphere. He looked through the haze of cigarettes and garlic but didn't see Kate. "One?" the waiter asked suspiciously.

"No, two. Is Jean-Paul here?"

"Non," the waiter said with a little extra respect. He had the kind of French accent that would leak during a difficult evening. "He is on vacation."

"No smoking, please." Jack sat down at the table, facing the door. His skin felt a little slick from the humidity.

"Will m'sieu have a cocktail now?"

"A vodka martini, up, please. With Absolut."

"A twist?"

"No thank you."

"An olive then?"

"No vegetable matter at all, thank you."

The waiter stood just long enough to allow Jack to admire his miff, then stalked away to mutter conspiratorially with the bartender.

The place wasn't very crowded at that hour. At a table nearby, a young man in a black turtleneck was furiously reading a book in French — Jack couldn't tell what it was — and marking it occasionally with a red pencil, breaking off every now and then to gulp at a beer or bite off the end of a breadstick. He was obviously waiting for someone and seemed prepared to be angry at her (him?) for being late. A little farther down the wall, two women sat facing each other. One of them, much younger than the other, was talking hesitantly, shaking her head, her left hand flat on the table. The older woman reached out and covered it, reassuring. Beyond, in the corner, a tall man with a balding head stared rudely out at the world. And what did they see if they looked at him? An elegant young man in a pale gray suit, staring with wary green eyes over the edge of a large, damp martini glass. Kate came in the door.

Immediately, and all at once, he forgot why he'd come, what he'd meant to say to her, that he was in love with someone else. All he could remember was how beautiful she was. That was the way it came to him, as he sat watching her shake the rain out of her umbrella, not as the beauty he saw standing before him, but as the recollection of her beauty in the long months of their

courtship. Kate, in the close warm light of a theater, or by candlelight at a dinner in someone's apartment overlooking Central
Park, or asleep in bed, unconscious of his watching. Even before
he'd known who she was, on that first night, he'd stood in the
back of the theater, wondering at her beauty.

"You are the most beautiful woman in the world," he'd said to
her one night the previous February. Her parents were in Palm
Beach, and she and Jack had moved into their house. It was a
wintry night, with snow blowing hard against the windows, the
wind drifting it up in the streets, and the noise of the plows
muffled beneath the windows. They had taken a long bath together and were lying, wrapped in robes, on the floor before the
fireplace in the sitting room where she kept her jade collection.
He had a damp strand of her hair in his hand, playing idly with
it, looking at the curve of her breast through her open robe. He
felt warm and drowsy and steamy and comfortable. Around them,
the carved stones winked in a hooded darkness, the firelight flickering on their oblique corners. There was no bright clarity, none
of the faceted transparency of diamonds: jade was a water stone,
clouded like a river, shadowy in its beauty, more lovely the more
unclear it was. "Like jade," he went on.

"The Chinese say that the spirit of jade is like a beautiful
woman." She spoke with the authority of an expert, with the
passion of a collector. "They have stories about women and jade."

"Tell me one," he demanded, a little boy at bedtime.

She pushed her knee between his, nestling against him. She
spoke as if reciting, as if giving up a story she had fashioned in a
long silence until it was ready, full-grown, for display. "A jeweler
made a beautiful jade bracelet, which he put on the arm of his
little girl. The wonder of it spread all over China, until an imperial
concubine demanded that the emperor obtain it for her. But the
girl had grown, meanwhile, and the bracelet couldn't be removed,
so a soldier hacked off her arm to get it. The man to whom she
was engaged refused to marry her in her mutilated state, so she
retired to a monastery, where she became a master of the art of
fencing. One night she disappeared, and the next morning the
emperor and his concubine were found murdered in the palace."

It brought back to him the tales from the *Arabian Nights* that he had loved as a child, his mother's voice reading to him of Aladdin and his lamp, of Sinbad and the Roc, pictures of black-mustached Chinese men with long fingernails, adventures he lived over in a thousand and one nights of dreaming. "Go on," he said softly.

She paused again, gathering her thoughts, and he thought that she could tell these stories a thousand and one times, and each time they would vary by not a word. "A beautiful girl was betrothed to the emperor's heir, but when the Son of Heaven himself saw her, he couldn't resist her, and she became his concubine. Even that didn't satisfy her and, despite the dangers, she began an affair with a beautiful young man of the imperial guard. He was banished, and rebelled. The army blamed her for this disaster and refused to fight for the emperor unless she was killed. Even when her jade ornaments were thrown at their feet, they were adamant. In desperation, she hanged herself." She paused. "I like to think that one of the bracelets I have here belonged to her, that she would love even to destruction for the sake of love."

Jack thought of Harriet pretending to be Cleopatra. "Tell me another."

"The king made war for the sake of a girl. He was so enslaved by her that he built, at her command, a seven-story tower, the tallest building in China, the tallest in all the world. Then his kingdom was defeated in battle while he dallied with the girl. Remorseful, he climbed to the top of the tower, arrayed in thousands of jade ornaments, and set fire to himself. The emperor, the tower, and the jade all burned. Sometimes I think I'll do that, make my funeral pyre out of all this jade, burn it up with me."

"You can't take it with you," he said, laughing at her extravagance. But in fact she could. All that jade, all the lore of the stone, was an element of her beauty, along with all the other bright objects that surrounded her. Her aura of possession was part of her always; those things that her family owned — the people they acquired, all the massed collections of the Wellands — were latent in her, she blazed with them. That was the true source of her beauty, the way in which she so completely summed up the world to which they had both been brought up.

Now, seeing her standing in the front of the restaurant, that was all he saw. The past two weeks dropped away, and the previous six months came flooding back. Everything had been settled. Ellen, he thought, why did you make me do this? Then Kate walked over to the table, and as he stood and hugged her and kissed her cheek, the negative reversed itself, and now it was the last two weeks that seemed settled, and Kate a far-distant object.

"John," she said, sitting down next to him and taking his hand. "I missed you so much."

"I missed you too. Would you like a drink?"

"Dying for one." He signaled for the waiter while she went on. "I spent all afternoon in a tiny little studio — no air conditioning, of course — and we couldn't get the lighting just right, and then there was a problem with — I don't even want to talk about it." She stopped and leaned a little closer to him. "I love you, John."

"A gin and tonic with lime. And I'll have another martini," he said to the waiter. He suddenly felt frightened, the enormity of what he had to tell her emptying a void beneath his breastbone. He took a deep breath and told himself to act normally. "You look great."

"Thanks." She touched his face, and he moved away slightly, telling himself not to flinch. It was something he'd never liked, public touching. She knew that, it wouldn't bother her. He didn't want to give her any signs, there was no point in an emotional Chinese water torture. It would have to come all at once, and coolly. He felt his heart beating hard, as if he'd just finished a swim race.

"You look tired," she said.

"I had a virus last week. Nothing serious."

"Where were you?" she demanded. "I tried calling you, but all I ever got was your machine."

He thought of her voice in his apartment, while he had hidden, guiltily listening. "I was visiting Timothy Archer at his parents' house in the country."

"Timothy Archer? Really?" Timothy had never counted much for her. Their drinks came.

"Well," Jack said trying for a light tone, "you'd abandoned me. And he asked me."

"Did you have a good time?"

"I did, yeah." He was usually so attuned to what other people were thinking, but now he felt completely out of sync. He'd thought of her, all during the last couple of days, as Elizabeth's partner. He'd had a vision of the two of them planning everything over lunch at some soigné restaurant in the fifties, a sort of female equivalent of 21. He could see them, perched (the word passed this time) on a peach-colored banquette, breaking crusty rolls while they sipped Bloody Marys in a room full of women. He would have been disposed of between the sole meunière and the cappuccino. First he would have to be separated from Ellen. Elizabeth had achieved that nicely. Then there would be a grand reconciliation with Kate, to be followed, no doubt, by an early wedding. Perhaps he would even be permitted a renunciation scene (in Hollywood this would have happened while the church was filling with guests, against the background of Bach organ preludes, and intercut with scenes of the happy bride-to-be dressing), a last interview with Ellen before he and Kate rode off in her father's limousine to a cabin on the QE2. Cut. Print.

It had been easier to think of Kate that way — but now, seeing her as she really was, the whole conceit collapsed. She wouldn't have connived with Elizabeth, she was probably just as much the object of Elizabeth's plots as Jack was. She was acting as if nothing had changed between them because for her nothing had. And she loved him. "How was Switzerland?" he asked.

She wrinkled her nose. "Terrible. There was nothing to do — the people were dull, there were a million tourists everywhere. Everyone was talking about Poland."

"It sounds awful."

"Don't tease me." The waiter walked along the aisle next to them, carrying a plate of snails to the bald man in the corner. The smell of garlic descended on them. "London was wonderful, though. I love London. Maybe we should move there." She was leaning forward over the table, her arms resting flat in front of her, her hands wrapped around the base of her highball glass. "I spent the whole time shopping."

He laughed. This is all hollow, he thought, but how can I tell her? Forming words in his head and rejecting them. That we won't be moving to London, that we won't be moving anywhere. I don't love you, get out of my life? But she was his life, and she seemed so full of life, of his life, that he almost succumbed. He forced himself to say something else. "What'd you buy?"

"Well, I got a lace tablecloth in the Burlington Arcade, for those people whose wedding we're going to in September."

"What people?"

"I don't remember. Your friends from Yale. And I sent home a huge supply of things from Fortnum — I got that tea your aunt Clara likes."

He was noticing the fine, fair hairs on her arms, the way she seemed to sparkle as she leaned forward. "And jade?"

"Well, just a small piece. And something for your birthday."

He always pictured her like that: leaning forward over something, surrounded by rich fabrics and smelling of faint, exotic perfume. It was odd, how fixed in his mind this image of her was (the first night, in the theater, he had imagined her lighting candles over a dinner table; it was the same). She leaned into life, just as he leaned back from it. Where did that leave Ellen, then? — standing upright, he supposed, between them.

He took another deep breath. His face still felt damp to him, and he was scared again. A group of people came in, NYU types, he thought, boisterous, happy, crowding around the table next to theirs. He caught one of them watching him and thought, This is impossible. I can't tell her something as serious as this in a restaurant.

Kate was saying, "I can't believe this day I had. Four hours for three crummy photographs. It was worse than that night at the monument. Remember that?"

He did, even though he didn't want to. They'd been going out for three months and had reached the stage where they were very absorbed in each other. She had started to accompany him to events he covered for the magazine, and it only seemed right that he should go with her to a shoot she was supervising. The gallery was opening an exhibition of architectural drawings of New York monuments in connection with a book they were publishing, and she was arranging the cover photo for the catalogue. So he found himself, late one winter afternoon, on a height above the Hudson, at the Soldiers' and Sailors' Monument, waiting for the sun to set.

He was sitting on one of the cold marble benches at the side of the small rectangular plaza that faced the monument. The floor of the plaza was tiled in big white rectangles surrounded by thinner strips of brown. To his right the monument reared up: a thick round base with a small iron door that was always locked; then great columns, capitalized in Corinthian excess, surrounding a narrow inner core; and then, above, vigilant eagles with thrust-out chests and beaks. The dome was unseen. Around the pediment was carved the dedication: To the Memory of the Brave Soldiers and Sailors Who Saved the Union. Across from where he sat, Sherman's name was carved on a massive plinth above the names of battles: Gettysburg and Vicksburg, Chickamauga and Chattanooga, Spotsylvania, Cold Harbor, and Atlanta. The roster of the victorious Union.

Kate was standing on a lower terrace — he could see the top of her head — surrounded by her crew: a photographer, a couple of techies with various kinds of lighting apparatus. She had told him that there was a moment, just after sunset, when the color of the sky and the color of the monument were perfect together. She'd scoped it out for days, she said, catching cabs up here to wait, with her watch, for the exact moment. She knew when it would come. All they had to do was wait.

But he couldn't wait, not any longer. Not here. He had avoided, as much as possible, looking around him, his head down and his eyes on his shoes, but he couldn't keep it up. He had always tried to be careful, to avoid places with the associations this one had, but love had trapped him into coming here. He stood and went up the steps to the base of the monument. He looked down at Kate and her entourage for a moment, then walked around to the back.

It was much quieter here. A flight of steps with a curving stone balustrade descended to a beautiful little terrace, paved with exactness in white and brown. He went down lightly, not wanting to make a sound. The place was very classical, perspectives of stone in different configurations. The curve of wide, graceful steps ending in an uncompromising cube of inscribed marble, the squared corner of the foundation thrust against the roundness of the monument, a bare stone banister supported by vase-shaped pillars. Through the stripped branches of the trees, he could see the Hudson and the unremarkable end of the Palisades. The little terrace was empty. He sat down on a bench.

This had been one of his father's places. Every year or so, usually in the springtime, they had come here. It had been typical of his father to pick one of the city's less beloved landmarks, hardly a landmark at all, since so few people knew about it. One couldn't, for example, give directions by saying that something was three blocks from the Soldiers' and Sailors' Monument, the way one could with Grand Central or the Empire State Building. Perhaps his father had liked the view of the Hudson — the North River, as he sometimes called it, in deference to genealogy. Perhaps the visits were in tribute to his career in the Navy during the war in the Pacific. Jack had gone with him more or less dutifully: it was the sort of "outing" New York children are occasionally subjected to, like visits to the Zoo or the Natural History Museum. His best friend, Dougie, was taken every year to the Statue of Liberty, and Jack went along, just as Dougie came here with Jack and his father. He remembered one of their last visits, when he was eleven or twelve. He and Dougie had brought their baseball gloves, and they climbed down the embankment to a level space next to the West Side Highway, tossing the ball back and forth while the cars rushed by and his father sat up on this same terrace (on the same bench Jack was now sitting on). When they got too hot, they came back up here, and his father talked to them about the Navy. Usually he told them about Okinawa, where he'd served on the *Indianapolis* and the *New Mexico*, on Spruance's staff. But that day he talked about the Civil War instead. About Farragut, and the *Trent* Affair, and mostly about the *Alabama*. "In a three-month cruise, *Alabama* captured twenty-six Union ships and burned twenty-one of them. People thought she was invincible, a miracle of some kind. But the good guys got her in the end. *Kearsarge* went broadside to broadside with her for over an hour and sunk her in forty fathoms off the French coast." For a moment, Jack felt as if he were back on that day — hot, feeling stretched, happy, the cool of the stone on his bare legs, and Dougie sitting next to him. His father's voice, calmly describing glory, full of pride and the familiar smell of scotch.

Abruptly, he stood up and shoved his hands in his pockets, feeling cold. Asshole, he thought. Sitting on a stone bench in the middle of February. He realized he was shivering. And what the hell was Kate doing?

He found her surrounded by a bunch of men all huddled at the base of some steps. There was a camera on a tripod, a bunch of other equipment. The photographer was saying unhappily, "Kate, you've got a sensational shot here. You've got ten sensational shots. We wait any longer, the light dies completely and we end up with a floodlight effect. It's a cliché, it's been done. What you have is original."

She put her hand lightly on the photographer's arm. "You guys are terrific. But if we wait another ten minutes, we'll get what I want. Trust me."

Jack was shivering even more. He held his arms close to his sides, trying to control it, sucking in his lips. Above, the monument seemed to have elongated, to have grown monstrously against the darkening blue of the sky. It hadn't been like that when he was a kid, he thought, those days with his father.

The photographer was saying something, and it took him a minute to figure out the guy was talking to him. "Let's ask your boyfriend here. Come on, take a look through the lens. Tell me if that isn't the greatest architectural photo since the Flatiron Building."

Jack held his hands up in front of him, declining to get involved, then put them down to hide the shaking. But he knew that, just for an instant, he'd let his impatience show on his face. And the photographer had seen it. Jack looked at Kate apologetically and walked away. A minute later she followed him. "I know what I'm doing."

He nodded. "Yes."

"You're cold. Why don't you ever wear a coat?"

He shrugged. "I couldn't find it. I must've left it somewhere."

"Go home, John. Take the car and go home. I'll meet you later."

He shook his head. "No, don't be silly. I'll stay. It's what I came for."

She led him toward the curb, where the car was parked. "You're being silly. I think it would be better if you left."

He suddenly saw it from her side. He'd been feeling useless, sitting on the bench, and probably looking it, too. He'd disappeared behind the monument, coming back with a ghost at his shoulder and a case of the shakes. He'd behaved badly, at least he could exit gracefully. "OK. Will I see you later?"

"I'll call you." She kissed him, and he got into the car.

He stood in his apartment, still shivering, wondering what he was going to do with the rest of his evening. With the rest of his life, he thought, now that he'd let Kate down so badly. If he'd thought a little bit more about her, if he hadn't thought so much about his father. If he hadn't gone at all, knowing that in that place he would inevitably think of his father.

The doorbell rang. He was shaking, he didn't want to see anyone. He answered the door. It was Kate.

"I decided not to go home," she said. "I'm freezing. I'm going to make some tea or something."

As if nothing has happened, he thought, following her into the living room. "How'd it go?"

She took her coat off and tossed it across a chair arm. "Terrific. I was right, there was enough light. Barely, but enough." She went into the kitchen and put a kettle on the stove. He could see her through the pass-through, she looked so at home.

"I'm sorry."

She came back into the living room, sat down on the couch, and kicked off her shoes. She sighed, pointing her toes. "For what?"

"I mean for butting in. About the picture."

"What are you talking about?"

And he saw that she really didn't understand. That he couldn't, for her, intrude where he wasn't wanted, because she wanted him everywhere. He looked away.

"What's the matter, John?"

He shook his head. "I don't know."

"Come here and sit down."

He sat next to her, and she put her arms around him, holding him. He said, "I'm sorry. Just that — I was thinking all these rotten things at the monument, bad things that happened to me." He wouldn't tell her, he couldn't. Any more than he'd been able to tell Ripley or the psychiatrist. "It just seemed like I was doing bad things to you too."

"Sh. It's OK. You can't do any bad things to me." And he'd believed her then, that it was possible with her. That he wouldn't hurt her, or anyone else, ever again. And now, sitting in the restaurant, listening to her, he knew it wasn't true. The rule of his life (one of those inflexible rules learned from the close examination of recurrent phenomena) reasserted itself: he would do bad things to her, he would hurt her. "Kate," he said, "let's go."

She looked at him, and he wondered what she could see in his face. "You don't look so hot. Are you feeling all right?"

"Yes, I just want to leave. Let's go to your apartment."

She finished her drink. "What about Billy? It's dinnertime."

He'd forgotten Billy. "He'll be OK."

"Well, I think we should at least feed him. We'll pick up a couple of pizzas on the way to your place. How's that?"

Something was giving way in him, he felt the way he did sometimes in dreams, trapped in a dark, constricted passage. He just wanted to get out of there. "Sure, fine. Let's just go. Please." And they went uptown.

"Great, I'm starved," Billy said when they got home, taking the boxes and opening one. "How you doing, Kate?"

"Fine. How's Hank?"

"At camp." Billy, standing over the pizza box, took a slice out and started chewing on it.

"It might be nice," Jack said, "if you offered some to somebody else."

"Oh yeah. Sorry." He finished his slice and headed for the kitchen. "I'll get some plates."

"That," Jack said, "is what it's like to have a teenager in the house."

She sat down on the couch, where she always sat. She had

appropriated the spot months ago on her first visit to his apartment. "He's cute."

Jack snorted, and sat down at the other end of the couch, the spot to which she had assigned him. When her feet got cold, she would stretch them out and bury them under him. He nodded at the closed door, behind which lurked the wreckage of Billy's occupation. "You should see what he's done to my study."

Billy came back into the room with plates and napkins. "So, Kate, I want to go to Val's. Will you take me?"

She looked at Jack. "I don't know. What do you think?"

Billy interrupted. "I already asked him. Besides, I'd rather go with a beautiful woman than some old guy."

Kate smiled. "Well, Billy, I don't know if they'll let you in. Are you old enough?"

"Sure I am — they will. Please, Kate." His voice chose that moment to crack up an octave, and he blushed.

Jack was starting to feel sick, imagining the words he would use, knowing that he was running out of time, that sooner or later Billy would go to bed or Kate would want to go home. He forced himself to get into the spirit of things. "Anyone else you want to invite, Billy?" Jack looked at Kate. "He's got a girlfriend."

Billy turned even redder. "Shit."

"Don't tease him, John." She twisted her head around and looked at Billy. "Would you like to invite her, Billy?"

He shook his head. "She's away."

"Well," Jack said, "think about it. We'll go maybe in a few days." Putting it off.

After dinner, he took Kate home. It was still raining, and he watched the windshield wipers of the cab instead of thinking. The doorman of her building said hello to him. The elevator boy was new and didn't know either of them. Inside her apartment, she turned and held him. "It's great to be alone, finally," she said and reached up to kiss him.

He stepped away, feeling miserable. He knew he shouldn't do this, he knew that he should go along with her. She was here, and Ellen was far away: the choice between causing immediate hurt and postponing everything at the expense of Ellen, who would never know if he took a few days more or less to tell Kate. He said, "I need to tell you something."

"OK. Come sit down." She led the way down the hall into the living room.

Another mistake, he thought right away. This room was hers. Knowing her, you could walk in and know that it was made in her image. There were two large yellow sofas and two white chairs. An antique étagère in the corner held specimens of her jade collection. But more than the furnishings was the ensemble, the way everything had been put together so exactly, so characteristically. He felt like a traitor here, as if he should have chosen any other place. She sat down and kicked off her shoes. "Is something worrying you? You haven't seemed yourself all evening."

"I —" He pushed his hand up through his hair. "I'm not sure we should get married," he said. And thought, Pretty weak, Jack. "I think we should call off our engagement."

Blunt and stupid. But there didn't seem to be any gentle way to do this. He could talk about how much he loved her, what a wonderful person she was, what a shit he was — all kinds of formulas from soap operas occurred to him.

"But why?"

Because I'm in love with someone else: the one thing he could never say to her. For Ellen's sake, he had to leave her out of it. And he'd had no assurances from her anyway. She'd said he should come back afterward, and they would see. "I don't think it's the right thing to do."

I sound like an idiot, he thought. I don't want to be doing this.

She said, very gently, "John, it's OK. I know how you feel. At least I think I do. It was obvious to me, all those nights at clubs with Amy and Boyd, or when we had dinner with Elizabeth and David, the way you are with Hank, that something was making you unhappy. But I guess I feel you're entitled to that. You don't talk much about your parents, but that doesn't mean I can't feel your pain. We don't need to rush into anything. We can take our time. And I love you."

He felt himself starting to cry and knew it was the wrong reaction. He got up and walked to the window, looking out.

She waited a moment and then said, "I would never pressure

you. We'll just go on with our lives. We haven't told anyone —
well, I told Elizabeth, but that doesn't matter. We'll be together.
All I want is for us to be happy."

And she would make them happy, he thought. She always knew
exactly how to place everything and everyone, and now she was
placing him. A secret engagement had a place, as did a public
one. So too, it seemed, did a broken one. They'd go on with their
lives, she'd protect him if she could from his own unhappiness
until he was ready to propose again, a matter only of time in her
mind. Everything was worked out — except Ellen, except the
real cause of his unhappiness. "I don't think we should see each
other so much. For a while."

But she was ready for that, too. "It seems to me we haven't
been together enough, and it's my fault. I should have known —
I shouldn't have gone off to Europe right after you proposed like
that. I should have been here —"

"It's not your fault," he interrupted.

"We need to be together, at least for a while. I don't blame
you for feeling like this, the way I've deserted you. At least for
a little while. And then we'll see."

And then we'll see, he thought. Ellen's message to him, and
Kate's. He wanted a conclusion — at least that's what he'd thought
he wanted when he came here. Women didn't want conclusions,
they wanted situations. And he thought of Ellen's other message:
You have to be fair to her. "All right, Kate. Oh God, I'm sorry."

She came over to the window and touched his shoulder. "Don't
be. It'll all work out. And don't think you're the first man to get
cold feet. It happens all the time, I bet, but men do get married."

She didn't want a wedding, he thought, so much as she wanted
him. She was happy now, he had made her happy. But it was all
a zero-sum game, in which one person's happiness would have
to be paid for by someone else's pain.

He was numb the next day, as if he were pretending it hadn't
happened. He kept thinking that he was setting Kate up, that by
letting her believe they could go on, he was only making her
ultimate unhappiness worse. In the afternoon, doodling in his
office, he got a phone call from Blanche Morgan, Anne's mother,

inviting him to stop by for a drink. It was a summons he couldn't refuse, especially not that day, knowing why she called, as she did every year on this date. It was the anniversary of the day his parents had been killed. He had been pretending all day that she wouldn't call, that he wouldn't have to think about it on top of everything else. Didn't he have enough to deal with? — or not deal with, he thought miserably.

She was waiting for him in the living room of her apartment, sitting stiffly in an old wooden wheelchair, to which arthritis had finally confined her. She had been his grandmother's friend from childhood, his mother's godmother, just as her daughter had been his mother's friend and Elizabeth's godmother. He had grown up in and around her home, she had told him stories of her girlhood, linking him to his ancestral past. Of days when private homes still lined Fifth Avenue and ladies spent their afternoons paying calls up and down its length. Of long afternoons in the summer at Newport, when the sea breeze blew unpolluted over wide empty fields. Of the great parties, crushes, held in the huge ballrooms of the forgotten mansions, of the golden horseshoe at the old Opera House, where the wives of self-made men paraded their jewels in displays more elaborate than anything seen on the stage. Of titled Englishmen trawling for wealthy American girls, and the scandals of divorces and fallen women. A world in which everything had its place, sure and certain. She would tell him that he was the only young man she knew who would have fit into that world, who understood it, that was why she consulted with him on matters of taste, invited him to her dinner parties at which the few remaining relics of that world gathered over table settings of great elaboration, finger bowls and menu cards, oyster forks nestled in soup spoons, and four wine glasses each. He would sit there, the starched collar of his dress shirt biting into his neck and the white tie tight around the collar, talking first to the lady on his right and then (next course) to the lady on his left, and would feel, ridiculously, that she was right, that he did understand this world. He wondered what would happen if he told them about his nights at Val's, about cocaine in dirty men's rooms, about having sex with people whose names he couldn't even remember two months later, but even as he thought of their expressions, he knew he would never do it, out of politeness, of course, but more because he loved a life where everything was prescribed for him.

He bent down to kiss her cheek. "Blanche, you look wonderful." She did, too. Her face had gotten a little puffy these last years, not marring its beauty but softening it, and her skin was still as smooth and unlined as a child's.

"Thank you, John. Would you like a drink?"

"Yes, please. I had a crazy day." He told her about it. She loved his job, took a kind of malicious pleasure in his skewering of the vanities of a world she didn't care for, the made-up society of arrivistes who strove without success to imitate the sophistication of her life: in aping, they became merely apish.

"Where is Milton?" she asked abruptly.

Jack looked around. She had a bulldog, one of a litter that had been born, much to her surprise, in her kitchen, of a bitch that belonged to her cook. The dog had been born blind, and Jack, in an attack of sentiment, had persuaded her to keep it. He had named it Milton, after the poet. "He's probably in the fireplace." The dog had a habit of wandering into the fireplace and then being unable to find its way out again. This caused endless problems in the wintertime, when it would trail ashes around the house. Jack was sure that one day the dog would incinerate itself. He went over to the fireplace and helped it out. "I see Andrew Toller has finished his masterpiece."

She looked around in lieu of gesturing. "He's wonderful, don't you think? His work, that is. I think he's rather a disagreeable person."

"He wants me to write an article about him, with pictures of your apartment."

"How very vulgar."

He grinned. "I told him you wouldn't like it."

She raised her hand from her lap and rested it on the wheelchair arm. "I said it would be vulgar. I didn't say I wouldn't like it. There's a world of difference, you know."

He sipped at his drink, then put it down on a rococo, marble-topped table that rested on three thin gilt legs — Andrew had probably sent specially to Rome for it, it had a genuine look. "You've never done anything vulgar in your life."

"I'll tell you a secret. The only way to be flawless is to do something vulgar every now and then. It proves that your taste is true." She looked at him shrewdly. "I needn't tell you that. I know why you wear those awful shirts with those plaid ties every now and then. Am I right?"

He laughed. "You taught me everything I know, you must have taught me that too."

She sat still for a moment. The afternoon was bright, but the room seemed dark — Andrew had had the walls painted a deep blue — and now a shaft of light, reflected from some source outside, fell on her face. She never hurried anymore. He sometimes thought that she drifted in and out of a kind of doze, rousing herself only when she needed to, conserving herself. "What's this I hear about you and Kate Welland?"

He sighed. "What have you heard?"

"Are you going to marry her? Or not?"

No one else would have asked him so directly, and he was sure that Elizabeth wouldn't have approved. Certainly she hadn't put Blanche up to it. Blanche made her own rules or, rather, the rules by which she lived were so archaic that they seemed quaint, personal, and sometimes outrageous. He would meet her at her own game then. "Tell me, Blanche. Why is it so important to everyone? Elizabeth, you, David. Even my friends."

"I don't know," she said in a very dignified voice, "that it is especially important to me. I want your happiness, dear boy, just as I always have. Kate will make you happy. Happier than you know. The two of you understand each other, and understanding is more important than you think it is. Young people marry for love, and they make each other unhappy over it. Love comes and goes"— she made a motion with her hand, a conjurer's pass making love disappear and then reappear, her bracelets jangling against her wrist, and he had the impression that she was telling him something very private about herself — "and comes again and goes again. But understanding remains. You were made for each other, I've never known two people more suited. That means more than love, John."

It was an old woman's argument, he thought ungenerously. "Have you ever been in love?"

"Don't be impertinent. Have a biscuit."

"I don't want a biscuit." He looked at her, sitting upright in the wheelchair with its wicker back and its uncompromising size. "Is that why Elizabeth is being so pushy about it?"

"As for Elizabeth, I couldn't say."

He stood up and walked across the room. A beveled mirror hung over the fireplace, but he didn't look in it. A small painting of a ship in shallow water, Dutch, hung near it, but he only glanced at it. "But she is being pushy. It seems so — important to her, out of all proportion. Why? You understand her better than anyone, I think, better than I do, anyway. Tell me." He felt ridiculous, pleading with her like that. He wouldn't have asked anyone else, but he knew she wouldn't go to Elizabeth with the story, even if she wouldn't answer him.

"Your sister has had a very difficult time, I don't have to tell you. Did you know that your parents disapproved of David, that they didn't want her to marry him? They thought she was too young, that he wouldn't make her happy — that he didn't, as I said before, understand her. Whether they were right or wrong, I couldn't say." She said this last in a changed tone, as if continuing an old argument. Then she went on in her normal voice. "She never got a chance to show them, to let them see how things turned out. She's lived all this time with that hanging over her. Perhaps she's trying to rectify that with you, to do for you what they tried to do for her. I know you haven't always appreciated it, but she has been very concerned about you, ever since that terrible night. She's always said that it was worst for you. She wants to make sure you're happy."

Arranging his life, he thought. She had always done that. Now he was upsetting her calculations. Well, he didn't want to be bound by her guilt. "I have to do what's best for me," he said lamely.

"Do you know what's best for you?"

He heard a noise and looked down. The dog had gotten stuck in the fireplace again. He lifted it out.

She said, "If you've finished your drink, we could go outside."

He pushed her wheelchair out through the French doors and onto the terrace that surrounded the apartment on three sides. It was widest here, and there were stone boxes planted with flagrant annuals, and trained trees in pots against the wall. Below them, Central Park spread out its treetops toward the West Side. "I love this balcony," he said as he pushed her along. "It always reminds me of something from the thirties, from a Gershwin movie, *Shall We Dance,* or Cole Porter."

She laughed. "Cole Porter had a wheelchair at the end, but he never let anyone see him in it. You'd go to dinner at his place at the Waldorf, and he'd be charming all through cocktails. Then everyone would have to adjourn to some side room, and the next time you saw him he was already seated at the dining room table. Silly man."

There was a picture, somewhere, of Jack with Cole Porter. He had been two years old and didn't remember its happening — the photo was his only evidence.

"I don't much mind this wheelchair," she went on as he pushed her slowly across the stones. "They say it's not as comfortable as a modern one would be, but I'm not in it for my comfort."

"It's old-fashioned and beautiful," he said, looking out over her head at the buildings across the park. "It suits you."

"You may stop here." He did, and then sat down on a very low stone bench in front of her. "You're the only one of your generation who appreciates things like this."

He didn't know whether she meant her antique chair, her terrace, or her life in general. "What about Andrew?"

"Oh, Andrew. He can design the set, my dear, but he can't command the stage. You can. You should."

He looked up at her, feeling a little as if he were sitting at her feet. "And would marrying Kate make me, as you say, command the stage?"

"Of course it would. What are you thinking about, John, you seem to have gotten very woolly lately. How can you ask?"

He had gotten woolly, he thought. He was in love. He confided in Blanche as much as he did in anyone, but he wasn't going to confide that. He said, "If I ever own a boat, I'm going to name it after you."

"Blanche?"

"No. *Indomitable*."

She smiled thinly. "Do you think I'm indomitable? I know my children do, and my grandchildren even more. But I don't feel it anymore. The world has changed. I have my havens, but even here I have to let the Andrew Tollers of the world in. John, if I asked you to push me off this roof, to walk away, would you? If I call you up one night and say, Do it?"

"No, darling, I won't," he said gently. She had these moods, more and more lately. Age, he thought, the passage of time. The world had rotated out from under her and left her placeless. She could ignore that most of the time, but occasionally she would call him to her and bemoan this fate that she hadn't deserved.

There was a noise from inside. "That's Anne," she said. "She wants to talk to you about something. Kiss me and you may go." She never apologized for her moodiness, and he didn't want her to.

Anne was waiting in the living room. "Hello, green eyes. Having a nice summer?"

Don't you know all about it? he thought, suddenly defensive. From Andrew and Elizabeth. He wondered if she were the next move in their game. "Your mother said you wanted to see me."

"Yes. My friend Randy died last week. I don't know why, but it strikes me fresh every time." She had a varied acquaintance, in the theater world, the fashion business, all the places where AIDS had hit hardest. Each time she seemed bewildered by it. She would always make a contribution to the home in their memory. He felt sorry, suddenly, that he had misjudged her — that he had assumed she was after him for some cynical purpose when she was only bereaved. He watched as she wrote the check and then said, on impulse, "Anne. Was my father —" He stopped. When it came to the point, he couldn't ask straight out.

"Was he what?"

"Before he died. Was he sick or anything?"

"Oh, Johnny," she said, using his little boy's name. She touched his hair. "No, he wasn't sick." Then she remembered. "Oh, sweetheart, I'm sorry. I forgot. It's today, isn't it."

He nodded unhappily. He shouldn't have asked.

Kate came to his apartment for dinner that evening. She brought a steak with her and cooked it, which was a sign, to him, of something. She wasn't the cooking type, ordinarily, preferring restaurants, take-out, and Jack's cooking, in that order. But she seemed to want something different that evening, and he let her, contenting himself with his bourbon. He kept thinking that he was a coward, that he was afraid to say anything more to her. But it had been bad enough the night before, he could wait at least a day or two before making it worse.

At nine o'clock, Billy yawned elaborately, said he was tired, and went into the study. Kate watched him go, then said, "Do you know what Amy told me yesterday? You remember that friend of Boyd's — the accountant with the red beard? Amy told me he has a mistress."

"A mistress?" It was a word out of an old novel. "Didn't he just get married at Thanksgiving?"

Kate nodded and yawned. "Mmm-hmm. Then he met this other woman at an office Christmas party. Boyd said they went into the boss's office and used his couch, and they've been at it ever since."

"That's revolting."

"I talked about it with Amy. She said she wouldn't be surprised if it happened to Boyd someday."

"I don't think Amy has much to worry about. Boyd's pretty in love with her."

She sat up. "You know him awfully well, don't you."

He nodded. Boyd was his oldest living friend, except for Dougie. And Dougie was from the time before his parents died, and that was a different category entirely.

"I should go, John." She gave him a little kiss, as if observing a self-imposed restraint on his behalf. He went downstairs with her and waited while the doorman got her a cab. Then he went back to the apartment, poured himself another drink and stared into the window at his own reflection. The sleeves of his shirt were rolled up carelessly and his hands were stuck into the pockets of his trousers. One shirttail was untucked in the front, and his feet were bare. What a mess I am, he thought, what a mess this is.

A mistress. He didn't want a mistress, the idea disgusted him, even if there were plenty of examples from which to choose, among his parents' friends (and now, it seemed, maybe his own friends). Couples one saw around, and everyone knew that one or the other was having an affair. He remembered one woman who had conducted an openly concealed affair with one of her husband's friends; the husband, knowing and not knowing, had seemed to wither away, as if he were a plant suddenly deprived of all but an occasional watering. At a party one night, Jack had seen him sitting alone smoking a cigarette. Jack had wanted to go over and talk to him, be friendly, but that would have been out of character and an acknowledgment of the very thing that everyone, the husband most of all, was keeping quiet. That was how these things went most of the time.

Not, he imagined, with Kate. She would not, under the circumstances, dry up, lose leaves, and fade. She would glow more brightly, in pride of possession. She would display him as her own, with an innate confidence that would distract if it didn't completely deceive. Her family for years had owned rare items — paintings, porcelain, jade — and if for a time they consented to lend these things, to museums or exhibitions, the loans only enhanced the ownership, for wherever they went they carried little brass markers with the Welland name. Her father and grandfather were, after all, bankers, very skilled in the ways in which property, surrendered for a time, returns enhanced in value.

He shook himself. That was a compromise which would suit Elizabeth, maybe, but it wasn't what Kate wanted at all. What she wanted was what they'd had that evening. Dinner together, a kid around the house. She was showing him, as graphically as she could, what life with her would be like. Not the parties and benefits and pictures in the paper, but life at home, dinner, a child. She'd made it all clear to him without his even realizing it. He felt as if generations of experience were being brought to bear on him, a whole history of women skilled in gentle manipulation, all aimed at one end, all personified in Kate. He had no cause to complain, it was what he loved about her, what he'd loved from the first. She was the personification of her world, with a place in it as hard and unshakable as the jade she collected. But like jade, she was cloudy and impenetrable, the result of years of deposits in the riverbeds of their ancestry, most comfortable in a watery world where life achieved balance through obscurity.

He turned away from the window and noticed that light was showing under the door to the study. He knocked and went in.

Billy, wearing a torn pair of sweatpants and an old T-shirt, was sitting cross-legged on the pulled-out couch. He looked up innocently at Jack. "Oh. Hi."

Jack took a big swallow of his drink and tossed his head back. "Who do you think you're fooling?"

"Huh?"

"You weren't the least bit tired. Why'd you excuse yourself so early?" While he waited for an answer, he prodded a pile of dirty clothes with his bare foot. "Well?"

"You really want to know? Mom told me I should, you know, not be in your way. Leave you and Kate alone, since you hadn't, like, seen each other in a long time."

Jack relented. It wasn't Billy's fault. "Thanks. Kate's gone home. You want to go to sleep, really?"

"No."

He finished his bourbon. "We could play cribbage if you want."

"Sure."

Jack gestured toward the desk. "The board is in the second drawer. With the cards. I'm going to get another drink."

Billy frowned. "You want to change your clothes or something instead?"

"Oh. Yeah. I'll just be a minute." He could see the trace of concern in Billy's face, but he didn't want to respond to it. They sat on the floor, Billy's long legs stretched out, his smooth arms reaching to move a peg. Here I am, Jack thought, playing cards with a sixteen-year-old boy, pretending to a semblance of normal life, counting out fifteens and thirty-ones. He stopped, his hand in midair moving a peg, and stared out at the room, not seeing anything.

"Uncle John," Billy said.

"I was thinking — my father taught me how to play cribbage. He loved to teach me things. How to play cards, how to hit home runs." Billy stirred a little uneasily. Jack couldn't remember ever talking to him about his father before. "I hit a game-winner once, in Little League, when I was eleven." Random memories, he thought, shaking off the important ones. "Do you remember him at all?"

Billy nodded. "A little. Not much. There's pictures and all, sometimes I'm not sure what I really remember."

"I know what you mean."

"But one thing I do remember, I'm sure of it because there isn't any picture. I remember sitting in his lap under a tree in Connecticut — the big horse chestnut tree in the back? — and him reading to me. A book of poems. Sometimes when we have to read poetry in school, I think I hear his voice."

He looked at Jack, wanting approval, wanting the stamp of validation put on his memory. Jack said, "He loved to read, almost anything. History, novels, poetry. I remember him reading to you."

"You do?"

"Sure. I'll bet I know what book it was. A. A. Milne. *When We Were Very Young*."

"I don't remember," Billy said.

Jack stretched out on the floor, his head propped on his hand. Behind Billy, through the sliding door that led to the terrace, the lights burned in complicated patterns in buildings across the street. "He loved you so much. He was so proud of you. Hank, too, of course, but you were first. That's what I remember best about him, I think. How much he loved everyone — you, your mother, Mommy, even your father."

"And you," Billy very tentatively offered, unsure probably where the conversation was going or even where it had come from.

"Yes." He looked at Billy, seeing an adult for a moment. "Me most of all, I think. He loved so much."

Billy was very quiet. His face was puzzled, and he was obviously following all this closely, and trying to read between the lines. Wait ten years, Jack thought, then you'll be adept at reading between the lines; there won't be any lines, just what's between them.

Billy said, "Are you in love with Kate?"

Jack rolled onto his back and looked at the ceiling. "I'm engaged to her."

"Are you in love with Ellen?"

"Yes," he said, even more flatly.

"Poor Uncle John," he said, sounding very grown-up. "What are you going to do?"

"I don't know."

"Well," Billy said very definitely. "You should do what you want. Everybody's always telling you how to live your life, but it's not their life. You should do what you want."

Jack smiled. Fourteen years ago, half a life, his friend Dougie had said almost the same thing to him. Teenagers always had all the answers. "Listen, tiger, it's been a long day. I'm going to bed."

But he couldn't sleep, and after fifteen minutes he stopped trying. He went back into the living room and got out a glass to have some bourbon, then changed his mind. He sat down on the floor and played with the TV remote, but he didn't turn it on. In front of him, on the coffee table, the cribbage board was where they'd left it. His father had taught him to play cribbage, his father had taught him how to hit home runs, his father had taught him everything except how to be a man. That was for him to find out himself now. He had been pushed to the very edge of the hole in the center of his heart and was looking at last into that deep well.

XIV

HE SAID GOODBYE to Vinnie, the elevator man, and fished his key out of the pocket of his uniform. He opened the door and banged into the apartment, his baseball shoes clattering on the floor. He walked back toward the kitchen, tossing his mitt up in the air and catching it. The almost-best part of the day had been hitting a home run in the fifth (and last) inning of the game. But the really best part had been walking home from the park with Dougie and Ted and Skip, bumping shoulders with them, giving Dougie a shove and getting shoved back, making jokes and all. It had been his first home run of the season, and they'd all stepped back just a little bit to let him know they thought it was cool. He'd wanted Dougie to come home with him and talk about it, but Dougie had to go home and practice the piano. He stopped outside the library door, which was half shut. Through it he could see his father's briefcase, which wasn't exactly right because his father usually wasn't home that early. "Daddy?"

"Yes, Johnny. Hello."

He went in. His father was sitting at the desk, talking on the phone. He was holding one of those glasses with all the diamonds and points cut into it to sparkle the light, what he called an old-fashioned glass, and it was mostly full of scotch. He waved Johnny in and said into the phone, "So put a hundred-thousand-dollar penalty in. We're not going to kill the deal over a hundred thousand dollars."

Johnny sat down on a leather hassock and wondered why his father was home. It was happening more and more, that he'd come home after school and find his dad there. He frowned. It wasn't exactly in the order of things, and he wondered whether something was wrong. He tossed his glove into the air again, too high up and a little behind him. He missed, and it fell into the brass fireplace tools, one of which rattled to the floor. He laughed, but his father held up a hand for quiet. Johnny spread out on the hassock, lying on his back, and reached out over his head for the glove, stretching his arm pretty far. His shirt came out of his pants, and he felt the air brush his stomach. He retrieved the mitt and then, still upside down, tried to stand the poker back up where it belonged. He lost it at the last minute, with more loud noise. He didn't look at his father this time. He left the poker where it was and instead prodded one finger experimentally into his bellybutton. A little sand stuck to it, from a diving catch he'd made in the outfield. It had been a cool-looking dive, even though he'd dropped the ball. Dougie's mother had been there with a movie camera. Usually it was the dads who had the cameras, but Dougie's father had moved in with his new girlfriend, and now his mom came to the games. Johnny scratched himself under one arm. Dougie came over a lot now that the divorce was going on. He practically lived with them, sitting in Johnny's room and saying bad things about his father. It wouldn't ever happen to him, even if Dougie said it could happen to anyone. He would have to go over to Dougie's and watch the movie.

He got up off the hassock and went into the hall bathroom. It was a small room, and his mother and the new decorator had just finished redoing it all in mirrors — to make the room seem bigger, she said, which he thought was dumb, because it wasn't any bigger — and he wasn't used to watching himself. He unzipped his fly and took out his penis and then caught sight of himself in the mirror. He held his arms up to his shoulder, as if he were standing in the batter's box with two out in the bottom of the ninth at Yankee Stadium, a three-two pitch on the way, fifty thousand watching, and his dick hanging out. He and Dougie, on a mutual dare, had once walked around Central Park with their pants unzipped. It'd been a little weird. He peed, watching himself in the mirror, and not watching what he was doing so that he missed a little — well, more than a little. He thought about wiping it up but just put the seat down instead.

Back in the library, his father was off the phone and pouring himself another drink. "Daddy. Let me tell you this."

His father turned around, and his face looked a little funny, as if he were thinking about something else and wasn't quite sure who he was looking at. "What is it, Johnny?"

He faltered a little, as his father put another ice cube in the glass, then, remembering the hit, went on. "It was the bottom of the fifth. With one guy out and Teddy Hirsch on second base. We were losing by one run? So I —" Already, in his mind, the hit was taking on mythic proportions. Out on the mound, the pitcher had pulled off his cap — he had really short hair, which was usually dumb looking, but on the mound it made his head look sort of dangerous — and wiped his forehead with his arm before putting the cap back and pulling it down over his eyes. All during the game, a bank of clouds had been hovering beyond the buildings of Central Park West; now it had moved, gray and menacing, over the diamond. It made everything seem smaller to him, closer together. A gust of wind had lifted his shirt off his back. "— it was a new pitcher and he has this fancy wind-up, like he thinks he's Luis Tiant or something — so I took the first pitch. Like you told me to? To get used to him." His father nodded. "And then I whacked the second pitch to left center and got a homer out of it."

His father smiled. "That's great, Johnny. I'm really proud of you."

"Yeah, it was great."

At that, his father seemed to wake up or something, because he came over and put his arm around his shoulders and gave him a little hug. "A game-winner. I wish I'd seen it."

"Mom too," he said. "Where is she?"

"Out shopping. She should be home soon."

"Hey." He bounced away from his father and picked up his glove from the floor next to the hassock. "How come you're home so early?"

His father took another swallow of his drink, then put it down on the desk. Johnny thought that was strange, because his father always got mad when anyone didn't use a coaster. "I got tired of being at the office. Things there are — Don't you think you should change your clothes?"

"Yeah. Sure." He went into the bedroom and took off his uniform. He stood in the middle of the room in his underpants, a skinny, compact little kid, shivering in the air conditioning. He kept seeing the wet glass on the desk.

A little later, he heard voices in the library, his mother's voice. He could tell from the sound she wasn't happy. (A few months before, he'd awakened in the middle of the night to hear his parents arguing about something — he wasn't sure what it was, only that they were angry at each other. He'd wanted to get up and make them stop, he thought if they knew he was listening they would stop, but the only thing worse than hearing them would be for them to know he'd heard. He'd buried his head under the pillow, which only worked a little. This time wasn't like that, but he caught the note of irritation in his mother's voice, of resignation in his father's.) He stood a moment in the hallway, listening.

"A fine young man," his mother said. "Of course he's a fine young man. That's no help."

He couldn't hear his father's reply, only the clinking of an ice cube.

"She's twenty-one years old," his mother said. "She's still in college. Don't you think she's a little young to get married?"

"Darling." His father's voice sounded funny. "The invitations are printed. The engagement's been announced. The wedding is in seven weeks. What are we talking about?"

"You think it's too late, then. That's all you have to offer?"

"It's none of our business. She's old enough to make up her mind."

Johnny frowned. The conversation had been going on for five months. It had started one afternoon, in January, he thought. He'd come home from school with Dougie. It was sleeting outside, and they were cold and pretty wet, too, and they started for the kitchen. Elizabeth met them in the hallway.

"Hello, Johnny." She bent down to kiss his forehead.

He wriggled away. Elizabeth didn't usually kiss him. "What are you doing home?" he said without stopping. She wasn't supposed to be here.

She followed them into the kitchen. Dougie had that look — she's OK but when do we get rid of her — that they all adopted in the presence of family members. Johnny dipped his head apologetically and got the milk out of the refrigerator.

"Johnny," she said, leaning against one of the kitchen chairs, "I've got some good news."

"Yeah? Dougie, get the cookies, 'K?"

"David and I are going to get married."

"Congratulations. That's really good. When?" He poured the milk into a couple of glasses.

"Well, we haven't set a date yet."

"D'you tell mommy and daddy?"

She shook her head. "Not yet. You're the first. Keep it a secret until I tell them."

"Sure."

"Cool," Dougie said.

The conversation had started that night at dinner, and it had gone on, in different ways, ever since. It seemed like something was wrong with David, but Johnny couldn't figure out what. David and Elizabeth had taken him and Dougie to the circus that spring — that had been OK, except that David had seemed a little tight about it, like he didn't want to step in any elephant shit, Dougie had said, and Johnny had giggled. They said words like shit to each other. He didn't much care either way about David. Their friend Teddy's sister had gotten married to a guy they all liked, but he had played football in college and was pretty cool — unlike David. Johnny only half paid attention to the argument, Elizabeth on one side and their mother on the other. His father had sunk more and more into the background. "Thomas Welland trusts him," Elizabeth kept saying. "He just made David a vice president, that's why we decided to get married. And I love him."

The wedding was supposed to be the week before Johnny's eleventh birthday, and he had figured out already that he wasn't going to get much of a party this year. He went into the library. "Mommy. I hit a home run today."

At dinner, they took it up again, as if he weren't there. "Thomas Welland trusts him," his father said.

"As a vice president. Half the people in that bank are vice presidents." His mother served him some salad with two silver forks. He watched carefully to see how many cucumber slices he was getting; if it was only a couple, he could probably get away with hiding them under his knife and fork on the plate. "He may trust him with that much responsibility. But there's no future in that. He has no connections, no family, no friends — not in Thomas Welland's world."

"That world's disappearing." His father swirled the scotch around in his glass and put it down very precisely above the tip of his knife. "Or hadn't you noticed. Hippies, free love, coed dorms — five years ago they were great causes, controversial. Now they're taken for granted. They're even running their own candidate for president this year. Thomas Welland's world is going the way of the horse and buggy." He added, in a different voice, "So is mine."

Johnny decided he would have to eat one slice of cucumber. But his mother wasn't paying attention, so he got away with none.

"Yeah, well," Dougie said combatively, "would you go to the movies with Sarah Klein?"

"Sure. If she paid."

They were in the Museum of Natural History, looking at bones. Or supposedly looking at bones. They had sneaked away from the rest of the class and were sitting on the floor, their backs to a grizzly bear, making paper airplanes from pages torn from his spiral notebook. They were daring each other to go out with the ugliest girls they knew. They were twelve years old and had recently discovered sex.

"Well, would you, like, make love with her?"

Johnny shook his head. "No. Too gross. I heard she got her period in the middle of gym class one day." He wasn't exactly sure what was involved in getting a period — whether it was the kind of thing that could happen all at once in the middle of a gym class — and he looked out of the corner of his eye for a reaction, ready to take it back if it wasn't right. But Dougie was bent over a new airplane, folding it carefully, the tip of his tongue showing in concentration. Johnny realized they were sitting so close together that their shoulders were touching. He didn't move.

Dougie finished the plane and held it up for inspection before tossing it toward a family of caribou that was grazing across the way. The plane nose-dived halfway across and slid noisily along the hard floor. He said, "Do you think girls really, you know, put their mouths on your dick?"

Johnny pursed his lips, imagining this. "Is that what it says in the book?"

"Yeah. But —"

They were silent a minute. "Some girls, maybe," Dougie finally said.

There was another pause. Then Johnny said, "You don't, like, have to do it to them, do you?"

Dougie shook his head. "No way. What about Jan Richards? Would you go out with Jan Richards?"

Jan Richards was, in Johnny's opinion, the ugliest girl he knew. He made a gagging sound, and Dougie sniggered. Johnny looked across at the caribou. The male was standing on top of a rock, looking out at the fields and mountains painted on the back wall of the diorama. The wall was curved, and it made him a little nauseous to look at it too long. The male standing guard over the female and the two babies. They came here every year from school, and one year Mr. Fischman, who everyone thought was a fag, told them that sexual stereotypes were invalid, which made them all giggle and stare at the big balls hanging down beneath the male's belly. They all knew better, whatever Fischman said — that men were supposed to look out for the family, be in charge, teach the babies how to hunt and find food and fight. All the females did was have more babies. He pushed his shoulder a fraction of an inch closer to Dougie. The silence was starting to seem a little scary, and he had a question he'd been avoiding asking all day. "You going to California? Or not?"

"Not," Dougie said flatly.

"Yeah? What did your dad say?"

"Fuck him."

Dougie was supposed to spend Christmas vacation with his father and his father's new wife, and his father's new son. He didn't want to go and had been fighting with his mother about it for weeks. His mother had done the unforgivable, had appealed to Johnny. "You tell him, Johnny. He has to go." He had been totally embarrassed, not wanting to get into a big argument with an adult (who was buying him dinner at the time) but not wanting to betray Dougie. He had squirmed down in his chair, hoping she wouldn't notice him again. Yesterday had been the last day for Dougie to decide. "Did you tell your dad?"

"Yeah. He said I should come see my new brother. I told him I already had a brother, I didn't need another one. I told him I wasn't coming."

"So what did he say?"

Dougie slumped his shoulders. "He didn't even try to make me. He just said OK and hung up. I mean, I wouldn't have gone, no way, but I thought he'd try to make me."

Parents were supposed to make you do things even if they were dumb things. The young caribou probably thought it was dumb to have to stand on a rock all day. Dougie's father didn't care.

His own father cared a lot, he thought. He was always teaching him things. Like how to play cribbage, which they'd been doing the last few weeks. It was a grown-up game, you had to pay attention to a lot of different things, counting the cards, figuring different ways they added up to fifteen. When his father taught him how to play, it was like being let into a world only men inhabited (he didn't know any girls who played cribbage). Most kids he knew, their fathers would come home and at most maybe sit in front of the TV with them. But his father talked to him, played games with him, once he brought home an abacus for him. It was black with brown counters, squashed beads with a ridge around their middles. The instructions were in Chinese, with an English translation that sounded weird, and they spent a whole week, every evening, doing the problems in the little book. There was something very satisfying in the way the abacus worked, a finite machine with infinite capabilities, his father said. Johnny liked the way it let you see the computations, not like a calculator where you just pressed buttons and an answer came out. At first he didn't like it, it seemed threatening because it had to do with math, and he didn't do too well at math. He felt stupid a lot of the time in class, especially because he was so good at all the other subjects. (Dougie, on the other hand, was a whiz at math; when Johnny showed him the abacus, he took about ten minutes to figure the whole thing out.) His father showed him things about math, like how to do complicated fractions or shortcuts for long division. And he never got too mad, even when it took him a long time to figure something out.

He sneaked a look at Dougie, who was still angry about California, about his father. Johnny had been at their house once when Dougie's father had hit him, not really hard, but enough. Dougie had gotten some money for his birthday, which he was supposed to put in the bank. They bought some junk with it instead. When Dougie's father found out, he hit him for lying. Dougie ran away, to Johnny's bedroom, for a whole night until they were found out. When his parents came to get him, he could see the look on Dougie's face, wondering if he was going to get smacked again. It was one of the things Dougie talked about, all that time when his parents were splitting up, how he wanted to hit his father back.

His own father lectured him instead of hitting him the one big time he lied, which was almost worse. "We're responsible for what we do," he said, sitting next to Johnny on the swing set that was slowly rusting away behind the house in Connecticut. It was after dinner, the sun was behind them, and long summer shadows stretched out across the lawn in front of them. He watched his shadow slowly swinging back and forth while he tried not to cry. "If you do something wrong, own up to it, and usually it can be fixed. But if you lie about it, no one can fix it, and you're just cheating yourself in the end. Always be honest." He didn't hit Johnny either, when he ran away one day when he was seven. His mother had made him wear a stupid pair of pants she'd bought at Saks that he wouldn't have been caught dead in. He ran away on his bike as far as Bailey's, the general store on Main Street in Westfield, and then he called home. His father came to get him, bought him an ice cream soda, and asked why he'd done it. Then, his father bought him a kite, an elaborate box kite, which they put together with airplane glue and balsa struts and tissue paper, and they went down to a field below the house and flew it, all the way to the end of the string, Johnny holding tightly to the wooden spool, his father's hand resting on his shoulder.

He didn't know why he was thinking about all those things. Just that his father was different from Dougie's. He said, "You want to be with us at Christmas? Up in Connecticut?"

Dougie sniffled, wiping the back of his hand across his nose, and nodded.

Later that winter, he was sitting in the living room of Dougie's house. He had his feet up on the couch, and a history textbook balanced on his knees. A bag of cookies and a can of Coke were in easy reach. He was reading inattentively: "Cornwallis surrendered on October 19, 1781. As General Washington accepted the surrender, a military band played the song 'The World Turned Upside Down.' " Behind him Dougie was practicing the piano for a recital at his music school. He was playing a Haydn sonata, and he kept getting stuck over one measure. Finally he stopped, muttered something to himself about being a dickface, and played the few problem notes over and over, first very slowly and then gradually up to tempo. Johnny looked back at his book. Something about the sentence he'd just read bothered him. Whose military band? The British wouldn't have played that unless they had a pretty weird sense of humor. And a military band didn't exactly fit his picture of Washington's ragtag and bobtail army. He frowned at the picture, on the opposite page, of "The Spirit of '76": a recently beaned fife player and a couple of drummers, one of whom looked as if he'd had all his teeth kicked out, didn't constitute a military band. He closed the book and dropped it on the floor next to the cookies. He listened to Dougie, who'd gone back to the beginning and was now sailing easily through the difficult part. Johnny nodded to himself. Dougie was getting really good.

"The World Turned Upside Down," he thought. Not a bad name for a song, the way things were going. First Elizabeth getting married, and now having a kid — Billy was almost ten months old, and Johnny counted on his fingers the nine months back from that. They hadn't wasted any time. Supposedly you couldn't get pregnant unless you wanted to, if you used rubbers and all that. Dougie said that sometimes it still happened by accident anyway, but Johnny didn't think David did anything by accident. The baby was making his mother more happy about the whole thing — talk about the world turning upside down. Then there was the way his father had been acting lately.

Dougie was playing the third movement now, and Johnny counted the variations to himself — he'd heard it so many times that he practically knew it by heart himself. He concentrated on the music instead of thinking about his father. The way he'd started coming home early from the office again, but almost every day now. He dragged his mind back to Haydn and kept it there until Dougie finished. Johnny said, "That was great. You're really getting it."

"Thanks. If I don't forget it all by tomorrow."

"Get outta here. You're on a roll." The recital was in two weeks. He and his parents were going.

Dougie walked over and bent down to get a cookie. He looked through his legs at Johnny, who said, "The World Turned Upside Down."

Dougie stood up. "What?"

He explained. "Think how old Cornwallis must've felt."

Dougie nodded and munched his cookie. He said, "You going to the dance Friday night?"

Johnny shrugged. "I don't know."

"You taking Blair?"

"I don't know." He sat up straight on the couch. "Jesus Christ."

Dougie looked down at him. In the last few months Dougie had grown a couple of inches, and now, in the afternoon sun coming in through the tall windows that looked down onto Seventy-fourth Street, he seemed out of proportion, elongated and enormous. Dougie shrugged and sat down in an armchair, putting his feet, big in white sweat socks, on the coffee table. The room, already full of light, became full of silence. Johnny finally said, "It's my father. He's been acting — kinda strange."

"Yeah? How?"

He hadn't thought it would be so easy to tell Dougie, but when it came to it, they were best friends and all. They had talked about Dougie's father, and the rest of their families — Dougie's brother, Elizabeth — this was just part of being best friends. "I don't know. He comes home from the office early. He just sits in the library and makes phone calls. I mean, business calls. But still."

"Maybe he got fired," Dougie said practically.

"Mm-nn. I was there a couple of weeks ago. At his office. I mean, his name's still on the door and everything. Wouldn't he tell me if he got fired?" He said this hopefully, wanting to believe it.

Dougie thought a minute. "They don't always tell you things." He reached for another cookie. "What else?"

"Sometimes he forgets things. Just dumb things. He promised to get a book for me, and he went to the bookstore, but he didn't get it. He said he forgot. Things like that."

"You think he's sick or something?"

"You mean like a tumor?" The father of one of the kids in school had had a brain tumor. He'd died.

Dougie shook his head. "No, 'course not. If he had a tumor, he'd be in the hospital and getting chemotherapy. His hair would come out. Just sick."

"I don't think so." Johnny looked down at his feet, which he tapped together a couple of times. He could see Dougie out of the corner of his eye, sitting in the chair. He seemed really calm and safe — Johnny thought how great it was to have a friend you could tell anything to, even the worst thing. "I was in my room yesterday afternoon, doing some homework. And I heard this crash in the library. So I go to look? My father was standing there — he dropped a glass and there was this puddle on the floor, and his suit pants were all splashed, and there were a million pieces of glass — I mean everywhere. He didn't see me, I think." His father had been standing very still, not moving at all, just looking down at the floor. It had been scary as hell. "I didn't know what to do."

"So," Dougie said after a minute, "what did you do?"

"I went back to my room." He frowned. "What was I supposed to do?"

"Yeah. Right. That's probably what I would have done." He stood up and walked over and picked up his can of Coke from the piano where he'd left it. Then he sat down on the couch next to Johnny. "At least he's there."

"Yeah," Johnny said dubiously.

"Sometimes they just do strange things. My dad once broke all the coffee cups, the china ones she uses for dinner parties."

Johnny remembered that. Dougie's father had sat in the pantry and broken off the little curved handles from all of them, one by one. Dougie said, "I heard my mom talking about male menopause."

"What?" Johnny didn't like that, it sounded wrong to him.

"You know, like when women get old they can't have their period anymore and it makes them nuts."

"Yeah, I know. What does that have to do with guys?" He tried to figure it out. Men got old and they couldn't — what? Do it? Not have wet dreams? He was still waiting for his first one, and now Dougie was telling him he would run out at some point?

"Not literally," Dougie explained. "Just that middle-aged men sometimes get wacky too. They do crazy things. Like run away from their families and move to California, or drop cocktails on the floor."

Johnny leaned his head back on the couch pillow and looked at Dougie's profile. "So you think this is just, like, normal."

"I guess." He looked up at the ceiling. "My father is nuts. Your father just seems as crazy as everybody else."

Johnny sighed a little, relieved. He'd told Dougie the worst thing, and it was going to be OK.

At the end of that summer, after he came back from camp and before school started, he spent a weekend alone with his father. The rest of the family was in Westfield — his mother, Elizabeth, David, and Billy. His father said, "Let's spend some time together, just the two of us, whatever you want to do." On Saturday afternoon they went to a Yankees game. The Stadium was crowded, but his father got them great seats behind the Yankee dugout by tipping the guy in the ticket booth (he winked at Johnny when he did it, and Johnny winked back), and then he tipped the beer guy to keep coming by and bringing him more cold beers. Johnny ate a bunch of hot dogs and the Yanks won. Then they went back to the apartment for a couple of hours before dinner. They played cribbage, the sweet smell of his father's scotch hovering over the board, and at one point Johnny had a hand he couldn't believe, especially when he cut a five out of the deck. His father said, "A perfect hand, Johnny," and ruffled his hair, and he thought, a perfect hand on a perfect day. Then they went to a restaurant on Third Avenue for dinner, a place with a long wooden bar and shelves with tons of bottles on them, and a fancy mirror on the wall behind them. The bartender said, "Good evening, Mr. Newland. The usual?" and poured a glassful of scotch. His father said, "This is my spot. I never brought your mother here, or your sister. Just you and me, son." He put his hands on Johnny's shoulders. "This is my boy," he said to the bartender.

After dinner, they started walking toward the movie theater on Sixty-eighth Street. It was a late summer night, warm and blue, with an occasional puff of breeze from the tops of the buildings, and a sickle moon hanging over the avenue. Johnny was talking about the baseball game, thinking what a great day it had been. Lately, going anywhere with his family had become a drag — he always felt as if everybody thought he was just a kid. It had gotten worse after Billy was born, traipsing around with a baby carriage and diapers and all, everybody always watching him just when the baby threw up or farted or something. But going out alone with his father was totally different. It was man to man. His father had even given him the money to buy the movie tickets. They stopped at a corner, waiting for the light to change, and when it did, he started to cross the street. Then he looked back.

His father was half lying, half sitting in the gutter, holding up one hand and looking at it. He ran back. "Daddy. What happened? What's the matter?"

"I don't know. I must have tripped." There was blood on his wrist from a deep cut on the edge of his hand beneath the little finger. "I must have cut myself on something when I fell."

A small crowd had gathered, and someone offered to call an ambulance.

"No." His father took out a handkerchief and held it over the cut, wincing. "We'll get a cab. Help me up, John."

They hailed a cab and went to the hospital. A nurse looked at the cut and then took them through some swinging doors to a big room divided into cubicles by hanging curtains on curved rods. "Wait right here," she said and gave Johnny a clipboard with a form on it. An old pen dented with toothmarks hung from it on a dirty string. His father was lying down on a bed that had a thin mattress and big wheels. His face was very white and the hand-kerchief very red. Johnny was scared. He said, trying to sound normal, "What's your social security number?"

"I'm going to be fine, son. Don't worry."

A doctor came in, a tall, heavy black man with a stethoscope draped around his neck. He asked some questions, looked at the "wound" (it's not a wound, Johnny thought protestingly, it's just a cut). Then he said, "We're going to stitch this up, but first I'm going to examine it, have some X-rays taken. Just to make sure there was no bone damage when you fell." He looked at Johnny. "Maybe you'd like to wait outside."

He pushed his way out through the curtains and found a place to sit down — a group of three molded plastic chairs bolted to an iron brace. Two of the chairs were orange and one was beige. One had a chunk missing, as if someone had taken a baseball bat to it. He sat in the beige one.

He sat still, hoping no one would notice him, watching the activity around him. Two nurses were sitting behind a curved counter drinking coffee. A doctor came along, dressed in a green scrub suit with the sleeves rolled up. He reached up with his arm and leaned against the wall, bending over the nurses. Johnny could see a tuft of curly black hair on his chest. The nurses laughed. A policeman came in, his light blue shirt looking bright, his gun big on his hip. He had a mustache and soft brown eyes that stared at Johnny before looking away. Two orderlies wheeled a bed by; the man lying on it had a bandage around his head, and a nurse walked next to him holding up a plastic bag full of clear liquid, which ran into the man's wrist through a tube. A woman was walking behind, sobbing loudly. I hate this, Johnny thought, frozen in his seat. For the first time in his life he thought that nothing bad would happen to him if he pretended he wasn't there. He concentrated hard on not being there at all, on not existing, and, after a while, it worked.

The curtains in his father's cubicle were pushed aside, and his father came out in a wheelchair pushed by a skinny young guy in a blue uniform, much duller than the cop's. His father smiled and said, "We're going to X-ray."

"Might be a while," the orderly said. "You could come with us."

So Johnny tagged along through a maze of corridors that zig-zagged strangely, and they crossed a bridge over the street into a different building and then went down in an oversized elevator to the basement. The orderly nodded him toward a waiting room, and his father disappeared through more swinging doors.

The waiting room was labeled Lounge, but no one did. He thought that was funny as soon as he thought of it, because the people in it were all sitting stiffly and silently, waiting — for bad news, which is what everyone expected in a hospital, it was what he was expecting. The room was full of cigarette smoke from a middle-aged man who sat in one corner, looking at a copy of *Time* with a torn cover. A young couple sat opposite Johnny, and an older lady sat next to him. He coughed — cigarette smoke made him feel sick to his stomach.

The only person in the room who seemed at all relaxed was an old man in a wheelchair. He had a blanket over his legs, and nothing showed under it — maybe he didn't even have any legs. He was tapping his fingers, but not impatiently, waiting.

Johnny sat very still again and practiced not being there.

After a while, the smoke started making him feel really sick, so he got up and left the room. A long wide corridor stretched in either direction, with rooms opening off it. As he watched, a man in a bed was wheeled into one of the rooms on the right. He turned to his left and walked along the hall.

In the first room he came to, a man lay flat on a bed with a bandage around the top of his head. White stubble was scattered thinly over his cheeks and chin, and his lips were drawn into his mouth a little, as if he didn't have all his teeth. His hands lay outside the covers, thin and tendony and spotted with age but even more with the grime that had gotten under the skin and now would never come out. Johnny wondered if the man even remembered what it was like to lie in a bed, with white sheets and a pillow, instead of on a steam grate with a hard building at his back and the feet of strangers all around. The man turned his head and looked at Johnny, and his mouth worked as if he were trying to talk, but no sound came out.

In the next room, a fat woman in pink polyester pants stretched tightly over her ass was standing in the doorway talking to a man whose clothes were too big for him. Jack Sprat and his wife, he thought. The woman said, in a Brooklyn accent, "An X-ray machine." Behind them, on the bed, a young woman was lying, facing straight up at the ceiling, her arms crossed over her stomach, her eyes shut so tightly he could see the squint lines. Then she relaxed and opened her eyes, listening to her mother. "They're bringing in an X-ray machine to find out why she's in distress. I'll tell you why she's in distress." She looked at Johnny rudely, and shut the door.

A nurse was walking down the hall toward him. "Can I help you?" she said, in a friendly kind of voice.

No one can help me, he thought, surprising himself. He said, "My dad's in X-ray. I'm waiting for him."

"OK." She smiled. "You have beautiful green eyes. Did anyone ever tell you that?"

He blinked, but she was already down the hall.

The next room was very dark, and he couldn't tell what he was looking at, all he could hear was a strange, obstructed breathing noise. He'd read in some book that you could tell when someone was going to die because of the death rattle of their breathing — death rattle, he'd remembered the words. He wondered if he was going to see someone die, wondered if he should call a nurse about whatever was happening indistinctly in the room, but then he remembered that he wasn't there. He'd thought it would be cool to see someone die, now he only wished it would never happen. There was an especially difficult gasp, and the form on the bed moved, and he realized what he was looking at. A man lay on his back, dressed in one of those flimsy hospital gowns. He had lifted his knees up, evidently to help him breathe, and the gown had opened a little. Johnny could see, up between his raised knees and his thighs, his naked crotch, dark and strange-looking, bearing no resemblance to the bodies he knew, his own, the other boys in the shower room. The man's penis was shrunken and discolored, his anus dark and dirty, his scrotum old and withered and dying. Johnny looked away quickly, it was indecent and degrading to leave people alone like that where anyone could see them, it made them less than human.

The next room was the strangest of all, and later he wasn't always sure that he hadn't just imagined it. All the lights were on, and he could see a boy lying in the bed. The boy had very white skin, very clear and translucent. His face (Johnny could see his profile as he stared up to the ceiling) looked familiar. He wondered why a kid his age would be in the hospital all alone, and he took a step nearer the door. Then, for a long time, neither of them moved. Why are you here, Johnny thought, concentrating as if the question were visible in the air between them. The boy turned his head and looked at him. His hair was brown and red and gold like Johnny's. And he had bright green eyes.

They looked at each other, and then Johnny shook his head, feeling panicky. He turned away and walked quickly back toward the lounge, almost running. This is Hell, he thought. A huge building with demented, twisting corridors that led nowhere, but where you weren't allowed to stop walking. Where people lay sick in bed while loudmouthed mothers hectored them. Where men exposed their genitals to the world and the world watched, and no one had any shame. Where your father disappeared into a lab and left you all alone to wander the endless halls. Where you could look through a door and see yourself lying, sick and alone, in an empty room; where you could lie, sick and alone, in an empty room and see yourself standing in the corridor outside.

He leaned against the wall next to the lounge, breathing hard. He put his hands up to his face and grabbed the front of his hair, covering his eyes with his wrists. This is stupid, he thought. A hospital was a hospital, Hell was Hell. He'd never thought that way before, the world as it was had always been enough for him. Now the world had turned upside down, it was no longer right in itself, and for the first time he hid the world behind an image of the world. I'm not really here, he thought again. I'm not really here.

"Hey, bright eyes," someone said. "Everything all right?"

He blinked twice and took his hands down. It was the nurse he'd met in the hall. He managed a fake smile. "Yeah. Not too bad."

"Would you like a cup of coffee?"

He shook his head. He didn't drink coffee.

"How about a soda?"

"Yeah. Thanks."

She led him down the hall the other way to a nurse's station, where another woman sat in a battered swivel chair at a low desk. "Look what I found," his nurse said. "What's your name, bright eyes?"

"John Newland," he said.

"His father's the one with the hand injury." He thought he saw some kind of look pass between the two nurses, but he wasn't sure. "He sure is cute, don't you think?"

"A real heartbreaker," the other said, smiling a nursely smile. They gave him some Coke.

A long time later, the big doctor who had examined his father came into the room. "Are you John Newland?" he asked in a tired voice.

"Yes."

"I'm Dr. Baker." He put out his hand and captured Johnny's in a dry handshake.

"Is my dad OK?"

"His hand'll be fine. Five stitches. No broken bones." The nurses had both disappeared, and the doctor sat down next to him. "How old are you, John?"

"Thirteen."

"Thirteen." Dr. Baker sighed. "What we need to know is why your father fell."

That was an unnecessary question. "He tripped."

"Well, he says he thinks he tripped. He can't remember exactly." Dr. Baker reached out a long arm and poured some coffee into a Styrofoam cup. "Can you help us out?"

"No." The doctor didn't say anything, so Johnny elaborated. "I just looked back and he was on the ground."

Dr. Baker nodded. "You had come from a restaurant, I believe. What else did your father do today?"

"We went to a ball game. The Yanks won." Johnny yawned. " 'scuse me."

"Did your father seem dizzy at all today?"

"Nope."

"The thing is, John" — he poured some Sweet'n'Low into his coffee and stirred it with a brown wooden stirrer — "when people fall down for no reason we like to know why."

"I'd like to know why, too."

Dr. Baker smiled and sipped at his coffee. "Has he fallen before?"

"No. Did you ask him?" Johnny began to wonder where all this was leading.

"Yes." There was another pause, but this time Johnny decided not to fill it. There was something not right about all this. He felt as if he were in a very small room in a very small house in the middle of the night in the middle of the wilderness, and outside some huge shadowy monster with a bloody mouth was lurking, prowling. He would be all right as long as he didn't open the door and let it in. Then he thought again, That's stupid. I'm in an office in a hospital, not a — a whatever.

"Do you mind if I ask you some routine questions?"

Johnny pushed his back against the chair a little. "If it'll help my dad."

"Good boy." Dr. Baker drank some more coffee and made a face. "Do you know if your father has been seeing a doctor?"

"No. I mean, I know he hasn't. Just checkups."

"Good. Do you know if he's taking any medication?"

Johnny shook his head. "No. I mean, aspirin and stuff sometimes."

"Has he ever passed out before?"

"No." It wasn't a brain tumor, he kept thinking. He was sure it wasn't.

Dr. Baker went on, starting to seem a little scary now. "Has he been treated at a hospital in the last two years?"

"No — I mean, sort of. We were skiing last winter and he twisted his ankle. We went to the emergency room, is all."

"He's never been treated for cancer."

"No way," he said quickly.

"Has he ever been treated for a drinking disorder?"

He felt an instinctive flinching from this, as if he were part of a tribe of nomads gathered round a campfire and a stranger had come accusing. Loyalty to the tribe was more important than any truth — and for the third time he told himself not to be silly, not to pretend the world was something else. But he couldn't help it, not really, because even as Dr. Baker finished asking the question, Johnny knew what the truth was, that his father didn't have a tumor, that the doctor was right. Johnny had had the whole picture in front of him all along, but he hadn't had a name for it until the doctor gave him one. Now he knew: My dad's an alcoholic. He said, "What do you mean by that?"

"We're trying to help your father, John."

He shook his head rapidly twice, like a little kid, feeling scared again the way he had in the corridor. Was this guy used to seeing thirteen-year-olds come in with their fathers and be in charge, kids who looked after their parents instead of the other way around? Maybe that's who Baker thought he was. His father's doctor would never have asked him all these questions, they weren't things he was supposed to know about. I'm only a kid, he thought, leave me alone. "Ask my dad."

In the cab, Johnny sat in the corner pressed against the door, not laughing at his father's jokes, pretending to be sleepy. He didn't even want to look at this man riding next to him. His father had become alien, not so much from Johnny as from himself, and Johnny was afraid that if he looked too closely he would see that it wasn't really his father at all but someone different. Maybe, he thought exhaustedly, everyone is different. Maybe that had been him lying in that bed in the brightly lit room, maybe that had been his father lying in the gutter.

He woke up early, having spent a lot of the night looking at the ceiling and thinking. He put on his shirt and his underpants and then sat on the bed, still feeling tired. He imagined what his father would do if Johnny were sick instead of the other way round. Make breakfast. He wanted to call his mother, but he couldn't because he would have to lie to her. Make breakfast. He finished dressing and padded into the kitchen. He'd never made breakfast before, just cereal or toast. His father liked scrambled eggs, it was something special he would appreciate, it would make him feel better. He looked under the counter and picked out a cast iron skillet, put it on the range, and turned the gas on. Then he got some eggs out of the refrigerator and put them down on the counter. One rolled into the sink and broke. Shit, he thought.

His mother always used a knife to crack eggs. He tapped experimentally, and nothing happened. He hit it harder, and the shell dissolved in his hand. But most of the egg went into the bowl and only a little shell went with it. He tried to get the pieces out with his finger, but they were stuck in the gluey mess of the white. He cracked another egg, then beat them together with a fork. By the time he finished, the skillet was smoking, even though he hadn't put anything in it. He dumped in the eggs.

There was a loud hissing noise and a big cloud of steam that turned to smoke, and a minute later the kitchen filled with a terrible smell. He poked at the eggs with a spatula, confirming that they were burned. He angrily picked up the skillet before he realized how hot it was. He dropped it noisily into the sink and said, "Ow. Shit." His hand was burned, and he shook it hard in the air. "Fuck. Shit." He started to cry, partly from pain, partly from frustration. He put his hands over his eyes, leaning on the counter thinking, God, what am I going to do?

He had repaired most of the damage by the time his father came into the kitchen. He'd washed the burned eggs down the sink and started a new batch over a lower heat. And the big fan had sucked out most of the evil smell. "Good morning," his father said.

"G' morning." He picked the skillet up, using a mitt this time, and slid the eggs onto a plate. "I made you some breakfast."

"Thanks. You didn't have to do that."

"Yeah." He put the plate on the table with more of a clatter than he intended. "If I were sick, you'd do it for me."

"I'm not sick," his father said, holding up his bandaged, damaged hand. "Just a cut."

"Yeah, sure." He poured a glass of orange juice and put it on the table. "Is that what Dr. Baker said?"

"Dr. Baker? Oh, you mean the doctor at the hospital." His father paused in the middle of salting the eggs. "Why? Did he say anything to you?"

"Just some questions," Johnny said. Like whether you're a drunk. Then he added, guiltily, "Like whether you'd been to an emergency room before. I told him about when you hurt your ankle skiing. Just stuff."

"These eggs are good. What did you have for breakfast?"

"Nothing. I'm not hungry."

His father looked up. "Here, have half of these."

"I said I'm not hungry." He leaned against the counter, his hands in his pants pockets. He felt like a kid in a TV movie, one of those kids who has to support a family, who wins a scholarship to college and reunites his parents and beats the drug pushers or whatever, one of those kids Dr. Baker had thought he was — he felt like anyone but himself.

His father was still looking at him, smiling. "Sounds like you got up on the wrong side of the bed."

Johnny turned his head away. "I hate it when you say that."

"Are you bothered by what happened last night? It really was nothing —"

"Nothing," Johnny interrupted. "Oh, sure. Nothing. Except we go to the emergency room, you get a bunch of stitches, I have to walk around with people who are sick and — and sick and disgusting, and hear horrible — and all because —" Because you had too much to drink, because you drink too much and it's catching up with you. But he didn't say it. He thought if he once said that, he and his father would forever be separated by the deepest imaginable chasm, that however much they loved each other, once said, the words would always lie between them, unrecallable.

"Because what, Johnny." His father's voice was threatening, or warning.

"What's wrong with you, Daddy?" he burst out. "Why are you coming home early from the office so much? Why did you forget to buy that book for me? Why did you drop a glass on the floor? Why did you fall down in the fucking street —" It was the first time he'd used a word like that in front of his father, and it stopped him. Tell me the truth, he thought, say it and then we'll deal with it. I'll be the kid in the movie, the hero of the family, but you have to tell me.

"Is that what's bothering you?" His father smiled. "Come here." He held out his arm, wanting Johnny to come and be held. But

Johnny stayed where he was. His father waited a moment, then went on. "Did you think I was sick or something? It's not that at all. It's just coincidence." He looked levelly at Johnny. "I've been leaving work early because, frankly, there's some tension in the office over business matters and I'm happier working at home. I just happened to drop a glass — I've done it before, so have you. I tripped in the street last night. That's all."

You're lying, Johnny thought, staring at the yellow eggs spread on the white plate.

"I appreciate your concern, son, I really do." His father kept talking, although it seemed mostly irrelevant now. "I'm glad you're old enough to think about looking after other people, and I'm very, very proud of you. But I don't need it. Not yet. Wait a few years, till I'm old and gray."

Johnny looked away from him, down at the floor. He didn't want to be patronized on top of being lied to. He said, "I told Dougie I'd meet him. I'll be back later." One liar to another, he thought.

Outside in the street he took a deep breath. His only thought had been to get away, and the idea of meeting Dougie had seemed a convenient excuse. But now that he thought of it, there really wasn't anywhere else to go. He went off down the block, keeping his head down, feeling it bob strangely on his neck.

Dougie's mother answered the door. "Hello, Johnny, you're up bright and early."

"Hi. Is Dougie home?"

"He's still asleep. You can go up and wake him if you want."

"Thanks." He went upstairs.

There was enough light in the room for him to be able to see the familiar posters on the wall, one of Jagger on a stage, backlit and bare-chested, one of a skier leaning into a turn, advertising Kneissl White Stars, and one for a Rudolf Serkin concert at Carnegie Hall, with a lowering Beethoven in the background; the schoolbooks piled neatly on the desk in order of size, like a pyramid; the TV in the corner, seeming luminous even when turned off; the stack of stereo equipment next to it. One of the advantages of the divorce, Dougie had found, was that everyone involved, from his parents to his grandparents to his older brother, kept giving him stuff to make him feel wanted. The television was the latest acquisition.

Dougie had kicked the covers off, which he always did in his sleep, even in the winter, and he was lying on his side with his hair tumbled all over his forehead. Under his thin pajamas, Johnny could see that he had a hardon. He grinned. "Hey, Dougie. Wake up."

Dougie rolled over on his stomach.

"Wake up," Johnny said more loudly. "Hey. It's me." He heard a noise from the kitchen, a pan rattling.

"Whuzzuh?" Dougie said.

Johnny shook him by the shoulder. "Wake up."

Dougie woke up. He twisted his neck and looked at Johnny. "Oh wow. What's going on?"

"Nothing. I just dropped by."

"Great." He pressed his body into the bed and stretched. "Oh wow, I was having the weirdest dream."

Johnny grinned again. "Yeah. About Debbie Allen, right? I saw the evidence."

"No. I just have to take a leak is all." He got up and went into the bathroom, leaving the door open. "What's going on?" he called back while he peed.

"You won't believe what happened," Johnny said.

Dougie flushed the toilet and ran water in the sink. "What?"

He hesitated, wondering how to tell it. "Well. It's about my father."

Dougie came to the door, a toothbrush in his mouth and foam on his lips. "Mmm?"

"We went out to dinner last night, at this cool place on Third Avenue. Then we started walking to the movies. And my dad —"

Dougie waited, then turned to the sink and spit. He came back into the room. "He what?"

"He sort of fell down. In the street. He cut himself."

Dougie pulled his pajama top over his head. He had a tuft of pale hair under his arm. "He fell down? What do you mean?"

Johnny shrugged. "He just fell down. We went to the emergency room. It was gross."

Dougie put on a shirt, then took off his pajama bottoms. He

picked some underpants up off the floor, looked to see if they were dirty, and put them on. "Like sick people and all."

Johnny nodded. "Old guys and even kids like us. One guy came in with a cop, I think he had a bullet wound."

"That sounds cool."

"It wasn't." His eyes went blank as he remembered. "His wife was there."

"Bummer."

Johnny sat on the floor, his back against the desk. It was where he usually sat in Dougie's room. He said, "Remember when your dad told you about getting a divorce, and Carolyn and all."

"Yeah, sure." Dougie sat down on the bed and pulled on his socks. Dougie's father had taken him to Tavern on the Green for lunch one Sunday. He listened to everything his father said and then went into the men's room to throw up. He wasn't mad at his father, that came later. The more he thought about it, the more he talked to Johnny about it, the angrier he got. He sometimes said that the worst part of it had been blowing a good lunch, but he only said that when he wanted to act tough.

"Did you, like, have any idea, before then, what he was going to say?"

Dougie sat thinking a moment. Johnny leaned his head against the desk, wondering how he was going to tell. Dougie said, "I knew that things were weird. I mean, I knew he wasn't coming home some nights and they were having fights. I guess I sort of knew. How come?"

"Did you ever talk to him about it? Before, I mean."

"No way." Dougie shook his head. "I guess I thought if I didn't say anything about it, it would go away. Besides, I was only ten. It's not the kind of thing you can really talk about. I just pretended it wasn't happening. But it did. Anyway."

Like in the hospital, Johnny thought. "Like nothing bad would happen if you pretended you weren't there." When Dougie looked puzzled, he said, "I kept thinking that in the hospital last night."

"Sounds deranged to me." He yawned. "What's with your dad?"

He was drunk, Johnny wanted to say. He's an alcoholic and

that's why he acts so strange. But even as he opened his mouth, he knew he couldn't say it. He hadn't been able to say it to Dr. Baker, and now he couldn't say it, not even to his best friend. He watched as Dougie lay on his back on the bed, kicking his legs up and into his pants, and thought: they'd shared everything together, even the worst details of the divorce, but divorce was different, divorce was normal, lots of kids had parents who were divorced, but no one had a father who was a drunk. It was a secret only he and his father could share, Dougie could never know. He felt alone — not the loneliness of being homesick at camp, but a real aloneness here with his best friend. He felt his face go all funny, but Dougie was bending over to tie his sneakers and didn't notice.

"So how is your dad?" Dougie asked again.

"Oh. He's OK. He had some stitches and all that. No broken bones. He just tripped," he lied. His father had lied and now he was lying. He said suddenly, "I'm sorry, Dougie."

"What for?"

"I don't know."

Dougie tipped his head to one side. "You don't look so hot."

"The hospital was the pits. And I got up real early. And I didn't eat breakfast."

"Well, come on." He bounced up from the bed. "If my mom will let me eat."

"Why not?"

"Yesterday she bought bagels and all this stuff to put on them — lox and whitefish and cream cheese with chives and stuff, and all I wanted on my bagel was butter. So she got really pissed off and said she wasn't going to make me breakfast anymore if I didn't appreciate it." They went out of the room and noisily scrambled down the stairs.

After breakfast, they went out and wandered aimlessly through the streets. It was a beautiful September day, warm and breezy, with a lot of small white clouds that moved rapidly across the sky. The streets seemed especially clean and fresh, as if a wind had come and swept them. Dougie seemed content to just walk next to him. Johnny was having a new idea. There were things you could do, weren't there? You could go to AA or a psychiatrist or something. He'd seen pamphlets in a rack at the church they went to when they were in New York on weekends, pamphlets for different things like that. He could go home and talk to his father about that, real casual, maybe even just leave the pamphlet lying around. Without saying anything, he turned a corner and headed for the church. That would be an added bonus, he thought: Dougie would see him take the leaflet and figure it out, it was a way of telling without telling. Even though it was Sunday morning, they might be able to sneak in without anyone seeing. But it was later than he thought, and there was a crowd of people coming out, so he walked past the church without saying anything to Dougie.

They wound up in the park, sitting on the hillside watching kids and old men float toy boats in the pond. They talked about baseball and school. Dougie went to get some ice cream, and Johnny sat with his knees drawn up, hugging his legs.

He had to do something. AA wasn't such a bad idea, but he didn't know anything about it. There was no one he could ask — if he couldn't discuss it with Dougie, he certainly wasn't going to talk it over with anyone else. His own doctor was just a pediatrician. The guidance counselors at school were no good — they were always encouraging you to talk to them, they'd even made Dougie go for a couple of appointments, but that had been a laugh. He could call his mother — but he skipped away from that idea without even considering it. There wasn't anyone he could trust, not with this. He'd have to do it himself. He would go home and pour the scotch down the sink and force his father to say something. It was his responsibility.

"Johnny. Hey." Dougie prodded him with his sneaker. "I've been standing here talking to you for like five minutes."

"Oh." He looked up and blinked at the bright sky.

"Here, have an ice cream."

"Thanks." It was coffee, his favorite, already melting over the top of the cone.

Dougie sat down and pushed his hair off his forehead. "You're pretty bummed out, aren't you."

He didn't say anything.

"It's about your dad, right? You figured out something, because of him falling, right?"

Johnny said, weakly, "What are you, Sherlock Holmes or something?"

"Doesn't take a genius." He waited, licking his cone. When Johnny didn't answer, he said, "Well, my advice is to forget it. They don't listen to what you say. You can talk to them till you're blue in the face, but in the end you're just a kid and they don't give a fuck what you think. They like to talk to you about politics and civil rights and shit like that, but when it comes to anything important, like how the rest of your life is going to turn out, they don't want to hear it. Guidance counselors and shrinks and teachers, even your parents, they pretend they want to hear what you have to say, but they don't. They just want you to talk so they don't feel guilty about things, but they don't really listen, 'cause they know they can't do anything about it. They just, like, pat you on the head and collect their forty dollars an hour. Besides, you probably can't do anything about it either."

But he could, he thought later, as he let himself into the apartment. He had to, just because there was no one else.

The apartment was quiet. He had rehearsed what he was going to do. He was going to get rid of the booze. Then his father would ask why. And he would tell him: what Dr. Baker had said, what he thought, how he wanted to help. The words were all there, he'd tried them out all during the long afternoon as they walked through the park and then watched the ball game on Dougie's new TV. It all fit together. He would save his dad.

He went into the library. It was empty. The bottles were kept on shelves in a recess above the sink. He took the scotch bottle down and looked at it.

"What are you doing?" His father's voice was sharp and unexpected.

He turned around, and they looked at each other. Everything was implicit in that look, and everything that would happen afterward. He could tell that his father knew exactly what he was doing, what he was thinking. Up to that moment, Johnny had only half-believed his own suspicions, he had more than half-believed that Dr. Baker was wrong, and now he realized that what he really wanted from this stunt was a flat denial from his father. All he saw now was confirmation, as surely as if the words had been spoken. And he also saw the impossibility of it all. He couldn't discuss it with his father. It would be their secret, all right, but they would keep it secret even between themselves. He'd have to look out for his dad, but furtively and without the drama he'd envisioned, which he now saw was just a hopeless attempt at distraction. I'm only thirteen, he thought, I'm just a kid. He put the bottle back. "Nothing."

"What time is the concert?" his father asked for the second time since they'd come into the deli.

"Two o'clock," Johnny said.

"We have plenty of time." His father picked up the coffee cup, one of those thick white cups in deep saucers that they had in places like this. His hand shook a little as he held it up to his mouth.

Just a little, Johnny thought, watching, as the noise of the crowded restaurant closed around them. He didn't know what to make of it, or of any of the other indications he'd noticed in the eight months since the night at the hospital: the trembling hand; the cold his father had had in January, which he hadn't been able to shake; his watery eyes and the way he suddenly seemed to disappear from his body for minutes at a time, staring blankly out over the cribbage board or the magazine; the funny pattern of small blood vessels in his cheeks that might or might not have been there all along. Johnny saved all these moments to take out and examine when he was alone. It was as if he were keeping a scrapbook full of clippings from someone else's life. He could puzzle over the pages, the yellowing notices torn from old newspapers and held to the page by dried-out tape, and he could recognize here and there a pattern seeming to emerge, as if of a life; but then the image that had been forming itself receded and the scrapbook lost all coherence and became again a record of events without cause: a trembling hand, burst veins. If he stood on the ground of his secret, a high and lonely place where the wind whispered unintelligibly, everything connected and was explained. But if he was just a normal kid, his father a normal dad, there were no explanations and really no events, just the random coincidences of a normal life. In the half-light of unspoken knowledge, everything had significance and nothing had meaning.

"They think I'm old-fashioned," his father said, sipping his coffee. "New ideas, new blood, that's what they want. Sometimes they forget that I founded that firm. I know a little bit about new ideas myself." He smiled as if he'd made a joke, and Johnny dutifully smiled back at him.

"Do you know what Melville wrote, in *Bartleby?*" his father said out of the blue.

"*Bartleby?*"

"Yes," his father said impatiently, "*Bartleby*. What the hell am I paying such exorbitant school fees for, don't they have you reading Melville?"

"I'd prefer not to," Johnny said, not looking up.

His father opened his mouth and then paused. "That's very good, Johnny. Very good." He laughed loudly. "Listen to this." He recited from memory: "I am one of those unambitious lawyers who never addresses a jury, or in any way draws down public applause; but, in the cool tranquility of a snug retreat, do a snug business among rich men's bonds, and mortgages, and title-deeds. All who know me, consider me an eminently safe man." He finished and waited for applause, but Johnny didn't have any to give — he'd noted the lines when they'd read the story in English class a few months before. His father returned to the main theme of his argument. "They want to make Grayson head of the department. The two of them, Grayson and Burdett, came into my office on Friday, very friendly, full of compliments." A waitress in a white uniform that had seen better days squeezed by them and put a huge corned-beef-on-rye down on the next table, her ass in Johnny's face. His father lowered his voice. "Burdett — my friend —" he snorted, "we were in the Navy together, went to law school together, started Newland and Burdett together — with my money, by the way." He stopped talking, as if he'd lost the thread of his sentence, or thought he'd completed it.

Johnny had been listening to this sort of thing for months now. It had started right after that night at the hospital, his father discussing business with him. He hadn't talked about the law firm much before, not to his mother or Elizabeth, and certainly not to him, he'd always said that he didn't want to burden his family with dull office details. Now it all came out, the pent-up triumphs and discontents of twenty-five years spewing out. Johnny didn't understand a lot of what he talked about; his father was usually pretty good at explaining things, but when he talked about work he used a lot of legal terms. He did understand that things weren't very good at Newland & Burdett. His father was concerned that his partners, or some of them, were pushing him aside — out of greed, he said.

His father put the coffee cup down but kept holding on to it. "They said that the firm was in terrific shape, thanks to me. That we had terrific clients, again thanks to me. They were terrifically appreciative. Terrific: it's one of Grayson's words." His father peered at him across the table, as if he wanted to be sure that Johnny didn't suspect him of using a word like that. "Then the punch line. I should take it easy. Things were so terrific they don't need me anymore. I should relax, turn some of my clients over to the younger men, let them sweat for a change. We all laughed at that." His father didn't laugh, so Johnny didn't either. "They want my partnership share. That's really what they're after."

The noise in the deli — the clatter of plates being dropped on tables, the high voices of women shepherding children, the whirring of the meat slicer, the ringing of the number box behind the counter — dropped away, and he was left alone again, with another indecipherable clipping for the scrapbook. Maybe his father's partners were greedy, maybe they wanted him out of the way so they could get more money. But maybe they knew, maybe they'd seen his father come back from too many lunches with too many scotches. Maybe they didn't want to entrust their business to a lush (he'd increased his vocabulary in the last few months, too). The worst part of it was the doubt. He should be feeling indignation on his father's behalf, he should be able to damn Burdett and Grayson for the SOBs his father thought they were, he should be able to stand proudly at his father's side and tell the world to fuck off. But he couldn't, not when he knew that whatever their motives, there was a good reason for them to be worried. He hated himself for that, for disloyalty. What kind of a son was he, especially when his father was so proud of him?

He always reached this point sooner or later: if he were a better son to his father, he wouldn't have these doubts. When this happened, he retreated into that strange place he'd discovered in the hospital, the place he went when he wasn't there anymore. He'd said to Dougie, "Like nothing bad would happen if you pretended you weren't there." What he'd discovered was that if you weren't there, you had to be someplace else. It was a place where he wasn't exactly himself and where the world was obscured and became other than it was. Where he could look at real things and see deeper meanings behind them. While he was in that other world, nothing bad could happen, and that was why he went there. And yet, it was also a place he hated, an obscene place that terrified him with the completeness with which it took him away. He was dragged into it against his will, and it left him feeling disgraced and humiliated. It wasn't a place that other boys he knew would ever go; for them the world of school and families and girls was enough, right in itself — they never had to go someplace to hide their shame at what they had to do.

"Well," his father was saying, "I still know a thing or two. I told them that I'd love to stay and chat but I had an appointment with Thomas Welland. That made the point very neatly, I think."

His father was looking at him expectantly, waiting to be asked. "What point, Daddy?"

"The North River Trust is the largest client of the firm, always has been. Accounted for nearly half our billings last year. And who founded the North River Trust? Your great-grandfather and Thomas Welland's grandfather. The Newland Trusts are the largest shareholders of the bank after the Welland family. And I control the Newland Trusts. If I go, Welland's business goes with me, and that for Stan Burdett." He snapped his fingers.

"Yeah, right," Johnny said bitterly. What did any of it matter. He was tired of hearing about his father's problems. I'm just a kid, he thought, I don't want to know any of this. He would be going to sailing camp again that summer, and then he would start at Westfield in the fall, he could get away. "Leave me alone," he whispered.

"What's that?"

"Nothing, Daddy. We should go." He slurped the last of his ice cream soda through a straw.

In the end, he didn't go to camp. His parents tried to find out why, but he'd read one of those books about teenage development and pretended that it was just adolescent stubbornness, and they bought it. He stayed in Westfield with his mother, his father drove up on weekends, Elizabeth visited from time to time. One afternoon, a few weeks before school was to start, he drove up to Lenox with his mother, to an antique store. He watched her in the shop as she moved among the highly polished wooden tables, the ceramic bowls with bearded Chinamen painted on, the little jade carvings in the glass-fronted highboy, the gilt-framed ancestors without descendants. Here and there a ray of light from the deep bay window in the front picked out a patch of gold, or a brass finial, or the crystal teardrops of a chandelier. His mother passed from light to shadow to light again, and her hair seemed to gleam — it was like his hair, not any one color, but with threads of gold mixed in. He had his mother's hair, he thought, putting his hand up to his head for a moment.

He adored her more now than ever. A year before, he had felt himself, without stopping to think of it, growing away from her. She was always so much there in his life that it was impossible to avoid her. He hadn't, at the age of twelve, much wanted parents, a necessary evil to be borne patiently or impatiently, as the advantage turned. He had been prepared to leave her behind. But then a piece of his love for his father had fallen out, and he'd transferred it, as best he could, to her. There had grown up between them a mysterious complicity centering on his father. What it consisted of on her side he couldn't know, because he had determined from the moment he put the scotch bottle down in the library that his only safe course of action was never to acknowledge the secret openly. He always, in her presence, mounted special sentries on the walls of his knowledge to be sure nothing escaped. Maybe she, on her side, was being equally circumspect, which suited him perfectly. His asking her to dance at Mrs. Pauling's had been a tacit acknowledgment of their conspiracy.

They left the antique store, he carrying a bulky, heavy package for her and feeling like the man of the house. In the car she said, "I have a surprise for you. A place that your father and I used to go to." As she drove out of town, they passed Tanglewood. "Would you like to go to a concert next weekend?"

"What's the program?" He wouldn't mind it, picnicking on the lawn maybe. As long as Elizabeth wasn't coming up. Hank had just been born and he didn't want to have to be with any babies.

"An all-Tchaikovsky program on Saturday night."

He wrinkled his nose. "I hate Tchaikovsky. Dougie says he's the most overrated composer."

She laughed, and he looked at her quizzically, but she didn't explain. She said, "When I was — oh, twenty-five, Daddy and I came to a concert here. Bernstein was conducting the Pathétique, and you know how he is. During the third movement" — she made a bup-bupbup-bup-bup-buppa sound, like the music — "he kept bouncing up and down, bending his knees and jumping around more and more in time to the music. We thought he was going to fall off the podium. I'm afraid we disgraced ourselves badly."

"How?"

"We were laughing so hard that Daddy had to excuse himself. He ran across the lawn between the picnic blankets, trying not to howl. I wrapped myself in our blanket. I don't know what the people next to us thought."

"Dougie says Bernstein is the best conductor to listen to on records and the worst one to watch in person."

"Well, there's something to be said for that." She turned the car into a drive. "Here we are."

He looked at the sign. "What's Chesterwood?"

She parked. "Daniel Chester French was the sculptor of the Lincoln Memorial and Alma Mater at Columbia and the Minuteman Monument at Concord. This was his home and his studio."

They walked around the gardens and peered into the studio. There was a tour going on, led by a lady with white hair who seemed to be some kind of curator. They listened for a while, then went back outside to a strip of lawn with a small fishpond.

He dug into his pocket and pulled out a penny, tossing it into the water.

"What did you wish for?" she asked.

"I can't tell or it won't come true." He wouldn't tell anyway.

She stood next to him, looking into the pool. "You've really become a man, Johnny."

"What do you mean?" he asked, his voice picking that moment to crack.

"Oh, you're getting so tall, and handsome." She gestured toward his reflection in the pool. "I'll bet all the girls are after you."

"Yeah, right."

"And you seem much more grown-up to me," she went on. "Don't grow up too fast."

"Why not?"

"Well, for one thing, the faster you grow up the faster I get old." He noticed, in the water, how much alike they looked, the same hair, the same face. She wasn't getting old, she was just as familiar as she'd always been. She put her arm through his. "Growing up means taking responsibility for new things. There are some things you can't be responsible for, not until you're a lot older. Maybe not ever. Don't take on more than you can handle. Don't grow up too fast." She leaned against him while he deciphered her meaning. Then she laughed. "A mother's advice upon her son's leaving for boarding school. I'm going to miss you."

"Maybe I shouldn't go," he blurted out. He knew it was the wrong thing to say, but he couldn't help it. "I could stay in New York with you and Daddy."

"That's very flattering," she laughed, teasing him. He'd known she wouldn't take him seriously, but there had been a slight possibility she would. It was a thought he'd been having more and more often, all spring and summer.

He'd even discussed it with Dougie a few months before. He had been in Dougie's bedroom, sitting on the floor, his back against the desk, a French textbook propped on his knees. Downstairs, Dougie was practicing a Mozart sonata. It was the end of May, and the window was open. A warm breeze blew in, ruffling the edge of the Mick Jagger poster, blowing down occasionally through his hair, touching his scalp.

Dougie finished playing, and a few minutes later came upstairs with a bag of potato chips, which he tossed to Johnny. "How's it going?"

"Lousy," he said. "I can't figure out this goddamn verb. I keep staring at the page and it still doesn't make any sense. You gotta help me."

Dougie sat on the floor next to him. "Lemme see." He looked at the page where Johnny pointed. "It's an irregular verb."

"So give it a laxative." They still found that funny, even though Dougie pretended not to.

"Lame, Johnny, lame. Look." He started to explain, very patiently. Johnny tried to concentrate, but couldn't. He gave up and listened to the sound of Dougie's voice, the most familiar voice he knew, almost. He looked away from the book at Dougie's face. Dougie was concentrating, intent on his explanation — the most familiar face he knew, except his own. He was suddenly filled with enormous affection, love, he would have said if pressed, his best friend. He would stay here forever, just the two of them in the warm breeze of the spring, where everything was safe and familiar, itself.

"Got it now?" Dougie finished.

"I don't know. How'm I going to do at Westfield if I can't even conjugate irregular verbs?"

"I wouldn't worry if I were you. Westfield is the brainiest school and you're the brainiest kid around, so it's the perfect match."

"I'm not the brainiest kid," he said. It was, actually, something he was proud of, but it wasn't the kind of thing you were supposed to admit.

"Bullshit. You know everything. I've never seen you in class without an answer."

He shrugged. "I make them up."

"Yeah, right."

He didn't argue any more. He sat, still basking in the feeling of Dougie next to him. "Listen, Dougie. Seriously. Do you think it's too late to change my mind? About going to Westfield. Maybe I should just stay here and keep on going to Collegiate with you all. Who needs boarding school anyway?"

Dougie looked at him. "Seriously? I think you're just nervous."

He touched Johnny's stomach, just below the breastbone. "Right here, right?"

They had talked once about being nervous — the way Johnny felt before he went away to camp every year, the way Dougie felt before a recital. He shook his head. "It's not that. Everything is working out OK, maybe if I go away —" He gave up. He didn't have the vocabulary to say what he meant, even if he'd wanted to.

Dougie said impatiently, "Is this about your father again?"

Johnny didn't answer. Dougie knew everything but the truth. He knew that Johnny was spending all his free time at Dougie's house, after school most days, and that he didn't especially like to have Dougie come over, that Johnny didn't talk about his father much anymore. For Dougie, all that was familiar, the mirror image of what he had done when his parents were splitting up. He'd figured it all out except the basic cause.

"Look, Johnny. Just do what you want, and it all works out in the end. Like me and my dad. I didn't even want to speak to him for two years, and now we're friends again." It had happened because of Dougie's bar mitzvah. At first Dougie hadn't even wanted his father there. Johnny sat on the floor in Dougie's room during the transcontinental phone calls in the weeks before the ceremony. He listened to Dougie complain that he was being forced into something, that it was his life, his bar mitzvah. He didn't say anything when Dougie yelled that it was his father who had walked out, not him. He watched, just before the service, while Dougie and his father hugged each other, and Dougie said, "I love you, Dad." That had been a year ago, and Dougie had spent last Christmas vacation with his father in California. Johnny knew there wasn't any possibility of that kind of reconciliation for him. The situations were totally different. Dougie said, "It's your life, you should do what you want. And what you want is to go to Westfield. I should know. I'm your best friend."

Now, as he stood with his mother and thought of the conversation, he knew he was doomed to Westfield, there was nothing he could do about it. He said to his mother, mimicking the voice of some movie actor in one of those thirties films she liked so much, "I'd give up anything for you, darling," and they both laughed.

When they got back to the house, she said, "If you're coming to dinner with us, you'd better change."

" 'K." He headed for the stairs, then turned. "Thanks for a nice day."

She was putting her keys in the porcelain bowl. She had yelled at him for doing it at first, because the bowl was old, but now they all did it, which made things easier for him. She said, "Are you sure you want to go with us tonight? Would you rather stay home?"

"Why? Do I embarrass you or something?"

"No, of course not."

"If you don't want me to come, I won't."

"Johnny, don't be like that. Of course you may come if you like. I just thought you might be bored with us all the time."

"Well, I'm not." He turned and went up to his room. He was doing her a favor, even if she didn't know it, and he didn't want her to stop him. He shut the door, frightened a little at how angry he'd been over nothing. He took off his clothes and sat on the bed, picking at a toenail. They were going to a dinner party at the home of some friends of his parents. Almost every weekend all through that past year, when they'd come to Westfield, his parents had gone out and he'd gone with them. It was his responsibility: not being there, going to that other place, worked if he kept it in his head, but it was part of his job to be with his father as much as possible in case anything happened. In case he was needed. That was why he had stayed home instead of going to camp.

He showered and looked in the mirror, wondering if, since the morning, he'd suddenly developed the need to shave. Then he got dressed and went downstairs. He heard his father in the living room, the familiar clink of ice in a glass. He would have two drinks before they left, on top of whatever he might have had during the day. Then two more before dinner, and wine, and maybe cognac or his new favorite, Cointreau. Or two or three. That was the way these evenings went.

Johnny walked softly over to the porcelain bowl and took out his father's keys. He put those in one pocket of his jacket. Then he took his mother's keys and put them in another pocket. His mother had commented on how nice he looked in a blazer. She didn't know that he only wore it because he needed the extra pocket space.

His father was standing at the living room window, which overlooked a short lawn and the edge of the woods. He said, "Did you have a nice day?"

"Yeah. We went to Chesterwood."

"Chesterwood." He came away from the window. "I remember when I was eighteen, my father had to go to Washington for something. It was right before the war, and he took me with him. I remember looking up at the statue of Lincoln in the Memorial." He seemed to run out of memory at that point. Johnny tried to picture his father at that age, but he couldn't. There were photos in an old album in New York, and he'd heard some stories, but he couldn't independently of those bits of family lore form any image of his own. He could barely remember his father a year ago — his other father, he sometimes thought, the one before the hospital.

His mother came in. "Johnny, how nice you look. Is that blazer getting too small for you?"

He looked at his sleeves. "I dunno."

"We just bought it, when? Before Easter. You're growing too fast." She was fastening a bracelet as she talked. "I called Mrs. Cornwell and she told me that Boyd will be there tonight, so you won't be stuck with just us old folks. You know Boyd, don't you?"

"Yeah."

"He seems like a nice boy."

He was two years younger and therefore out of the league. Johnny didn't like him or dislike him, he just wasn't a factor. Except to the extent that he would be a distraction.

They sat in the living room and watched one another. His father was very mellow that night, unaware, it seemed, of the scrutiny he was under. He remembered some more of his trip to Washington before the war, a visit to the White House, even, where his father had had a meeting with Mrs. Roosevelt. Johnny didn't listen to all this talk about the past, it was the future that loomed in front of him, and he wondered what would happen, on evenings like this, when he was away at school. That was the real reason he didn't want to go to Westfield: not nervousness about what lay ahead but fear for what he was leaving behind.

When it was time to go to the Cornwells, he added up what he'd seen and made a decision. "I got your keys, Daddy," he said, taking them out of his jacket pocket. It had become a part of their routine — helpful Johnny, no one questioned it. His mother never took her keys unless she was driving, so she wouldn't miss them. It was easy for him to be in charge.

Dinner at the Cornwells' was about as bad as he'd expected. The men all talked about the economy. The women talked about children and prep schools. He didn't know what Boyd talked about because he didn't listen. After dinner, Boyd suggested they go up to his room and listen to music or something. Johnny didn't want to go, he wanted to keep watching, but his mother more or less insisted: he could see her getting ready to lecture him on the obligations of a guest. So he went. He sat on Boyd's bed and listened to a Who tape and then a Rolling Stones tape, and fortunately Boyd liked the music loud so he didn't have to talk much. Johnny kind of thought he would like Boyd if he got to know him, but he didn't have time for it now, and he couldn't really concentrate, wondering how his father was.

When they went down again, he could tell he'd missed something, but he wasn't sure what. His father never got drunk, the way guys got drunk on TV. He never slurred his words a lot or got sick or fell down (except that once), and he certainly never got loud or rude. Whatever had happened had been something small, probably something no one else would have noticed. He scowled. Probably nothing had happened, he was just making the whole thing up. His father had another Cointreau.

Still, when it was time for them to go home, he wasn't sure. If he hadn't left the room he would have known, one way or the other. It was his job to know and he'd muffed it, and now he had to make a choice. Johnny put his hand in his pocket and closed his fist over his mother's keys. They were at the door, saying goodnight, he was saying see-you-round to Boyd. He took his hand out and gave the keys to his mother. "You drive," he said. He didn't look at her. He wasn't there.

"The thing is, John, to hold out for the slow dances." He and his roommate, Jeff, were getting ready to go to a dance at the girls' school across the border in New York. "You have to ask her for a couple of the fast ones, so she knows you're interested. Then, when the slow dance comes, you just act cool." Jeff had gone to a coed school in New Orleans, so he instructed Johnny when it came to girls.

Johnny was brushing his shoes. "I know about slow dances," he said, waiting for Jeff to tell him more.

"Yeah, right. You know about dancing classes and snooty New York girls, I'm talking about real action."

"Get outta here. Half those girls tonight are from New York."

"Well they like this coon-ass boy real well." Jeff had picked up a girlfriend at the first dance they'd gone to. Her name was Corkie, and he wrote her long letters, which he showed to Johnny before he mailed them. Mostly they were full of stuff about swimming (they were both on the freshman team) and about how great Jeff did in classes and stuff. Johnny never commented on their accuracy.

"Here," Jeff said, handing him a bottle of English Leather cologne. "Try some of this."

He rubbed it on his face, feeling it sting a little. He had shaved the day before and hadn't needed to again, but he had anyway. He wondered if anyone would notice the little cut next to his Adam's apple, and pulled his shirt collar up a little higher. He put his breath spray in his jacket pocket.

Outside in the hall the phone rang. Johnny froze. It was a Saturday night. He didn't know, but he figured his parents were here at the house in Westfield, that they would be going out to dinner. He usually imagined that the call would come to the headmaster's house, and then he'd get a summons to go over there, but it was possible, in an emergency, that his mother would just call the hall phone directly. He heard someone call out for Baumann, so the call wasn't for him this time, and someone else yelled that Baumann was taking a shit. He went back to polishing his shoes.

"Well, tonight's your chance, John. Just ask Sheila for that slow dance and you'll be in her underwear in no time."

Sheila was a girl he'd met at the last dance, and she seemed to like him. Jeff had been giving him pointers all week. He took a last look in the mirror and pushed down his hair.

"Ready?" Jeff asked.

"Ready."

He danced three fast dances with Sheila and then let someone else ask her for a while. When the first slow dance came, he held her tightly, imitating Jeff in a sort of rocking back and forth motion. He could have done a fox trot, like in Mrs. Pauling's class, but this was better, he could feel her body all the way along his. Jeff and Corkie were dancing next to them. It was turning out pretty well.

Near the end of the evening Jeff came over and said, "Corkie knows a way we can sneak out and go somewhere," and, feeling daring and scared, he got Sheila, and the four of them slipped out through a side door. Corkie led them down a hall toward the locker room and then into a side room that was full of athletic equipment. The lights were all out, and there was only one window, through which an exterior light gave some illumination. He had never been in a girls' locker room before.

Sheila put her hand in his and intertwined their fingers. Behind them he could hear Jeff and Corkie doing something. Then Sheila heard a noise outside in the corridor. They waited about five minutes, none of them moving, and then they went back to the dance.

He and Sheila became an item, and he sent her the same kind of letters Jeff sent Corkie. He even wrote to Dougie about her, and got a letter in return, which he read while walking back from getting the mail. Dougie said that he was going out with Blair Phillips. Johnny stood still, the wind blowing around him on the top of a little hill, the torn envelope in one hand, squinting a little in the bright, cold sunlight. He'd always thought that Blair would be his girl — hadn't they danced together all those nights at Mrs. Pauling's? Dougie hadn't even gone to dance class. He tried to imagine the two of them together, his best friend and his girl. It didn't seem right, Dougie had a lot of balls to try that. The wind came up and fluttered the letter in his hand, and he shoved both his hands, still holding the letter and envelope, into his pockets. Then he thought, what the hell. That was New York, he'd left that behind. Westfield was better anyway — everything about it. He liked Jeff, he liked the swim team, he liked Sheila, he liked his classes. He even liked knowing that he was as smart as anyone else in their class, except maybe Ripley Lewis, but Ripley was a showoff and Johnny was just as happy to let him be brain-of-the-year (and incidentally mouth-of-the-year). He avoided Ripley as much as he could — he was weird. But it was all far away from New York, from Dougie. Let Dougie have Blair, good luck to him. It just made Johnny feel farther away from all that, from his father especially. He went back to his room and wrote Dougie a letter about slow dances.

Thanksgiving vacation wasn't too bad — they went to visit his grandparents in Palm Beach — but Christmas turned out to be a disaster. It was just the three of them (Elizabeth was with David's family, and Dougie was in California) and there was a lot of snow, and the hours seemed empty. His father looked older, worn down. Even his skin looked funny, a little yellow and papery. In as roundabout a way as he could, Johnny mentioned it to his mother, but she acted as if she didn't understand him. One afternoon he went up to the attic to look for her and found her sitting on the floor, crying. He wondered if he should put his arm around her shoulders, not wanting to. He did it anyway. "Mommy, what's the matter?"

"These were your favorite clothes," she said, "when you were a baby."

"Why're you crying?"

She leaned against him a little. "Life is complicated, Johnny. I'm just tired, I guess."

He thought, It can't come from me, she has to bring it up herself. Silently, he willed her to do it, but nothing happened. She was protecting him, he thought, or maybe she was protecting his father. The moment slipped away, and they put the baby clothes away, laughing about them now, and gathered up Christmas ornaments instead. It was only much later that he wondered if she wasn't after all protecting herself. His father drank no more than usual, no less either, the same indecipherable straws in the wind. The one good thing was that they didn't go out much, his mother entertained at home a lot, and he was mostly spared his hand-is-quicker-than-the-eye trick with the car keys.

Corkie broke up with Jeff. He showed Johnny the letter — something about a Taft boy she'd met. "Taft faggot," Jeff said. They went down to the hockey rink and checked each other into the boards for an hour, and then Jeff stood in goal while Johnny took slap shots at him first from one face-off circle and then from the other, and the cold air rose off the ice like blood in his nose. It was the hard, confined wintertime. Staring out a classroom window one day, across the wide dry lawns, over the frozen lake to the whitened mountains, it occurred to him that they had all been cryogenically suspended, reachable only by the dry hum of English history or the narcotic declension of Latin nouns. The long nights were filled with soft yellow light, study, and desire.

Sheila broke up with him in May. He would have broken up with her, but he didn't know how. The heartbreak of spring, he thought, as buds popped pitilessly around him. Jeff took him down to the track and they ran about six miles, and he felt better, ready for exams anyway, and the baseball game that seemed to go on and on as different guys took study breaks and filled in. He hit two home runs in one afternoon and almost forgot her. When school ended, Jeff came and spent a week with him in the city. They went to a couple of ball games and a couple of Westfield parties, and to a Jerry Jeff Walker concert with Dougie, but he and Jeff didn't hit it off for some reason. His father was great about all this, more his old self. He went with them to the Stadium one night and told Jeff the story about the time he'd met Ted Williams.

His father was taking the last two weeks of June and all of July off. "It's what Burdett wanted. I decided to go along with him." His father was trying to sound cunning, Johnny thought. "Give him some rope and see who he hangs — it won't be me, I can promise you that." Their first Saturday night in Connecticut, there was a dinner party, and Johnny went with them as usual. His parents' friends asked him about Westfield and told him how grown-up he must be, a boarding school boy, and he answered them very politely. But he was in that other world again, the place where no one could see him — it had all the old feeling of safety. Not being there, he thought, was like riding a bike was supposed to be, you never forgot how.

Dougie came up for Johnny's birthday weekend. On the Saturday afternoon he played the piano for Johnny, a Beethoven sonata. He'd just won a competition for young pianists, and this was the piece he'd played in the finals. Johnny didn't know the music, and he lay back on the couch with his feet up and listened, until suddenly Dougie stopped playing in the middle.

"What's the matter?"

"What's the matter," Dougie echoed, leaning his elbows on the music stand, his chin on his hands.

"You're playing great. You've really improved." The words sounded hollow, made up.

"Oh, thanks a lot. That's a great compliment coming from a Westfield man." Dougie wouldn't look at him. "I don't even know who you are anymore."

"That's crazy. I'm not any different." Maybe he had been wearing his Westfield-ness a little obviously, but that didn't change who he was.

"Yes, you are. Everything about you is phony. You say things like how much I've improved, but it's not what you're thinking. Maybe at Westfield they have their noses too far in the air to notice, but I notice."

"It has nothing to do with Westfield," he said glumly.

"Yeah, right." Dougie started playing again exactly where he'd left off.

With Jeff, with Stephen, with any of the guys at Westfield, he didn't have to worry, because none of them knew or could possibly even guess about his father. But Dougie was on the edge of knowing, and had been all along. That was what had happened, without Johnny's even knowing it. He was doing it to Dougie too, not being there. It made him feel a little sick.

Dougie went home to New York. Johnny spent his days at the swim club, practicing, lazing. He met a girl named Julie, and they spent a lot of time together, swimming laps, sitting on the float that was anchored a hundred feet offshore, dangling their feet in the water and talking about things: how adults didn't really believe in anything except working, how values were the only important thing in life, and how when they grew up they were going to have ideals. Julie was the first girl he'd ever met who really understood him. Around them, little kids jostled, climbed the ladder and jumped cannonball-style into the black lake. From across the water came the smells of hamburgers cooking, of cigarettes and coconut oil, the French-fried scents of summer.

They went to the movies in Westfield and held hands. He bought the tickets, even though she offered to split it. They went for ice cream after, standing outside the little store in a crowd of other teenagers, while kids rode by on bicycles and families sat at picnic tables nearby with dripping cones. They were, the two of them, a couple in the crowd. A little sticky with ice cream, they held hands again. She invited him to a party at her house the next night, Saturday night. Then her father came by and picked her up.

He walked home on air, floated up to bed. He couldn't get to sleep, all he could think about was that the next night he'd be in a room full of kids, holding her hand, maybe he would even put his arm around her. Then maybe on Sunday, he'd call Jeff and tell him about it.

He didn't wake up until almost lunch the next morning. It was a hot day, and he dragged a lawn chair out into the sun and gooped himself up with suntan oil and turned the radio on. He lay back and closed his eyes, spreading his arms and legs a little and rolling the waist of his shorts down to let the sun get to him. Bees buzzed in the hydrangeas nearby, and the music had the flat, unresonant sound it always did out of doors. He felt great.

After a while he heard the mail come, and he walked gingerly in bare feet down the gravel driveway to get it. There was a letter from Dougie, more or less apologizing for what he'd said, which made him feel bad because he knew that Dougie had been right the first time. But he couldn't feel too bad, not today. He went back to the sun, he wanted to look good for that night.

His parents came home around three. He went into the house to say hello, standing in the kitchen in the air conditioning, wearing a pair of shorts and nothing else.

"I forgot to tell you, last night," he said, opening the freezer.

"Julie's having a party tonight, I'm going. Can one of you give me a lift?"

His father was holding a glass of scotch and soda, something new for him. It looked like ginger ale.

"We're going to the club tonight, with the Wellands," his mother said.

"OK." The steam from the freezer was reaching out, touching his bare shoulders. He got out the ice cream. "You could drop me on the way." He shut the freezer.

"Johnny, you know you're supposed to come with us tonight. We discussed it a week ago."

She looked as if she were about to give him a lecture, so he went over and kissed her. "I've got to go to this party. You won't really miss me." That usually worked. She liked it when he went out on his own, at least she said she did.

But his father intervened. "You'll have to call this girl and tell her you can't come."

"No, I can't do that." She was his girlfriend, although he wasn't ready to tell them that.

His father looked back with his watery stare. "Of course you can. Thomas Welland is a friend of our family. He's also an important client of mine. As I recall, you asked to be invited to this dinner."

Johnny recognized the symptoms — a drink, maybe a few, at lunch. He dug a spoon into the ice cream. "Well, I'm asking to be uninvited." He banged the spoon against the bowl to get the ice cream off. For a moment, he hoped the bowl would break.

"You might show a little consideration, John." His father swallowed the last of his drink.

Johnny dropped the spoon. "Consideration. What about me, consideration for me? All I do is show consideration for you." And then, eerily, it was as if they were back in New York, he with the scotch bottle in his hand, his father staring at him, having the same unspoken conversation: I know; I know you know. He stalked out of the room and went upstairs.

He lay on his bed looking up at the ceiling. First Dougie, now Julie. Was he supposed to give up everything in his life, everyone? It was bad enough that he'd given himself up. It wasn't fair.

He heard his mother come upstairs and go into her room to dress for dinner. After a while he got up and knocked on the door. "Come in," she said.

He went and sat down on the bed. She had changed her clothes and was standing in front of the closet trying on shoes. "Well, have you changed your mind?"

"No. I'm not going to."

She poked her head out a moment and then stepped back in front of the mirror. "Your father wants you to be there. It's important to him."

"Is it important to you?" He lay down on his side, catching a glimpse of himself in the mirror over her dressing table. His face looked dirty — a combination of suntan oil and tears. He rubbed one cheek.

"Don't use that tone of voice with me."

He hated it when she said that, it made him feel like a little boy. "You're always telling me I should do things on my own. Now what's happened? You change your mind?"

"You made an appointment —"

"I want a life of my own," he said loudly, then stopped himself. It was the wrong thing to say.

She let it pass, though. "At least go downstairs and apologize."

"You're being so unfair."

"And you're being discourteous. You knew we had this commitment. Why did you make other plans?"

"I don't care about his commitments. Some stupid client." He bit a fingernail, knowing that the Wellands were more than just some client.

"That's enough, young man. I would have thought you were old enough to behave properly." She came into the room and opened her jewelry box.

"I am old enough, I'm fifteen. I can make my own plans."

"Well, you're not being very responsible, considering that you are fifteen."

He watched her as she took out her emerald necklace. He wasn't going to change his mind, at least not yet, anyway, but he wanted to make up with his mother. He stood up from the bed. "Can I help you with your necklace?"

"Yes, thank you."

He stood behind her and fastened the catch. She looked back at him from the mirror. "Please change your mind and come with us."

He wavered — it was part of his life now, and he'd chosen that — as much, he thought, as anyone ever chose anything. "I'll see."

"At least go and apologize to your father."

"I'll see."

He went downstairs, his hands stuffed in the pocket of his sweatshirt. At the bottom, he stood for a long time in front of the bowl. Then he looked out through the windows at the back of the hall. It was that end-of-day time that seemed to happen only in the summer, when the sun started to go down, it was as if someone rolled a rock away from the mouth of a cave and the gleaming gold of a dragon's hoard came shining out. As a kid, he'd looked up at this time of day and thought how much more there was of time, how much before his mother called him in. He heard his father, in the living room, cough. It was also the time of day when his father, on Fridays, had arrived at the house after driving up from New York, when they'd go out on the lawn for a game of catch after dinner, their shadows before them on the grass. He took the keys out of the bowl and put them in his pocket.

His father was sitting in an armchair looking straight ahead, a highball glass in his hand. It was a good thing he had taken the keys, he thought, this was a bad one. "Daddy?"

"You have ten minutes to change." He drank from the glass.

Johnny felt he at least owed it to himself to put up some fight. "I think I want —"

His father put the glass down hard on the table. Some of the scotch spilled over the side. "You want. You want. I don't care what you want. I'm tired of your thinking the world revolves around you and what you want. Don't be so selfish."

He stood there, not answering, knowing finally what it felt like if your father hit you.

"If, however, you choose to think only of yourself, you may stay home. But you may not go out. You can keep your commitments or be punished."

They looked at each other, and this time there was no tacit understanding between them, only his father's words. He turned and left the room, feeling empty. He tripped over something that wasn't there and nearly fell, then stopped to get his balance. Through the haze, he saw the porcelain bowl and dropped the keys back in noisily, not caring who heard. Hoping someone would.

After they'd gone, he made himself a sandwich and then showered and changed. Julie only lived a couple of miles away, he would walk, someone would give him a ride home. His face in the mirror looked very grim to him, but as he walked through the warm night, with the smell of flowers and early dew in the air, he began to feel better. His father had been drunk, he hadn't known what he was saying, he hadn't meant it. Someday, when he's all recovered, he'll thank me for helping, for being such a man about it. A single star appeared whitely above the horizon. A huge orange moon rose next to it.

It was an awesome party, he'd never had a better time. Julie acted as if he were her boyfriend, holding his hand, keeping him next to her, showing him off to her friends. Words like poetry floated in his head as he imagined what he would say to her when they were alone. At the end, when everyone else was leaving, he stayed. He wanted a minute alone with her, just a minute. And he wanted his parents to get home before him.

They said goodnight, standing on the front porch, her parents inside. He put his arms around her waist and kissed her.

"I really like you," she said.

"Me too."

He walked home. Someone had offered him a lift, but he'd wanted that last moment, and the romance that went with the moonlight on such a night as this. Isn't it romantic, he hummed to himself, his father's favorite song. He was still humming as he turned into his driveway.

Later, everyone commented on how brave he was, it almost became his only identity for a while. But it was only because he knew, immediately, without thinking, the minute he saw the two strange cars parked in front of the house.

XV

HE WAS STILL in his living room, lying on the floor, as the sun came up the next morning. He watched incuriously as the gaps between the buildings across the street filled with a dead gray light. He went to the window and looked out the sliding doors, at the narrow terrace and the black railing that always seemed dangerously short to him. He saluted the dawn, whispering, "I'm sorry," and then, "Goodbye, Johnny." He went into his bedroom, exhausted, and fell asleep. When he woke up a few hours later, he was still exhausted. He went through the motions of showering and shaving and putting on his tie. In the mirror, he imagined he could see his cheekbones beneath the skin, a hollowness at his temples. "Goodbye, Johnny," he said again softly.

He was empty now, as if he'd given up the last of himself and had nothing left. It wasn't that he was afraid of losing too much, although that was part of it. It wasn't, in the end, that he thought Blanche was right, that understanding was better than love. All along he had been telling himself that he would give up Kate, that he could pay the price, thinking that the price would be exacted only from him. But he knew better. In his life it was always someone else who paid the price. Over the last few weeks, revisiting his memories, he had remembered the one unshakable lesson of his past, that everyone he'd ever loved had gotten hurt, and some of them had died, because he'd loved them. It was something essential in himself, something that had been implanted in him at the age of thirteen and that had grown now to a ripe maturity — his legacy from his father.

That was why he needed this world in which he lived so comfortably, the world of Kate Welland and Blanche Morgan, where nothing ended badly because everything was arranged. All along, he'd thought that he accepted the arrangements because they kept him from getting hurt. Now he knew the truth, that the rules were necessary to prevent him from hurting someone else.

That other place he'd first discovered in the hospital, to which he'd gone as a boy when he wasn't there, was no longer for him a kind of dream world of illicit fantasy: he had made it his real world, where Kate and David and Elizabeth and Billy could live safely, because the rules of that world made it impossible for him to do any more damage. That was why he couldn't abandon his life. Because if he broke the rules, they would all get hurt, and Ellen most of all.

That was the irreducible minimum of his predicament. Because he could love Ellen only if he broke the rules. And if he broke the rules, there would be nothing to prevent the cycle from starting again: love, hurt, and someone else's pain. It would be Ellen this time, she'd be his victim. He'd sacrificed enough, hadn't he? enough of other people's happiness, enough other lives. How many more people were going to have to die on the altar of his love, as Ripley had died, and his parents. It was better not to love at all.

There was only a little time left until Ellen came back to town. Then he could see her, and he'd know. Until then he could afford to let them all drift. Clean up the loose ends, put his affairs in order. Wearily, he went to the office and began going through the motions.

He spent most of the day racing around the city in his new capacity as political reporter. In the morning, he went to a rally in Queens, an inhospitable affair at which the mayor alighted from a helicopter, waded through indifferent crowds, and gave a rambling speech over an inadequate sound system. The mayor was beginning to seem dispirited. Jack rode the subway back to a press conference at the World Trade Center at which the governor either was or wasn't going to say something that either would or wouldn't be an endorsement of the mayor or of one of his challengers. In the event, it was none of the above — the governor spoke with great conviction and wit and with all the clarity of cold oatmeal. Jack duly noted that the mayor's entourage was heavy on security and short on style, while the governor's men all had the hungry look of people whose eyes are fixed on a higher prize, probably involving an oval office. Then he went back to the mag-

392 • *The Rules of Seduction*

azine to type up his notes. It was more fun than he'd expected — maybe he'd gotten tired of the same kind of stories all the time. It was certainly more real, or seemed to be anyway, than a charity affair at the Library or a première at the Met.

And through it all he kept thinking: I love Ellen, I need Kate.

He was finishing when Elizabeth called. "When are you going to send my boy back to me?" she demanded, in her usual style of conversation.

"I didn't know you wanted him back," Jack said.

"What a cruel thing to say, I'm his mother, of course I want him back. He's not boring you, is he?"

"One thing about Billy, he's never boring. How's Hank?"

"Better," Elizabeth said. "He says he found your initials carved in a tree from your days as a camper."

He tucked the phone into his shoulder and started typing again. "That was fifteen years ago, Elizabeth." His midnight boat ride with Donny Schaefer.

"Maybe he said it was painted on a wall," she said elliptically. "I told him to call you."

"Thanks." He kept typing, not giving her any help.

"Well. How is Billy?"

"Healthy as an ox," he said, beginning to be annoyed. "He practically ate a whole steak himself, Kate had to fight him for the last piece. What else do you want to know?" Steady, he thought. Don't antagonize her.

"Oh, well, if Kate was there, I suppose it's all right."

He stopped typing and took the phone off his shoulder, holding it in his hand. "What's all right?"

Elizabeth laughed, just a second too late, pretending to make a joke of it. "I don't want you leading him down the path to sin. I know all the trouble you can get into. As long as Kate's there, I won't worry."

"Trust her more than your own brother?"

She laughed again. "It's just that I don't want you turning my son against me."

"That's ridiculous."

"Oh" — he could imagine her in the house in Westfield, waving her hand airily, as if dismissing her own remarks — "I know you talk to Billy behind my back. That he tells you things he wouldn't tell us, that you tell him things you wouldn't tell us. It's not that I object. But as long as Kate's there, I'll know that some female restraint is being applied. You know what I mean. You do want him to stay, he's not in your way?"

"Sure." He went on casually, not wanting to make too much of it. "He's fun to have around. I think he's having a good time with us. We're having a good time with him." Tacitly enlisting Kate on his side.

"Well, if you're sure. As long as Kate's there."

"Look, I'd love to chat, but I have to get Billy, and then we're going out to dinner with Kate and Boyd and Amy. Amy's found this terrific new restaurant or something. So —"

"Have a nice time, John. Say hello to Kate for me."

He hung up, deciphering the conversation. With Elizabeth, nothing meant what it appeared to, there was always a subtext. Billy could stay as long as Kate was there. But if Jack gave up Kate altogether, wasn't there the hint of a threat that he'd be giving up Billy too, and not just Billy but Elizabeth and David and Hank? That they would in some way cut the tie, or at least diminish it, and that along with Kate he would be giving up his family. What was left of it.

It was impossible to get a reservation at Amy's new restaurant — it was her specialty, impossible reservations; restaurateurs swooned at the sound of her voice. It was a narrow place in the Eighties off Second, with a black ceiling and a hand-lettered menu and German Expressionist–inspired art on the walls. The clientele looked German Expressionist too, Jack thought. At the next table, a group of young men with very sticky-looking hair and black shirts buttoned to the neck and totally unblemished faces (their skin looked as if it never moved) were solemnly drinking wine. Across the way, a young woman with short black hair, gamin-esque, with enormous purple-tinted glasses, was being enter-tained by a shaven-headed older man not her father. At the table in the front, evidently the choice spot, sat a large-faced woman with prominent teeth and fake jewelry who greeted Jack enthu-siastically. She had been a friend of his mother's in a previous life. And at another table nearby, an actress who had starred in the latest punk movie hit was eating alone, or waiting for someone, with the same aura of apathy that had distinguished her screen performance. (Jack had written: "The movie is like one of those long-exposure shots of highways, the taillights red streaks and everything else blurred. Only she stands absolutely still, at the center, and we see her with great clarity. But she has no point of contact with the world of the film which rushes by her.") Billy watched all of this, especially the actress, a little open-mouthed.

Kate and Amy sat across the table, their heads close together, talking. He remembered what Timothy had said about them: "Kate talked to Amy about you. A lot. And I overheard them." Were they talking about him now? This night seemed no different from any of the hundred other nights they'd all spent together, his best friends, his world, and on the surface it was no different. Only underneath, inside him was there any difference. And this was a world that didn't acknowledge anything beneath the surface. What would they do if he stood up and announced that he was breaking their engagement because he loved someone else, if he broke the nice smooth surface of their lives? It was ridiculous, he would never do that.

Boyd was sitting next to Jack, reading the menu. "Looks good. I think I'm getting fat. Do you think I'm getting fat? I'm starving."

He'd probably smoked a joint before they came, Jack thought, and now he has the munchies. He did look paunchier to Jack, but that might only have been in comparison to the sixteen-year-old he'd been. "You're not fat, Boyd."

"Yeah. Thanks." Boyd shut the menu. "That was pretty bush of you, Newland, walking out on me at Val's. Where'd you disappear to, anyway?"

"Sorry," he said.

The waiter came with their drinks and a basket of crusty bread. Boyd broke off a piece and buttered it. "We were worried about you, buddy. Wandering off in a thunderstorm. You have some kind of seizure or something?"

"Or something," he said, drinking his bourbon.

Boyd looked at Billy. "I even had to call Billy, remember? Wondering if you'd fallen into a manhole or something. I kept looking for you in the subway — one of those guys with a burlap suit and a cardboard co-op and no teeth."

He sounded really angry. Jack said, "No big deal. I went up to the country for a while. What's the matter?"

"You went to Westfield?"

"Yeah." He put his drink down. "Come on, Boyd. Chill out."

Boyd tore at his bread with his teeth. "It's been a shitty few weeks. I think I might get fired."

"What? Why?"

Boyd shrugged. "Read the papers. The market is dogshit. Wall Street's up to its ass in alligators and their solution is to fire people. Cost control. Fucking assholes." He put his head down toward the glass in his hand, and drank.

"Have they said anything to you?"

"Not exactly. It's not like my boss has to come and piss on my Quotron for the message to get through — you can tell. Maybe." He frowned. "What am I going to do, I mean I can't live without my income. We don't have a big wad packed away for a rainy day, we use the CICO method, cash in, cash out."

"You're being a little premature."

"Easy for you to say."

The atmosphere in the restaurant was hectic, with people going from table to table, everyone seeming to know everyone else, loud greetings, endless huggings, while the waiters moved, unnoticed, among them. How insular this world was, he thought, how limited. It pretended to welcome the new, but really only fed off it — running after fashions in art or music or drama. But if the object of fancy changed, the fanciers never did, it was always the same crowd making the running. They might today be attracted to this restaurant or that club, to the charity of the week, the disease of the month, but tomorrow they would remain unchanged, a little the worse for wear, perhaps, hung over or strung out, but essentially the same. No one ever tripped and fell in this race, the press of other runners held up the faltering. As long as you were one of them. And he was, he always had been. He'd been easy game for Kate because she was so much a part of this world in which he had chosen to hide himself that she could slip into his life with barely a ripple to disturb the surface.

He remembered a party they'd gone to in February, in Palm Beach. They'd been staying at her parents' house, and they'd all gone to the tennis club for a dance: Kate and Jack, Kate's parents, her brother George, and two or three assorted cousins. Kate seemed wrapped up in her family, while Jack sat back and watched.

"You get a haircut or something?" George asked him.

"No. Just something Kate did." George was twenty-one, an undergraduate at Sarah Lawrence majoring in drama. He wanted to be an actor. He had on a cream-colored evening suit with a lavender bowtie and a matching cummerbund, and his hair was a little long and artfully disheveled. He'd brought a girl with him to Palm Beach, one of his classmates, and the two of them spent hours lying on the beach together talking, and glaring at any of the rest of the family who came near them. Jack had pointed out the symptoms to Kate, who'd pooh-poohed them, saying that the girl wasn't really George's type.

"I like it," George said. "Wouldn't hurt you to be a little more radical."

He's stoned, Jack thought, looking at his eyes. His girlfriend was even more stoned. Mrs. Welland was trying unsuccessfully to engage her in conversation and looking puzzled at the responses she was getting — mostly of the "Oh wow" genre.

George stood up. "Kate. Uh, yeah. I need to talk to you a minute."

They walked away, skirting the edge of the dance floor. Jack watched them leave the room, then reappear on a terrace outside a large window. Kate was talking vehemently to George, who looked unhappy and then angry.

Kate's cousin Jenny sat down next to Jack. She was a painter, it seemed, and she had a problem with a column he'd written about the Contemporary Arts Institute. He only half-listened, trying hard to be polite, watching the couples dance. The familiarity of it all.

After midnight they left the party and went home. Kate led him through the silent house, out past the pool. She kicked off her shoes and went down onto the beach. The air was muggy and full, the moon obscured, the stars invisible. He stood on the crest of a small dune, his hands in the pockets of his black jacket, looking down at her as she stood just beyond the reach of the wavelets.

"Jenny is a pain in the ass sometimes," she said, not looking at him.

"She seems OK to me."

"You don't really think that, so why pretend?"

He retired into silence, feeling stung. She knew he didn't much care for discussions about his work or for people who wanted to argue with him about things he'd written, but he'd been making an effort for her sake — it was her family, after all, and he wondered what he'd done to make her angry.

"It's Georgie," she said after a while.

When she didn't go on, he said, "What about him?"

"He's fallen in love. He says."

Jack sat down. Something about this lower vantage point made the sand look smooth and featureless. "That's great."

"It's not. He wants to marry her."

"Oh." He lay back, his hands under his head. A plane flew over, its wing lights blinking. Beyond, through the murk, a single star gleamed.

Kate came and sat down next to him. "He wants to tell Daddy. He wants me to help him."

"Will you?"

"He's twenty-one, John. He's been sleeping around since he was fifteen, and he's always made sure to let me know about it. He's screwed more girls in six years than most men do in a lifetime." He wondered what she knew about most men, but let it pass. "I told him to go to hell."

"That's pretty rough."

"I just don't want to go through this again."

"Again?" He could see the lights of ships on the water, vague in the yellow haze: a freighter and two tankers. He was sleepy and a little drunk, and he wasn't following her.

"People keep walking out of his life — Daddy's, I mean. It's not fair. Look at Edward. He's not here this week, he wasn't even with us at Christmas. He avoids us. When he is with us, it's almost worse. He keeps needling all the time. Medicine is superior to banking, that's his theme. He's a doctor, he helps people, but sup-

posedly Daddy's only interested in money and corporations —
things. When you talk about charity, he says it's hypocritical — as
if serving on the board of the Natural History Museum is some kind
of moral tax write-off. He can think what he likes, I don't care, but
he gets nasty about it, and that just seems childish." She paused,
then went on. "Then there's Tommy."

Jack had heard the facts of Tommy's case, everyone in New York
had heard them. Tommy had been captain of the football team at
Groton when Jack was at Westfield, and they'd overlapped at Yale.
Tommy had gone to work for his father after college, he'd married
the daughter of one of Thomas Welland's closest friends, he'd
seemed poised to carry out gloriously all the best Welland tradi-
tions. And then his wife asked for a divorce on the grounds that
Tommy was having an affair with her eighteen-year-old sister. The
case was avidly reported in the tabloids and became sensational
when Tommy testified that the pressures of working for his father
had unbalanced him.

"He was Daddy's fair-haired boy all along, he was everything
Daddy wanted him to be: a hero at Groton, at Yale, he loved
working at the bank. Then, when everything happened with his
wife, he ended up blaming Daddy. You probably know all that."
Her voice became defensive. "Tommy made sure everybody
would know about that. But nobody knows that it was Daddy who
arranged the divorce settlement after Tommy made such a baby
of himself. And it was Daddy who got him his job at the Chase.
Now Tommy won't even speak to him. If Georgie goes ahead
with this stupid idea, it'll be the same thing all over again, and
Daddy'll have no one left."

"He'll have you," Jack ventured.

"I could do it, too," she snapped back, arguing with someone
who wasn't there. "I know I could, if I wanted to run the bank,
I could. Better than any of them."

She was her father's child, it had been obvious from the beginning. Jack had seen the two of them together at parties or on
weekends at their house in Long Island or here in Palm Beach.
The way she and her father moved around each other without
any hesitations, any trippings-up. As if their minds were so well
attuned they were thinking each other's thoughts. She was his

successor, whether they ever acknowledged it or not — and they wouldn't, because even in this age of enlightenment it was unthinkable that a woman would run the North River Trust. On the day when Elizabeth's dreams came true and David became president of the bank, Elizabeth would stand as close to that pinnacle as any woman ever did.

Kate said, "I went out last year with a man who went to Westfield. You must have known him — Ricky Torrance?"

"I knew him." There had been guys he'd liked and guys he didn't care about one way or the other — and then there had been the ones he hadn't liked at all. The Ricky Torrances.

"He was like every boy I've ever gone out with," she went on. "They all come from good families, they all went to good schools. They all go to the same parties and they'll all grow up to sit on the same boards. And they all seem so —"

She couldn't find the right word. He said recklessly, "I come from a good family, I went to a good school. I do all those things everyone else does."

"You are the same as everyone else, only more so. They do things, like my brothers do, because they have to, but they live in their own worlds. My world, my father's world, isn't real to them. Edward thinks it's contemptible, Georgie thinks it's a joke. God knows what Tommy thinks anymore. But that world is real to you, you're perfect for it. That's why I love you so much."

Thinking back on that now, sitting here in a trendy restaurant, he felt overwhelmed by irony. He'd always been able to fool people, to make them believe that he was what they wanted, and now, it seemed, he'd achieved the ultimate success with the most discerning of collectors. He had become, for Kate, the quintessential inhabitant of that world of money and men and private clubs that she associated with her father. But she went beyond even that, she represented the final promise: if he would only step into the role, she would guarantee that he would never need to leave it. She loved him because she thought he fit so perfectly into her world. And he loved her because she could make him fit in. It didn't matter who he really was: she was an authority, no one would question her authentication.

There were never any questions with her, her world was so

complete that everyone knew where they stood. He thought, I know where I stand in this world. And where did he stand in Ellen's world? Was there any place to stand in that world? Only the eternal shifting of possibility, an expanding universe with no steady state and no rules.

Much later, he was sitting on the banquette next to Boyd, who had his arm around Jack's shoulders. He was obviously feeling no pain, he was happy with the whole world, he'd forgiven Jack for running out on him the night of the thunderstorm, he'd forgiven the market for being so bad, he'd forgiven everyone. He said, "I love it here, with everybody. This is the best it can be."

"You sound like a beer commercial," Jack said. "Listen, why don't I talk to David, or Kate's father, and see if they'll talk to you about a job? I mean, if you want me to?"

Boyd squeezed his shoulder. "God, Newland, thanks a lot. I can always count on you, I know I can, even when you act like an asshole sometimes, you're always there for me. I love you, pal."

Always, Jack thought. It would go on like this forever. He thought of Rob's crazy idea about the president. He thought about asking Thomas Welland to talk to Boyd. All the connections — and he wasn't breaking them, he was only making them stronger.

He called David from the office the next morning and arranged to meet him for a drink at the Yale Club that afternoon. Then he got a note that Rob wanted to see him. He loosened his tie to journalist length and casually sauntered down the hall.

Rob's office was in the front of the building, overlooking the street below and the bay windows of the New York Yacht Club. Jack hung in the doorway and said, "You wanted to see me."

Rob looked up at him dubiously. "Are you still a writer?"

Jack looked himself over, starting with his shoes. "I guess. Why?"

Rob pretended to rummage around in what appeared to be a messy pile of papers on his desk. He had developed a careful system for ordering his work in such a way that it looked completely disorganized. This gave him time to keep hapless writers waiting, wondering if their precious manuscripts had been lost forever beneath a pile of more worthy submissions, old restaurant receipts, and back issues of competing magazines. Jack had recognized this trick early on, and now he ignored it, looking critically at a drawing that had been approved for next month's cover, trying to establish his own kind of psychological superiority.

"This essay," Rob said, finally, holding it with his fingertips. It was Jack's piece on Bogart and Bacall.

"Yeah. What about it?"

Rob dropped it on the desk, neatly conveying the idea that he couldn't bear to hold it any longer. "It stinks, is what."

Rob had two chairs in front of his desk. Jack sat down in the uncomfortable one. "I'm tired of hearing it's been done before."

"Well, that's not what you're hearing from me. Want a candy bar?"

Jack nodded, and Rob got one out of his desk drawer, went through the ritual of breaking it in half, and gave some to Jack. Jack said, "Then what am I hearing from you?"

"The writing. It stinks. The idea —" he held his hand out flat, palm down, and then twisted it a couple of times, "the idea's not so bad. But the writing. Jesus."

They went through this all the time. Jack would submit something, Rob would tear it apart. Jack would rewrite it, Rob would grudgingly admit that maybe if he worked on it some more they might publish it, and Jack would rewrite it again. Rob took a lot of trouble with him, treated him as part apprentice, part disciple, part mascot, and in return Jack was fiercely loyal to him, defending him when other writers called him narrow-minded and uncreative. He settled in for their usual battle. "So what's wrong with the writing?"

"It's dull. It's flabby. There are about three good sentences in the whole thing. You write as if you're in love."

Jack looked up sharply. He hadn't discussed Ellen with Rob, how could he have known? But Rob meant something else.

"Never," he was saying didactically, "never fall in love with your own writing. You lose any critical faculty you might have. I mean, face it, Newland, if you're hot for some girl, you don't usually see that she's got the IQ of a frozen pizza, or one ear bigger than the other. You gotta keep your distance."

Rob tossed him a photocopy of the essay, and for the next half-hour they went through the piece sentence by sentence, and then Rob, as unenthusiastically as possible, said, "I guess it's worth a rewrite," which meant he wanted to publish it.

Jack stood up and started to walk out of the office. Then he turned and leaned on the back of the chair he'd been sitting in. "Can I ask you a question?"

Rob snorted. "Advice to the lovelorn? Need a loan? What?"

"No." He shook his head. "Nothing like that."

"Sounds serious. Sorry if I was my usual sarcastic self."

Jack turned around again. "It's not important. Never mind."

"Hey, come on back here. What is it?"

Jack went back. "Suppose — well, what if I wasn't well connected, as they say. What if I couldn't go to all these parties and things that I write about?"

"Yeah?" Rob looked at him carefully. "What are you getting at?"

"Would you still want me around here?"

Rob shook his head. "What, you need an ego boost? You really think we keep you around here because of your friends?"

Jack looked away. "I kind of —"

Rob waved his hand in a kind of a circle. "I'll give it to you straight, right? You're a writer, pal, I should know one when I see one. And believe me, I don't see them very often. Now get out of here. And lighten up a little."

Back in his office, he sat down and looked at the computer screen. At least Rob thought he was a serious writer, even if no one else did. His aunt thought he was being tasteless, displaying himself and their friends in an unflattering light. His family thought he was threatening the foundations of society with his pinpricks. Boyd thought it was a joke — "I can't believe you get paid to go to the movies," he said every time the subject came up.

Kate, on the other hand, was his biggest fan. "They're always so touchy," she'd said when he told her about David's criticisms. "It's like they're still living in the nineteenth century, worried that the masses will riot and take everything away if we don't keep things quiet. Like those women who put French fries in the little paper containers at McDonald's for minimum wage are really going to rise up in revolt because you write about a museum benefit? I mean, come on."

"Aren't you worried that some Jacobin mob might storm your house one day and take your jade in the name of the people?"

She tossed her head. "Let them try. Besides, if David were a woman, he'd understand how much society needs you. All those people you write about love to be noticed. Not just the arrivistes, either, but the old-timers too. You're perfect for them — if you flattered them, they'd feel guilty, as if their altruism was all for the sake of an honorable mention. That little touch of snideness is perfect, it salves their consciences."

As he walked across Forty-fourth Street toward the Yale Club, he thought he would tell David what Kate had said. He would use Kate to defend himself to David — and wasn't that what he'd always envisioned doing, relying on her? Ellen, he thought — Ellen offered him nothing except love. She never encouraged him, never told him what to do, only told him what she would do. How could he know what to do in a world like that?

At the club, he got himself a drink in the bar and then went into the lounge. The huge room was starting to fill up, and he snagged a couple of chairs near a window. David came in. "How are you, John?"

"I'm good. And you? How was Seattle?"

"Fine." He looked around the room. "It's so different from the Knick. More crowded, it seems more alive."

"It's the women," Jack said randomly.

"You think so?"

"I don't know. It's just bigger maybe." The waiter came with the drinks. Jack said, "I have a favor to ask you."

"What's that?"

"My friend, Boyd Cornwell, is thinking about a job change. I wondered if you'd talk to him about it. No commitments. Just a chat?"

David smiled. "We heard things weren't going so well over there. Has he been axed?"

"No, no." Then he amended, "Not yet, anyway. He's a little worried, is all." It suddenly occurred to him that this conversation was totally out of character. The only confidential information he ordinarily shared with David had to do with the trust fund, discussions that were always, unlike this one, initiated by David. Now, for some reason, it seemed natural to be talking to David almost as an equal. "Would you be willing to do it?"

"Of course. Have him give me a call." He put his glass down on the table. "Is he good?"

"I don't know how good a bond trader he is, except what he tells me. He's a good guy." David was waiting for more, assessing. Jack thought, he really wants my opinion, he's asking me for my judgment, and he's going to act on it. He said cautiously, "He's not the most creative guy in the world."

David laughed. "I don't think we'd especially want creativity in a bond trader. You have him call me. Maybe we can find something for him. Don't tell him that — just that I'll see him. I don't want to get his hopes up."

"Thanks."

They sat silently for a while. Jack looked around the room, at the group of eight men and women gathered around a table across the room, looking like they were four or five years out of Yale, at the two old gentlemen with martini glasses who could have been fifty years out, at the couples, trying to guess which one of each pair had gone to Yale. He saw one of his own classmates come in and wave at him, and Jack waved back.

David asked, "How's Billy?"

"He's fine. He's fun to have around."

David lifted one eyebrow. "If you don't mind arguing about everything, cleaning up after him, and being treated half the time as if you aren't there."

"He's a teenager, it goes with the territory. I probably treated you the same way. And besides, you're his father, you get the worst of it. He's not so bad with me."

"He's a great kid," David said quietly. "I'm very proud of him."

Were you ever proud of me? Jack thought, and for a moment wanted to ask the question, wanted David to say yes. A question he couldn't ask his own father.

David said, "It's a difficult role to play, being a father. You never know exactly where to draw the lines. Too few rules and you have a delinquent on your hands. Too many and you end up with a wimp."

"Billy's not a wimp," Jack said loyally. "And he's certainly no delinquent."

"I'm glad he has you," David said, looking at the glass in his hands. "I think it's good for him to have someone, besides me, he can ask for advice."

"Oh, David." This wasn't the kind of thing David ever said to him. "I'm not his father. I don't even try to be."

"Well, of course you're not. I didn't mean that. I meant only to thank you for being so good to him." He sipped meditatively at his drink. "It's important that he have his own life. That's really what I meant when I said it's a difficult role. As much as you love your child, in the end that's what you want for him, that he have his own life."

"I love him, too," Jack said simply, and then caught himself. The conversation had gone completely off the tracks. They'd never talked like this before. Who had made it happen, he or David?

But David accepted the comment on its face. "I'm glad. If you want, though, I'll take him to Westfield with me. I'm taking a few days off."

"I'm happy having him with me. I told Elizabeth, he's welcome to stay as long as he wants. It'll give you and Elizabeth some time alone together."

But David didn't appear to be listening to him. He asked, in an odd tone, "How's Kate?"

Jack didn't answer for a minute. He'd been so caught up in the sudden intimacy of the conversation that he was sorry to have it ruined with some gambit about Kate. He said carefully, "She's fine."

But David, it seemed, had something else in mind. "Billy isn't the only person who needs to have a life of his own. You do too." And now he looked directly at Jack. "It's your life, John. I want you to live it the way you want to. Even if I haven't always approved" — he gave a kind of self-deprecating smile — "I wouldn't approve if I thought we were pressuring you."

None of this made any sense to Jack. He'd always seen David

as a voice with rigid standards and an uncompromising approach to life, the exemplar of disapproval and the closest person to a father he had left. He thought of his friends from school, the fathers they had all wrestled with while his own father lay quietly and inaccessibly in the cemetery. David was solidity and sureness, and the heir presumptive to the North River Trust. Could he really be telling Jack not to marry Thomas Welland's daughter? It didn't fit with Jack's image of him, but then nothing in the conversation fit that image. Maybe, he thought as he walked home, his image of David had been wrong all these years. That would mean, of course, that Jack's image of his own relationship with David had been wrong as well. The idea opened up such a wide set of possibilities that he couldn't take them all in. But he knew that somewhere among the possibilities might be one in which he spent his life with Ellen, and made her happy.

He saw Ellen the next day. She didn't want him to come to her apartment, and he respected her feelings, so they met in front of her building and went for a walk, heading east toward the river. Everything about that walk was fixed in his mind, the details of the brick buildings that ascended in elegant setbacks to high penthouses, the rose he bought for her, dripping from the bucket at a sidewalk grocer, the clanging of love in his head. Ellen talked about her vacation, Jack thought about their life together. Maybe they would buy a farmhouse somewhere, she'd said she liked farmhouses. They'd have beautiful children, two or three or four, he liked for the moment the idea of a big family. Boys who would be like Billy, and a girl who would be like Ellen and perfect. She'd work for Con Tech and win the Nobel Prize. They'd always be together.

At this point reality intervened, because missing from the picture was any context. His family, his friends, his world, had nothing to do with the idyllic vision of the two of them locked in an eternal embrace. There they'd be, in their farmhouse with their kids, with nothing around them but their love. Who would he be in that situation, what would happen to her when he proved undependable? Which brought him around to what he had to tell her.

They came to the river and walked uptown a little way, along the esplanade beneath the apartment buildings. Then they sat down.

He told her about his parents. It didn't have the same texture as his memories, it didn't take as long as he'd thought it would. But the facts got across. He finished, telling her finally about the night they died. He paused, then added, "I've been thinking about something you said to me, that children should, at least for a little while, hate their parents. It's the age when kids establish themselves, right? That's what the books say, separate from their parents, that's really what you meant, isn't it? Well, I couldn't. My father needed me too much. I felt like my whole personality was being taken away from me. I was being swallowed up instead. And then they died, and you can't hate the dead, it's not allowed. I just stopped believing in myself. If you don't believe you exist, you'll do anything if someone wants you, it's the only affirmation of self that you have. So I put myself out, like bait, waiting to see if anyone even would notice. I let myself be seduced because that would be the proof. And no matter how many times I was seduced, I kept having to go back for more, to be sure." He didn't add, because it made him think of Kate, that if you offered yourself, you had to deliver. Those were the rules.

She sighed. "But if you've always known that, why —"

"Didn't I change? Because I haven't always known. Just because of you, these last few weeks."

She sat for a long time after that, looking out at the river, at the collapsing lighthouse on Roosevelt Island. He'd told her everything and now, he felt, the balance rested in her hands. "You've told yourself," she said at last, "that you're not responsible, that it's silly to blame yourself."

"Of course." Anyone who'd ever even glimpsed the truth had told him that. "It doesn't change the facts."

"Oh," she said gently, "the facts. Your father drank a lot. You tried to protect him from the consequences. One night when you weren't there, he drove off the road. Those are the facts."

The scientific method, he thought. He waited for the conclusion she would draw from the facts.

"People have accidents all the time," she went on. "You nearly had one yourself, driving home from the club that night."

"I was watching the ghosts."

"Maybe your father was too."

"I know how it was," he said stubbornly. "I knew then."

"How?"

"I just did." He stood up and leaned against the black railing, looking down at the dirty water. An oil barge went by, sunk almost to the gunwales with the weight of its load, twisted piping on the deck, a tug pushing from behind. "You're trying to tell me that my whole life has been meaningless. Or," with a stab at her kind of precision, "at least based on a false premise. That can't be true. I know it's not."

But she wouldn't let it go, not as long as there was a fallacy to be nailed or a term to be defined. "Precisely. But not the false premise you think. Obviously your father was drinking that night. But I don't care if he was an alcoholic or the man in the moon." He turned to her to protest, but she went on. "I care about you. It's been thirteen years. You can't build your life on something that happened thirteen years ago. The past is data, some of it good, some of it bad, but it isn't some kind of slavemaster with a whip, driving you forward on an inevitable path. You choose your present. You have to assimilate your past."

"I have assimilated my past," he said. That's all he'd been doing the last three weeks, remembering Ripley, and Harriet, his mother and his father. What more did she want of him?

"No, you haven't. You've just buried it."

"You bet," he said bitterly, thinking of the grave in the cemetery in Westfield, the single stone.

"Buried it," she insisted, "so you can dig it up and look at it every time you want and then put it back."

"Look," he said angrily, "I didn't tell you this because I want you to make me feel better. I wanted you to know the truth about me."

"Oh, the truth," she said, just as she had said, a few minutes before, "Oh, the facts." She touched his back just above his belt. "Come and sit down." He did, and she held his hand. "The truth. What truth? Timothy said that you wanted absolution, is that the truth? That you think you killed your parents." When she said that, he had a quick image of himself in L.A., hitting Ripley for saying the same thing. "That you're a terrible person, lugging this burden around? I'll tell you a different truth that has nothing to do with anything that happened to you before this month. That I don't know anyone even remotely like you. That you care deeply about things most people don't even think about. That you have an infinite capacity for love, whatever you may think to the contrary and, all right, maybe that hurts you. That I love you more than I've ever loved anyone."

"Oh, Ellen," he murmured, his head bent over their hands, his face hidden.

"I never thought I'd fall in love. I thought, I'm too logical for that, my mind is under control, my emotions too. It would happen slowly, one step at a time like evolution, maturing over months or even years. I didn't want men to tell me they loved me because that would only force the issue, not give me the time I needed. And then you came, walking across the deck at the restaurant in Cornwall, with your Westfield tie and your hair just brushed and the evening sunlight in your face, and my heart turned upside down. And an hour later, after talking to you for just an hour, I knew I'd never love anyone but you." She stopped. "It's silly, isn't it."

"I felt the same way."

They sat there silently. Then she said, "Shall we walk some more?"

They walked uptown again, past the asphalt basketball courts where the usual enthusiastic games were going on, past the swings, the sandbox. It reminded him of the parks of his childhood. They came to the shaded lawns by Gracie Mansion and stopped again, leaning against the railing, both of them now looking up the river toward the bridge.

"How's Timothy?" he asked.

"He's fine. He's got a date this weekend with your friend Susan. You did a good job of matchmaking there."

He shook his head. "I didn't mean to."

"I was only teasing. He gave me a message for you, a quotation from Schiller: 'Who reflects too much will accomplish little.' "

"That's no help."

"No one ever said Germans are forgiving. Timothy says they're mostly a bunch of Romantic, heartless bastards, but they're not wrong."

She still loved him, he thought. Despite what he'd said, despite his warning. He wasn't persuaded by her that he wasn't responsible, that it wasn't his fault. Too much history lay between him and that conclusion. He thought again of what their life together would be, and the choice became very clear to him. He could marry Kate and live an assured life, with no surprises, no cracks, no accidents. Because whatever happened, in that world things didn't smash, they never got to any point nearly so dramatic. They were settled by unacknowledged accommodation. Or he could marry Ellen, with her world of facts, where everything was acknowledged, where the light fell into every corner and people were what they were, stand or fall. He said, "I can't tell her. I don't know how."

He should have known what her response would be. "Tell her."

"I don't want to hurt her. I want her to break it off herself. To hurt me instead."

She had picked up a stick, and now she was swinging it like a pendulum over the water. "She won't. Didn't you see it in your sister that day?"

"Oh, Elizabeth thinks I was just having a last fling. She's waiting for me to get over you."

"No. She doesn't even remotely think that. She knows that this is different." She broke off a piece of her stick, and he watched it float away on the current. "So does Kate. That's why you have to tell her."

"I can't," he said, thinking of Ripley, of his father, of the people he'd let down.

It was her turn to be angry. She snapped the stick again and said, "That's what they're counting on, isn't it?"

"But if I have to hurt Kate in order to love you —"

"Yes?"

"It just proves what has always happened to me — that you hurt the people you love. Sometimes you kill them. I can't do that again."

Ellen tossed the last of the stick away. "She'll get over you."

"Yes, but will you?" He heard what he'd said, and added, "I mean, I don't want you to get hurt. And that's the way it always turns out."

She paused, thinking so long that he began to wonder. Then she said, "Are you telling me that you love her?"

When he didn't answer, she leaned forward, and kissed him, and then walked away. He let her go.

He had one more thing to do, one more obligation to fulfill. It was a way of avoiding everything, a way of putting off the reckoning (and he gave himself a little credit for recognizing his own procrastination). He didn't want to think about Kate when she said she loved him, or about Ellen as she walked away from him. He got up early and lay in bed for a while, debating whether to take Billy with him. As a rule, as a surrogate older brother, he didn't believe in object lessons. Still, he thought, it wasn't entirely a bad idea. He knocked on the door of the study and went in.

Billy, lying on his back, looked blearily at him. "What's up," he said groggily.

"I have an appointment downtown. I thought you might want to come."

Billy sat up, bunching the sheet around his waist. "Do I have to? It's the middle of the night."

"It's eight o'clock in the morning —"

" 's what I said."

"I'm going down to the AIDS home. Just for a couple of hours. You want to come, or what?" Jack didn't even know himself why he thought Billy should come. While he waited for an answer, he looked around the study that in the last week had ceased to be his and had become Billy's. The books, the room he'd vaguely thought of as his refuge, now looked down on scenes of teenage occupation: soda cans in a growing pyramid on the desk; an open duffel bag, trailing clean clothes; the shade negligently drawn so as to let in too much light; and a pile of dirty clothes that lay on the floor like body parts from a demented battle scene — shirt arms reaching over the rug, blue jeans gaping stiffly, boxer shorts turned inside out.

"I guess," Billy said cautiously. Jack had the feeling of being humored, but he ignored it.

The home was in a rundown building on a crummy block downtown on the West Side. The building next door was vacant. Across the street, an empty lot was surrounded by a decaying fence, its pavemented surface strewn with the broken glass of smashed wine bottles. Garbage collected mysteriously at the curbside and then, equally mysteriously, disappeared. Even here, though, the home had had resistance, a protest from the neighbors — nobody wanted AIDS patients next door. Every Saturday morning he came by, visited the sick, counted the living, and mourned the dead. On most Thursday nights he went for dinner. In service to Ripley.

Inside, off the front hall, was a lounge or living room. It was furnished, as was most of the place, in other people's castoffs. Furniture that didn't match, that looked used up; old posters — rock bands and Metropolitan blockbusters — stuck to the walls with push pins; a pile of games, Scrabble, Monopoly, in broken boxes. They had found that it didn't work to overpersonalize the decor, turnover was too high.

A boy about Billy's age sat on a faded couch under the front window. "Hello, Chris," Jack said.

"Hi." The boy stood up.

"This is my nephew."

Billy stuck his hand out. "Hi. I'm Billy Lorburn. Pleased to meet you."

"Chris Holden." He shook Billy's hand, then looked at Jack. "He passes the test. Did you coach him?"

"Huh?" Billy looked blank.

"I've told you, I don't think the test is fair. You can explain it."

Chris sat down on the couch. "Some guys come here, they don't want to shake your hand. They look at the floor or they, like, try to hide their arms behind them. Sometimes you catch them wiping their hands on their pants afterwards. Maybe they go home and boil themselves. What do you think?" he said to Billy, challengingly.

Billy shrugged. "I think if you can get AIDS by shaking hands then we're all in deep shit." He stared back at Chris, and then they both started to laugh.

Jack said, "I have to go see Buzz. I'll be back in a little while."

He went upstairs and spent half an hour with the director of the hospice, a psychiatric social worker with prematurely gray hair and a paunch, and a penchant for plaid flannel shirts even in summer. An air conditioner in the window moaned ineffectually — every so often Buzz would stand up and change the setting just to test whether it was still alive. There was a white Styrofoam cup on his desk — little droplets of coffee formed mysteriously on the outside and ran down to the desk, squeezed through some invisible pin-hole.

One of their clients had died during the week. He had been with them a month and a half, Jack hadn't known him very well. Buzz seemed to be taking it especially hard. Now and then one particu-lar death would stand out, not for a reason anyone could name, sim-ple randomness maybe. Jack suggested, for something to do, that they clean out the vacated room, the symbolic mourning of those who have no claim on the deceased other than having cared for him when no one else would. So for the next hour, they stripped the bed and remade it, folded clothes to be sent to a homeless shelter, washed the floor and the windows to make things clean for the next occupant and, at the end, sorted through the few personal things in a drawer under the socks. Some letters written in an unformed hand, a few photos of a boy with sandy hair standing on a sandy beach, and a clipping from the *Times,* a small-print death notice that concluded: "In their death they were not divided." He identi-fied the quotation with a flash of annoyance, then felt ashamed of himself: why should AIDS make people any less sentimental? He knew what epitaph he would choose for himself. He wouldn't want a mawkish, nineteenth-century vision of death redeeming love, but simply the bare fact: The End of Love Is Death. Standing here amid the meager wreckage of a life, in this halfway house to the grave, he thought it could be the epitaph of everyone he knew.

Buzz was squatting on the floor, holding the artifacts in both hands, looking blindly at Jack from behind his glasses. He seemed to have lost all his initiative. Jack said, "Put them in the scrap-book."

They kept a notebook and pasted remembrances in it. Ac-knowledging their guilt.

He went downstairs and found the two boys talking, evidently very seriously. Chris had his feet up on the sofa, his knees tucked under his chin, his arms wrapped around his legs (he's getting thinner, Jack thought clinically). Billy was staring up at the ceiling, his body almost a straight line down to his sneakers, which were spread wide apart on the floor, his hands clamped together over his stomach. They looked at him as if he were intruding on something private, and he had a quick image of his father interrupting Dougie and him, one of those moments when an adult is completely irrelevant. He went away for a few minutes, and when he came back, Chris was gone. "He'll be right back," Billy explained.

"We're going to have to go anyway."

"OK. I'll just say goodbye, OK?"

Out on the street, as they picked their way among pieces of old newspaper and little piles of dogshit, Billy was unusually quiet. "You like Chris?" Jack asked.

"Yeah."

"Did he tell you how he got sick?" Chris had run away at fourteen from his home in Pennsylvania, on a Greyhound bus that had dropped him at the terminal at Thirty-fourth Street. It didn't take the talent spotters more than an hour to pick him out, pick him up, give him a hot meal, become his friends. He resisted the payback, but what, in the end, was a fourteen-year-old going to do in New York to keep body and soul together? So he went back to them, was beaten up for his trouble, and put to work, mostly in hotel rooms where the sheets were still stained from the last time and where nameless men gave him money that a watcher took away practically before he was out the front door.

"A little," Billy said. They were walking up Ninth Avenue. It was one of those hot, windy days when the air seems full of dust. The sky was white. "We talked about music — he's never heard the Radiators, I said I'd bring him a tape."

"Oh. You going back?"

"I guess." Billy kicked the sidewalk with his toe. "He's going to die, isn't he?"

Jack didn't say anything.

"He's going to die," Billy said, this time accusingly.

"You're not invincible, Billy. No one is."

"I don't want to know," he shouted, and a couple of black kids carrying skateboards turned to look at him. "Why'd you have to bring me here?"

"You have to be responsible for your own actions," Jack said didactically, which he thought had been his purpose in bringing Billy.

"That's such bullshit." They passed a Korean grocery, its produce splayed out in boxes, shining nakedly in the sun. Billy smacked the side of a tomato crate with his open hand. "He had no choice, did he? He couldn't say, excuse me a minute while I get this condom. Could he?" he shouted again.

"No. But you can."

Billy looked at him, incredulous. "I can't believe this. You're preaching to me? Jesus. Is that what Chris is to you?" He wiped his eyes with the back of his hand. "He's just a kid, why does he have to die?"

Because, Jack thought involuntarily, the end of love is death. And even in the heat he shivered a little at his own coldness.

He sat in the park while Billy jogged around the reservoir. The day had gotten hotter and dry, it seemed as if it hadn't rained in weeks, and the ground by Jack's feet was hard, and busy with ants. They kept crawling up his Top-Siders and onto his bare ankles, and he kept brushing them off. His cuffed khaki pants and his sockless feet in his shoes made him look very boyish, which was the last thing he felt. It had been three weeks since his birthday. He sat for a long time, thinking about the last month, about all the memories that had been stirred up, about where they were leading him. He was coming to the conclusion that the best approach would be to do nothing, to escape back into the world of shadows. He didn't exactly see how that would turn out, or even what it would mean in this context to do nothing, but it would be a familiar, the most familiar, response: to not be there, to pretend he didn't exist.

He looked up at the trees, which were being blown now with the kind of dark, gusty breeze that precedes a summer storm. The undersides of the leaves were showing, lighter colored, like the eyes of an animal seen by headlight. He thought the rain would not come for another hour — or not at all.

Billy, finished with his run, came jogging back. He sat down on the bench and threw his head back. "Four miles," he said.

"Great."

"Yeah." He was breathing hard, the sweat running in two lines down either side of his face.

Jack grinned. "You're beautiful, Billy."

"Thanks." He leaned forward, resting his elbows on his knees.

Jack put his hand on Billy's back. He was thinking of Ripley, oddly enough, since he couldn't imagine two people more different. But beauty had been Ripley's word, adopted at second hand from Socrates and Plato. Jack said, "Beginning from beautiful things, to mount ever upward until he at last understands the essence of beauty."

"Huh?"

"A quotation. From Plato, it used to be a favorite of a friend of mine. I think I left a lot of it out."

Billy said, "You're just showing off."

A teenager's sin. He'd really only been speaking his thoughts. He pushed his hand up until it touched Billy's damp hair. "You ready to go?"

"Sure."

They walked back slowly. Billy said, "Maybe I should enter a ten-K this fall. What do you think?"

"Great. You'll blow 'em away."

"Yeah, sure." He looked at Jack a minute, wondering perhaps at his mood. "Would you run with me?" he asked a little shyly. "If I do it."

"I couldn't keep up."

Billy frowned. "You could if you worked at it. You're in great shape for a guy your age."

"Thanks a lot."

"If you ran four or five times a week and cut out drinking so much booze and partying all the time."

"You sound like my uncle now."

Billy laughed. "We could do role reversal, what do you think?"

"No way. I'm easier on you than you'd be on me." Do thou stand for my father, and examine me upon the particulars of my life. He thought of Ripley again, how they had talked, that first day, about Shakespeare. Banish plump Jack, and banish all the world.

They reached the edge of the park and walked toward Sixth Avenue, the sun in their faces. A hansom carriage came clopping by, stinking of horse. Billy said, "Don't they know what century this is?"

"Supposed to be romantic." Love and marriage.

"Yeah, sure." They crossed the street and wandered down Sixth. "Uncle John, what's going to happen to Chris?"

Jack frowned. "You know, Billy. He's going to die."

"But, I mean, how?"

He wanted information, facts however unpleasant as a bulwark against the unknown. CMV maybe. Lose his eyesight first, or most of it, then lose his mind. Of pneumonia. Of some exotic fungal infection. Of just exhaustion, Jack had seen that too — after a long illness. "It could be anything," he said. "Your body has all these diseases in it, things we never see because the immune system suppresses them. When the immune system shuts down, your body just goes haywire."

"So there's no chance?"

"You know that. Unless some cure comes along, or some drug that helps."

They turned into Jack's building and rode up silently in the elevator. When they got inside the apartment, Billy said, "The thing is."

"What?" Jack put his keys on the table in the hall.

"I don't think he should die alone."

They went into the living room. Jack sat down on the couch. "Most of the people at the home go to the hospital when they get very sick. It's our policy. He'll have doctors, nurses, whoever the hospital provides."

"That's not what I meant. Someone who cares about him. A friend."

Jack looked up at him as he stood in the light from the sliding doors. He looked awkward with the awkwardness of his thoughts. "Like who?"

"Like me," Billy said.

Jack sighed. "You can't save him, you know —"

"Oh shit." He sat down hard on a chair. "I don't want to save him. I just don't think people should die alone."

"Listen to me. This is a big commitment you're making. You can't know how big until you've done it. And if you go into it thinking that this time'll be different, that your being there will save him, that it won't happen, you're going to have your heart broken. And I don't want that to happen to you."

"It's my heart," Billy said sulkily.

The phone rang, and Jack got up to answer it. It was Elizabeth, calling for Billy. Jack gave him the phone and then went to the bathroom. This wasn't what he'd expected when he'd taken Billy to the home. He didn't want Billy to get hurt, not ever, but it was, as he said, his heart. He went back to the living room and found Billy yelling into the phone. "I don't want to. I'm sixteen, I can make my own decisions." He looked at Jack and held out the phone. "She wants me to come to Connecticut again. Now. Dad's driving up for a couple of days or something. You talk to her."

Jack took the phone. "Elizabeth?"

"John, you've been wonderful with him. But we want him home now. Maybe he can come back later in the summer. If you still want him."

He wondered what would happen if he called her bluff. Said, Great, take him, it'll give me a chance to entertain Ellen. But he would be bluffing then, wouldn't he? Can you call a bluff with another bluff? The stakes were too high. "I'll miss him."

"Come visit us. You know you and Kate are welcome anytime."

We better be, he thought, it's half my house, after all. And I'll bring anyone I want. "Thanks."

"Love to Kate. Goodbye."

Billy was looking at him angrily. "How could you do that to me?"

"She's your mother."

"Great." He went into the study and started picking up his clothes. "I don't even get to shower. Just, meet Dad at home in twenty minutes. This really sucks." He looked at Jack. "I want you to know I think this really sucks." He pulled off his sneakers and his running shorts and then looked around for some clean clothes. "Jesus."

"Come on, Billy. She said you could come back in a few weeks.

Tell you what. Go up there for two weeks. When your folks go to the Cape to get Hank, you come back here."

Billy was pulling up his underpants, hopping from one foot to the other. "Great. What am I going to do for two weeks in West-field?"

"Hang out at the swim club. Go running. Find a girlfriend. Why are you so upset?"

"I don't like being told what to do. You're always telling me to take responsibility for my own life. How can I if my parents always order me around?"

"Parents do that." Jack thought, Don't take it personally. You were a convenient watchdog for me. Now she wants the watch lifted. That's all. It has nothing to do with you. He wondered what had happened to make her change her plans.

Billy pushed the rest of his clothes into his duffel bag and looked around the room. "If you find anything, send it to me in Siberia."

Jack put an arm around his shoulders and hugged him. "Listen, baby, I love you." Whatever I do, he thought. "Right?"

"Yeah, right. Take care." And he was gone.

The emptiness in the apartment was immediately overwhelming. Maybe that alone was the point, why they'd called Billy away, there had to be some reason. Especially given the suddenness: not tomorrow, today; not later, now. Did they just want him to feel how alone he would be without them? He went back into the study and started cleaning up, stripping the sheets, folding up the couch, clearing away some of the mess from the desk. Then he noticed that he had a message on the machine. He played it back.

"Jack? This is Ellen." Her voice, on tape, sounded exactly like her. "I had a call from your fiancée." He didn't like the way she used the word, or that she used it at all. "She invited me to meet her for a drink at her apartment, at seven." Don't go, he thought. "I said I'd go. Call you later."

Oh God, he thought, sitting down on the couch. He looked at his watch. It was quarter to seven. He could get a cab, get to Kate's first — and what? He still didn't know, was still telling himself, stubbornly, to do nothing.

Across from him, on the wall over his desk, hung all the pictures of his life: Billy, Elizabeth and David, Kate, Hank, Ripley, Peter. He shut his eyes, he'd seen enough of them in his thoughts the past month. He tried to remember the way the sun rose at camp in New Hampshire; the way the birds sang at twilight on a summer night in Connecticut; the way ice kicked up under the blades of his skates when he made a quick stop on the rink at Westfield; the moment between the sound of the gun and the push of his feet at the start of a swimming race. He couldn't hold any of them in his head.

He went into the bathroom and looked at the tub, at the toilet. He thought: John Newland, a young man with a penchant for long baths and the propensity to throw up at the wrong time. He started to laugh but stopped himself, and went into the bedroom and lay down on the bed. Kate and Ellen would settle matters. He would lie on the bed like a pagan offering until one of them came for him, opened the door, and climbed in next to him. The rules of seduction. He heard footsteps in the hall and tensed his stomach muscles. There would be a pause (there was) and the sound of a key in the lock (it was too soft for him to hear) and then the closing of the door. But it turned out to be his neighbor across the hall, or nothing at all, just his imagination, because no one came into the bedroom.

He stayed very still, and after a while he saw himself, as if from above, lying in the center of the bed, the wrinkled sheets con- voluted around him, his arms straight at his sides, stripes of light falling across the room through gaps in the curtains. If he stayed here forever — in his imagination, a ceiling fan rotated slowly above him, and a cigarette burned in an ashtray on the nightstand, a woman was about to enter the room. But there was no fan and no cigarette, no woman. He would just lie here. Do nothing, he told himself. The end of love is death.

The thought frightened him, and he sat up. Without thinking where he was going, he grabbed his keys and left the apartment. The ride down in the elevator seemed endless, he kept tapping his hand against his leg, feeling that he had to get out. He walked quickly down the block and turned north up the avenue. At the corner of Fifty-ninth Street the light was red, but he was going too fast now to stop and he weaved his way through the traffic, putting his hand on the hoods of cabs that honked at him, stepping through the exhaust of a departing bus. Once in the park, he started to run along the pathways and then, even more impatient, across the grass. He came to a little valley and tripped on a root, rolling on the ground a ways, feeling something tear at his cheek, but getting up quickly and going on. He still didn't know where he was going, he was being pursued, driven like game into a net of his own devising. He heard an animal scream in the zoo, a siren wail from Central Park West, prophecies of doom for somebody else, his doom was ahead of him, he thought, the end of love is death. Then he was out of the park, running up the sidewalk on Fifth Avenue, dodging kids with cones, homeless men with tattered trousers, fathers with families. He was breathing hard, but his body was working by itself, pumping his legs and his lungs and his heart — he could keep up with Billy if he were being chased hard enough. He ran across the street, against traffic again, hearing somebody curse and not caring. He stopped in front of a building.

It was an elegant apartment building with an awning, and brass poles holding up the awning, and a doorman who looked at him suspiciously. He wiped the sweat off his cheek and his hand came away bloody, from where he'd fallen in the park. He walked up close to the building. It was the right one, everything about it was familiar — the color of the stone, a pale brown, the lines, deeply indented, where the stones came together, the street number on the brass plaque next to the door. He felt the sun behind him, the wind blowing harder now, lifting the hair off his head, the heat in the air. But he wasn't there at all, he was seeing something different in the spaces between his breathing.

It was late afternoon, the year he was thirteen. It must have been around Christmas, because he remembered the sky being dark and the air having that December snap of immediacy to it. He had been walking up Fifth Avenue with his father. Maybe there had been snow in the park, black ice on the sidewalk, he couldn't remember. And in front of this building they'd met a man, a business colleague of his father's. He hadn't paid much attention to the conversation, maybe he'd been cold or tired, he couldn't remember what they'd been doing all day. He'd forgotten nearly everything except the one detail that had driven him to come here. His father, standing behind him, putting his hands on his shoulders and saying, "This is my boy, Johnny. My keeper. I don't have to worry as long as Johnny's looking after me." It was the one slip his father ever made, the one acknowledgment. It was all the proof Jack would ever need.

"God damn you," he said, but no sound came out. God damn you. Then he made a fist with his right hand and swung as hard as he could, the hardest punch he'd ever thrown. His fist smashed into the stone side of the building, and he heard a cracking noise, felt blood on his hand and knew he'd broken some bones. He couldn't see anything for a minute, and when his eyes cleared, the doorman was telling him to get away or he'd call the cops. He started walking again.

He felt better, even though his hand hurt like hell. He didn't look at it, it didn't matter. He concentrated on feeling how much it hurt, because he didn't want to think, he'd had enough re-membering, enough of the past. He started to run again, and the impact made his hand hurt more. The pain matters, he thought, nothing else. He turned down a side street, slowing to a walk and catching his breath before turning into the building. He hid his hand from the doorman, who knew him, and from the elevator boy, who didn't. He got off the elevator and leaned against a wall to catch his breath. He shook his head to clear the spots out of his eyes, then walked down the hall. His keys were in his pants pocket on the right side, and he had a lot of trouble getting them out with his left hand. Unthinkingly, he held his right hand up to his chest, to keep the pain alive. Still with his left hand, he put the key in the lock and opened the door. He could hear voices from the living room. He walked softly, an intruder, down the hall. The two women were sitting on the yellow couch, their backs to him. He made a noise, and they turned their heads and stared. He couldn't see Kate clearly, it was as if she were already receding into the pain. He only looked at Ellen and held out his mangled hand. He said, "I'm here."